PENGUIN BOOKS

The Forgotten Lies

The Forgotten Lies

KERRY JAMIESON

PENGUIN BOOKS

PENGUIN BOOKS

Published by the Penguin Group
Penguin Books Ltd, 80 Strand, London WC2R ORL, England
Penguin Group (USA) Inc., 375 Hudson Street, New York, New York 10014, USA
Penguin Group (Canada), 90 Eglinton Avenue East, Suite 700, Toronto, Ontario, Canada M4P 2Y3
(a division of Pearson Penguin Canada Inc.)
Penguin Ireland, 25 St Stephen's Green, Dublin 2, Ireland (a division of Penguin Books Ltd)
Penguin Group (Australia), 250 Camberwell Road, Camberwell, Victoria 3124, Australia
(a division of Pearson Australia Group Pty Ltd)
Penguin Books India Pvt Ltd, 11 Community Centre, Panchsheel Park, New Delhi – 110 017, India
Penguin Group (NZ), 67 Apollo Drive, Rosedale, Auckland 0632, New Zealand
(a division of Pearson New Zealand Ltd)
Penguin Books (South Africa) (Pty) Ltd, 24 Sturdee Avenue, Rosebank, Johannesburg 2196, South Africa

Penguin Books Ltd, Registered Offices: 80 Strand, London WC2R ORL, England

www.penguin.com

First published 2011

1

Set in 12.5/14.75 pt Garamond MT Std
Typeset by Palimpsest Book Production Limited, Falkirk, Stirlingshire
Printed in Great Britain by Clays Ltd, St Ives plc

ISBN: 978-0-141-02604-6

www.greenpenguin.co.uk

Penguin Books is committed to a sustainable
future for our business, our readers and our
planet. This book is made from paper certified
by the Forest Stewardship Council.

This book is dedicated to Rory Jamieson
who I love and admire as a man and a dad.
You've inspired me with your courage and
perseverance. You're the world's best big brother.

You should have what you love

I must lie down where all
ladders start,
In the foul rag-and-bone shop
of the heart.

W. B. Yeats

Author's Note

In the early 1930s, the House of Caron – one of the great perfumeries of Paris – created a singular new fragrance. Its name, Fleurs de Rocaille, was intentionally contradictory. It translates literally as 'flowers of the rock' or, perhaps more appropriately, 'flowers from the rubble' – a name that conveys the ambivalence of a particular feminine type: the woman who can be both fragile and cruel, ruthless yet utterly desirable.

Foreword

Sonora, Mexico
Sunday, 22 September 1935

Usually, the road was quiet – a winding stretch of sand potholed by jack-rabbit burrows and spiked with saguaros – but now there was a car. Hector watched it approach his bridge with some interest. It was already dusk, late for a driver to be so far from home. There were no villages nearby and nobody attempted the road at night. The going was too treacherous.

This wasn't an official United States border crossing, like the one in Nogales twenty miles to the east. The rancher who owned the land had simply posted Hector at the bridge to watch for cattle rustlers. He was also expected to check the passports of any visitors who passed and record their names in a book. A few times each year, a minion of the United States government flipped through the book and marked the last page with an official stamp.

Hector removed his boots from the window ledge where he habitually rested them. The orange clay of the sill was scuffed raw in places by his spurs. He stood up and placed a palm against the wall to stop the room spinning. He had attended a wedding the night before and the celebrations had continued into the early hours of the morning. He was still drunk.

Hector left his shelter and waved the car to a stop. It was painted a colour he had never seen on a vehicle before – a pale, glittering gold like Yucatan beach sand. He saluted the driver, who saluted back uncertainly. Hector was suddenly distracted by the vehicle's hood ornament – a silver angel, her vestments billowing out behind her. He tickled the angel's chin with one greasy forefinger. The driver drummed his knuckles on the wheel in agitation. It was then that Hector noticed the woman curled up on the back seat. She had a scarf around her head and dark glasses on her face. The driver smiled at him. Hector smiled back and winked. They were both men of the world.

'Your papers, please, *señor*,' Hector said.

The driver handed over two American passports. Hector opened them and copied the travellers' names into his book: Liam John Michael Malone and Charlotte Ava Caine. His printing was painstakingly slow.

The woman stirred on the back seat and groaned. Hector was sympathetic. Perhaps she, too, had overindulged the night before. She rubbed the back of her hand unconsciously across her nose and her sunglasses fell off. Hector saw a face disfigured by bulbous red lumps. Both cheeks were marked with the crusty lines of dried tears.

Suddenly Hector was sober. He glanced at the driver. Had the man beaten this poor woman? He was a *gringo*, and he hadn't stopped smiling for a second, but that meant nothing. Americans were always coming into Mexico to make trouble. Sometimes they crossed the border with their dark needs and did this sort of thing to the local women. Sometimes they did worse.

On the back seat, the woman turned over lethargically

in her fever. The scarf slipped down over her chin, revealing hugely swollen lips. Was she drugged? Hector was no longer certain her condition was the result of loose fists. He snatched his hands away from the window and covered his mouth with a rag from his pocket. It smelt of rifle oil but he didn't care. Another possibility had occurred to him: the woman was coming to Mexico for a cure. Desperate *gringos* sometimes crossed the border in search of a *curandera* – a traditional medicine woman – usually after they had exhausted all other options. They brought their maids along as translators.

Hector handed the passports back to the driver and waved him on. As soon as the car had pulled slowly away, he went back into his hut and retrieved a bottle from its hiding-place beneath his blanket. He swigged deeply from it, washing away the grit he had swallowed in the car's wake. He thought of the silver angel on the car's hood, flying away into the shimmering desert. It was a long time before the dust settled.

Two weeks later, Hector saw the car again. He saw it in a grainy photograph this time, on the front page of an American newspaper somebody had left on the counter of his favourite bar. Hector asked his sister to read the article to him.

'Was it stolen?' he asked. He was fearful that he would be blamed for letting the car pass.

'It's only lovers run away,' his sister explained. 'Two famous picture stars. The police are trying to find that special car of his. They've maybe come to Mexico to live together in sin.'

Hector felt relieved, until he remembered that the woman

had been sick. Or had she been the victim of a vicious beating? He couldn't recall the details clearly.

Whatever the truth of it, Hector thought it best to keep his mouth shut. He worried about the names he had copied from the Americans' passports into his book. He agonized over it for weeks. He could not remove the evidence: a torn-out page would beg questions. But the authorities never showed up to check his work that month. When an inspector came by in December, the page with the names of Charlotte Caine and Liam Malone had been turned over. The official didn't glance back.

After that, Hector determined never to mention his odd meeting with the couple again. When he thought about them at all, he chose to believe that the runaway lovers had made a home together near the ocean. That was easy in Mexico, especially if you had money. You could buy papers for identification. He imagined them living in a lovely house. He imagined them making beautiful children. Hector was often accused of being sentimental, especially when he drank, but he had a romantic heart. Charlotte and Liam's relationship was a love story. What could be simpler, or happier, than that?

I

Far along the canyon, a string of electric lights suddenly appeared like a glowing line of tinsel in the dusk. They were stretched out at regular intervals, like a row of streetlamps running through the dry, vacant hills. A group of burly men hauled the cable through the dust of the valley floor. They yelled to one another but their words were swallowed by the wind.

Charlotte, Ivy and Verbena had come out on to their deck, dressed in bathrobes, to watch the unexpected activity. They gazed across the canyon, looking west together towards Glendale, unsure as to the purpose of the lights.

'It's a dogfight,' declared Ivy. 'They're setting up for one of those ghastly dogfights the Mexicans like so much.'

Verbena flopped into one of the wicker deckchairs and watched Ivy, who bounced on the balls of her feet like a girl. 'It's too big to be a dogfight,' she said. 'And too organized.' Her hands hung listlessly over the arms of the chair. The glass she was holding tilted. She almost spilled her gin.

'It's probably just people living rough,' said Ivy. 'If we had binoculars, we could spy on them.'

'Which means they would be able to spy on us, too,' replied Verbena.

The pinpricks of light began to rise from the ground in a long, sagging swathe. The men hollered instructions back and forward as they hoisted the line aloft.

'We should call somebody,' said Charlotte. 'This is a studio house. We don't want vagrants sleeping in our canyon.'

'It's not our canyon,' said Verbena. 'Besides, we're in the middle of a depression. People have lost their homes. They have nowhere to go. There are families living under bridges. What do you think Mr Roosevelt's been prattling about on the wireless?'

'Please let's not argue tonight,' begged Ivy. She was tired of Charlotte and Verbena's constant sniping. There had been friction in the house ever since the Warner Brothers studio had initiated its search for an actress to play Rahab in David O. Selznick's upcoming feature film, *The Walls of Jericho*. All three women were actresses contracted to Warner Brothers and Rahab was a wonderful role – a smart, assertive woman who had hidden the Israelite spies when they infiltrated Jericho. With her savvy, Rahab had earned salvation for herself and her family when Joshua eventually sacked the city. It was a serious, substantial part. Verbena wanted the role desperately. She felt an affinity with Rahab, who was strong and independent. Also, the gorgeous Liam Malone had been signed as the leading man. He would play Joshua, the leader of the Israelite army, and whoever played alongside Liam would become a star.

As the lights reached their destination high above the ground, they took on a distinctive shape – an enormous canopy with two pointed summits. Now two crimson flags unfurled at the pinnacles and began to flap.

'It's a circus!' squealed Ivy. She clapped her hands in delight. 'You can make out the big top quite clearly now.'

'What?' said Charlotte. Her voice was almost a shriek. 'I hate circuses.'

'What kind of person hates circuses?' asked Verbena.

'I do,' said Charlotte, unhelpfully.

'Maybe they'll give you a job, Charlotte,' said Verbena. She was feeling especially contrary. Her head still ached from too much booze the evening before. She had felt queasy all day and now she was drinking again. She knew she ought to stop. 'They could dress you up in a sparkly costume and you could show off your assets.'

'Bee!' said Ivy. 'That's an awful thing to say.'

Verbena liked it when Ivy used her special nickname because it evoked danger. She prided herself on her ability to sting.

'Verbena's trying very hard to be contentious,' declared Charlotte. She had made sure she understood the meaning of the word before she spoke it. Her schooling had been patchy and she was always afraid that her inadequacy would show.

'Which is better than being pretentious,' said Verbena.

'Let's play at being nice,' interjected Ivy. 'The nicest girl wins.'

'That hasn't been my experience,' said Charlotte, quite seriously.

'But you're as nice as pie, sweetie-pie,' Ivy told Charlotte.

'You're as sweet as sugar, sugar-plum,' Verbena added.

Normally, Verbena hated platitudes but employing clichés in her everyday conversations with Ivy had become a private joke between them, a subtle condemnation of the dire script dialogue they were both forced to parrot at work. Sometimes they talked insincerely like this at Charlotte's expense. It meant they were still a pair. Charlotte was the outsider.

Charlotte Caine was the most recent arrival at the house on Lantana Drive. She had moved in that April. The Warner brothers expected their contracted actresses to share accommodation in homes the studio owned. They moved them in and deducted the rent from their salaries. Ivy and Verbena had lived together quite happily for a year but there had been an empty room in the house during that time and they had known a new girl would be assigned to them eventually. They had anticipated just another pretty young woman from the suburbs who thought she could make it in the movies. Instead, they had been landed with Charlotte Caine, and Charlotte Caine was altogether different. Ivy thought of Charlotte as bold. Secretly she admired her. Verbena said that Charlotte was obvious and pushy.

Charlotte's arrival had made an impression. Finding the front door locked, she had walked round to the deck where Ivy and Verbena habitually relaxed. She had cut a lovely figure in her tweed suit, whose simple lines were indicative of great expense. The jacket had a russet fox-fur collar. An angled cloche hat had covered most of Charlotte's golden hair and one of her extraordinary chestnut eyes.

Despite Charlotte's dramatic ensemble, Verbena had immediately noticed that the woman's clothes smelt. She had clearly travelled a long way in them. Her makeup had been perfect, though, her complexion even beneath a mask of powder.

'Welcome to the party,' Verbena had said, by way of welcome.

'Is there a party?' Charlotte had asked, and she had actually looked around her, as though she might have missed a few dozen people enjoying themselves on the deck.

Verbena had smirked at that. Her role as resident wit seemed secure – that was something. Both Ivy and Verbena had detected a slight Southern accent in Charlotte's voice. They didn't especially like belles at the studio. Tough Yankees were popular that year. Both Ivy and Verbena had relaxed. Charlotte would work through her year-long contract, then marry some rich man who'd put money into one of her pictures. Most of the Warner Brothers girls married money. But Charlotte hadn't dated anybody since her arrival – which bothered Ivy. Pretty girls had no reason to be alone. Ivy sincerely believed that if Charlotte and Verbena both found themselves suitable men, life on Lantana Drive would be far more pleasant. Men didn't take to Verbena, though, despite her handsome appearance, and Charlotte's single status was a complete mystery.

Ivy felt a sudden tenderness towards her friend. She knew that Verbena was lonely. She was drinking more these days. It was nerves about work. When Verbena landed her next part, she would stop. It was only 'resting' that made her cantankerous.

Ivy reached out to touch Verbena's cropped black hair, which was as sleek as sealskin. 'Your hair looks lovely in this light,' said Ivy. 'You look like a . . . What do you call that animal, Charlotte?'

'A rat?' offered Charlotte.

'No!' said Ivy, with a giggle. 'A panther. Verbena looks like one of those jungle panthers, the black kind that shines.'

Verbena smiled the sly, secretive smile that meant she was deeply contented. Her green eyes, when narrowed, exactly resembled a cat's. 'I still say Rahab should be dark,' she said. 'She should be slim and dark.' Verbena was describing herself. She was proud of her tall, athletic body. She favoured Katharine Hepburn in that way. She looked like a serious actress, a stage actress. Charlotte looked like a tawdry pin-up girl, in Verbena's opinion, all bosom and lips.

'They have to choose a brunette. After all, Rahab was Jewish, wasn't she?' Verbena asked Ivy.

'No, I think she was a prostitute, actually,' said Ivy. She was trying to ease the tension. It worked. Verbena laughed out loud.

'What?' said Charlotte.

'Oh, for God's sake, Charlotte. Haven't you read the bloody Bible? Don't you know anything?' said Verbena.

'I don't own a Bible,' said Charlotte.

'Then stop pretending to be so bloody pious. I can't stand it!'

'Nobody told me the character was a prostitute,' said Charlotte. 'I'm not auditioning for a part like that. It isn't seemly.'

'Wonderful,' said Verbena. 'Then call Madge and say you're pulling out. One less chancer in the running suits me just fine.'

'Oh, you'd love that, wouldn't you, Verbena?' said Charlotte. 'On principle I won't give you the satisfaction.'

Ivy had decided not to put her name forward for the part of Rahab. She had settled into accepting the bit parts she was evidently destined to play – the sister or friend or rival of the leading lady. Besides, Ivy had recently met a man – a junior congressman from Pasadena named Nathaniel Whitewood and, at twenty-five, she had started to think of retiring from show business. She would never share that particular thought with Verbena. Ivy knew that Verbena still held some hope of achieving real acclaim, but Verbena was almost twenty-eight – far too old. Sometimes, it seemed that the youngest of them, Charlotte, had the greatest shot at stardom but Charlotte was an enigma. It was hard to tell why she had come to Los Angeles or what she really wanted.

'They'll definitely go with somebody dark,' reaffirmed Verbena, trying to reassure herself most of all. 'And I've got the monopoly on dark at Warner's. You're just not right for it, Charlotte. I'm sorry, darling.'

'Oh, haven't you heard?' said Charlotte, ignoring the slight. 'They especially want a blonde. I'm certain Madge mentioned that to me.'

So Madge St Claire had coached Charlotte about the audition. Verbena's anger exploded inside her, sudden and bright like a magician's flash paper igniting. Madge was the agent the three women shared and Madge was a favourite with the Warner brothers. They had signed Charlotte as a contracted player on the basis of Madge's recommendation. Since then, Madge had proved to be an attentive representative. Charlotte had appeared regularly in the studio's smaller projects. Madge was doing well for the newcomer. Verbena had to acknowledge, begrudgingly, that Charlotte had begun to edge her out of parts for which she would once have had no real competition.

'They're lousy with blondes over at Warner's,' interjected

Ivy. 'Charlotte and I are just two of a dozen. We'll all just have to wait and see what happens.'

Ivy wanted to change the subject. She was tired of her role as cheery mediator. She flapped the edge of her robe and enjoyed the breeze the gesture generated. It was barely June and already it felt as if they had endured a long summer. In Santa Monica, the temperature at the beach had soared past a hundred degrees. The concrete of the city had baked to a white-hot glaze. The sprinklers ran all day in the landscaped gardens; the pools had to be topped up before the weekend swimming parties.

'They'll see sense,' said Verbena. 'Liam Malone can actually act. He won't agree to being paired with some vacuous little upstart. He'll want an actress with substance and a brain. All I know is that my audition went very well, and they haven't even called you in, have they, Charlotte?'

'Should we go to one of the circus shows, do you think?' Ivy said. 'We could make an outing of it – all the girls together.'

'I won't go,' said Charlotte, vehemently. 'Those places are full of undesirables and conmen.'

'I hope their tent blocks our view of that bloody sign,' said Verbena. 'It's nothing more than a tawdry billboard.'

Charlotte leaned over the railing of the deck, which projected out into Beachwood Canyon. She looked across the valley to where the giant Hollywoodland letters were displayed on Mount Lee.

'Did you know an actress killed herself there a few years back?' Verbena added.

'I never heard about that,' said Charlotte.

'It's a fact,' insisted Verbena. 'Now they're putting up a bloody circus tent right where her body lay.'

'Peg,' said Ivy. 'Peg Entwistle was her name. I made a point of remembering it.' Ivy thought about Peg from time to time when she was feeling blue. She imagined the girl had hiked up to the sign to have a private cry. Peg had apparently found a maintenance ladder propped up against the H. She had climbed to the top of the giant letter and thrown herself off.

'I heard the coyotes got to her body,' Verbena added casually, though she was directing the comment at Charlotte. 'They gnawed her pretty face right off.'

Charlotte's lower lip trembled. 'I don't like coyotes,' she said. 'They frighten me. You know that, Verbena!'

'They'll be out tonight,' said Verbena. 'Wait and see. There'll be coyotes in all the gardens, eating the neighbourhood cats.'

'Stop it, Verbena!' said Charlotte.

'Well, if we can't talk about circuses or coyotes, what can we talk about?' asked Verbena disingenuously.

Charlotte flounced through the French windows into the kitchen, where their new maid, Allegra, had just taken off her apron and folded it on to the table in preparation for the next morning's work. 'Why are you still here, Allie?' said Charlotte, louder than she meant to. 'Go home to your family. Verbena can wash her own dirty glass for a change.'

As Charlotte passed her, Allegra looked out of the window to see Verbena's reaction. She saw her toss the glass over the deck railing into the canyon below.

'All done!' Verbena shouted, as she settled back into her chair.

Ivy threw the last of her gin over the railing, too. She didn't let go of the glass, though – she didn't want Allegra to have to clamber under the deck to retrieve it. Ivy always imagined diamondbacks down there. She thought she heard the sound of their rattles at night, though she knew it was more likely the scratching of the seedpods from the bottle-brush trees.

2

Charlotte went down the passage to her bedroom and slammed the door behind her. She rested her back against it, tried to calm her breathing. It wasn't Verbena's spite that had unsettled her. It was the appearance of the circus. It was so close. The circus people might easily walk right up to their deck. Charlotte decided she would talk to Madge about it. The studio could send a security man to patrol the premises until the circus moved on. The canyon hills were quiet at night, barren and isolated. It was dangerous.

In an anxious state, Charlotte sat down at her dressing table. She opened the bottom drawer and pushed aside the velvet pouch that held her combs and brushes, her curling tongs. There, beside the pots of eye-colour and a jar of gardenia talcum powder, lay the perfume bottle. It was nestled in its original gold organza bag, and shaped like a crimson tulip bud on a stand of green glass leaves. The stopper was made of red glass, too, so that the impression was of an ornament without function. The wax seal was still intact.

Whenever Charlotte thought she might open it she remembered what she had done to buy it. It had cost far more than its price tag indicated. Charlotte couldn't bring herself to use the scent, even now. She placed the bottle carefully back in its place. She suspected Verbena's skinny-fingered hands liked to snoop. Those hands explored the contents of cupboards and diary pages, Charlotte suspected. This was a house in which a woman had to keep her secrets hidden. The other two had cemented their friendship before Charlotte had arrived, which made her feel like an interloper.

'Is there anything you need before I go, Miss Charlotte?'

Without warning, the new maid had appeared in her bedroom doorway. Charlotte jumped. She could not get used to the girl's presence, her stealth. Allegra del Rio was her full name – a beautiful name, a name like a river, Charlotte thought. Allie, as they all called her, was a tiny, burnished girl with a slick of long hair like a tar waterfall and eyes like black coffee. She wore a neat uniform with pretty lace edging. Charlotte wasn't sure how to manage her. She had never employed a servant. It was Verbena who knew about such things.

'I need something laundered,' Charlotte said.

She went to her closet and slid the hangers along the rail until she found the fox-fur jacket she had been wearing on the day she had arrived at the house on Lantana Drive. How embarrassing that Verbena had commented that day that it smelt of smoke! Charlotte had been mortified. She sniffed it. Even though she had aired it a dozen times over the intervening months, it still reminded her of her train journey to Los Angeles.

'You must know a reliable laundry,' Charlotte said. A Mexican housemaid was sure to. 'It's very expensive. It's very precious to me.'

She tossed the jacket on to the bed. Allegra picked it up.

'I know a good laundry lady,' said Allegra. 'She stays near me.'

Charlotte wondered where the girl lived. It crossed her mind that it might be a long commute, and it was already dark outside, but she didn't ask. She went over to her purse and handed Allegra a dollar bill. Allegra took the money. Charlotte tried to decipher the maid's expression, and could not. The girl's face was a stone wall. Charlotte found her enigmatic expressions disconcerting. Had she given the girl enough money? She immediately handed over another dollar bill. Allegra took it with a bob.

'I will bring your change,' Allegra said quietly, and Charlotte wondered whether she should have entrusted her with the jacket. Would the girl run off with it? Perhaps it was too soon to give her such an errand. It would be so nice, though, to have somebody to ask about things – other than Verbena, who wouldn't even share the name of the salon that waved her hair so well.

It occurred to Charlotte that Allegra was likely newer to Los Angeles than she herself was. For Allegra, the whole country and everyone in it was foreign. For some reason, this thought was comforting.

Madge St Claire arrived on Lantana Drive the following morning dressed, as usual, in a man's suit. It fitted her perfectly; her body was lean and hipless, all angles and edges. Madge was tough. She worked in an industry dominated by men, one of the few female 'ten-percenters' – talent agents who squeezed the studios for every dollar and who were seen as a necessary evil, tolerated by their clients and universally loathed by their clients' employers. It took a unique kind of woman to relish this abuse. Madge St Claire was that woman. On her short nails, she wore polish so dark it was nearly black. Her lips were painted the same deep colour. She wore powder too pale and dyed her hair too red.

Madge found Ivy and Verbena in the kitchen.

'Good morning, Madge,' said Verbena. 'Have you been in the sun? You look quite life-like.'

Ivy tried, but failed, to hold back a grin.

Madge looked scornfully at the bathrobes Ivy and Verbena still wore. 'Which is more than I can say for you two. It's nearly ten o'clock, my darlings,' she noted.

They heard Charlotte coming down the stairs. She appeared in a sundress the colour of a strawberry milkshake with wide-legged white trousers beneath it. Her hair was tied up in a pink floral scarf. Both Verbena and Ivy adjusted their robes self-consciously.

'At least Miss Caine is presentable,' said Madge.

'You know that Charlotte is the good one, Madge,' said Verbena, rolling her eyes. 'Charlotte is one of God's special angels, sent as an example to us all.'

'Apparently you could use one,' said Madge. She took an empty vodka bottle from the sink, holding its neck between two fingers, as if the contents might be poison. She threw it theatrically into the garbage can. As studio actresses, the three young women were contractually obliged to behave in a decorous manner. They were expected to turn up for their calls on time, avoid staying out late, and live clean, decent lives. Madge St Claire did not, however, view herself as a housemother.

'Have you girls been eating?' She opened the refrigerator to reveal a slab of butter and two bottles of tonic water. She closed it in a slow, sad rebuke. 'I have some important announcements to make.' Madge slid a cigarette into the thin glass filament of her holder as she spoke. 'They liked you, Verbena. They really liked you. That's the honest truth, my darling.'

'Good,' said Verbena.

'But . . .' Madge paused to pick a speck of tobacco from her tongue. 'They want to see Charlotte.'

'What?' shouted Verbena.

'I'm sorry, my darling,' said Madge. 'But Charlotte is my client, too.'

'That part is mine,' said Verbena, furiously.

'It may still be,' consoled Madge. 'They've asked to see Charlotte, that's all. She's been assigned a time tomorrow with Selznick. Word came through to my office this morning.'

Madge St Claire had no office. She worked from her home in Echo Park, where she lived with a menagerie of exotic caged animals.

'They want you at three, Charlotte. I'll make sure they send a car.'

Charlotte looked modestly at her shoes. She had been hoping for this; Madge had hinted at it but now it had actually happened. Charlotte had her chance. If they liked her, if the public liked her, she would be in a position to re-negotiate her contract. She would have some real money of her own for the first time. Perhaps there would even be enough to secure a house like the one she coveted on Cherry-bowl Lane. 'Coveted' was the right word. Charlotte had wanted a home of her own for as long as she could remember. She wanted it more than she had ever wanted anything . . . except for the red scent bottle, she thought. And the suit with the fox-fur jacket. She had wanted those things very badly, too, and she had got them. She ought to feel proud.

'If I get the part, I'll be able to buy my own house,' Charlotte blurted out.

'Oh, I'll get a husband to do that for me,' said Ivy.

Verbena shot Ivy a scathing glance.

'But it wouldn't be yours then, would it?' said Charlotte, earnestly. 'You could be kicked out on his whim. The bank could take it away from you. You would never feel safe.'

'I thought your father treated you to all the best places,' said Verbena.

Verbena was always trying to catch Charlotte out in a lie. It was getting tedious but it had become a bad habit and Verbena found she could not give it up, even when she could see that Ivy found it mean-spirited and irritating.

'I don't expect you to understand, Verbena. You were given everything.'

It was true. Verbena's family was extremely wealthy. She came from Boston. Verbena didn't dwell on the fact that her family had all but disowned her for becoming a movie actress. Only her maiden aunt still corresponded. Monthly letters arrived in her spindly hand. 'Maybe you should land the part before you start spending the pay,' she said.

'I'm an expert at screen tests. I'll give you a few pointers, Charlotte,' twittered Ivy. 'Don't do your own lipstick. Pretend to forget it and then ask for some once they've started filming. Put it on in front of the camera.' Ivy lit a cigarette and sucked on it deeply to draw attention to her own mouth as she spoke. It worked. Charlotte watched Ivy's lips as they moved. Verbena was transfixed. 'That way they think you're seductive without being lascivious. Oh, and smoke in front of them. Really suck on a cigarette, and let them see you do it. Your mouth is everything in this business and I don't mean the way you speak. You'll have that screening panel squirming in their breeches . . .That's free advice.'

'You're a dirty girl, Ivy,' said Madge, not without admiration.

'It's a dirty business,' commented Verbena.

Ivy stubbed out the cigarette she had just lit and flicked the butt on to the dishes in the sink. Madge shook her head. The kitchen counters were littered with breadcrumbs. Nail-polish bottles stood at the centre of coffee-cup rings. Cupboard doors hung open. The sink hosted a balancing act of porcelain plates.

'I'm going to lie by the pool,' said Ivy.

'Don't get too dark,' said Madge. 'If you're not careful, you'll look like a fruit picker and there's no acting work for Mexicans in this town.'

'I'll wear a hat,' said Ivy. 'But I have to get outdoors.' She turned to Madge and added, in a soft sing-song aside, 'You don't know what it's like living with these two. They're at each other's throats like two she-cats.'

'What time does your maid arrive?' asked Madge, changing the subject.

Just as she said it, Allegra hurried across the deck and came into the kitchen through the French windows, to discover them all awaiting her. Allegra tried so hard not to be noticed that she found their anticipation of her arrival most uncomfortable. She had no way of knowing that the three actresses found her presence equally disconcerting.

She was like a mute ghost in the house, a disapproving conscience.

Allegra kept her eyes down while she explained, 'The bus was very late today.'

'It's fine, Allie,' said Charlotte.

'It's not fine,' said Verbena. 'Get on with your work at once.'

Allegra scurried into the pantry to change from her forlorn little dress into her uniform.

'Don't take your personal dissatisfaction out on the help, Verbena,' said Madge, as she gathered up her cigarette case and prepared to leave. 'Now, is there anything else anybody needs?'

'Oooh, oooh,' said Ivy, remembering. 'I need some binoculars to spy on the circus that's moved into our canyon.'

Madge didn't enquire any further. She didn't require details. No request was too odd or too obscure. She had been dealing with actresses for ten years and the breath-taking scope of their demands and insecurities no longer surprised her. 'Binoculars. Fine,' she said. 'Toodle-oo.'

Madge left the kitchen and strode along the hall. Verbena stood up to follow her. She hurried after her and caught up with her on the drive, where she took the agent so hard by the arm that her fingers left red stripes on Madge's white-blue skin. 'It's my part, Madge,' Verbena said. 'You know it's my part. It's the one I've been waiting for, the important one. The one that's going to count.'

'That's the business, Verbena,' said Madge. 'I'm so sorry.'

Madge touched Verbena's cheek but Verbena pulled her face away.

'I don't know what will happen if she gets it,' said Verbena. 'I just don't know what I'll do.'

'How can I help, my darling?'

'Get me the part, Madge. I need it.'

Madge's face contorted in real empathy. 'Only you can do that, my darling.'

'But I tried so hard!'

'I know you did. Nothing's been decided yet. They may not like her. Is there anything else?'

Verbena steadied herself. She swallowed her anger. As it cooled, it turned to stone inside her. 'Circus tickets,' said Verbena. 'Charlotte especially wants to go and I'd like to surprise her.'

3

Charlotte stood at the centre of a halo of light. Beyond the focused spotlight beam, a row of chairs accommodated four men.

A young production assistant, a pretty, wide-eyed boy in a harlequin sweater, stepped into the light and snapped a clapperboard in front of Charlotte's face.

'Miss Charlotte Caine reading for the part of Rahab in *The Walls of Jericho*,' he called out. His announcement was followed by silence. Charlotte heard the cameras' whirr out in the darkness. Click, click, click, they went, as the film ticked through.

'Carlie.' It was Madge St Claire. One of the masculine shapes in the darkness belonged to her. Charlotte was relieved by Madge's presence. 'I think Carlie is better. Carlie Caine,' Madge said. 'Charlotte's too English. Carlie is fresh, snappy. Carlie is American.'

'Hello, Madge,' said Charlotte, in her lowest, most alluring voice.

'Hello, my darling. Just you relax now. Mr Selznick will give you a few directions.'

Charlotte turned to the nearest camera lens. She posed for its blank, enormous eye. She didn't swallow: nothing made a woman look less sure of herself or more vulnerable. She held a flood of saliva in her mouth.

'Look down a little,' said a man, from the darkness.

Charlotte presumed this voice belonged to David O. Selznick, the studio's *Wunderkind*.

'Give me coy and bashful,' Selznick's voice commanded.

Charlotte was an expert at that particular look. She dipped her chin in a barely perceptible gesture of submission.

'Head up again,' said the voice.

Charlotte grew haughty as she pulled herself up to full height.

'Turn right.'

'My right or yours?' Charlotte asked. She could feel her heart pounding against the fabric of the plain black shift they had made her wear. Could they see her pulse thumping in her temple?

'Your right side to the camera, darling.' This in Madge's familiar voice.

There was some discussion and a titter among the men as Charlotte turned. She made sure her breasts were pushed out; her shoulder blades were almost touching. Charlotte knew her face was perfect, her long neck beautiful. They knew it, too. She wanted her body to be admired. Charlotte understood what most men wanted from her. She hoped these men wanted it enough.

Charlotte moved like a puppet for a further ten minutes. They hadn't put any makeup on her yet; they hadn't asked her to speak a word. She saw Madge's shape move towards the director's in the dark. Madge leaned over the man's shoulder and spoke into his ear. Charlotte thought she heard the word 'sensational' hissed in the gloom. Selznick's reply was a 'hmmm' of indecision. Charlotte thought that was it. She was done for. She had failed. They hadn't even let her do a reading.

Charlotte recalled Ivy's snippet of advice from the day before. 'Is there anyone from Makeup on hand?' she asked. 'If we're done, I'd love some lipstick.'

A girl scurried forward and handed her a silver tube.

'Thank you,' said Charlotte, as she gracefully spooled it open. The lipstick was rosy crimson, a peculiar shade that was neither red nor pink. Charlotte applied it and smiled. 'I feel quite naked up here without it,' she purred. 'Isn't that silly?'

In a flash, every man in the room imagined Charlotte Caine naked. The tension in the room grew almost palpable.

'Moving on,' said Mr Selznick. His voice came out in a squeak as he cleared his throat. 'Moving on,' he repeated more deeply.

'Carlie,' said Madge. 'You can go into Makeup now. They want to see what you look like in blue.'

'I look sensational in blue,' said Charlotte.

Charlotte sat for an hour in a chair while a stylist played with her hair, weaving it into complicated plaits and binding them with lengths of copper cord. A makeup girl spent ages on her eyes. Charlotte daydreamed as the girl worked. They didn't let Charlotte look in a mirror when they were done. The camera was her only mirror now. The opinions of those behind it were all that mattered.

The wardrobe master swathed her in a floor-length blue robe. Charlotte followed the boy in the harlequin sweater back to the soundstage. She passed a pane of glass and caught a glimpse of her face reflected in it. The makeup was heavy and tawdry. It turned her eyes into hard, aggressive holes. Charlotte went in front of the cameras once more. The boy in the harlequin sweater raised his clapperboard for the second time. Charlotte noticed that he had rubbed out 'Charlotte' and replaced it with her new name – 'Carlie'. She followed more directions. She read the few lines they had given her. She stood before the selection panel, hot and exposed, while the men conferred.

'She deserves some bigger parts, Madge,' she heard one of the men whisper. 'I agree with you there. She's definitely got something, but Rahab is special. This movie is big. It needs a star . . . Perhaps we should see Verbena Marsh again.'

Charlotte remembered more of Ivy's advice and, in desperation, she decided to try it. 'Does anybody have a cigarette?' She tried to sound bored.

The clapperboard boy handed her a Chesterfield. Charlotte pressed close into him as he lit it for her. She tilted her head back to expose the deep fulcrum V at the base of her neck, and exhaled a perfect O of smoke. It rose, expanding yet holding its shape, until it trembled in a disintegrating cerulean halo above her head. The camera caught the moment – the exposed throat, the exhalation of blue, and the adoration of the clapperboard boy, who looked on, transfixed. His body stiffened in response to the experience. He winced in embarrassment and had to scurry away.

Mr Selznick knew rampant sex appeal when he saw it. 'I don't believe Rahab was a smoker, Miss Caine.' He chuckled uncomfortably at his own observation.

'If they'd had cigarettes back then, she would have been,' said Charlotte. She put the cigarette back into her mouth and drew on it with gentle, sustained suction. 'I believe Rahab was familiar with all of life's vices.'

The men were silent for a few seconds more. David Selznick was at a crossroads. The girl would be absolutely perfect for something – and he believed he knew what that something was – but did she have the necessary vulnerability to play his Rahab?

'It's good to watch potential leads side by side. I'd like to see her read with Liam,' Selznick said. 'I've called him in today. He'll be here shortly.' He wanted to watch the pair together. That would decide him. Sometimes what Selznick thought of as 'natural fizz' existed between two actors and sometimes it did not. It couldn't be manufactured.

When Liam Malone did arrive, he made his entrance quietly and with artless ease. He greeted the casting director and the man adjusting the lights with the same apportionment of grace. He shook hands with several people; he smiled at everybody. He knew names. Liam was dressed in a pair of smart pinstriped trousers paired with a white cotton sweater. The sleeves were sloughed up to his elbows and the fabric was taut across his chest and around his biceps. Liam was a man of unconscious personal style. His black hair was a pleasing, wavy muss; his teeth were white and even – a triumph of good blood over childhood deprivation.

Liam made his way towards the lighted area where Charlotte had been awaiting his entrance so anxiously that she had, at the crucial moment, almost missed it. Charlotte had her back to his approach. She had dropped her script and the sheets had spilled out across the floor in a perfect fan. Liam bent over to help her collect them. At first, flustered, Charlotte didn't identify her gentleman helper. Then she met Liam's eyes over a single piece of paper they had both taken hold of. Charlotte's mouth opened slightly in wonder and the beginnings of an uncertain smile, but Liam was very serious in his contemplation of her perfectly beautiful face.

They stayed frozen like that for a few seconds before Selznick stepped in to make the formal introductions and cover the awkward moment of mutual attraction. He had seen it, though. Nobody present could have failed to notice it. It was fizz! It sizzled.

The screen test between the two players clinched the deal. Liam Malone left the set immediately afterwards and the studio lawyers were called to draft the contracts. Madge St Claire acted as Charlotte's representative and signed on the line for her ten per cent.

4

Back at the house, before they got out of Madge's enormous black Ford, the agent turned Charlotte towards her and said, quite solemnly, 'Let me tell Verbena, would you, Carlie? She had her heart set on landing the Rahab role.'

Charlotte wanted to say, 'Good!' She wanted to breeze in and toss her success on to the kitchen table under Verbena's nose, but she was feeling so light, so overcome by happiness, that she could be magnanimous. Madge went into the house first. Charlotte felt ridiculous, hovering outside her own front door, but after a few minutes she heard Verbena's bedroom door slam at the end of the hallway. The sound shook the house. As generous as Charlotte thought she felt, she couldn't help smiling to herself. When she entered the house, she saw Allegra. The girl bobbed a curtsy and said, in her slight Spanish accent, 'Congratulations, Miss Caine.'

'Thank you, Allie.'

Ivy was there, too, and embraced her warmly. 'This is it, Charlotte. This is your big break. You'll be able to buy your house now.'

Charlotte hadn't really considered the financial implications of landing the part. Now she saw that what Ivy had said might well be true. Somehow she couldn't consider a house: her head was filled with Liam Malone.

'There's a bottle of champagne in the refrigerator,' said Ivy. 'Allie can bring it out to us.'

Ivy, Madge and Charlotte went on to the deck. It was growing dark and the lights of the circus tent in the distance twinkled against the dusty hillside. Charlotte's stomach flipped over like a pancake at the sight of it, but her excitement overshadowed any qualms.

Allegra delivered a bamboo tray with three crystal flutes. She scurried back inside to make a second trip with an ice bucket containing a bottle of Bollinger. Madge popped the cork, which flew into the canyon and drew all their eyes to the distant tent once again.

'Oh, that reminds me,' said Madge. 'Before we toast, I bought something for Ivy.' She scratched about in her capacious handbag and retrieved a moulded leather case. 'Don't ever say I don't meet your every need, darling girl,' she said.

Ivy opened the case and retrieved a pair of binoculars.

'You remembered!' she squealed, and immediately placed the binoculars to her eyes. She turned them towards Charlotte, who sat across the table from her with her champagne glass raised, waiting for her moment.

'I'm sorry, Charlotte,' said Ivy, putting the binoculars down and raising her own glass. 'To Charlotte,' she declared.

'Carlie,' Charlotte corrected her. 'The studio wants me to be called "Carlie" from now on.'

'I convinced them today,' said Madge. 'I decided I liked the sound of it.'

'I suppose "Carlie" has a certain sass,' said Ivy. '"Carlie" can be playful or seductive. Carlie Caine – it rolls off the tongue.'

'To Carlie, then,' Madge announced.

The chink of their flutes confirmed it.

'So, what's Mr Malone like?' asked Ivy.

Madge let out a snort of disdain and lit a cigarette, placing it in her signature glass holder. 'He may be a star, darling girl, but he's still just a bloody man.'

'I'm only asking,' said Ivy. 'Is he a dish?'

'He's perfect,' said Charlotte. 'The kind of big man you feel really safe with. He has the darkest hair, the bluest eyes.'

'So he's as gorgeous in person,' stated Ivy. She sounded a bit melancholy at hearing it. 'He's like he is on the screen.'

'No, he's not. He's entirely different,' said Charlotte. 'He smiles so easily,' she added, in a tone of near astonishment. Smiles were not easy for Charlotte. She had to practise hers. Joy did not come naturally.

'They're always different in the beginning,' said Madge. 'Very different and . . . and . . .' She sought the right word. 'Less, usually.'

'No,' said Charlotte. 'That's where you're wrong, Madge. He's not less. He's more. He's so much more than I could have dreamed.'

'He was on the soundstage with you?' asked Ivy.

'Yes. We didn't get to speak much with all the fittings and scene blocking, but I watched him with other people. He was kind to them when he didn't need to be.'

'He's an actor, remember that,' said Madge. 'He was on view. That's about as authentic as an "I love you" at the moment of penetration.'

'Madge!' shrieked Ivy, and let out a glissando of giggles. 'That sounds like something Bee would say.'

At the mention of Verbena, all three looked towards the part of the house where Verbena's bedroom was.

*

That evening, Madge took Charlotte out to dinner. They drove down through the twisting canyon roads into West-wood Village. There was a quaint courtyard restaurant there, covered with slipper vines and lit by candles. After their wine had been poured, Madge rested her elbows on the table, steepled her fingers, and leaned forward with sincerity.

'It's my opinion that you may go far, Miss Caine.'

Charlotte smiled. It was a novelty to be dining with a woman. Sometimes she felt as if she had spent half her life looking across tables at the veined noses and turkey throats of old men. Madge was lean. There was not an ounce of softness to her. In some ways, Madge reminded Charlotte of her own mother. It was true that Madge was a redhead when her own mother had been blonde but they were of the same type. Charlotte's mother had also been ambitious and cool and generally dissatisfied.

'I'm here to make money, Madge,' said Charlotte. 'I want to buy my own home. That's why I came here in the first place. Can you help me do that?'

Madge's lip tweaked up on one side. It was the closest she ever came to a grin. 'You're direct, Carlie. By God, you're direct. Normally, aspiring actresses tell me they want to act more than life itself. They'd do it for free, they tell me, just for the love of it.'

'I don't do anything for free,' said Charlotte. 'I have my future to consider. There's nobody to take care of me.'

'Good girl,' said Madge. 'Practical girl. Which brings us to the point of our dinner.'

'I thought we were celebrating,' said Charlotte. She was always afraid when people said things like that, when they implied there was a reason for a private meeting, or a need to discuss something. She always imagined the worst, that something terrible had been found out.

'I need to know everything,' said Madge.

So it was true. Madge had her suspicions about Charlotte's past, just like Verbena. Charlotte sipped her wine. She wanted to cry.

'Personally, I don't care what you've done,' said Madge. 'But I need to know so that I can protect you.'

'Know what?' asked Charlotte. She was going to play it out to the very end.

'Whatever it is,' said Madge. 'Everybody has a past. There's usually something that's better left hidden. Tomorrow or the next day, *Variety* will announce that you're to be Rahab and you'll suddenly be somebody worth sniffing around. The press will pounce. If there's anything to find, they'll find it, Carlie. It would be better to let me know first.'

'I can't think of anything,' said Charlotte. 'Do you mean scandals?'

'I mean anything,' said Madge. 'Anything,' she stressed.

'I'm too young to have a past.'

'If that's true, you'll be the easiest client I've ever managed,' said Madge. 'Only it isn't. It never is.'

'I'm an open book, a daddy's girl who lost her mother very young.'

'How did you lose your mother?' asked Madge, almost casually.

'She died when I was twelve. She was very ill. She had been very ill for a long time.'

'Ahhh,' said Madge, her forehead wrinkled in compassion,

but Charlotte couldn't help suspecting that the older woman didn't believe a word of it.

'I've made my money spotting opportunities, Carlie. I see where the wind's going to blow and I'm there waiting for it. This depression's brought the country to its knees. People are going hungry. There are Americans without enough food to eat. Imagine that! It's a disgrace. But do you know the one industry that's flourished?'

Charlotte leaned forward to meet her with breathy expectation. The lights fell softly on her face, the lips she had just wetted, her eager-to-please eyes. 'I do,' she said. Charlotte relished knowing the answer, any answer. 'Moving pictures.'

'Spot on. And why do you think that is? Escapism, that's why. Things are so God-awful that people will spend their last penny for a laugh or a love story. They need to feel normal again. They don't feel so poor in those darkened theatres. They're swept away by the stories, the magic of it. They're transported.'

Charlotte put down her empty wine glass. 'How much will I make, Madge?' she asked bluntly. 'Will I be able to buy a house?'

'Yes,' said Madge. 'I believe we can arrange that. If that's what you imagine will make you happy.'

'It will make me happy,' said Charlotte. 'I know it will. I can't live with Ivy any more. Well, not so much Ivy as Verbena.'

'Verbena,' said Madge, with a sigh of fondness. 'I understand the Verbenas of this world. Tossed out by their families, used to privilege but doing without for a principle or a career that's viewed as unsuitable. I was a

Verbena once, until I decided to be myself, to be a scandal.'

'I thought it was your job to avoid scandals,' laughed Charlotte.

'That's something I do for my clients, Charlotte,' Madge said. She emphasized the old name to bring Charlotte back to earth, to remind the girl that she was nothing more than a Madge St Claire invention. 'So, can you assure me that there are no awkward brothers or sisters?'

'I'm an only child.'

'There's no embarrassing drunken mother? I can't tell you how seriously the studio views these matters.'

'I've already told you that my mother has passed.'

'What about your father? How is he doing?' Madge knew Charlotte's father was no more than a body in a bed, a living corpse that needed to be fed and bathed.

'The situation with my father has been difficult,' acquiesced Charlotte. 'He's doing as well as can be expected. I simply must go to the home to visit him tomorrow.' Charlotte hadn't seen her father for months; it was painful to see him.

'You absolutely have to go,' said Madge. 'We don't need accusations of neglect from the press.'

'They wouldn't dare!' said Charlotte.

'Let's not give them the chance,' said Madge. 'A little visit might be just the thing your father needs. There's nothing the public loves more than a doting daughter.'

Madge dropped Charlotte back at her house. She watched the young woman go in through the front door and waved her goodbye. As she turned her car around in the drive, somebody stepped into the glare of the vehicle's beams. Madge had to stand on the brake pedal to prevent the bumper hitting Verbena, who was in her nightgown, holding an empty glass. Her drooping eyelids and slightly slurred speech told Madge she was drunk.

'Been celebrating with the little angel?' Verbena asked.

'You need to get some sleep, Verbena,' said Madge, gently but firmly.

'Ivy's gone out,' said Verbena. Madge could hear tears in the woman's words. 'She has a beau now, did you know that? He's very good to her, apparently.'

'So are you,' said Madge.

'Ha!' declared Verbena. 'She doesn't want me. The studio doesn't want me.'

'We'll find you something, my darling,' said Madge, reassuringly. She was deeply concerned by the despair she heard. She tried to think of what she could do to make Verbena feel better. The woman was at a low point. In the harsh headlights, she looked – for the first time – haggard. 'You're on the cusp of something wonderful,' said Madge. 'I feel it.'

Verbena smiled wanly. 'Really?'

'I'd like you to make friends with your friends again,' Madge suggested.

'That woman is not my friend,' said Verbena.

'Do it for Ivy, then,' said Madge.

'Ivy is my friend,' Verbena stated.

'I know, my darling. I know.'

Madge eased her Ford past Verbena and turned on to Lantana Drive. Verbena's sadness bothered her as she drove. What could she do to help her through this bad patch? Madge knew how Charlotte's success must burn Verbena, who had been working in the business far longer but had never had her big break. Suddenly it came to Madge. It seemed bizarre, but Verbena, who exuded grace and elegance, had especially asked her for circus tickets. Madge decided she would rustle up a few of the best seats for that Saturday night's show. An evening at the circus, however incongruous it seemed, might be just the thing to cheer Verbena up.

5

Charlotte followed a nun down the sanatorium corridor. Her heels sounded very loud to her as they clicked along the tiles. Glamour was inappropriate here.

Ahead of her, the nun came to a standstill. She turned to face Charlotte with her hands clasped discreetly across her stomach and her eyes downcast. Charlotte didn't know this particular woman. All nuns looked alike to her. Their skin was grey without makeup. They were old beyond their years. While some people Charlotte had known – the Catholics especially – claimed that nuns glowed with innocence, Charlotte had always thought of them as deeply bitter people, and sly. They had reached the door to her father's room. Charlotte went in without thanking the sister for her escort. Her father's figure was serene in the bed. His eyes were open but they stared right through Charlotte. He seemed focused on the wall behind her, where a solitary crucifix looked like a black crack in the plaster.

'I'll leave you to your visit, Miss Caine,' said the nun. She had an Irish accent. 'And I'll tell Sister Olivia you're here.'

Charlotte nodded at her and the nun slipped away. Charlotte knew the sisters here saw her as a special case, one assigned directly to them by the hand of the Almighty. Miss Caine and her dear father were living proof of the Lord's mercy, if poor Mr Caine could be thought of as living.

Patrick Caine's head injuries were still evident, though

healed. His body had repaired itself during the preceding months. Scars ran like pink veins through his hairline. The obstinate stubble on his cheeks and chin had been shaved.

One of her father's hands lay where it had been placed over the taut stretch of snowy sheet. The other had atrophied into a claw that rested motionless on his chest. His mouth moved, though, chewing and chewing at the non-existent tobacco some undamaged part of his brain clearly missed.

Charlotte didn't know what to do when she was in this room. She pulled a chair beside the bed and took her father's normal hand in her own. She squeezed it firmly. It did not respond. Charlotte caressed the knuckles with her fingertips. There were old calluses between the joints from long-ago fist fights. The nails had been cleaned. The man's eyes didn't flicker as Charlotte pressed her lips to his forehead. His mouth moved continuously, producing saliva that dribbled down his chin. Charlotte saw that he had travelled a vast distance and would not return. He could not find his way back to the world they had shared for so many years. Perhaps he did not want to.

Charlotte took some lotion from her purse and warmed it in her hands. She pushed the sleeve of her father's nightshirt up and began to rub the cream into his arm, massaging gently with smooth, regular movements. She wished he could understand her success. Sometimes, when she was feeling lonely, she wished he was around to share in her achievements, but her father was all but gone. Comprehension came and went in him like the shape of a cloud. Charlotte told herself she would visit him more often if she owned a car. Borrowing the blue Jordan from Verbena all the time was awkward, especially given the recent acceleration of their mutual animosity. Charlotte had taken a taxi that morning and the fare had been expensive. Perhaps she would buy herself a car. The boldness of the idea shocked her, but why not? Might she not be able to buy herself a new home and a new car? It all seemed possible now.

It was a blessing that her father could no longer talk. Suppose he had become one of those half-witted mental cases who tried to tell everybody their sad story? Charlotte didn't know what she would have done then. But, no, her father only muttered sounds to himself. He couldn't disclose anything, nothing coherent at least. In that one way, she was a very lucky girl. Even if her father remembered any of her secrets, he was in no condition to compromise her with them. She had told Madge the truth. There were no scandals in her past that might resurface and cause ripples.

They had been travelling together on a train when Charlotte's father had sustained his dreadful injuries. They had been crossing the country from Miami to Los Angeles for Charlotte's screen test with the studio when they had been attacked by bandits. Three men had beaten her father; one had been armed with a broken bottle. It had been a sordid, ugly tragedy and Charlotte still felt nauseous when she remembered how sticky and fiercely red her father's blood had been as she tried to staunch it. They had been nearing the terminus by then and the train had stopped.

'Please.' She remembered repeating that one word, though nobody was there to help, and their attackers had fled, jumping from the slowing train as it approached the station.

Charlotte had moved to the nearest exit and slithered down on to the station siding. She had almost collapsed – her legs were jelly – but her fall had been broken by a figure standing on the platform. The woman had been wearing black, so the blood from Charlotte's hands barely marked her clothes.

'Please,' Charlotte had repeated to the body she had seized. 'Please.'

She had looked up into the astonished eyes of Sister Olivia, who was only there to greet a visiting priest from Sacramento.

If Charlotte had absorbed any of her early religious schooling, she might have considered her meeting with Sister Olivia to be a miracle. Instead, she thought of it as a lucky break.

'It's my father,' she had stammered, and the sister, sensing the girl's shock and being of a stalwart disposition, had taken charge of the situation. She had arranged immediate attention for the injured man and soothed the hysterical girl. Now Charlotte's father lay in that same sister's sanatorium, as he had done for the preceding six months, with little change and little expectation of change.

'He's doing very well,' said Sister Olivia, from the doorway.

Charlotte turned to look at her, returned from the past to the sterile surroundings of the present. Sister Olivia took in Charlotte's dress and grooming, her beautifully made-up face. This girl was an angel. Sister Olivia had read about Charlotte's latest success in *Variety* that morning. The girl was to play Rahab in a very important new picture. Sister Olivia had a weakness for the pictures – only the decent, more respectable ones, of course. Charlotte's face up on that big screen made Sister Olivia want to burst with pride, though pride was sinful, she reminded herself.

'You're doing well, too, I believe,' Sister Olivia added. The comment wasn't snide; she seemed really pleased for Charlotte. 'A little bluebird told me some lovely news about your acting work, Miss Caine.'

'Oh, yes,' said Charlotte. She, too, had pored through *Variety* that morning. The announcement regarding the completion of casting for *The Walls of Jericho* had mentioned her name, but the accompanying photograph had been that of Liam Malone, since the article had reiterated his participation in the project, too. Charlotte hadn't minded that her photograph had been omitted from the article. Soon she and Liam would be seen together all the time.

'They say the picture will be a triumph. And I do believe you'll be the loveliest thing in it,' said Sister Olivia.

Charlotte blushed prettily. 'Oh, I don't know about that. I can only try to do the part justice.' It was something she had once overheard Verbena say during a telephone interview.

'You're so lovely, Miss Caine. I think people would watch you no matter what you were doing.'

That idea made Charlotte uncomfortable. For some reason, she thought about the circus in the canyon again. 'I've brought some money with me today,' Charlotte said, partly to quiet her own anxiety and partly to shut the old woman up. They loved their money, nuns. 'To help the convent . . .'

'Put it in the poor box as you leave, Miss Caine. We don't count dollars here but we do appreciate your help.'

'He can't come home,' said Charlotte, in a matter-of-fact voice, turning her attention back to her father.

'No, dear. Your father is better off here where we can give him constant care. He's doing as well as can be expected. It's been almost six months and he's still with us. Often, they don't last very long, you know. Still, you should prepare yourself for the inevitable.'

'I try and focus on the future,' said Charlotte.

She was thinking of Liam Malone again, his sheltering body and his boisterous laugh. He had a way of attracting all the attention in a room. Yes, her father's passing would be a blessing, Charlotte thought. Sister Olivia was right about that.

'Of course, sometimes they hold on for years and years,' added the sister.

That thought made Charlotte shiver.

'Would you like some tea, Miss Caine?' asked the nun. 'You look a bit chilly in that light dress.'

Charlotte interpreted the remark as a criticism of her summer clothing. She took the cardigan from where it was draped around her shoulders and pulled it on. Perhaps she had been displaying an immodest amount of shoulder. She followed Sister Olivia back down the corridor, retracing the way she had come. The nun's traditional habit hid Charlotte's view, so she didn't see the group of journalists until she was almost upon them. The men stood in a rumpled clump in the reception area, their shirts untucked and their ties splotched with breakfast ketchup.

The Irish sister who had escorted Charlotte earlier chastised them.

'This is a house of the Lord!' she remonstrated. Her voice was drowned out by clamouring questions.

'Miss Caine, have you been with your father?'

'Is he doing better, Miss Caine?'

'Can we get a picture with him, Miss Caine?'

'Does he know about your new role?'

Flashlights snapped in Charlotte's face. She put up a hand to cover her eyes, then thought she must look like a criminal. She dropped it and smiled instead, pretending she had only been startled for a second. In truth, she was horrified. How had they found her here, and so quickly? Charlotte wasn't used to the press. In the past few months, she had conducted only two polite interviews over coffee with fawning women from the ladies' magazines.

Behind the crowd of photographers, Charlotte suddenly saw Madge St Claire standing coolly by with her arms crossed and a cigarette pluming smoke from her glass holder.

Madge stepped forward at the sight of Charlotte's diffidence.

'Miss Caine visits her father often,' Madge announced. 'She's quite devoted. Despite the good news announced in *Variety* this morning, she still made her dear father a priority.'

Pencils scribbled furiously in notebooks.

'Miss Caine, I'm Alf Weathers with *Screen Weekly*. Our readers are enormous fans of the moving pictures. Any tips for them about dealing with an ailing parent?'

'I find love to be the best remedy,' said Charlotte, and Madge winked happily at her from beside the press pack.

'Can we have a few pictures? Our readers love pictures.'

'Oh, I'm not dressed . . .' said Charlotte, smoothing her skirt self-consciously.

'Nonsense, you look lovely. Doesn't she, boys?' Madge goaded.

The men hummed their agreement. One whistled in saucy appreciation and everybody laughed.

'Could I have a minute to prepare him?' Charlotte smiled her most delicious smile. She held it on her face until she turned her back and started along the corridor towards her father's room once more, with Madge at her side.

'How could you do this to me, Madge?' she hissed. 'I'll never forgive you!'

'Why not?' asked Madge, utterly astonished. 'It's a fabulous story. They leaped at it the moment I called.'

'You ambushed me,' said Charlotte. 'I'm very private about my father. I don't like him exposed. I don't want him spotlighted because of my professional life.'

'You'd better get used to it, my darling,' said Madge. 'You're entering the big-time now. Is he very ugly?'

They had arrived at the room and Madge saw the answer to her question lying before her. 'Oh dear,' she said, having second thoughts about her well-staged impromptu photo opportunity. 'This is unfortunate.'

'I told you he was scarred in the attack.'

'Verbena didn't seem to think he was that bad,' said Madge.

'Verbena?' said Charlotte.

'Yes, all this was Verbena's idea to get you some free publicity. She spoke to me about it this morning. If you're mad, have it out with her. She seemed to think you'd love the idea.'

'I should have known she put you up to this,' said Charlotte.

Charlotte had confessed to Verbena how she felt about her father when they had first met. She didn't like to talk about him or what had happened to him. She hoped he would die quietly and be at peace. She had opened up to Verbena on this point; there was no way that Verbena could have mistaken her position. For Verbena to be disloyal to this extent was a betrayal of enormous proportions. Charlotte felt it as a knife thrust between her ribs.

Still, Madge had beckoned the journalists, and Charlotte could already hear their shoes clattering down the corridor. She smiled for them. She posed beside her father and smiled. She smiled and thought that she would kill Verbena for this. She would kill her.

Unfortunately, Verbena wasn't at the house when Charlotte returned from the sanatorium, so there was no way to confront her. Charlotte had seethed the whole way home; Madge had driven her.

'I think it went fabulously well,' said Madge. 'I'm sorry you found it so distasteful but the coverage will do your career a world of good. You'll see, darling girl. When this month's rags hit the newsstands, half the country will know your name.'

'I don't mind them knowing my name,' said Charlotte, as she slammed Madge's car door shut behind her. 'It's my father's name I'm concerned about.'

'Carlie,' Madge tried to appease her, 'you have to let it go. It's done. It's a good thing. And next Friday night is Charlie Chaplin's party. You need to be at your best.'

*

Sitting at the dressing table in her room, Charlotte tried to think positive thoughts. She was Rahab. She had won a significant role, acting beside Liam Malone. Liam Malone was a dream and they would be working together for the next few months. As a salve, Charlotte took the Fleurs de Rocaille from its organza bag and held the cut-glass bottle in her hand. It glowed like a red coal; it ought to have burned her but it was cold and surprisingly weighty. Charlotte felt a physical quiver beneath her skin as a thought hit her: she could have the bottle on display now. She could look at it as she lay in bed. It would be the last thing she saw before she drifted off. Its convolutions were endlessly fascinating, changing with the angle of the crystal corolla.

She still would not open it, though. She could not. She had come to fear the contents a little. If the perfume was not as sweet as she remembered, she didn't think she could bear the disappointment.

Charlotte looked around her bedroom. Allegra had replaced her sheets that day. She could smell the sunshine on them. The bed stood crisp and replete between a pair of mahogany side tables. The room was stylish but Charlotte did not own it. She was only a renter here. She would not put the perfume bottle out in this room, she decided. The place simply wasn't good enough for it. She would save it until she had her own home. Then it would feel right to have the Fleurs de Rocaille on display.

Charlotte tried to stay awake to confront Verbena when she returned, but by the time she heard the engine of the blue Jordan pull into the drive, she had decided against it. She was too tired for a scene.

6

Charlotte and Verbena started to argue over breakfast. Charlotte attacked Verbena about informing the press of her father's condition and his whereabouts. Verbena claimed that she only had Charlotte's best interests at heart. She had thought Charlotte would appreciate the free publicity. Charlotte scoffed at that excuse, refusing any explanation that involved pure motives. Verbena was as wily as a fox. Verbena accused Charlotte of stealing the part of Rahab from her. The fight became so intense that poor Allegra had to cover her ears. The maid felt sympathy for Ivy, who was always in the middle when Charlotte and Verbena had a tiff.

Eventually, the antagonists retreated to their separate bedrooms to fume. Ivy shuttled between them like a nurse with two patients, carrying messages of apology that she embellished greatly. By the time Ivy had done her best work, all three of them had agreed to go out together for the afternoon. It was only after Charlotte accepted this mollifying gesture that she realized Verbena intended to take them to the circus.

'Madge got me special tickets,' Verbena said, when they all met in neutral territory in the hallway. 'I think a day of fun together will clear the air.'

Since Ivy had agreed, Charlotte didn't feel she should be the difficult one. Besides, it was preposterous to assume that this circus would be the same one she had known all those years ago. There must be dozens of small family circuses operating throughout the country. She was being a goose for even worrying about it.

The three women left the house at two o'clock. Verbena drove. Ivy nattered continuously. Charlotte sat, sullen and solitary, on the back seat. She would get through the day, the performance, and then they would go home. She would see Liam Malone in a few days. A cast meeting was scheduled. The blue Jordan followed the curves of the canyon road as they snaked down Beverly Glen before turning east on Ventura Boulevard. As they entered the narrow pass that channelled traffic through the mountains, Verbena slowed.

'We should start to see posters soon,' Ivy said, and just then, one appeared. It was tacked to a lamp post, its edges curled by wind.

When Charlotte saw the sign, she refused to acknowledge it. It showed a disembodied hand in a white glove thrust forward out of preternatural darkness, displaying for the viewer a fan of playing cards – all four were sevens. In white, a message proclaimed 'Magic Sevens Circus' and below that: 'Experience the Marvels! Explore the Horrors!' Charlotte's heart thumped in her chest. As they sped past the poster, she realized that she had stopped breathing. She tried to convince herself that she had not seen the familiar name, the well-known poster. They passed another. The same ghostly, dismembered hand, the same fistful of sevens. Charlotte felt tears rising in her eyes. There was a poster on every second lamp post now, interspersed with white arrows indicating the way. How could it be? Charlotte wondered. How had he found her?

Verbena turned the Jordan through an open gate, and they drove off the tarred road and into a field of dry, ankle-deep grass. She followed ruts in the field left by preceding vehicles until they rounded a gentle hillock and saw the tent. Verbena parked beside a row of ageing cars. Charlotte found her voice. 'I'm not going in,' she said.

'Don't be ridiculous,' said Verbena, as she grabbed her purse and opened the car door.

'I'm not being ridiculous,' said Charlotte. 'I didn't want to come in the first place.'

'We're here now,' said Ivy. 'Come with us. It'll be swell, you'll see.'

'No. I'll wait in the car.'

'It's ninety degrees,' said Verbena. 'Don't be a mule.'

'I'm staying right here,' said Charlotte. 'Leave me alone.'

'Suit yourself,' said Verbena, with perverse satisfaction. 'It'll be a long wait.'

'I don't care,' said Charlotte.

'Let's go, Ivy.' Verbena got out of the car and slammed the door as hard as she could behind her. She remembered Charlotte's response when they had first seen the circus. Now, at the last minute, the woman had bowed out of attending the show, obviously due to some obscure personal terror. Sometimes, Verbena thought, even the smallest torments could be deeply satisfying.

Before following Verbena, Ivy turned round in the front seat and studied Charlotte. 'Don't you feel well?' she asked, noting the sheen of sweat along Charlotte's hairline.

'Come on, Ivy!' Verbena shouted.

'We'll hurry back,' Ivy said. 'Or you can come and find us, if you change your mind.'

Charlotte slithered down on the back seat and curled up into a ball.

A man was approaching them, a large man dressed in a shiny tuxedo jacket and red and white striped stovepipe trousers. He was enormous but squat. He had no visible neck and his bald, polished pate reflected the sun like a gypsy's crystal ball. His collar was choking him and he held a pork-pie hat that looked several sizes too small for his head. Beneath the incongruously elegant tuxedo jacket, the man's shirt was white, or perhaps the palest blue, and it strained against a pair of red elastic braces. He looked like a comic figure – an Oliver Hardy type with a round face designed to wear a cheery grin – except his face was not beaming. It was pointed. The man's nose and ears ended in sharp tips. Even his teeth, when he chewed on his bulbous cigar, seemed filed to spikes.

'Welcome, ladies,' said the man, expansively. He spoke with a strong Cockney accent. 'I've been expecting you.'

Apparently Madge St Claire had arranged not only for tickets but also for a personal escort. 'I'm Theodore Pike,' said the man. 'Teddy Pike to those who know me, and to my new friends, such as your good selves. The Magic Sevens Circus is glad you're here.'

'You're the ringmaster, Mr Pike?' Ivy asked.

'I am, dear lady,' said Pike. 'And the owner of this unique establishment.' His accent was so strong that Verbena believed it must be affected. 'I was anticipating three special guests,' he added.

'Our friend isn't well,' explained Ivy. 'She's resting in the car.'

Pike glanced past Ivy but Charlotte was curled up so

tightly that she was barely visible. 'Oh, that's too bad. Would she care to rest in one of our trailers? She might be more comfortable without the sun beating down on her.'

'No,' said Verbena. She'd be damned if she would allow Charlotte's posturing to receive any notice. 'She employs this sort of attention-seeking all the time. She's absolutely fine where she is.'

'Then allow me,' said Pike. He presented both his arms and Ivy and Verbena looped their elbows through his, one on either side of the ringmaster's bulk. The man was such a dandy that Ivy couldn't stop herself smiling. She was having a good time already.

It was Verbena who noticed that the man wasn't fat at all. The bulges beneath his clothing were all muscle. He must weigh two hundred and fifty pounds!

'I have a few surprises up my sleeve for you today,' said Pike, as he led his charges towards the back of the tent, passing a patient row of regular attendees waiting to buy their tickets. 'It's not often we have the pleasure of two lovely movie stars among us.'

Verbena was aware of the wild stink of caged animals. It mingled with the mulchy smell of damp straw and dried feed.

Pike opened a tent flap with a flourish and beckoned Ivy and Verbena through. Up close, the jewel-like colours of the canvas were not nearly as alluring. The panels were dulled with dust and grime, the drops stitched and repaired in dozens of places. They entered a staging area where various circus performers were preparing for their roles. The faces, which stared silently as Ivy and Verbena passed, were painted. A forlorn clown tied the laces of his tatty, too-big boots. A young girl in a daring, sequined costume soothed a skittish mare by blowing gently into its nostrils.

In the wings, beyond where the lantern light reached, Ivy and Verbena sensed other members of the troupe. It was dark inside after the bright daylight and the sidelined figures were misshapen forms. A grotesque face moved half into the lantern light and Verbena flinched. Ivy had seen the man, too. She pressed closer to Pike, and he clamped his elbow firmly against her arm, a protector. 'Sometimes we have a sideshow,' he said, 'what some call a freak show, but there aren't enough punters here to make it worth my while to set up the midway.'

'So, not everybody is performing today?' Ivy asked nervously.

'No. The freaks have time on their hands,' Pike said dismissively. 'Now, I've saved the best seats for you right up front. I just thought you might like to see behind the scenes first.'

'That was thoughtful of you, Mr Pike,' said Verbena.

'I have work to do, dear ladies,' said Pike. 'I'll have Celeste take you to your seats.'

He motioned to the woman who had been petting the horse and she came over to them. He spoke slowly to her and she smiled and nodded. She was a tiny sprite of a girl, very young, her body barely into puberty. Celeste seemed delighted to be entrusted with the responsibility of escorting the two actresses. She motioned to them with overt hand signals, and Ivy realized that the girl did not, or could not, speak. Celeste pulled Ivy and Verbena insistently towards her mare. Verbena petted the creature's neck with her gloved hand. She was used to horses. Back in Boston, they had rented a stable on the Common and ridden there every weekend. Her brothers had taken their polo quite seriously.

Ivy was nervous of horses and chose to engage Celeste instead.

'You don't speak, Celeste?' she asked kindly.

The girl shook her head. Her pretty curls bounced on her shoulders. Then Celeste opened her mouth into a disconcerting maw and leaned forward right into Ivy's face. Ivy stepped back at the sight. Inside the red cavity of Celeste's mouth the stump of her tongue was torn raggedly across, halfway down its length, and blackened at the edge as if by fire.

'I'm sorry,' Ivy said, and Celeste closed her mouth and smiled prettily, though Ivy noticed that she smiled with her lips closed. How could an injury like that occur without any damage to Celeste's face? Had she chewed her own tongue off during some kind of fit? But that blackening . . . had the injury been cauterized? Or was the organ rotting, slowly decaying in the girl's mouth? What must it taste like?

The girl reached out suddenly and touched Ivy's lips with her fingertips. It was an inappropriate gesture but made with such tenderness that Ivy did not move to push the girl's hand away. With the curiosity of a small child, Celeste parted Ivy's lips delicately and stood on tiptoe to peer into her mouth. She did not touch Ivy's pink tongue but, upon discovering it in its place, stepped back and clapped her hands happily.

'I believe she's a simpleton,' said Verbena. 'Poor girl.'

Celeste flung her arms around Ivy and hugged her close.

'I think she likes me.' Ivy laughed uncomfortably.

Pike noticed them again. He stood behind the stage curtain, about to go into the ring. 'Celeste!' he shouted. 'Take those ladies to their seats now.'

Celeste obeyed him immediately. Ivy and Verbena were seated apart from the crowd, surrounded by a barrier of empty seats. For the next two hours, both women were transfixed. It was an ordinary circus. There were clowns and performing poodles and a sullen tiger. A family of Chinese tumblers, wearing shiny green costumes and black topknots, performed amazing contortions. But it was Pike who stole the show. He strutted back and forth across the circle of sand. He swooped the tails of his coat like a matador. Sometimes, when the spotlight caught him at a particular angle, his teeth glittered and grew elongated, lupine, until Ivy felt sure they would prick his lower lip and draw blood.

7

The show lasted just over two hours and the finale was a spectacular parade of all the performers through a rain-storm of confetti. The audience had cheered itself hoarse. The ring darkened and the crowd woke from its trance and began to leave the tent, stuffed with cotton candy and caramel corn and Coca-Cola. Children were buoyed up by the magic. Mothers were flushed with excitement. Exhausted babies howled.

Mr Pike came over to Ivy and Verbena, who had stayed behind to thank him. He had sweated profusely during the show and, now that his jacket had been removed, Verbena could see that the man's body was covered with tattoos. Through the soaked fabric of his shirt, she could make out blue lines that swirled like a splash of ink poured into a glass of water.

'Did you enjoy the show?' asked Pike.

'It was wonderful!' declared Ivy.

'Most enjoyable,' said Verbena.

'Do you have to rush off?' Pike asked.

'Oh,' said Ivy, thinking of Charlotte in the car. Even inside the shade of the tent, she had felt the heat. She could only imagine how hot it must be in the Jordan. 'Our friend is still in the car . . .'

'We can stay a little while longer,' said Verbena, thinking of precisely the same thing. 'Be polite, Ivy.'

'We have a little event planned this evening,' said Pike. 'And Celeste seems to have taken to you, Miss Ivy.'

'An event?' enquired Verbena.

'A wedding,' said Pike. 'A genuine circus wedding.'

'How splendid!' said Ivy.

'Yes, our little Miss Celeste is tying the knot.'

'Oh,' said Ivy. Celeste was barely a woman – a girl far, far too young for marriage – but Ivy did not think it was her place to say anything. Circus people had their own way of doing things.

'Do you think your friend would join us?' Pike asked. 'I could send someone to fetch her from your car.'

'No', said Verbena, emphatically. 'She's right where she wants to be.'

They trudged across the grass, dodging tent ropes. Roustabouts were moving props from the ring and packing them into caravans. Keepers, some of them children, were watering and feeding the animals, penning them into corrals formed with insubstantial uprights and twine.

'Excuse me for a few minutes, dear ladies, but a sartorial modification is required,' said Pike. He doffed his pork-pie hat and bowed deeply. 'Miss Dainty Delightful will take care of you. And don't ask her if that's her real name – it is.'

He indicated a caravan unlike the rest. It was painted pink but the paint was flecked with road dirt and worn by time so that the caravan resembled a flaking piece of candy. On the top step, just inside the open door, stood the smallest woman Ivy had ever seen. She reached no higher than their hips and she wore her hair in baby-doll ringlets. She looked like a baby-doll, but when Verbena examined her face, she saw wrinkles around her eyes and at her neck, which indicated maturity, if not middle age.

Dainty Delightful – could that really be the woman's name? – worked hard to convey the doll-like impression. She wore a pink ribbon in her hair and lacy socks under buckled patent-leather shoes. She wore false lashes, too; they fluttered about her blue eyes, which were her prettiest feature.

'Make them some tea, Dainty,' Pike ordered.

Without a word, Dainty Delightful went inside her caravan and Verbena and Ivy followed her awkwardly.

'Come in, ladies,' Dainty said formally. 'I need to change, so I can't offer you any tea.'

'That's fine,' said Verbena. 'We're after the shade, really.'

Everything inside the caravan was pink, too. There were pink chintz curtains blooming with cabbage roses and pink satin pillowcases on the bed, embroidered with pink poppies. Even the enamel kettle on the stove was pink. The appliance was regular-sized but the rest of the furniture in the caravan was built to accommodate a child. Ivy sat on the only full-sized chair – an obvious courtesy for guests – while Verbena perched on the edge of the bed when Dainty directed her.

'We have a carpenter. He made my furniture. I've paid him for several very good pieces over the years. I'm the only person here who doesn't complain about how small these caravans are.' Dainty giggled. 'When you're my size, they're cosy but roomy enough.'

'How did you get into the circus trade, Miss Delightful?' Ivy asked.

Verbena glared at her. The answer to that was obvious.

'You don't "get into the circus trade", ma'am, if you don't mind me saying. You're born to it or you run to it for refuge.'

'I see,' said Ivy.

Dainty unbuttoned her little pink costume and slipped into a yellow dress that hung all the way to her ankles. Verbena caught a glimpse of her gnarled body. It was built around a twisted skeleton. Her knees and elbows resembled malign growths. Every movement she made seemed to comprise a series of painful convolutions.

Somebody rapped on the caravan door and Ivy answered it for Dainty. Celeste stood there. She still wore her sparkly stage makeup but she had changed into a simple white shift. She took Ivy by the hand and pulled her down the stairs, handing her a bouquet of wild daisies tied with ribbon, apparently offering her a role in the wedding party.

A crowd had gathered in the sandy patch beneath an oak tree, a short distance from the tent. A filthy boy was bounding around their ankles on all fours, bare-bodied but for a pair of tattered long johns. He was too old to be play-acting. He was in his middle teens but his odd behaviour drew no attention from the assembled circus workers. Some of them bent down to pat his head as he panted beside them in pleasure. When he sat still, the boy squatted on his haunches with his knees drawn up under his armpits like a waiting dog.

Verbena was thrown by the sight of him and by the gathering in general. She had stepped into a bizarre other-world where people behaved in unexpected ways, as they sometimes did in dreams. How had she come to spend her Saturday afternoon like this? She hoped that Charlotte had experienced an unendurably hot one in the car. Though perhaps she had stepped out and lain quietly in the shade of one of the oak trees. Verbena wanted to spit. She looked about for cameras and saw none. At least she would not be pictured standing beside a bunch of dirty freaks. She thought about the free publicity she had handed Charlotte the day before. Why did everything she attempted to do fall flat?

When the groom arrived, Verbena couldn't believe her eyes. It was too much. How preposterous could this fiasco get? The man bore a grotesque misshapen hump on one shoulder, though his face was sweet, she supposed. She looked at Celeste and was struck again by the loveliness of the girl. Was she really going to marry a hunchback?

Theodore Pike's change of clothing, though slight, was even more startling. He wore the same black jacket as before but now it had a preacher's collar beneath it. His bulk took up much of the shade as he assumed his position in front of the crowd. Ivy waved at Verbena in excitement from her place beside the bride. Verbena longed for the afternoon to be over. After a few minutes, she tuned out Pike's voice; she listened instead to the intermittent drone of a bee.

When it came to the part of the service where the couple exchanged vows, even Verbena was touched. Unable to speak the 'I do', Celeste nodded vigorously. Her groom, in an exclamation of joy, said, 'She does! She does!' as if her decision was a delightful surprise to him.

Instead of throwing the bouquet, Celeste pressed her bunch of daisies into Ivy's hands and insisted, with a series of adamant cooing noises, that she keep them.

Pike declared them man and wife and they kissed.

'Now there's tipple for everybody,' Pike announced. The crowd whistled and cheered. The freaks made harsh braying sounds, like a herd of cattle. 'But we're showing tonight,' Pike continued. The crowd hushed immediately at the sound of his voice. 'Don't any of you forget it!'

Distinctly subdued, the group moved to the trestle tables where mugs filled with beer were laid out. Ivy came over to Verbena, carrying the modest bouquet. 'It looks like I'm to be next,' she said, with a wink.

'Heaven forbid!' laughed Verbena.

'No, I mean it,' Ivy whispered back. 'I think Mr Whitewood plans to propose.'

For such a casual remark, it turned Verbena instantly cold. She rubbed her own shoulders with her hands, as if the shade of the oak had chilled her. She walked into the sun but felt no warmer. Was Ivy serious? Could she be considering marrying that milk-toast politician? The world seemed to tilt. Verbena, who hadn't ever swooned before except on stage, thought she might faint. She dabbed at her forehead with a handkerchief. Pike saw her and came over.

'Feeling a bit emotional, Miss Verbena?' he asked, mistaking her sudden sweat for tears.

'No, I suddenly don't feel well.'

'Come with me,' Pike said.

Pike led Verbena off behind the oak tree where a water pump stood on a cement tray. He removed his jacket and gallantly laid it on the grass. 'Please,' he said, helping her to sit. Verbena felt embarrassed but she didn't know when last she had felt so sick. Normally she was a stoic, but then Ivy was not just another friend: she was a best friend who was apparently willing to toss aside their closeness for a man. Ivy was the only person who made Verbena feel beautiful. She made Verbena feel soft, so that Verbena could almost imagine that she was. Ivy was extraordinary and now she was going to marry a mediocre man.

Pike rolled up his sleeves and primed the pump until water gushed into the tray. While he worked, Verbena could see the tattoos on his exposed forearms quite clearly. This artwork was not an ordinary sailor's inking, but a compact assortment of crazy images that covered every inch of the man's skin, creating a long sleeve of blue that ended in a cuff at his wrist.

'You're a ringmaster and a preacher, Mr Pike,' said Verbena. 'That's interesting.'

'Not really,' said Pike, as he accepted Verbena's handkerchief and wet it under the pump. He settled his bulk down beside her. 'Wipe the back of your neck,' he said.

Verbena, surprising herself with her compliance, obeyed. The sensation was delicious.

'That feels good,' she said.

'It works every time,' Pike replied.

'How does a man of God get into your current line of work?'

'Circus people marry one another. They always have done. For obvious reasons, many of them aren't comfortable in churches and some so-called Christian folk don't enjoy my friends' presence in their congregations.'

'Oh,' Verbena said.

'It helps to have an ordained preacher on site. Of course, I send all the paperwork to the proper authorities. We have a postbox in several towns we pass through. I collect the marriage licences and pass them on to the newly-weds when they come in. It's perfectly legal, I assure you.'

Pike put his pork-pie hat on to his head and got to his feet. 'Should I send Miss Ivy over to see to you?'

'No,' said Verbena. 'I'm better now. Thank you.'

'Then allow me.' Pike offered her his arm. Verbena took hold of it and saw a most extraordinary thing. On his right forearm, revealed below the turned-up sleeve of his shirt, there was a very good tattoo of a girl. It was a crisp job, neatly done with few lines or embellishments, yet Verbena was almost certain that the girl it depicted was Charlotte Caine.

As Ivy and Verbena walked back to their car in the dusk, Verbena's mind tried to process what she had seen. She didn't say a word to Ivy about it. Charlotte was still inside the car. She hadn't changed her position since they had left her almost four hours before. She sat up with a start when she heard the car doors close. Ivy began to chatter to her about the show and the wedding. Verbena glanced back and saw that Charlotte was bleary-eyed and disoriented. Then the smell hit her. Charlotte's silk dress was darkened with sweat all the way to her waist. It was not just the smell of body odour, though. It was the unmistakable reek of fear. What could have terrified her that much? Verbena felt once again a distinct prickling of curiosity about Charlotte's past. Ivy simply chattered on about pressing one of the daisies from Celeste's bouquet so that she could keep it for ever.

8

Charlotte could not sleep that night. Her heart was a drum. Her nerves jangled. Pike had found her. She did not know how he had done it, but he had. After hours of twisting and turning, she got up and took the bottle of Fleurs de Rocaille from its place in her drawer. She clutched it in her hand and examined its blood-red contents in a sliver of moonlight. Finally, she drifted off.

Charlotte awoke to Allegra's knock on her bedroom door. She sipped the tea the maid brought in and centred herself. Pike didn't know where she lived. His presence in the canyon might still be a coincidence. Charlotte decided she would prepare herself for him, steel her resolve. She would take him on, if he chose to confront her, and face him down. He had nothing on her. He couldn't prove a thing.

Charlotte felt a burst of strength when the studio car drove her through the mighty black gates of the Warner Brothers studio. A group of schoolgirls stood outside holding autograph books. Charlotte waved at them and they shrieked. They'd recognized her! Charlotte could only imagine what life must be like for Liam Malone. Was it possible that soon she would be as famous as he was?

Madge St Claire was there to meet her. Charlotte stepped from the car and noticed a magnificent gold Rolls-Royce parked in a reserved space directly in front of the office building. She saw her reflection in the car's side window. She ran her fingers along the curvature of its flanks.

'Whose car is this?' Charlotte asked Madge.

'That's Liam Malone's new toy,' said Madge. 'It's just this side of garish, I suppose.'

'It's beautiful.'

'You'd look beautiful in it,' said Madge, and she touched Charlotte's cheek in a way that Charlotte had thought only men did. Not for the first time, Charlotte found Madge's behaviour more attentive than was comfortable.

'Thank you, Madge,' she said sweetly. 'I'm awfully nervous.'

'You're a natural, Carlie darling. You've got nothing to be nervous about. The secret is to look as if you belong.'

All that day, throughout the meetings with producers and David O. Selznick himself, Charlotte acted. She acted as if she belonged. And the only one who noticed that she did not was Liam Malone.

She was sipping a glass of iced tea from the catering table when he approached her. 'Hello, there,' he said. 'How are you coping?'

'Oh,' said Charlotte, as she made a breezy gesture with her hand.

'That was well done,' Liam said. 'It made you look utterly carefree.'

'Good,' said Charlotte. 'Because I'm terrified.'

'Well, you're holding up beautifully.'

'I saw your car,' said Charlotte. She wanted to keep Liam by her side for a moment more. She knew men loved to talk about their cars. 'Is it really a Rolls-Royce?'

'It is. I have to confess, I'm in love with it. Rolls-Royce approached me, actually. It's something they do for "famous people".' He rolled his eyes at the description. 'You receive extravagant benefits you could never dream of. They designed it just for me, then gave it to me as a gift. Can you believe that? Now I have the money to actually buy nice things for myself, people are falling over themselves to give them to me for free.'

'I can't imagine that,' said Charlotte. 'I've been in the background till now.'

'I'll have to take you for a spin sometime,' said Liam.

'Oh, yes, please,' said Charlotte. She hated the way she sounded, as giddy as one of the girls clutching the fence rails and calling out his name.

'I remember my first really big picture,' said Liam. 'The first time the girls wanted my autograph. It was so odd. You'll get used to it, though, I promise. You'll learn how to deal with the attention. When I hear you reading Rahab, I think you'll have to get used to it . . .'

'Why's that?' asked Charlotte

'Because you're quite wonderful, Miss Caine.'

Before she could stammer a reply, Liam waved a cheery goodbye and left her alone.

As soon as Charlotte's car had pulled out of the drive that morning, Verbena pushed past Allegra, who was on her hands and knees in the hallway, sweeping the carpet, and went into Charlotte's room. Verbena had one objective in mind. Every actress she knew – Verbena was guilty of it herself – kept a scrapbook of her career or, at the very least, a collection of her publicity clippings. Newspaper articles that mentioned her name might be carefully underlined. A piece that included her picture, or an announcement in the *Hollywood Reporter*, would hold pride of place. Verbena slammed open Charlotte's closet door and searched for a keepsake box among her shoes; she flipped up Charlotte's quilt and looked under the woman's mattress. She opened every drawer in Charlotte's dresser and carefully examined its contents. She did not find any personal writings or souvenirs, let alone anything incriminating.

Verbena was about to give up when she caught sight of the edge of Charlotte's suitcase. It had been stowed away on top of a vast armoire, pushed so far back that only one corner was visible. She stood on Charlotte's bed, not bothering to remove her shoes, and stretched over. She couldn't reach the suitcase. She got down from the bed and took a spare hanger from the closet rail. Using it as a hook, Verbena finally pulled the suitcase to the edge of the armoire and allowed it to thump to the floor. It was a good case, leather and well travelled. Verbena flung the lid open. She found nothing inside. The suitcase was empty. Verbena slapped her hand against its silk-lined base in frustration and heard the distinct crinkle of paper. She ran her fingers along the edge of the suitcase. Where the lining of the sides met that of the base, the stitches had been picked loose along several inches of the seam. Verbena separated the silk and found a hidden stash of papers.

Verbena pored over the hidden items. She set aside a rumpled notebook filled with childish drawings, notations and magazine cut-outs; it was undoubtedly some memento Charlotte had kept from her school days. She ignored a wedge of postcards tied with a yellow ribbon. A carefully catalogued pile of magazine articles and newspaper clippings remained. Verbena paged through them, looking from one of Charlotte's publicity pictures to another. She went through the collection again, more carefully, and then for a third time. By the time she had finished her final assessment, Verbena was convinced. Not a single one of Charlotte Caine's public photographs in any way resembled the pose depicted in Teddy Pike's disturbing tattoo.

Satisfied, Verbena packed away the articles and replaced the suitcase. Allegra came into the room as she was finishing. 'Don't you breathe a word!' Verbena hissed. She pushed her pointed fingernail under Allegra's nose.

'No, Miss Verbena,' Allegra said. She kept her eyes down, unwilling to confront her employer's threatening gaze.

A few minutes later, Allegra heard the throaty sound of Verbena's car starting up in the drive and roaring away.

The circus campsite looked very different than it had a few days before. The workers were occupied with chores, watering and feeding the animals, rehearsing, conducting the activities of everyday life.

Verbena felt odd navigating the rough ground in heels. The peacock feather in her fabulous hat seemed ridiculous now that the performers weren't decked out in their outrageous makeup and costumes. Verbena hadn't taken time to consider how she would approach Teddy Pike. How could she explain her motives without appearing petty and mean-spirited? How could she get information from him? Verbena wasn't sure. She only knew that he must be a man, an unusual man to say the least, who had known Charlotte before she had arrived in Los Angeles.

Verbena had been suspicious of Charlotte's stories since the day she had moved in. The dreadful attack on Charlotte's father was something Verbena dared not question for fear of losing Ivy's respect for ever, but she often wondered about it. Charlotte's past seemed muddled. The woman mentioned dozens of towns across Florida and throughout the South. Her father's occupation seemed to change. There was no mother in evidence. It was all very peculiar and Verbena would be damned if a woman like Charlotte – a woman with a murky past – would usurp her position as Warner Brothers' emerging ingénue.

The man who worked in the ticket box accosted Verbena but, just then, she spotted Dainty Delightful emerging from her pink caravan.

'Miss Delightful!' Verbena called out.

Dainty carried a basin of dirty water. She had apparently been washing dishes.

'Miss Verbena, isn't it?' said Dainty. 'What brings you back here?'

'I had such a pleasant conversation with Mr Pike at the wedding the other day but we were interrupted before I could ask him a few questions.'

'Really?' said Dainty, suspiciously. 'I expect he was just being polite. Teddy doesn't usually take to uninvited callers.'

'Still, I'd like to see him,' said Verbena, strongly.

'Suit yourself,' said Dainty. She flapped a dishcloth in the direction of the far side of the tent, then tipped her water right beside Verbena's feet.

Verbena stepped over the mud and headed off, following the curve of the big top. The air was filled with the sound of animals. Verbena heard the neigh of a horse, the short, huffing trumpet of the circus's one lonesome elephant and then, suddenly, the high yips and yelps of dogs. They were in a pen of barbed wire and mesh. There were many of them. They nipped at each other, then hunched down, guarding their throats from attack. Pike stood beside the pen with his back to Verbena's approach. She saw his right hand rise above his shoulder. It held a cleaver and he brought the instrument down on to a wooden table with a dull, wet *thunk*.

'Mr Pike,' Verbena called out.

She didn't want the man to turn around, startled, with that cleaver in his hand. She had a vision of her dress being splattered with gore. Pike did turn but the cleaver remained at his side. In his other hand, he held the head of a coyote. 'Miss Verbena,' he said. 'What an unexpected treat!'

'Good God!' said Verbena, as blood began to trickle from the severed head on to the grass beside Pike's boot. 'You're busy. I can wait.'

'Just finishing up,' he said. He slammed the cleaver down on the coyote's carcass one last time, severing the rear leg from the haunches, then launched a hunk of flesh over the pen to the dogs. They boiled in a seething mass as they ripped at the carcass. Verbena turned her back on the shocking scene. Pike removed his bloody apron and took her arm in the crook of his own. He walked her towards a clump of trees a quarter-mile from the tent.

'A man has to ask himself,' said Pike, 'what a woman like you wants from a man like me and a place like this.'

'It was your most unusual tattoos, Mr Pike,' Verbena said coyly. 'I was astonished by them, quite taken with them, really.'

'Miss Verbena, Miss Verbena. They're mostly home-done, to tell the truth. Miss Delightful is the artist, if you can believe that.'

'Dainty does tattoos?'

'She does,' said Pike. 'Some of my early scratchings pre-date hers, of course. I've been a ringmaster for about ten years. I was a full-time preacher before that.'

Pike stopped walking. They were short of the shade. The sun beat down heavily on their heads.

'I was wondering, particularly, about the lady on your right arm.'

Pike looked at her then. He stared at her. Verbena felt her skin grow cold. Pike's eyes bored into hers. There was no option but to tell him the truth.

'I believe I know the girl,' said Verbena.

Now Pike seemed most interested. 'Do you really?'

'Yes. I think that tattoo of yours depicts a friend of mine. She's an actress, an emerging star, supposedly,' offered Verbena. 'I share a house with her. Her name is Charlotte. We call her Carlie . . . Carlie Caine. Are you a fan of the cinema, Mr Pike? Is that why you had the tattoo made? Or do you perhaps know her personally? That was what I wondered.'

'She was Charlotte when I knew her,' said Pike. 'Charlotte Caine, she was, and a beauty.'

'She's still a beauty,' said Verbena, reluctantly. 'I just wondered how you were acquainted with her.'

Pike paused, as though considering whether to answer her question. 'I knew her as a girl,' he said. 'Her father was a great friend of mine.'

'Oh,' said Verbena. She was disappointed. Charlotte couldn't be blamed for her father's eccentric taste in friends.

'Archie was his name and he was a first-rate bloke.'

'I thought her father was a Mr Patrick Caine?'

Pike closed his mouth so his bottom lip bulged out aggressively. 'I called him Archie.'

'Oh,' Verbena smiled at the answer, as if it explained everything, but there was more here. She could feel it in her bones. She decided to push a bit harder. 'I don't suppose you came all the way to Los Angeles to see her, did you? Could that be the reason for your sojourn here in the canyon?'

'My reasons for taking my crew anywhere are my business, Miss Verbena.'

'Of course they are!' said Verbena, pretending to be shocked that she might have engendered offence. 'I'm just curious because of the tattoo. It's unique. It doesn't match any public photographs of her, so I knew it hadn't been copied from a magazine. And I thought to myself, That man must have known Charlotte years ago . . .'

Pike laughed good-naturedly but the humour did not touch his eyes. 'You'd be no good in a circus, Miss Verbena. Circus folk don't encourage curiosity. We're private people. We don't care for gossip. And if privacy doesn't come natural to a woman she needs to be taught to keep her own counsel.' He swivelled Verbena around and started walking her back towards her car. 'You met Celeste, I believe.'

Verbena nodded. She couldn't make the connection between what Pike was saying and the lovely mute girl whose wedding she and Ivy had attended.

'Now Celeste was a girl who couldn't stop wagging her tongue . . .' Pike stopped walking. He said no more.

Verbena swallowed. Her throat felt coated in canyon

73

dust. Was Pike suggesting that he'd taken out Celeste's tongue? It could not be possible.

'You met my dogs, Miss Verbena,' said Pike. 'They love tasty little treats, my dogs.'

Verbena was too startled to say goodbye. She couldn't walk away fast enough. She stumbled to her car and fumbled with the door. She had made a terrible mistake in coming here. If this man did know Charlotte, then Verbena could almost feel sorry for the woman. Verbena would never return to the circus again. She would let Charlotte be. She would mind her own business. Pike waved a cheery goodbye but Verbena didn't wave back. Her hands were shaking and she kept them on the wheel.

9

Verbena avoided Charlotte for the rest of the week. Charlotte couldn't help but wonder what Verbena was scheming but she had other things on her mind, too. She had a demanding schedule for the next two months. Principal photography began on location the very next week and there was a party at Charlie Chaplin's house on Summit Drive that night.

It had become bizarrely fashionable in Hollywood for stars to avoid making an appearance at their own parties, but Madge St Claire, who had helped to book entertainment for the event, believed that Chaplin would be present. Charlotte was exhilarated. The man was an icon, though controversial, and Charlotte had loved his pictures since she was a child.

In the afternoon, Ivy and Verbena drove out to Glendale to look at a horse Verbena wanted to buy and Charlotte had the house to herself for a few glorious hours. She tried to clear her head. She mustn't worry about her father or Verbena. She mustn't worry about the coincidence of the Magic Sevens Circus. It would move on in a week or two and the threat would trundle away with it.

Charlotte was on her way to the kitchen to get Allegra to make her a salad, when she passed the front door and noticed something. It was a colour glimpsed from the corner of her eye – a ruby pink. The swatch of colour, mottled by the glass panel beside the door, was too large to be a blossom though apparently it adorned one of the bushes that framed the entryway. Charlotte pressed her face to the glass and recognized the item, with a spurt of shock, as a pair of her best knickers. She had bought them from Madame Parisian in Miami and they were real silk with black bows sewn all around the waistline. Charlotte looked about to see if any other items of laundry were on display. Had they dropped from the laundry basket as Allegra carried it from her bathroom? How had the garment got outside? Had it blown from her bedroom? No, there wasn't enough wind for that. Besides, the front door was closed; so was the window to Charlotte's bedroom. Also, there was something about the way the knickers were displayed. They looked to have been carefully hung from the end of a leafy branch so that they were fully open, exposed.

Charlotte felt afraid, somehow guilty, as she opened the door quickly and snatched the silky bloom from its place. She looked over her shoulder, feeling as if she had been caught in an unseemly act. That feeling of dirtiness made Charlotte furious. She had done nothing to feel ashamed of! Whoever had embarrassed her like that would be made to pay for it. Verbena! Charlotte thought. She stormed through the house, knowing that Verbena would not be there to face her rage. Charlotte wanted to strangle that vicious woman, scratch her face. But the more she considered the knickers, the less it seemed like something a woman would do.

'Allie!' Charlotte shouted.

The little Mexican maid came at her call. She had a rag

in her hand and wiped sweat from her forehead with her arm. She had been scrubbing the kitchen floor.

'Have you been in my things?' Charlotte demanded, and she waved the crunched-up fist that held the knickers in the girl's face.

'No, Miss Charlotte. I haven't been to your room yet. I will clean in there next.'

'Has Miss Verbena been in my room?' demanded Charlotte.

'I didn't see anything like that,' said Allegra.

'And nobody's visited the house?' Charlotte asked.

Allegra shook her head decidedly. 'I've been cleaning in the portico.'

The portico was beyond the kitchen at the far end of the pool, an open-walled room with a roof for shade where they had sun chairs and a changing room. Allegra wouldn't have heard anybody enter the house from out there.

'All right, all right,' Charlotte said, at Allegra's obvious distress. 'I'm not angry. Go on with your work.'

Charlotte went down the hall to her bedroom. She was being ridiculous. Finding the underwear had been a little disconcerting, even mortifying, but she mustn't get hysterical about it.

Charlotte examined her underwear drawer. Everything appeared to be in its place. She sat down on her bed. The pale paint of the walls was imbued with a sunset glow. Charlotte turned to the window. There, placed perfectly in a ray of sunlight, was her special secret bottle of scent. The red glass caught the light and bathed the room in blood.

In that second, realization hit her. Charlotte felt sure she knew who had paid her a visit. She was quietly and deeply

77

afraid now. She tried to breathe but her ribcage refused to open. It was ridiculous to assume Pike had been here. She was overreacting. One of the other women had moved her scent bottle from its drawer into the open. It was harmless. Charlotte mustn't keep assuming she was a magnet for monsters. Breath whooshed into her chest again. It might be better to prepare, though, just in case. She told herself she needed to be ready. With the man so close by, Charlotte felt she ought to plan a strategy to defend herself.

The studio had arranged for the three actresses to be collected from Lantana Drive at seven o'clock, but Charlotte wasn't nearly ready to leave and it was well past six thirty. She sat in a slip in front of her dressing-table mirror, applying makeup. She was quite composed now: she had spent the afternoon considering her options. There had been tears, of course, but she had beaten them. Now she was resolute with self-control. Only Allegra had borne witness to her fretful pacing.

Verbena came into the room uninvited and sat down in Charlotte's bedroom chair. She wore a man's suit and a trilby; her small dark nipples showed through her white silk blouse. She had strung a dozen strands of pearls casually around her neck. Ivy followed her in, dressed in more conventional attire – a low-cut fitted dress in rose satin with short, matching gloves.

Ivy let out a squeal. She had been paging through the latest issue of *Silver Screen* and now held up the magazine for the others to see. 'It's him!' she said. 'Look, Carlie! It's Liam Malone. There's a four-page feature with pictures.'

Charlotte swivelled in her chair and snatched the magazine,

devouring the photographs. There were several studio snaps in which the actor looked suave and disinterested with a cigarette in his hand. Charlotte turned the page and came across a candid shot taken in the man's house. A woman sat beside Liam. Half a dozen children were tangled together at their feet.

'I don't have time to read it now,' Charlotte said, as she tossed the rag back to Ivy.

'I'll read it to you, then,' said Ivy. She began: '"At home with his family, Liam Malone is perfectly content . . ."'

'Don't believe everything you read,' Verbena interjected.

'. . . "He loves nothing more than spending time with his beloved wife, Bernadette, and their six adorable children . . ."'

Verbena snorted. 'Bernadette! Women like that are always named after saints.'

'. . . "He's been blissfully wed for fifteen years,"' Ivy continued. '"No scandalous dalliances for this wholesome star! Mr Malone married his childhood sweetheart shortly after arriving in the United States from the Emerald Isle . . ."'

Charlotte squeezed her hands into fists to stop them trembling. Verbena saw the reaction. Ivy stopped reading and closed the magazine.

'Surely you knew, Carlie?' Verbena said. 'Everybody knows he's besotted with his wife. Liam Malone's the epitome of marital fortitude.'

'He's practically famous for it,' said Ivy, softly.

'Of course I knew,' said Charlotte, a little angrily. 'I'd just never seen her picture. That's all.'

Ivy felt bad. 'I'm sorry, Carlie,' she said. 'We all have the most awful crush on him.'

Charlotte flapped away Ivy's pity with her hand, but she felt distinctly blue. She had been so sure the man was intended for her, that the universe had decided – at last – to bestow a gift. But the photographs made Liam look so entrenched.

'Does it make it too real for you, darling?' said Verbena.

'Too real for what?' asked Charlotte.

'For what you were planning to do,' said Verbena.

The atmosphere had become uneasily charged. Ivy jumped up with her usual enthusiasm. 'You can still knock his socks off, Carlie. Have some fun tonight. Enjoy yourself.'

'Oh, I will,' said Charlotte, heartily.

Verbena changed the subject. 'I like the way you do your eyes, Carlie.' She said it casually, as if to change the subject. 'It's very . . . different.'

Charlotte's hand paused before resuming its work with the mascara wand. A compliment from Verbena always came as a surprise. 'I copied Mary Pickford.' Charlotte tried to sound sure of herself. 'I do them exactly the way she does. I saw a picture of her in *Cinelandia.*'

'You'll probably meet her tonight,' said Verbena.

Charlotte was determined to be unimpressed. It was hard not to feel quite giddy.

'When you meet her,' added Verbena, 'be sure to tell her you copy her makeup. She'll be so flattered.'

Charlotte put down the mascara wand with a bang. Ivy jumped. Charlotte would not let Verbena – the witch! – see her insecurity. She knew she was being needled. How dare Verbena lounge in Charlotte's own room, pretending to be supportive while undermining her with snide remarks?

Verbena unfurled from the chair and walked out. Ivy followed her but paused to squeeze Charlotte's shoulder. 'You'll be the most beautiful one there, no matter how you paint your face,' she whispered into Charlotte's ear.

Charlotte wanted to turn around and hug her. Instead she shrugged Ivy's hand away and sat up straighter. She took a long, deep breath of cold air into her lungs and held it there.

10

When their car pulled into Charlie Chaplin's drive, Charlotte spent a few moments looking at the house. It loomed like a Victorian monstrosity at the end of the drive. Uniformed parking attendants dashed to and fro, moving cars away from the house and into the vacant hillsides beyond the backyard.

Charlotte, Ivy and Verbena got out of their car. Two young women in sequined costumes and headdresses of purple ostrich plumes greeted them. The host himself couldn't be expected to await arrivals: he was already mingling.

'It's another circus!' declared Ivy. 'I wonder if it's our circus, Bee? Do you think Celeste might be here?'

'They're just showgirls,' said Verbena. 'A couple of those half-starved chorus dancers from Lulu-Belle's who all want to be actresses.'

'I think Madge had something to do with the entertainment,' said Ivy. 'She got you the circus tickets. She may have arranged for Mr Pike's people to entertain here, too.'

Charlotte was, by now, trailing behind. She thought she might throw up into the bushes at Ivy's suggestion, though she hadn't eaten anything that day.

In the entrance hall, Chinese tumblers in green satin suits were building pyramids with their bodies. They rolled and sprang and bent like jade-coloured pieces of liquorice. Charlotte watched them with her mouth open. She couldn't be sure if she'd seen this very display years ago. All acrobatic performances were alike, she supposed, and one Chinese face looked very like another.

Ivy recognized the act immediately, however. 'It is our circus!' she said, as she clapped her hands. 'Hurrah for the Magic Sevens! Hurrah for Madge!'

Verbena found a door off the hallway, which opened into a closet. She threw her coat on to a pile of other garments and Charlotte copied her. Charlotte loved her silver stole. She hated tossing it down that way but she was trying so hard to be carefree. When she closed the door, it came off its top hinge and she had to struggle to force it home.

Verbena laughed. 'Do you know what they call this place?'

Charlotte shook her head.

'It's known as "Breakaway House". I mean it. That's its actual name. Charlie is famously cheap. He hired studio carpenters as workmen and they built it like a set. It's been falling apart ever since. Apparently Charlie loves it! He can't wait to see which bit is going to break away next. Entire walls can literally come down without warning.'

Charlotte was stunned. That wasn't how a house should be! Her own house, when she bought it, would certainly be smaller than this but it would be perfectly maintained.

'Only the tennis court is properly kept up,' noted Ivy. 'Charlie takes his tennis very seriously. His court is world-class.'

Ivy and Verbena knew exactly what to do. They peeled away from Charlotte after five minutes. Charlotte accepted a glass of champagne and moved purposefully from room to room, trying to appear as if she had a destination in mind. She hovered at the edge of conversations but couldn't join in. She didn't know what to say. The talk was of politics, Chinese and Mexican immigration, and financing.

Ivy brought over a stern-looking young man in spectacles and introduced him. 'This is Nathaniel Whitewood, Carlie,' she said. 'You can call him Nate. He's in Congress and he's my beau.' Ivy clung to the man's arm. She was already unsteady on her feet and Whitewood was working to keep her propped upright. He held her as inconspicuously as he could – a real gentleman, Charlotte thought.

'Now shove off, Carlie,' Ivy said. 'He's definitely taken.'

Everybody laughed at that but Charlotte sensed that Ivy meant what she had said.

As it grew dark, Charlotte went out into the garden where she could watch the people in the pool and listen to their chatter. She sat on a bench. She knew she looked conspicuous. She lifted her chin, opening her long neckline to the moon, and attempted to appear fey and lovely – just another woman trying to get away from the hubbub, not one who wanted, desperately, to be part of it.

On the other side of the pool, on a corresponding bench, Charlotte saw another woman sitting alone. She was composed of angles under skin, a linen bag of bones. She wore a shapeless dress of palest peach, hardly a colour at all. She would look perfect clutching a Bible, Charlotte thought. Something about her brought Charlotte's own lean mother to mind, though this woman was a good deal younger than her mother would be by now, assuming her mother was still alive somewhere. There was no proof that she had died. That had been Charlotte's way of explaining her absence to Madge. In truth, Charlotte's mother had simply run off one day and never returned. The woman across the water tried to flatten down her unruly hair by repositioning the diamond pins she wore in it, but she couldn't seem to contain the frizz. It took Charlotte a few moments to realize that she was looking at Liam Malone's wife – Bernadette.

Unnoticed, a horse walked up to Charlotte and put its warm muzzle against her cheek in friendly greeting. Charlotte shrieked and nearly fell off the bench. The swimmers cackled at her. The horse was a grey, freckled with smoke. It had soft pink nostrils and wet black eyes, like a stone after the rain. There were blue ribbons tied into its mane and it wore a face-plate attached to its bridle, which had been carefully fashioned with a silver spiral horn that protruded from its centre. A unicorn in Hollywood!

Charlotte reached out and patted the creature's shoulder. She felt ashamed of her initial alarm. Liam Malone came over and swatted the horse's rump. It whinnied and kicked out its back legs, then trotted off, up the garden stairs and through the open French windows into the house.

'Bothering you, was he?'

'He simply startled me,' said Charlotte, and glanced across the swimming pool to see if Liam's wife was watching them, but Bernadette had disappeared. She went to sip her champagne but found she'd spilled it. Liam had a glass in each hand and held one out to her. He took her empty glass and tossed it into a flower bed.

Charlotte sipped gratefully.

'So, it's completely official. We're to be working together,' Liam said. 'All the documents were finalized with my lawyers today. I'm glad it's you, Charlotte. I really am.'

Despite knowing her new stage name, Liam had chosen

to stick with Charlotte instead of Carlie. She liked that. He looked comfortable in his white tuxedo, just as he had in his cotton jumper with its sleeves pushed up on the first day she had met him. 'They're taking a chance on me,' she said. 'Though it's not a very big part. It's mostly a man's picture, isn't it?'

'Mostly male characters, I suppose. But Rahab is the female lead,' said Liam. 'And they haven't taken much of a risk, believe me. They know a million-dollar face when they see one.'

He threw the compliment away with such candour that Charlotte had to believe it was genuine. Her cheeks were suddenly burning hot.

'I haven't seen a blush like that for many a year,' Liam said.

'I'm sorry.'

Charlotte knew she wasn't making a very sophisticated impression but Liam disconcerted her. She felt her stomach tighten. A man's proximity had never caused such sensations before. She realized, unexpectedly, that her body desired this man the way men had always desired her. It was a powerful feeling. That she could want a man, want his naked body beside her own, want him again in the morning after the night was gone, felt like a revelation.

Fireworks exploded in the sky, raining cherry sparks down on to the manicured lawns. The crowd aaahed in unison. Charlotte watched the flashes come and go in the dark irises of Liam's eyes, which were the same as the horse's, soulful and at peace. 'I should be off,' she said. She wanted to be away from Liam before she ruined things. She would leave him with a transient impression of her, a desire for more. It was one of the tricks her father had taught her.

'You need to go before you bore them, Charlotte,' her father had said. 'A few steamy remarks and then you're off. Understand? Intrigue them. You're the fantasy. Don't stay long enough to say the wrong thing.'

'You have somewhere to be?' Liam asked.

He sounded disappointed. Charlotte was surprised he would let his feelings slip free so easily. 'Just the party,' she said vaguely, and waved at the house as she walked in its direction.

Charlotte spent the rest of the evening watching him. She felt physically nauseous when another woman made him laugh. She tried to locate his wife among the crowd but she did not spot bony Bernadette again.

Charlie Chaplin had been in the swimming pool. He came up to her in a damp robe and introduced himself. His embrace left a wet mark on the front of Charlotte's dress and he pawed at it by way of apology for the rest of the evening. He didn't put his clothes back on either. He drifted about in the robe with bare feet, throwing back Scotch and snapping crab legs open with his hands. Charlotte tried to avoid him.

Ivy bounced up to Charlotte near midnight and asked if she wanted to play tennis. 'Everybody plays in their underthings,' said Ivy. 'Nate and I are partners in the mixed doubles.'

'I hope there aren't any cameras about,' said Charlotte. 'You might ruin his political career.'

'Nothing that happens at these parties ever ruins anybody's career,' said Ivy. 'Besides, if everybody's naughty then nobody gets to pretend they were good. Everybody has a vested interest in keeping the naughtiness a secret. You have to play!'

Charlotte smiled and declined. She didn't know how to play tennis.

'But you're wearing a good slip,' said Ivy. 'You might as well show it off.'

'Okay,' said Charlotte. She had no intention of joining in.

'See you on the court, then,' said Ivy. 'Or there's croquet on the lower lawn.'

The tennis courts were lit at night, but a group of tired-looking maids left their work in the kitchen and trudged into the garden carrying candles and torches to light the impromptu croquet game. Charlotte could see a glowing square taking shape on the distant grass. She heard Charlie's whoop in the darkness. She looked for a place to hide. The bedrooms were full of writhing bodies and foul-smelling smoke that gave her a headache. One of the bathroom doors was locked and a man was passed out under a running shower in another. Charlotte went guiltily to the closet and retrieved her silver stole from beneath a pile of coats and shawls. The thought of it lying there, rumpled, had bothered her all evening. Charlotte couldn't be casual about mistreating things the way Verbena was. She couldn't seem to get the hang of it.

On the upstairs landing, Charlotte encountered the bewildered unicorn again. It had knocked over a potted fern. A mound of soil darkened the carpet. The horse munched thoughtfully on the uprooted plant.

Eventually Charlotte found a comfortable chair in a stock

room off the kitchen and snuggled up on it, surrounded by shelves stacked with peach preserves.

Liam Malone located her in the small hours and watched her sleep. Charlotte's lips were slightly parted. She looked so young, unspoiled. Liam didn't want to wake her. He draped his tuxedo jacket over her body. The tennis games went on till dawn. Verbena had stripped down to her French knickers and nothing else. She trounced Charlie Chaplin in two sets. After the match, the players ended up back in the pool, but their drunken shouting did not disturb Charlotte. When the last of the fireworks went off at dawn she did not wake, although her body twitched in its sleep, as if jolted by gunfire.

Charlotte woke early. The house was silent. Her neck was stiff. Somebody had covered her with a white tuxedo jacket. She would have to find its owner. It was very large in the shoulders. She hoped it belonged to Liam. Charlotte picked up her shoes and crept out of her enclave. Two maids whispered to each other while they washed dishes as quietly as they could. They did not remark on her presence. In the living room, bodies were slumped across sofas and dotted here and there on the floor.

Charlotte stepped over them to reach the patio.

Charlie Chaplin and David O. Selznick, her new director, were looking down into the swimming pool. Two silver party masks floated near a large white shape that was half submerged in the shallow end. The forgotten unicorn had slipped on the pool deck sometime in the night and fallen into the water. It had probably broken a leg, or its neck. It lay crumpled on the wide top step, its face beneath the surface. The blue ribbons in its mane streamed like medieval banners in the wind-creased water, as if the horse was still cantering towards some faraway hilltop castle.

A female guest came over to the two men and pointed at the unicorn, laughing drunkenly.

'It's not funny!' snapped Chaplin. 'How are we going to get the bloody thing out of there? I'm going to have to drain the whole fucking pool.'

'What about its owner?' commented Selznick. He was also still drunk. He started to laugh, too. 'Try returning a soaking wet, slightly dead unicorn and getting your deposit back!'

Charlotte pulled her stole more tightly around her shoulders. She felt a chill. She didn't want the men to see her. She didn't want to speak to them.

She walked around the side of the house. It was so still that she could hear her bare soles slapping on the cobbled pathway. In the trees, birds sang. The fountains had been turned off, leaving the surface of their pools still, rippled by midges.

On the circular drive, Charlotte came upon Liam Malone. He was sitting on a wall with his bow tie in his hand, swinging his legs like a schoolboy, banging his heels against the bricks.

'You'll scuff your shoes, Mr Malone,' warned Charlotte.

'Careful, Miss Charlotte,' Liam said. 'You'll reveal something of your past with observations like that. You're not supposed to care about shoes, you know.'

'I always had to make my shoes last,' Charlotte confessed.

'Sssh,' said Liam, with a finger theatrically to his lips. He added, in a stage whisper, 'So did I.'

'Are you waiting for your wife?' Charlotte asked.

'She'll send the car back for me,' he said. 'She left early last night. She likes to be home with the children before nine.'

Charlotte noticed that Liam was wearing just his shirt and braces. 'I believe this might be your jacket?' She held up the garment she was carrying.

'It is,' said Liam. 'I came looking for you but you were asleep. I thought about kissing you goodnight.'

He was flirting but he didn't seem glib. Charlotte couldn't flirt back. Her face was stretched with misery.

'Aaah, you saw that poor horse,' said Liam. 'I hoped you wouldn't.'

Charlotte felt unexpected tears spring up. 'I think I'd like to go home now,' she managed. She was about to cry in front of the man. She was going to wreck everything!

Liam hopped off the wall and touched her arm with a caress of such kindness it made Charlotte turn her face away. He took his jacket gently from her grasp. 'I'll arrange a ride for you,' he said.

Once she was seated in the studio car, Charlotte let the tears come. The severe frame of the chauffeur didn't flinch at the sound of her sobbing. He kept his eyes on the road; the bill of his cap faced resolutely forward. Charlotte didn't have a handkerchief; she sniffled into the corner of her silver stole. The driver took a familiar route into the hills. They passed a neighbourhood sign that told Charlotte the area was called Enchanted Glen. The driver turned right on to a side road near the base of the canyon. The houses in this suburb weren't nearly as big as the palaces high up in the hills. Charlotte watched them pass her window with nostalgia for something she had never known, only imagined. Dogs dozed on doormats. Porch swings awaited swingers.

Halfway down the next block, far from the main road with its traffic, Charlotte saw her house. She knew where she was now. They had turned on to Cherrybowl Close. Both her hands went to the car's window. They pressed ten clear fingerprints of yearning there. 'Stop the car!' she said.

The driver braked and Charlotte got out with her shoes still clasped in her hand by their straps. Her makeup had rubbed off, leaving dark circles under her eyes. Her feet were blistered. She walked back down the road and stood on the sidewalk across from the cottage. It was painted yellow, pale as buttermilk, with white wooden lattice decorating its gabled eaves. The front door was as red as a postbox. An arroyo willow shaded the drive and Indian paintbrush flared along the fence.

Charlotte stared. She had driven past this house half a dozen times since her arrival in Los Angeles and each trip had felt like a pilgrimage. A balloon of happiness inflated in her chest. The house was still here, waiting for her – a consuming, and possibly attainable, dream. If she could have a house like this, she could have happiness, too.

A woman came to stand at one of the windows. She was working, washing dishes in a sink. Charlotte could hear her singing to herself. She didn't want to be caught spying. She walked back to where her car idled near the kerb.

'You spotted the sign, did you?' the driver asked. It was only then that Charlotte saw a noticeboard hammered into the front lawn. 'I see it's for sale.'

I I

Charlotte tried to get a few hours' sleep that morning but she could not. She was filled with the irrational fear that she would lose her chance to buy the cottage on Cherrybowl Close. Somebody else would make an offer that very morning, before she had the chance. She got up and placed a call to Madge St Claire, who offered her usual sage advice.

'Well, I'm not a real-estate specialist, Carlie darling, but why don't you write a letter to the owners, to find out if they'd accept an offer from you?'

'Yes, please,' said Charlotte. 'We're going to Palm Springs in a few days to start filming but as soon as I get back I will do that, Madge. The day I get back . . .'

Buoyed up with optimism, Charlotte hung up the telephone to find Verbena, in her nightgown, eyeing her from halfway down the hall. The rough night hung around Verbena's shoulders like a black shawl. Her eyes were still heavy with whisky sours.

'Leaving us, are you?' Verbena asked.

Verbena was the last person Charlotte wanted to confide in. Curiously, she felt the urge to tell Liam about the house, but Verbena was there and Charlotte had to blurt it out or risk exploding. 'I might buy a house,' she said. 'It's a little cottage on Cherrybowl Close and it's perfect. It has a red door. Can you believe it, Bee? A home of my own!'

'Don't call me Bee,' said Verbena. 'Only Ivy is allowed to call me Bee.'

Verbena had given up any chance of inheriting her family home in Boston when she had declared her intention to become an actress. For generations, the stately house had been passed down through her family's maternal line, but Verbena's mother had disowned her. Verbena had failed on the Boston stage, and failed off Broadway, but she had done quite well when she had first arrived in Hollywood. Now, the parts were drying up. Warner Brothers wouldn't release her from her contract but they didn't seem eager to put her in any of their projects either. The hardest part of Verbena's life, these days, besides watching her own dreams crumbling, was having to witness all of Charlotte's dreams coming true.

By the end of the week, Charlotte was entrenched in a rigorous work schedule. Verbena noted her comings and goings from the house. Charlotte was collected, transported to meetings, fittings and makeup trials. There were several formal press conferences, and reporters called the house when they could wheedle the number from one of their contacts at the telephone exchange. It was a relief for Verbena when principal photography began and Charlotte went away. It gave her the freedom of the house. She felt she could breathe freely again, and she had room to scheme.

While Verbena was plotting, the crew of *The Walls of Jericho* moved into the rocky desert of central California to shoot on location. They travelled in convoy – trucks of equipment, caravans, buses and a few gleaming cars that flashed like signal mirrors in the sun. Charlotte hung her left elbow languidly out of the car's back window, letting the air cool her perspiration. Temperatures were so high that they would only be able to film in the early-morning hours and at dusk. The cameramen were ecstatic about the blush of shadows on the rocks, the imbalanced colour palette of red hills, white dunes and olive-green scrub, the sky which was a glazed tile of duck-egg blue.

The studio had booked out the El Mirador Hotel for the principal cast. The crew would stay in a selection of dingy roadside motels. Charlotte stepped from her car and looked around at her accommodation. The hotel building had mission arches and a turreted Spanish bell tower. The gardens supplied a plush green vista; bright orange umbrellas surrounded the pool. The swish of sprinklers was constant.

Charlotte felt rumpled after the long drive. She took off her hat and fluffed up her hair. One of the dozen or more boy assistants who all looked the same – eager and ebullient – handed her a key and arranged for her suitcases to be unpacked.

Charlotte's room at the El Mirador reminded her of every hotel she had ever stayed in. She hated hotel rooms. She kept a mental list of things that unsettled her. They were random, disconnected factors nobody else would understand – streetcar bells, park benches, postcards, circuses, hotel rooms. There were many more, too, and each one carried with it an associated memory that was powerful enough to make Charlotte queasy. She never spoke about them, these tattered, rag-tag terrors she had accumulated. Hotel rooms . . . She feared hotel rooms because they represented a transient life where a woman might never have a bedroom of her own in a home of her own. Charlotte feared that eventuality most of all.

Charlotte couldn't sleep. She got up at midnight and dragged on a pair of loose trousers with her camisole. She opened her hotel-room door and slipped furtively into the night.

Charlotte walked across a courtyard towards a row of outbuildings, seeking the cool she expected would linger in hidden nooks. It was sultry outside. The warmth trapped in the sand comforted her bare feet.

She came across a rabbit hutch behind the grounds-keeper's office. Raised on wooden legs, it stood about three feet off the ground. A lamp buzzed above it. Hypnotized moths worshipped at the bulb; their shadows made the light flicker. Instead of sleeping rabbits, Charlotte found that one section of the cage housed a coiled snake, its skin the colour of a sun-dappled jungle. In the next section, a chameleon rolled its eyes at her and spat out its chewing-gum tongue. She stepped back. There was a rabbit in the last section. Its pale fur was pressed against the wire, its pink eyes rolled in terror. The rabbit scrabbled its back legs in a vain attempt to escape its frightening neighbours.

Charlotte leaned in closer to the cage. She felt brave, all alone, outside in the darkness. The thought of touching the snake made her skin crawl. She had to do it, though. Fear did this to Charlotte. Any awful thing that came to mind had to be done, confronted. That way, afterwards, she could say to herself, 'I did it! It was the worst thing I could imagine doing and now it's done and over. I'm free of it.'

Charlotte's fingertips touched the snake's scales. The skin shivered beneath her touch but the creature itself did not move.

Charlotte suddenly felt guilty, as if she had been caught out misbehaving. She looked over her shoulder. Somebody was watching her. A figure sat smoking at a rusty table. As the man inhaled, the cigarette's glowing tip illuminated half of his face and Charlotte saw that it was Liam Malone. He wore a white vest that exposed his wide shoulders, blue striped pyjama pants and, incongruously, a pair of black dress shoes without socks. He had obviously slipped them on as casually as Charlotte had donned her trousers before venturing out into the lonesome night.

'That was brave of you,' Liam called out to her.

'I've never touched a snake before,' said Charlotte. Her gaze was drawn to Liam's face. It was quite blue in the shadows.

'Different than you expected?'

'Yes. It's smooth and dry. I thought it might be slimy like a frog.'

'But you touched it anyway?'

'I do that when I'm scared of something,' said Charlotte. 'Or, rather, I do the things I'm scared of.'

She thought of streetcar bells and postcards and park benches and the red glass perfume bottle. She pushed the images away.

'There are no snakes in Ireland, you know,' Liam said light-heartedly. 'Thanks to St Pat.'

Charlotte didn't know what he meant. Was that a scientific fact? She felt at a disadvantage. So often people engaged in conversations from which she felt excluded; they talked about things Charlotte couldn't understand or hadn't even heard of. She had to pretend to know a lot. 'You were born there?' she asked. 'In Ireland?'

'I was. In a little Galway fishing village between the rocks of the Burren and the rocks of the sea.'

'I grew up by the sea,' said Charlotte. It seemed imperative to find connections with this man. She wanted things to match up between them.

'You're an American girl, though, right?'

'I'm from Florida,' said Charlotte.

'My da moved us to Limerick when I was ten, then on to London. How did you like Charlie's party, by the way?' Liam asked her. 'You were upset when you left.'

'I'm quite all right now. I was unhappy about the horse . . .'

'The unicorn,' Liam corrected.

'Yes, the unicorn.' Charlotte paused, considering his question. 'I found the party unhappy, too.'

'Parties often are,' said Liam. 'That desperate need to be communally cheerful – it's depressing.'

'They tell me you know Charlie Chaplin quite well.' She edged coyly up to him. Liam reached over and pulled out one of the rusty chairs for her. Charlotte sat down with her knees primly together; she noticed that her feet were pale with dust.

'Do they?' said Liam. 'They know almost everything, don't they?'

'It's just another rumour, then?' asked Charlotte. She felt one of those inconvenient blushes rise in her cheeks.

'No, I worked with him, all right, just before he left London to come here. Charlie was in his early twenties then, performing with the Karno Comedy Group. I was a lad of no more than twelve or thirteen. We did a bit together in an East End dancehall.'

'What's he like, really?'

'He's a bit of a lunatic, actually. A little mad, more than a little sad. A lot of these artistic types are.'

'Are you?'

'No,' said Liam. 'I don't pretend to be a thinker. I'm a workhorse. I do as I'm told. I learn my lines. I'm happy to have more money than I dreamed of to take care of my children.'

Charlotte didn't want to talk about his family. She didn't want Liam to be thinking about them. 'It's so hot here,' she said. She threw her head back and fanned her neck with her hand.

'What's the coldest you've ever been?' Liam asked.

The question puzzled Charlotte.

'It's a game me and my brothers used to play when we were lads,' Liam explained. 'There were five of us, and when any one of us was sad, we'd ask him about the time when he felt happiest. When you're hot, you think about a time when you felt cold, see?'

'I can't think of anything,' said Charlotte.

'I'll help you, then.'

Liam stubbed out his cigarette and turned to face her. 'It was one of those days when the wind was blowing in off the North Sea. It was far too cold for snow. I woke up frozen to the bone and never got warm. The inside of my boots felt wet when I put them on but there was a pheasant shoot on a nearby grand estate that day. God, I was maybe seven years old, too young for the responsibility, but they were short of men. I had to keep up, to keep the beating line straight. I couldn't afford to miss a covey hiding in the brush. Us beaters were positioned in a wood thicket at the bottom of a valley. The leaves were wet, the grass was wet, the trees were dripping ice, and the shooting party was two hours late. I couldn't move or stamp my feet because I might disturb the birds. I just had to stand still and turn to ice. The face of the man beside me was quite blue; my fingernails turned purple. When I moved my mouth to whisper a complaint, my lip split open and bled. Jesus, my hands were like two blocks of iron, and when the party came over the hill, their breath was like white smoke signals . . . and every one of the bastards wore a bloody fur coat down to his knees.'

Liam stopped talking and lit another cigarette. 'Are you still hot?' he asked.

'No,' said Charlotte. 'I'm freezing.'

Liam laughed, then covered his mouth. He didn't want them to be discovered.

'You're a great storyteller,' said Charlotte. 'I could listen to you all night. I'm no good at describing things like that.'

'What are you good at, Miss Charlotte?'

'Being pretty,' Charlotte said, quite candidly, and Liam felt pained for her. She exposed herself too easily. The girl didn't have any guile.

Unexpectedly, Liam stood up and positioned himself in front of the table. 'You have to picture Mr Chaplin beside me,' he said. 'It went like this.'

He began to perform a tap-dance routine, which grew in speed and intricacy until his feet were a blur. Charlotte giggled. Liam spun and reeled, putting his heart and soul into the performance. He seemed to remember the steps perfectly.

The man could dance. When he finished, Liam gave a bow and Charlotte clapped. 'You'll ruin your shoes,' she said.

Liam looked down at the coating of dust and performed the schoolboy's emergency polish, rubbing one toecap and then the other on the back of his trouser legs. He flopped back into his chair.

'You're preoccupied with the state of my shoes, Miss Charlotte,' Liam said, with a wink. 'That's the second time you've been concerned about them.'

'You can tell a lot about a man by his shoes,' said Charlotte. 'My father put cardboard inside his when the soles wore through.'

'When I was a boy, I had one new pair of boots each winter,' said Liam. 'If I outgrew them, I had to go barefoot the whole next summer.'

They looked at each other without speaking for a few moments.

'Have you always wanted to act?' Liam asked.

'I don't want to act. I only want a home of my own and a family.'

'Jesus, don't go telling anyone at the studio that,' said Liam. 'They expect your contract to be your life. Didn't you sign yours in blood?'

'I haven't told anyone else. I've only told you.'

Charlotte was sure Liam would understand. She felt safe entrusting him with a confidence. She wanted very much to touch his sharp cheekbones, to smooth them out with the pressure of her fingertips.

'I like the way your face looks,' she said, and instantly wanted to crawl away into the dunes. She was mortified!

But Liam said, 'I like the way your face looks, too.'

The girl's honesty had him stumped. Liam wanted very much to be truthful with her.

'From that first day I saw you, I wanted it to be you,' he said. 'For Rahab, I mean. I wanted it to be you very much.' Then he stood up quite suddenly. 'Goodnight, Miss Charlotte.'

'Please just call me Charlotte,' she said.

Liam wasn't willing to identify the powerful emotion he felt. It was, he told himself, only the result of the desert or the moonlight. He walked towards his room. He did a few steps of a jig, without looking back, solely for her amusement. When he reached the rabbit hutch, he looked in at the creatures. He opened the wire gate. The rabbit kicked at him and he hushed it in a soothing voice. He set it down on the dust where it stayed frozen for a moment before it loped away into the desert. Charlotte watched its bobbing tail until it disappeared. When she looked back, Liam was gone, too.

Sitting at the table, she gazed out to where the desert swallowed up the last of the buzzing lamp's moth-mottled light. The night was a long, sleek span – a black cat stretching. And Charlotte knew for a certainty, in the way a person can suddenly know something, that she had been lonely her whole life.

12

Filming was tiring, especially in the heat, but the desert had a calming effect on Charlotte. The week away from Lantana Drive softened her. Being near Liam made her happy, though they hadn't found another occasion to be truly alone together since that first night. The cinematography went well and Charlotte was surprised to find she felt fulfilled by the work; she was good at something. It was difficult to tell with an intense man like David O. Selznick, but the director seemed pleased with her. Selznick was notoriously difficult to satisfy. He had a reputation for demanding a great deal of sacrifice from his cast, but he had been over-heard to remark in the catering tent that he believed Charlotte had a natural gift.

Charlotte had the knack of being able to remove the cameras from any scene and play it as though she was there, experiencing in turn Rahab's trepidation, then her brassy, unsophisticated courage. She went to bed exhausted each night after long hours of enduring Selznick's temper and the soaring temperatures.

It was Liam who worked hardest, though. Charlotte watched his performances with awe, imagining hushed movie palaces full of people who would appreciate this moment in the months ahead.

Selznick left his most challenging project for the final day of scheduled shooting in Palm Springs. It was one of the two scenes Charlotte shared with Liam. In it, Joshua made good on his promise and led Rahab from the sacked city of Jericho. The crew had assembled and dressed two hundred extras to form the Israelite army. These men had mostly been commandeered from the local bars and Relief Agency offices where the unemployed spent their days. Selznick filmed his pivotal scene six times that Wednesday, but he wasn't happy with the result. It was an expensive scene, with live fires and black smoke. They had spent a fortune in wasted film. The actors kept moving off their marks and the drifting smoke fogged up the lenses so that the action was barely visible. Eventually Selznick lost the daylight before achieving the footage he wanted.

That evening, because of the disappointing day, everybody was tense. Charlotte ate alone in her room. She looked from her window to see if the light was on behind Liam Malone's curtains across the courtyard. It was not. His dark window made her melancholy. There was a subtle knock on her door. Liam stood in the corridor, holding a bottle and two wine glasses.

'Somebody left some wine in my bathroom,' he said. 'I thought I'd bring it over and share a drink with you.' He straightened up suddenly and cleared his throat. 'Now it seems like a bad idea.'

'Why?' asked Charlotte.

'Because bringing liquor to a woman's hotel room at night . . .' Liam sounded disappointed in himself. 'It's not a thing I would normally do. You probably think . . .'

'I was thinking how nice it was that you stopped by. I've been wondering if you're as anxious about tomorrow as I am.' Charlotte took the bottle from Liam's hand and closed the door behind him. 'Somebody left wine in your bathroom?' she asked, puzzled.

Liam nodded and put the two glasses on the table, his hands returning shyly to his trouser pockets. Charlotte examined the bottle's label and tried to suppress a smile. It did indeed look like a wine bottle but that was only clever packaging. 'Are you sure somebody didn't leave bath bubbles in your bathroom?' she asked, and showed him the label. Liam read it with chagrin.

'I don't think it's untoward to show up with bath products at a woman's door,' teased Charlotte. 'It's a very acceptable gift.'

Liam covered his eyes with his hand but he was grinning now, too.

Charlotte twisted the bottle's cap and poured the thick, sweet-smelling goo into one of the glasses he had brought. She toasted him with it. 'I will enjoy this, with water, later tonight.'

Liam laughed. 'You're so easy to talk to, Charlotte,' he said. 'You're funny.'

Nobody had ever told Charlotte she was funny. She didn't think of herself that way, but the compliment made her happy. They sat down to talk, Charlotte with her legs curled under her on the bed and Liam at a chair near the table.

'How are your children?' Charlotte asked. It was best to acknowledge the complexities of the situation.

'They're with their mother in Napa this week. She has a brother who manages a vineyard up that way. They're going to pick grapes.'

'They'll love that!' said Charlotte. 'Fruit picking is so much fun.'

'It's Agnes who wants to try it,' said Liam. 'The boys are going along to please her. They're very patient with her. She's their little mascot. And she's my favourite. She's the only girl, so I can say that without upsetting anybody. She's my special one.'

'There's only one girl?'

'That's right. Five lads – Callum, Connor, Dashiel, Francis and Shea – and then, years after all those boys, my redheaded Agnes.'

'And none since her?' asked Charlotte. It was unusual that a Catholic family with the Malones' means would stop childbearing in their mid-thirties.

'Bernie had a tough time with the last pregnancy. We nearly lost her when Agnes came. The birth was . . . well, it was damaging to her . . .'

He cleared his throat and Charlotte, taken aback by this personal information, helped him move on. 'But you had your little girl,' she said.

'We did! These days, Bernie focuses on raising children, not making them.' He winked at Charlotte but it seemed an inadequate cover-up for an abiding sorrow.

They talked about other things. Sometime later, Charlotte found herself telling Liam about the circus trip, her inability to go into the tent. She hadn't thought the event was still at the forefront of her mind but clearly it was.

'You don't like circuses?' Liam asked.

'I'm afraid of them.'

'Agnes doesn't like clowns,' Liam said. 'She screams when she sees them. It's the face paint. It alarms her.'

'It started when I was young. Something happened . . . I never got over it.'

In that moment, it seemed that Charlotte might be able to tell Liam everything. She would tell him about the perfume and the streetcar and the park bench and the hotels and Pike. The story reached her lips, then stopped dead. It was only fair to tell Liam the whole story now, before their friendship, or whatever it was or would become, was fully established. Charlotte chose not to. Liam would not understand. He would not forgive her. She knew that. Nobody could, if they knew the whole ugly truth of it. Instead Charlotte chose to speak about Verbena. She told Liam about the awful tension in the house, the spite, and Verbena's apparent determination to make life uncomfortable for her.

'That's not good, Charlotte,' said Liam, with concern.

'There's always anger in the air. I feel watched . . .'

'You can't live like that.'

'That's why I've enjoyed being here so much, with you. It's an escape, a break from women, women, women all the time.'

'Well, you can't be expected to stay there,' said Liam.

'I'm going to buy my own house,' explained Charlotte. 'I've found one I love, so in a month or two I might be on my own at last.'

'Sometimes I go to my beach house in Malibu to escape. If I go this weekend, would you like to come with me?'

His offer was sincere, Charlotte felt sure.

'You can swim in the sea, even though it's freezing. You can rest and be away from people. I know how it was for me in the beginning. It's crazy with parties and demands. You need to escape sometimes.'

'I do need to get away,' said Charlotte. 'And I've never been to Malibu.'

'It's a sweet little village. Do you want to bring anyone along?'

Liam wanted her to know that the offer was a genuine one. It could be whatever Charlotte wanted it to be.

'I think I'd like to come on my own,' Charlotte said.

'I'd like that, too.'

Liam could not stop staring at her face. Those extraordinary eyes, like African gemstones, striated with yellow. He wanted to touch her, pull her against him. Liam had seldom been a casualty of such intense physical attraction.

Charlotte thought it was the most perfect invitation to an affair a woman had ever received. It wasn't tawdry or obscene. It was clean and clear and open. Her heart sang against her ribcage.

'It's settled, then,' said Liam. 'We'll have to fend for ourselves – there's no staff there.'

'We can live off sandwiches and tap water.'

'I could collect you at about four?' Liam suggested.

'Just park on Lantana Drive, a little way up the road. I'll walk along until I find you.'

She had made it so easy. With Charlotte, decisions were simple. They both wanted the same thing and neither of them felt the need to play coy. For years now, Bernadette had needed coddling and reassurance until, between her, and the work, and the children, Liam was exhausted. He was not a man but a strong place everybody came to with their needs and their demands. Not Charlotte, though. Charlotte was the answer to all that. She was what he needed. Liam did not see it as selfish desire: it was a rudimentary necessity that must be satisfied if he was to go on.

Liam pulled Charlotte to him, and kissed her. Her lips tasted delicious and he groaned.

'Until Friday,' Charlotte whispered against his neck.

Liam Malone was suddenly, wildly, crazy about her.

The following morning, Selznick got the shots he wanted. This time, when Liam made his way through the sacked city towards her, Charlotte didn't feel as if Joshua was coming to fetch Rahab from Jericho, she saw Liam – in costume, yes, but her Liam – coming to her rescue. He bent down and took her hand, helping her to her feet.

From his position behind the camera, Selznick watched Joshua and Rahab. The general kissed the woman chastely on both cheeks, his lips teasingly close to the edges of her own, so that if she only turned her head an inch, she would have his mouth on hers – but she could not. Neither could he. They were from different worlds, warring ones. Then Joshua took Rahab firmly by the arm and led her back through the rubble. The family members she had saved went cowering after them.

The small party, Joshua and Rahab at its head, walked off into the vastness of the desert.

'Keep going . . . Keep going . . .' Selnick whispered the wish to himself, as he watched the actors continue past their final marks. 'Keep going . . .'

Selznick saw that his intended finishing point for this shot was too close. They needed to go on for the shot to work, and they did. They kept walking until the blue of Charlotte's dress grew fainter and fainter, a tourmaline speck drifting slowly away until it blurred from view. They had done it! They had ignored Selznick's initial instructions and kept on walking, and they had perfected his vision.

When Selznick called for the camera to cut, Liam and Charlotte were half a mile away and still going. They were lost to the call of his bullhorn, alone together in a desolate place. Selznick sent a boy to run out to them with a flask of iced water and call them back. He wanted to embrace them! He couldn't wait to see the rushes back at the studio the next day.

He slapped his hands together in satisfaction. 'Everybody's earned the weekend off,' he said.

13

Liam Malone placed a call to his wife the next morning. His daughter Agnes answered the phone in the farmhouse in Napa. The sound of her voice was a joy to him.

'We made blueberry cream pie,' Agnes told him. 'It was better even than your chocolate cake.'

'Really?' Liam asked.

'No, not really,' said Agnes, with solemn loyalty. 'But almost better.'

After a while, Bernadette took the receiver. They talked about Agnes, then the boys.

'Do you have any plans for the weekend?' Bernadette asked.

'I may go to the Malibu place. I have some work to do,' Liam said. He held his breath.

'Oh, that's good,' said Bernadette. 'You always enjoy it there.'

Liam didn't know what to say next. It had been too easy.

'There's no help, though,' continued Bernadette.

'I'll manage on my own,' Liam said. 'A tin of beans will do.'

'That's good,' she said again.

'I need to get on top of this script.'

'I understand.' That was Bernadette – empathetic, compliant, malleable.

'It's easier for me to be on my own when I'm doing something like that.'

'Then you should definitely go,' she said.

Liam sometimes wondered how he had decided to marry her. Bernadette had been in his class at school when they were young children but she was a grey girl, not memorable. After her workday in the dairy, Bernadette would join the gaggle of girls in the street outside the pub where the boys drank their pints. She remained unnoticed. At fifteen, Bernadette had befriended Liam's mother. Liam would find the two women sewing together in their kitchen. They made pies together for the ladies' church mornings. They sipped their tea together in the priest's parlour. Bernadette never spoke to Liam. He never spoke to her. His brothers ignored her, too. She was not tough or flirtatious enough to tease, and they knew it. Bernadette would not cry satisfactorily or retaliate.

One night, after being unexpectedly rebuffed by a girl behind the dancehall in Killarney, Liam had stumbled home and found Bernadette stitching a piece of embroidery by their stove. His mother was in bed; his brothers and father were still out drinking. Liam had simply come across Bernadette there, kissed her, told her she was lovely. She had felt as pliant and comfortable as an old sofa and he had taken her. She did not participate and she did not protest. Afterwards, she adored.

Unusually for fecund Irish girls, Bernadette did not fall pregnant. Liam went off to London. He went on the stage. He came home a few times and saw Bernadette while he was there. She always had a needle in her hand. There was always a sock in need of darning in the Malone house.

When America beckoned, vast as a prairie, Liam had asked Bernadette to come along with him. He had married her to make it possible. She was a piece of Ireland he could transport alongside him and she was steadfast. There had been other women when Liam had lived in London, of course. They were educated, intimidating women, who painted their nails and drank whiskey and knew everything about a man's body – where to press, where to place their lips to drive a man into a frenzy, to make a bull of him. Liam thought of those women, always, as English. There was something of the oppressor in every one of them. But they were fickle, too. They grew tired of him quickly. They never wanted to be seen out with him.

Bernadette hadn't grown tired of him. She knew what loyalty meant. She had borne Liam five fine boys and a darling daughter, and Liam had fallen in love with every one of his children, without ever really having fallen in love with their mother.

In the house on Lantana Drive, it was three thirty on Friday afternoon. Charlotte had almost completed packing for her weekend with Liam when the doorbell chimed. She had asked Liam, for the sake of his own reputation, to wait for her on Lantana Drive, but perhaps he had decided not to. The thought of his impatience made Charlotte tingle. She might have felt more anxious about him arriving at the door but for the fact that Ivy and Verbena were both away from the house. Ivy had accepted a late luncheon date from Congressman Whitewood, much to Verbena's disgust. In a temper, Verbena had taken her car to Glendale to ride her new horse – the poor animal was in for a hard session. Allegra was somewhere about. As the maid, she would answer the door, but Liam's clandestine arrival wouldn't mean anything to her – a poor, simple Mexican girl.

The doorbell chimed again and Charlotte was annoyed. She looked out of her window and saw Allegra sweeping leaves from the swimming pool with a long-handled net. The woman hadn't heard a thing! Charlotte checked her image in the mirror for the last time and sped to the front door. She opened it wearing her most dazzling smile.

It was not Liam Malone who stood there. It was Teddy Pike.

'Mr Pike,' said Charlotte, in a deadpan voice.

Mr Pike tipped his pork-pie hat.

'So, you do remember your old friends, Miss Fancy-Panties – as we all used to call you in fond jest. I did wonder if you would.'

'I haven't forgotten you,' said Charlotte. 'I've been half-way expecting you, if I'm honest with myself.'

'But being honest isn't really your strong point, now, is it?'

From nowhere, Pike produced a card and bestowed it upon Charlotte with a bow. He liked demonstrating his sleight-of-hand skills. The card was from the tarot pack – the Lucky Lady.

It occurred to Charlotte that somebody – even Liam when he drove by – might see the odious man on her doorstep. 'You'd better come in for a minute,' she said.

Allowing Pike near her produced a sheen of sweat on Charlotte's skin. She ushered him into the living room, grateful once again that her housemates weren't present. She sat down but Pike stalled for a few minutes. He explored objects on display.

'You do look well, Charlotte,' he said. 'You should have seen my face when I read that article about you. You could have knocked me down with a feather.

'In fact,' he said, pulling a copy of *Starlet* magazine from where he had it tucked into the back of his trousers, 'I brought this along with me for your autograph.' He opened the rolled-up magazine to the page showing Charlotte standing beside her father's bed. 'Could you maybe scrawl a little love note to me, right there on that page? Maybe over the face of that unfortunate man.'

Charlotte refused to be rattled. She picked up a pen.

'Say something like "We'll always have our fond memories."' Pike paused and the nib of Charlotte's pen quivered ever so slightly above the page before she wrote what he had dictated. 'Then put "Love for ever, Charlotte Caine".'

'It's Carlie Caine, actually,' said Charlotte.

'A whole new name! How exciting for you! It must be nice to get the chance of a fresh start.'

'Yes, it's a whole new me,' said Charlotte.

'Yeah,' said Pike, and he crunched up his face as if reluctant, but obliged, to disagree. 'But everybody has a past, don't they? That's part of what makes us who we are.'

'I'm actually waiting for a friend to collect me, Mr Pike,' said Charlotte. 'I don't have time for you today.'

'Oh, oh,' said Pike, with exaggerated discomfort at having inconvenienced her. 'Don't let me keep you. It's been a treat just to see you again, Charlotte. There's no need to finish our reminiscences today. I'm staying in the area until the end of the month, which gives us plenty of time to catch up, time for me to meet your new friends. Past meets present, so to speak.'

'What do you do these days, Mr Pike?' asked Charlotte.

'I'm still with the circus. I'm the ringmaster now. I think you already know that, though. I've got my old top-hat-and-tails routine for the punters. Only these days I'm doing more and more charity work, accepting donations and the like for good causes. Perhaps you ought to start thinking about whether you'd like to make a little contribution.'

It was money. Charlotte felt relieved. If it was only money, she might be alright. But how much would he want? What if it was so much that she couldn't afford the house? What if he kept on asking, year after year? She would never be free of him. Charlotte wanted to cry but Pike was watching her intently, expecting some kind of an answer. Charlotte steeled herself. 'I'm expecting a payment from the studio shortly.'

'Awww, you always were a good girl, Charlotte, and so generous with what was yours.'

Charlotte felt a spider of disgust scurry up her spine.

Pike rolled up one long white sleeve to reveal a tapestry of tattoos covering his forearm. The man had always had tattoos. He had been painted with half a dozen when Charlotte had first met him, but now he was almost entirely covered with ink. Charlotte saw her own face depicted on his skin. Shocked, she walked to the front door and opened it. Pike got to his feet and went out. He stopped very close to Charlotte and looked directly into her eyes. When he spoke this time, all acting was gone. His voice was low and hard, his accent all American. It made it seem that these were the words he had come to speak, the only thing the real Teddy Pike had wanted to say: 'I'm not going anywhere, Charlotte. I will see you again.'

Charlotte found the courage to slam the door behind him.

As he rounded the corner of the drive, Pike encountered Allegra, who was returning the pool net to the garage.

'And who do we have here?' he asked, all affable Cockney once more.

'I'm the housemaid, sir – Allegra.'

'Allegra . . .' Pike twirled one hand in the air as if conducting an orchestra, trying out the name for its musical qualities. 'Sweet-sounding, that. Melodious.'

Suddenly his hand darted out and snatched something from the air. Allegra jumped. He opened his fist slowly and one of the dragonflies that drank from the swimming pool floated free, unscathed. The man had enormous hands, bigger than baseball mitts.

Who was he? Allegra was nervous. Had he been inside the house?

'Can I help you, sir?' she asked.

The man poked his cigar at her. Its glowing tip came very close to her eye. 'My name's Mr Pike,' he said. 'I just stopped by to talk with my old friend, Miss Caine. You might be seeing me again, so don't be alarmed.'

Pike continued walking. He whistled his way up the drive. He didn't seem to draw breath, but the eerie fluting maintained its force for several moments. Allegra heard the metal of the gate latch clang shut. The tune, which wasn't any song she recognized, drifted back to her – even when the man must have been halfway down the road.

Allegra took the pool net she still carried into the garage. As she was returning to the kitchen, Charlotte came out of the house carrying a suitcase. 'I'm leaving now, Allie,' she said. 'If anybody asks, say I'll be away for a few days. You can tell Verbena I'm dead, if you like. That'll make her happy for the weekend.'

Part of Charlotte didn't believe that Liam would be waiting for her, but he was. He sat behind the wheel of his gold Rolls-Royce, as if he had been born into wealth. 'Hop in, Miss Charlotte,' he said, as he patted the passenger seat.

Charlotte was glad he was relaxed; he didn't look regretful.

They glided down Lantana Drive. Charlotte worried that they might pass Pike on the way. Had he come on foot? Surely not! When they reached the freeway, she knew she was in the clear, but then Liam said, 'There was an unsavoury character loitering on the road outside your house. Do you know him – a stout fellow carrying a little round hat?'

'Oh,' said Charlotte. *Think of something to say!* she demanded of herself. *Think! Think!*

'I'm sure he came up from your drive,' continued Liam. 'I was quite alarmed for a moment . . .'

'He's nobody,' said Charlotte. 'He's a friend of my maid's, I think.'

'Your help shouldn't be having visitors to the house,' said Liam. 'Who knows what kind of people they associate with?'

'He doesn't make a habit of coming by. It was just today.'

'I don't like the sound of it,' said Liam. 'If I run into him again, I'll tell him to steer clear.'

'No, don't do that,' said Charlotte, a little frantically. 'I'll tell Allie to sort out her affairs away from work.'

'Good,' said Liam. 'I hope this Allie girl of yours doesn't

owe him money or anything, because he didn't look like the kind of man you'd want to cross.'

Liam Malone's beach house was reached by a one-lane dirt track. Malibu was a rural town with few permanent residents. The homes were old cabins and cottages; Liam's bungalow was charming. It was just the right size, covered in a blanket of bougainvillaea the colour of satsumas, with a big kitchen and small bedrooms, a single bathroom.

'When we visit as a family, we crowd in,' said Liam. 'It's far too small for all the children, really, but I loved it as soon as I saw it. Some of the boys sleep on the floor, Aggie on the sofa. We make do like only family can.'

Liam left Charlotte's suitcase standing just inside the front door. He seemed unsure where to put it. His manner was cavalier, but Charlotte could tell he was nervous. He opened the windows and doors. The sea breeze wafted in. The garden ran right to the edge of a cliff where a set of twisting stairs scrambled down to the beach.

Liam served her chilled root beer in a jar as they lazed by the pool, talking and not talking, until dusk settled in. Neither wanted to admit the situation was strange, mostly because it felt as good and natural as laughter. Charlotte waited for the night to come, the darkness that was necessary to draw her out and make her brave. At seven o'clock, Liam went through the pantry and placed an array of ingredients on the kitchen table.

'Do you like chocolate cake?' he asked.

'Who doesn't?' laughed Charlotte.

'Every actress I know,' said Liam. 'They're always watching their figures.'

Charlotte tossed aside the magazine she had been reading and went over to him. 'Well, I love chocolate cake. I'll eat the whole thing myself with a giant soup spoon!'

Liam laughed.

'You bake?' she asked incredulously.

'I don't exactly bake. I can make a chocolate cake. That's it.'

'I'd like to see that!' Charlotte said.

Liam demonstrated his method with great showmanship. Charlotte rested her chin in one palm as she watched him. She had never baked anything in her life.

When the cake came out of the oven, Liam took it on to the deck and together they watched it cool for an hour. They drank a bottle of Merlot from the vineyard Bernadette's brother ran. There was little conversation. Liam was acutely aware of Charlotte's physicality. He looked at her when she wasn't looking. She looked at him when he glanced away. Charlotte was conscious of Liam, too. She knew where his body was in relation to hers at any given moment. Her skin was infused with blood at his nearness.

They drank more wine and iced the cake at nine o'clock.

'Today was the best day,' said Charlotte, definitively.

'Compared to what?' asked Liam.

'The best ever,' she answered, and he knew what she meant.

Liam reached out the spatula to let her taste the frosting, and Charlotte took two of his fingers into her mouth instead. Liam shivered visibly at the softness and the wetness. She ran the length of her tongue down the tight groove between his fingers, deep into the fulcrum. Liam dropped the spatula and spread his fingers inside her mouth, pulling her lips apart. Charlotte gasped. She couldn't inhale. Liam's mouth came down over hers and she stole the breath from inside him instead. Their lovemaking was fast, all heat and friction. Then it was slow and unreal, an act completed half in reality, half in a dream.

Charlotte woke twice during the night that followed. The first time she was hot, her skin saturated with wine. The room into which they had retired was musty with disuse. Charlotte wanted water. She went into the kitchen and drank straight from the tap, splashing her face and neck. She felt feral and free in the dark rooms. The doors and windows were still open. The moon was a twist of lemon peel above the sea.

The second time Charlotte woke, there were stars. An unknown constellation was visible beyond the black cavity of the window. Charlotte clutched at the bedstead to prevent herself being sucked through the frame and out into space. There was a game she had played since childhood. She picked out two distinct stars and named them – Liam and Charlotte.

There was no clock to mark the increments of time, only Liam's steady breathing. The bed felt like a hammock. Charlotte swayed in it. She finally knew what it was to be happy.

Charlotte and Liam ate the chocolate cake for breakfast, sitting together on the grass at the cliff's edge. He wore nothing but a pair of shorts; Charlotte wore her satin chemise. One of the straps was broken; it hung down from her right shoulder, almost exposing her breast. Liam reached over and tied the halves of the strap back together in a clumsy knot.

They swam side by side in the pool and Liam held Charlotte's body against him in the water like a baby. They ate whenever they felt like it. They slept during the day. They made love over and over again.

On Sunday morning they walked barefoot to the Sidewalk Café and ordered scallops. Charlotte didn't wear a hat that weekend. Her nose turned pink in the sun. She didn't wear makeup either. In the evening, they shared a bath in the enormous tub. Charlotte lay against Liam's chest and traced her fingers along the patterns of the Malibu tiles on the bathroom wall until the water grew cold. Her lips felt bruised. Her body felt torn. She felt beautiful. She fell asleep with Liam's thigh between her own.

On Sunday afternoon, sadness descended. The weather conspired with Charlotte's misery. A sea fog came in off the Pacific and turned the garden into a ghostly graveyard with shrubs for tombstones. Liam sat reading Selznick's script changes. Charlotte rested against his shoulder, determined to maintain contact. Neither of them spoke about the future, or mentioned when they might find the chance to snatch another weekend away together.

'I want to buy a house,' said Charlotte. Liam lowered his script. 'I've been driving past this same cottage for months. It's right off Laurel Canyon, on the valley side. I'm in love with it.'

Liam kissed the top of her head. He liked the way Charlotte said she was 'in love' with it. 'When you really love something like that, you should have it,' he said. 'You should have the things you love,' he reiterated.

'Madge St Claire suggested I write to the owner and make

an offer. She gave me some idea of property values in the area.'

'I could look over the place, if you like.'

'Would you?'

'Of course I would. I'm not a builder but I can spot obvious problems. I can let you know if I think it's right for you.'

'I'd love that.'

Liam was a real man. Charlotte believed a real man was supposed to be helpful, to assist in decision-making. A wife might rely on her husband to do this sort of thing. Now Liam would help her with such things. She could lean on him.

'I can help you write that letter to the homeowners, too,' said Liam.

He extricated his body from hers and went over to a cupboard. He returned with a Royal portable typewriter, several sheets of blank paper and an envelope. 'You can type. I'll dictate.'

'I can't type,' said Charlotte. 'I can't do anything practical.'

'Luckily I can,' said Liam, as he sat down at the table.

'Chocolate-cake baker and expert typist,' said Charlotte.

'I'll always be in work,' said Liam. He crunched his knuckles in preparation. 'Do you know the address?'

'It's number four,' said Charlotte. 'Number four, Cherry-bowl Close.'

'We can stop by there tomorrow morning and you can pop your offer in their mailbox personally.'

After a few drafts, they had perfected the letter. Charlotte placed it inside the envelope. She asked Liam to lick the flap for luck.

*

On the drive back to the city early on Monday morning, Charlotte made a mental catalogue of her desires. She wanted the house – she had the offer letter in her purse – and she wanted Liam. Sitting beside him, so comfortable with each other, Charlotte felt that she almost had him. How would they work things out with his wife and children? Charlotte didn't know, but divorce wasn't that difficult any more, was it? The story would cause a media uproar for a month or two but things would settle down eventually. Some new scandal would supersede theirs. Charlotte also wanted to see her first picture as a leading lady completed. She would attend the première. Would Liam be on her arm by then? The idea thrilled her.

There were problems ahead, too. Charlotte admitted that to herself. She needed to speak with Madge's banker about consolidating the money to purchase the house. She needed to extricate herself from her current accommodation, from Ivy and Verbena. She needed to rid herself of the oppressive Teddy Pike. She would pay the man any amount of money to leave her alone.

Charlotte directed Liam to Cherrybowl Close and he parked discreetly across the road from her cottage. A grin split his face when he saw the place. 'It's just the kind of home I knew you'd choose,' he said, and he kissed Charlotte softly, his lips lingering on hers. 'It's so pretty. It's you, Charlotte.'

'I know!' said Charlotte. She pointed at the house. 'Promise me you'll bake me a chocolate cake in that kitchen.'

'I promise,' he said. The promise came too easily and Liam felt a twinge of guilt. The approach to the city had brought a return of the sense of duty that was his nature and his master.

Charlotte bounced from the car, crossed the road, and slipped her letter into the mailbox. Liam watched her skip back towards him. He felt perfectly happy in that second. There was a yellow ribbon in Charlotte's hair, which whipped in the breeze like a tattered strip of the sun. As she jumped into the passenger seat beside him, he reached his hand over to pull a stray strand of hair from the edge of her crimson lips. The flyaway ends were singed with scarlet. It was a gesture of such tenderness that it stilled Charlotte. She looked into Liam's eyes in the way that is only ever comfortable between lovers. Her joy overflowed. Her cheeks were flushed with excitement. Liam knew he could never let her go, but still he could not think of a way to have her.

'We should have the things we love.' Charlotte repeated Liam's words of the night before.

'In a perfect world,' Liam said.

That proviso was new. Charlotte thought he sounded a little sad. She knew she would be a little sad, too, until she could be with him again. But soon they would live happily ever after. Verbena would be out of Charlotte's life. Pike would be gone. Not a soul knew that Charlotte had any connection to that horrible man and his vile circus. That was the most important thing – nobody knew.

14

Allegra had walked home that Friday night through a perfect Californian evening. She thought, as she went, of her encounter with the alarming Mr Pike. It seemed strange that a man like that should, in any way, be associated with Miss Charlotte. How could those two vastly different people have met?

Allegra enjoyed being outdoors. The air was fresh. Only when she neared Stationville, beyond the freeway viaducts where the homeless slept, did the world grow hazy. There was always smoke in the township because the vagrant tenants, called Okies because a good percentage of them had fled the Oklahoma dustbowl, kept their fires going throughout the day.

During the months Allegra had lived there, Stationville had become a blot on the landscape, a scorched ring like a meteor crater. The trees that had once grown within its perimeter were now splintered and leafless, as if torn through by lightning. Wood was a commodity. Any fuel was precious. Sometimes the women of Stationville sent their children out to run alongside the coal cars that occasionally passed through, collecting the lumps that bounced free. The children found this chore exhilarating. The roaring trains jostled their teeth together in their mouths and smothered their shrieks. It was more fun than collecting water from the pump, but a year before a boy had been crushed to death beneath a locomotive. Another had lost his leg.

Allegra approached her neighbour, Mrs Dunn, who stood in her doorway smoking a cigarette as she waited for the trucks to return from the farms. Mr Dunn would be aboard one of them, along with the three Dunn boys, exhausted after a hard day of harvesting artichokes.

'Saw police cars drivin' by today,' said Mrs Dunn. 'They passed real slow, two of 'em.'

'Did they come into the camp?' Allegra asked.

Mrs Dunn shook her head.

'It's probably nothing to worry about, then,' said Allegra.

'Something's brewin',' said Mrs Dunn. 'They're plannin' to burn us out. I just know it.'

'The police wouldn't do that, Mrs Dunn, not to Stationville.'

'It ain't Stationville that pricks at 'em, it's Pipe City . . .'

'Then they'll clear out Pipe City,' said Allegra, 'and leave us alone.'

'Fire spreads,' commented Mrs Dunn. She stamped on her cigarette butt very deliberately and went back inside her room.

Allegra looked at Stationville, her home for the past year. Stationville itself was a settlement of forty ugly wooden boxes, standing in four rows of ten. Each box was a large room that stood on cinder blocks with the ground beneath quite visible through the cracks in the floorboards. The structures had tin roofs freckled with rust holes. Each was equipped with a coal stove. There was a central well with a pump at the end of the development. A pair of outhouses stood behind an old water tank at the far end of the scrubland lot. Stationville had been built as temporary housing for workers finishing a branch of the Pacific line, and should have been torn down years before, but the depression had hit, creating demand for even the cheapest form of shelter. The original forty dwellings were known as the Rows and they were at the heart of Stationville. The inhabitants of the Rows still had employment, however modest, but the township had grown far beyond this core. The place had swelled under the daily influx of Okies and Chinese and rootless pickers. The later arrivals had settled on the outskirts of Stationville, in a rough ring of shacks known as the Border.

Beyond the shunting yard there was a third distinct region called Pipe City, but nobody from Stationville went there. It was dangerous, inhabited by fringe-dwellers and dope smokers. Allegra's uncle Manuel had secured one of the cottages in the Rows for her when she had first arrived from Mexico. The place had no furniture except a table the former tenants had left in the middle of the room and three upturned buckets they had used as seats. The sleeping area behind a curtain was bare. The men had been dossing in bedrolls on the bare boards. The room smelt of burned wood where they had extinguished their cigarettes on the walls.

Since those first desperate weeks, Allegra had purchased netting to provide privacy at her windows, and a few bits of furniture from a second-hand store. With her last precious black-market dollars, she had selected an icebox, a wardrobe and two upholstered chairs. She hadn't splurged on a wireless. The cottages were so close together that she was able to hear the news on the wind and the Dunn family next door, playing 'Ain't We Got Fun' on their phonograph.

This was the place Allegra returned to after her day's work on Lantana Drive. She trudged up her two front steps and unlocked her door. She always left a basin of fresh water on the table before she left in the mornings, knowing she would be too tired by the time she came home to visit the water pump. She had placed a small bar of soap beside it. It had the logo of a hotel chain stamped into it. Soap was a neighbourhood currency. In the past, Allegra had thrown bars away the minute they cracked because she didn't like the way the grooves held dirt. She was shamed by that carelessness now. She took off her uniform and washed.

While she was drying, she heard a horse whinnying in the distance. She looked out of her window, across the stumps of felled trees the men used as gaming tables, towards Pipe City.

This settlement beyond the railway lines was a dark suburb. It housed despair. Pipe City had once been a storage yard for the construction company bringing a water-borne sewerage system to the suburbs in the Hollywood Hills. The company had left behind a dozen huge concrete pipes. Vagrants had rolled segments of these pipes apart then flanked their open ends with sheet metal and plywood. Each segment now housed a man who slept curved along its rough interior. These men had given up on finding employment. They smoked peyote bought from the ancient-faced Indians on La Cienega Boulevard. They mugged the jazz musicians in Compton for their reefer. They smashed the windows of drugstores and mixed pills together that helped them laugh at nothing or drift off into delirium.

Between the Border and the first concrete hoop of Pipe City there was a field – a patch of undeveloped crabgrass before the distant San Bernadinos. In this field, Allegra saw the horse. The corral that was his home had once been the parking lot for long-ago railway commuters. Now only one vehicle remained – a rusted-out Ford truck. The horse was a chestnut. He wanted company. He kept his tail high and his ears pricked. He trotted to and fro.

Allegra took a fall apple from the basket by the door and went out to meet him.

The horse came towards her as she approached. It was getting dark but his flanks glowed like a copper pot. He was cared for and friendly, happy to receive attention. Allegra held out her hand and the horse snorted at it in greeting, taking in her scent and liking it. Allegra wondered if some tiny remnant of horsy aroma still clung to her from months before, from all those years when she had been lifted up on to the backs of thoroughbreds in the winner's circle, her photograph in the newspaper the next day. The notion was unlikely but satisfying.

Allegra gave the horse the apple, talking to him softly in Spanish. She wanted to ride again; she wondered if she ever would.

A man came out from behind the rusted-out Ford. Allegra, who had believed she was alone, stepped back. The man appeared in silhouette, so short and slight that she thought he was a boy until he spoke with a low, mature voice.

'Evening,' he said, as he tipped his hat in Allegra's direction. He came forward out of the truck's shadow and into the last light of dusk. Allegra could see that he was grinning, though his voice hadn't held a smile. 'That's my horse. He's not for sale.'

'I can't buy him,' said Allegra. 'I live in Stationville, so I'm as broke as you are.'

'He's not for stealing neither.'

The man wasn't smiling after all. Now that he had drawn closer in the gloom, Allegra could see that he held a hammer in his left hand. She was glad of the paltry barrier the fence provided between them. It wasn't a smile that split the man's face but twin snaggles of scar tissue, pink and puckered, that ran from both corners of his mouth and disappeared into his sideburns in front of each ear. It looked as if he had hooked his fingers into the sides of his mouth and pulled until his face peeled in two.

'I'm not a wrangler,' Allegra said, determined to control her fright and remain civil. 'I used to ride and I miss it.' She moved forward; she reached out for the horse's muzzle again. He nuzzled her with his velvet nose.

'He's a fair judge of character, that horse,' the man said.

His face squiggled up on the left side when he spoke. The nerves on the right side were quite dead. Some of the tension had drained from his body. He turned and tossed the hammer casually back towards the truck. It clanged against a rusted hubcap. A plume of dust rose in the stillness. The man wiped his hands on his denim trousers and reached out to shake. 'The name's Holt,' he said. 'Just Holt. There's nothing more to it, so don't bother asking.'

'Allegra del Rio,' she said and then, to make herself more American, she offered him the nickname the actresses had given her. 'Allie.'

Holt looked at her with interest. His eyes were light green, the colour of quarry water when there were minerals in the stone. 'You want coffee?' he asked suddenly. 'It's the real thing. No chicory.'

'Yes, please,' said Allegra.

Holt lifted the loop of wire that secured the gate to the fence post and let her into the corral. He wore the thick leather gloves Allegra had only ever seen on professional horse breakers. 'Do you work horses?' she asked.

'No,' said Holt.

'But you're a cowboy?'

'No,' said Holt. 'I'm a carpenter. Born outside Dallas. Grew up on a farm, if that's what you take to be a cowboy. Know my way round horses and cattle some.'

As he talked, Allegra followed Holt towards the rusted-out Ford with the horse plodding beside her. She felt a momentary tingle of panic. Nobody could see her here. She had heard of girls being dragged off into the scrub by men or groups of men, left beaten and worse. Holt seemed to sense her apprehension. He kept talking to calm her, but he stumbled over his words; his voice was out of practice.

'Been making doors for Great Western Timber but they went bust. Got my last pay out of them yesterday. Start picking tomorrow, I guess.'

'My neighbours pick for a nice family. I could try to get you on their truck in the morning. I'll go out tomorrow, too, if they need extra hands.' Allegra didn't know why she'd said it. Unlike most of the residents in Stationville, she never picked fruit or vegetables on her day off.

'Obliged,' said Holt.

'Do you live in Pipe City?' Allegra asked. 'Or Stationville?'

His answer was important to her. She could learn a lot about him from where he chose to live. They came round the side of the truck and Allegra saw a canvas awning stretched from the Ford's roof and pegged into the ground to form a meagre shelter. A bedroll was laid out beneath it; a fire burned near the entrance.

'Live right here,' said Holt.

A portable Primus stove stood near the Ford's front wheel well. On top of it, a kettle piped. Holt went about making coffee. He had a string bag of beans and a single spoon.

'What you do?' he asked.

'I'm a maid. I have a good job in a house. I've been there for a month now.'

Holt poured the coffee and handed Allegra one of the mugs. She caught him looking at her hands. She had always been proud of them – she still tried to keep her nails neat and clean. 'You're no maid,' he said.

'I haven't always been. I am now.'

'Guess all this . . .' he gestured with his teaspoon to indicate their world of broken-down bric-a-brac and bindles '. . . is strange for you.'

Holt was right. It was very strange to her. Allegra was still in shock that she had lost everything.

'It might be a fresh start, though,' he added.

'I suppose it could be,' Allegra said. She hadn't looked at it that way before.

'Will be,' said Holt. He chinked his mug against hers in a toast.

They sat awkwardly side by side on the truck's peeling running-board. The silence went on for so long that Allegra wanted to gulp down her scalding coffee and leave. The horse poked his head in through the side of the tent and startled them both. Holt tapped the animal's nose and it pulled its head out again.

'That's Haywire,' said Holt. 'Had him four years.'

'He's lovely,' said Allegra.

'Last owner said he ran at Santa Clarita once. Came in second, which is just about good enough for the likes of me.' He scratched his face unconsciously.

'What happened to your face?' Allegra asked. It made no sense to ignore the obvious.

'Went through a wire fence.'

He wasn't going to say more and Allegra felt annoyed with herself for asking. Then he told her, 'I was riding through land I'd known from a boy. There weren't never any fences there. Had Haywire going full tilt and I guess he saw something I didn't. He put on the brakes and I went over the top, going twenty miles an hour, I reckon. Went straight through a stretch of high-tension barbed wire. One of the strands got me right between the lips and near sliced my head in two.' Holt laughed a bitter laugh. 'Didn't split my tongue or what the doc called my palate. They tell me that was luck. Convent hospital stitched me together and built my blood back up. I lay there, with nuns coming in and out, for near on two months. My face was wrapped up in bandages, like one of them Egyptian kings. I heard after that a bank had foreclosed on that land. Fences went up in less than a week. Nearly cut me apart, clean as a razor. Now I always got this grin on my face.'

'I think you have a nice smile,' said Allegra, solemnly.

'Thank you, Miss Allie,' said Holt, jovially, and he clinked her mug again. 'Your kin will be missing you.'

'I don't have a family any more. I'm on my own.'

Did that sound like an invitation? Was she offering this unknown man something? Allegra didn't know. He seemed strong. He moved like a man; Allegra sensed that his compact body was lean and powerful beneath his dirty work shirt and faded pants. He was tough and knowing. She liked being with him, as she had liked being with the jockeys when she was a child.

'People will talk,' Holt said, but he said it lightly and Allegra could hear that he didn't care.

'I find I don't mind so much about those things any more,' she said.

'Know what you mean,' said Holt. 'Notions about right and wrong, what the preachers teach, all that gets worn away in time. Went to France when I was seventeen. Thought I had life figured. Turns out life has lessons for you, and not one of them has anything to do with the improperness of a man and a woman having coffee together. Came back just wanting to be let be.'

They listened to the wind huffing through the scrub and Haywire's hooves rustling the undergrowth as he moved to munch on a fresh patch of weeds.

'Got to see Paris, though,' said Holt.

'I'd like to see Paris,' said Allegra. 'I've only been to Spain.'

'We'll take the Cunard over next year,' said Holt.

They laughed together. Allegra liked the way he assumed they would always know each other now that they had met. She felt connected, at last, to another human being.

'What I really want is my own business,' said Allegra. 'I think a restaurant would be wonderful. I used to be a great cook. When I was a little girl, I spent hours in the kitchen. Lately, the idea of a restaurant has been coming to me in dreams. I'd serve good Mexican food and people would have to reserve a table. I'd have my apartment right above the place. It would be somewhere near the sea.'

'Choose good wood for the tables,' said Holt. 'And the chairs. Get a wood where the grain shows out – redwood or mahogany. Put a nice deep stain into it, sand it down, then buff it up again till it shines like a Sunday belt buckle. Furniture done that way will last you for ever.'

'My house was full of beautiful things like that,' said Allegra.

She looked down at the parking-lot dust and saw the Cunard gangway and the water of a foreign ocean beneath her feet.

'We could scheme a way to do it, I bet,' said Holt.

'Scheme . . .' repeated Allegra.

She thought about the shrine in the house of her childhood, the waxy scent of candles, the heat in the church during mass, the ugly saints trapped in oil paint. Could she leave her Catholic morality behind, like a worn-out suitcase, and never look back?

Holt was speaking again. 'On the beach, I saw a crab eating a man's eye out. His face was caught up in seaweed. The foam at the high tide line was just blood bubbles. The broken shells were washed pink . . .' He stopped and started again, his voice still staccato from disuse. 'A boy from Fort Worth stood on a mine near Abbeville. We'd been through training together, shipped out together. They called him

Twang because of his accent. We were more than two miles from the army hospital, but I picked up Twang's foot and put it in my pack. Guess I hoped they could sew it back on him. They say they can do that now. Carried him over my shoulder with his own boot, which was sticking out of my pack, banging against his cheek the whole way. By the time we reached a medic tent, old Twang was long gone. I'd been carrying a corpse that last mile. Looked back over my shoulder and saw a line of red in the grass. He'd bled out down my back as I walked.'

Allegra was silent. She was not shocked. She felt glad that Holt would confide such an ugly, intimate thing.

'I don't know why I told you that,' Holt said, as he snapped back to the present.

'Sure you do,' said Allegra. 'Because it makes you sound heroic.'

Holt laughed unexpectedly. 'Exactly how old are you, Allie?' he asked.

Allegra considered her answer. 'I'm twenty-four,' she said. 'But I feel much older than that.'

'You want to take a ride?' he asked.

She eyed him suspiciously. 'For what?' she asked.

'For nothing,' said Holt. 'Just take Haywire out to stretch his legs. I'll trust you with him.'

Allegra wanted to ride again more than anything. She nodded quickly before Holt could change his mind. Whatever it might cost her later, she wanted to be on horseback again.

'I'll saddle him up for you,' said Holt. 'Sure you can handle him?'

'I'm sure,' said Allegra. 'I grew up around horses. My father owned a racecourse in Mexico.'

15

Riding felt as natural to Allegra as breathing. She turned Haywire out of his corral and traced the railway line west, asking the horse to follow the trail that ran between the tracks and the backyard fences of the neighbouring houses.

She had grown up surrounded by horses. Stables were her refuge – other children had tree houses or backyard forts as hideaways. Allegra had found both solace and excitement at her father's racecourse outside Tijuana. She went there in memory whenever she was afraid, and in the last few moments before she slipped off to sleep.

The racecourse was less than a mile from the del Rios' *hacienda* homestead and any given afternoon might find young Allegra's schoolbag slung against the wall of a horse's stall or her hat from the convent school of the Sisters of Santa Rosa tossed on a hay bale.

Allegra loved the whole place, not just the animals. She loved the sandy ring where the horses exercised or cooled down. She loved the owners' bar where the loud Americans chugged their beer. She loved the cheap, rowdy bench seats in the sun. The jockeys all knew her by name. The *gringo* gamblers took photographs of Allegra with her father. She would often carry the rosette into the winner's circle and place it around the neck of the steaming thoroughbred – a Mexican baby doll with a garland of victory roses.

Allegra's father had built the racecourse in 1920, just after the war, but in her memory it always looked brand new. It glistened. Its rails shone and the bleacher seats sparkled when they were wet with dew. The racecourse was called Camino Grande because it was built near the main road through Baja. There was a picture of a galloping horse painted on the road's exit sign, so the Americans could find it easily. They drove down by the thousand in their new cars to wager and to drink. Prohibition in the United States had turned alcohol into Mexico's main draw-card, and as the visitors grew intoxicated, they became careless with their money. They spent their dollars in the guesthouse Allegra's father had built. They spent them in his bar. Señor del Rio threw great glittering parties under the pochote trees, which were strung with lights. The American sailors on weekend leave from the naval station in San Diego would throw glasses of tequila into the nightly bonfire and shout, '*Olé!*' like Spanish matadors. Those were the nights Allegra remembered after her father was gone . . . the nights with the lights in the trees and the fires outside.

Señor del Rio liked to call his daughter 'polished'. He used the word to describe both Allegra's burnished skin and her accomplishments, though Lucia, their cook, complained that it made her sound like a scoured saucepan. Allegra spoke English with barely an accent. In Spanish, her words were a swift song. Allegra's mother had been educated in the United States but she had died of consumption. As she grew, Allegra became more and more like her father. Señor del Rio was tall in Allegra's memory of him – his body a soft toffee brown. He was dignified. Allegra never saw him with his sleeves rolled up or his jacket off.

Allegra knew she was loved but also that she was not like other girls. She was not popular at school. As a result of her differentness, Allegra was often alone. She was a reader and a rider, a loner. Allegra spent hours in the kitchen with Lucia. She loved to work with her hands, creating delicious food with fresh ingredients.

In some ways, Allegra was a doting Mexican daughter but she was precocious, too. She was exposed to the company of bookmakers and pundits at the racecourse and saw more than she ought to have seen as the privileged child of a privileged man. She saw despairing gamblers hunched over betting slips. She saw a man drink until he vomited blood. She saw a couple clinched together beneath the bleachers, the man's hand under the woman's skirt.

It was the jockeys who taught Allegra most about men, however. The jockeys were the opposite of culture and refinement. They spat on the sawdust. They dunked one another in the horse troughs. They spent whole nights with the women of the bawdy houses. The first man Allegra saw naked was a jockey.

She had been sixteen and knew the man's name. He was an American. Allegra's father didn't like the *gringo* jockeys but he housed them when they came down to Camino Grande with their mounts for a race. Some of them stayed on, listless and lazy, slouching over railings and drinking, always drinking. Starkey was one of these Americans. He was a fixture at the racecourse; he had lived there for years. Starkey would earn a race now and then from owners who fancied their horse's chances but couldn't afford a permanent rider. He was as spare as wire, and fascinating in his silent, sullen self-reliance.

It had been a saint's day – Allegra had forgotten which

one – and she had been sitting beside the water pump, holding one of the stable cats in her lap when Starkey emerged from the bathhouse with a blanket wrapped around his shoulders, his boots peeping out beneath it. His dirty clothes had been left in the empty feed bin they used as an enormous laundry basket. The washer-boy would collect all the jockeys' silks from there and do one huge, bubbling load each evening in a steaming cauldron.

Allegra knew Starkey was naked beneath the blanket. He was on his way to the bunkhouse when he saw her. He stopped and watched her. He had the wizened, starved face of all the jockeys, even the very young ones. He stood in front of Allegra and opened the blanket. He didn't check around to see if anyone was watching; he just casually exposed himself to her.

Allegra stared at his male parts. He didn't move; she didn't move. She just looked at his body for a moment and then raised her eyes to meet his. Allegra didn't know whether to be angry or ashamed or grateful to Starkey for the knowledge that had been kept from her for so long. Starkey closed his blanket again and grinned at her. She didn't smile back but she wasn't afraid.

'It's not that interesting,' she said in English.

Starkey let out a guffaw that broke the tension. His laugh was quite disproportionate to his size. It boomed. He reached out and tousled Allegra's hair. 'You've got some style, little sister,' he said. 'You've got sass.'

Of all the things her father had told her over the years about her beauty, after all his compliments about her ability with languages and her presence of mind, it was Starkey's description of her sass that kept Allegra going when everything crumbled. The compliment had come from someone who was little more than a stranger. That made it more valuable, more believable. Sass was modern. Sass was American. Sass survived.

When the racecourse was lost, sass kept her strong. After her father had hanged himself in an empty stable stall, sass helped Allegra get up each morning. When she had had to face the unpaid servants and then the debt collectors, sass was all Allegra had left.

After seven months of struggle, Allegra called her father's lawyer from town to help her close up the ranch. The money went straight to a bank in Mexico City. There was very little left over. Allegra paid the servants what she could – each one of them looked to her with the question of the rest of their lives. She had no answers. Some retainers had been on the ranch since long before Allegra's birth; some had known her father as an infant. Before departing, Lucia pressed a book into Allegra's hands. 'I had a teacher from the school write them all down for you,' she said, as she kissed Allegra's cheek, smearing it with tears. 'In case you started to forget.'

The book contained Lucia's favourite recipes, painstakingly printed out by hand. Allegra clasped it to her chest. Later, she kept it with her Bible.

It was hard to understand where all the del Rios' wealth had gone. It had once been a tangible thing: Allegra had seen it in their dinner silver and her leather-bound schoolbooks, but it was not really there at all. What looked like money was only an illusion, just stock certificates and bond documents – slips of worthless paper. Allegra del Rio was penniless. She had just turned twenty-three.

Now Allegra was a year older and a decade wiser. She

turned Haywire round and, with a nudge of her heels, asked the horse to take her back to Stationville. It had been a terrible year. It had been a year of crippling sadness and bitter disappointment, but at least she was back in the saddle again. The horse snorted with high spirits, and the familiar sound made Allegra unexpectedly happy. There was something about his master, too . . . The man called Holt reminded Allegra of the only man she had known as a lover.

On the night she had left Mexico for good, the night the last servant had finally departed from the house, Allegra had taken her father's yellow Packard – the only possession she had managed to hold on to – and driven down to the racecourse stables. She parked outside the fence and pushed through the narrow space between the chained gates. She walked among the empty bleacher seats. She walked past the bar. It was locked up, too. The fat Americans had packed their bottles of tequila into their steamer trunks and headed back across the border.

In the jockeys' bunkhouse, a few stragglers were still sleeping rough. They intended to stay until the law moved them on. They had water from the cisterns and – even though the generator's fuel tanks were dry – oil lanterns for light. The bunkhouse smelt of undercooked meat and eucalyptus muscle salve, the dank, mossy pungency of too many men living together in a confined space. When Allegra walked in, a few of the men got to their feet out of habit. Then, remembering that Allegra was one of them now, they sat back down. A game of poker was under way at a far table. Those who could read thumbed tawdry novels; those who couldn't listened to a wireless.

'Looking for work?' asked a surly man in overalls.

'I'm looking for Starkey,' said Allegra in English.

Most of the men who lingered were Americans; anyone with family in Mexico had drifted home with the tumbleweeds long ago.

'Starkey!' yelled the man. 'You've knocked up another one!'

The bunkhouse exploded with laughter.

Starkey got up from the card table and came over to her. He looked embarrassed. He pushed Allegra out through the door with a show of force but softened as soon as they were alone outside. Starkey pulled her down the side of the bunkhouse to the tack-room door. They stood close together in the alley. 'What you coming round here for? This place ain't safe for you. Boss's daughter don't mean too much round here no more. 'Specially since he decided to swing before wage day.'

'I need to ask you about America,' said Allegra.

'I thought you all were Mexican royalty or such. Why you still here?'

Allegra tossed her hair back defiantly then reined her neck in, as you would to show a horse who was boss. Lower your chin, she told herself. Keep your eyes down. 'There's nothing left. I'm alone.'

Starkey ran a match along the door jamb of the tack room to light it. Allegra had secretly tried this trick at home, but she could never emulate him.

'I have an aunt in California. My father's little sister, Tia Paloma. She ran away years ago and the family didn't speak of her again but she has heard about my father's death and she's written to me from Los Angeles. I need to know what that place is like.'

'You've never left Mexico?'

'I went to Spain when I was a girl to visit my father's family. We went by ship and train, and we stayed in the best places . . .'

'Maybe Spain's your best bet, then,' said Starkey. 'If you've got family there.'

'I haven't any more. My father's brother died in the Civil War.'

'Here are the rules of America,' Starkey said, as he smoked. 'Number one: you gotta stop talking smart. You hear me, sass?' There was that word again, their word. It was a kindness. 'The Yanks don't like their women too smart, especially their labouring women. They'll take a man over a woman any day – what with the big mouths you all seem to have – and they'll take a Mexican last of all. Number two: get yourself hitched lickety-split and let your husband worry about bringing home the bacon. That's my advice to you. Meet him somewhere nice, too, like at church.'

Allegra hadn't been to church in months. She had come to hate the *iglesia*'s useless carved saints with their pitiful, uplifted eyes and outstretched hands that did nothing, carried nothing, bestowed nothing. 'I just want to know about Los Angeles. What is the best way to get there?'

'You got dollars?'

'No, just pesos.'

'I'll be in Mexico a while longer. I'm no worse off here than there. I'll give you some greenbacks and you give me your pesos. Take your car north and try to look prosperous. Get all dolled up in one of your fancy dresses. Don't put too much stuff in the car. You ain't a bum, right? You ain't no picker.'

'Right,' said Allegra.

'Meet up with your auntie. Bunk down with her for a few nights till you find your feet. Pretty thing like you shouldn't have too much trouble making a living one way or another.'

Starkey reached out his hand and pushed Allegra's loose hair back over her shoulder. It was the hand holding the cigarette and Allegra was afraid that, if she moved, a strand of her hair might fall against the burning tip and catch fire. Starkey moved his hand down to her cotton blouse. Allegra's heart was thumping in her ears. The back of Starkey's knuckles touched her nipple and her flesh shivered. He still held the cigarette and Allegra didn't know what she would do if he put it out and freed the hand fully to fondle her further. She was frozen and alight at the same time.

Slowly, Starkey raised the cigarette back to his mouth and resumed smoking. He took Allegra's hand and led her into the tack room. The room was dark; its walls bulged with horse blankets. Girth belts and bits of sharp silver jangled against Allegra's fingertips as she felt her way. Spurs and buckles and stirrups were spiky white where the moon caught their edges. Starkey kicked the door shut behind them. Allegra could see nothing until her eyes adjusted to the gloom. Two lonesome stars became clear beyond the grey square of the window. Allegra named them: Allegra and Starkey. It was a game she sometimes played – this naming of stars.

Starkey unbuttoned his shirt. He kept smoking. The cigarette mesmerized Allegra, the way it moved from one of his hands to the other, then to his mouth, so that it didn't even singe his shirtsleeves as he slipped out of them.

He had a tight, compact body, marked with a dozen of

life's accidents. Nicks, burns and dents mottled his skin. His shoulders felt cool where Allegra touched them. Starkey crushed out his cigarette as she put her lips to his chest and ran her open mouth down to his navel to taste him there, the tobacco and the tang on her tongue of his cheap blue tattoos.

Starkey's stomach quivered and tautened. He pulled her blouse down roughly. The fabric cut into the flesh of her arms, scraped her raw. Starkey pressed her back against the rail where the pitchforks hung. The lines of the tines dug into her back, marked her with lashes. Starkey didn't care; Allegra didn't want him to. He pressed himself between her legs, then into her. The pain was sharp and deep – a long red tearing – then it was gone, replaced by an oily wetness that grew and grew, smoother and smoother, as he jerked against her, almost knocking her off her feet. Allegra climaxed in a rush of friction and pain and Starkey followed on the crest of her wave. They both quivered, burning with sweat, as sensitive all over as sunburned skin.

Starkey was both gruff and tender afterwards. He slid to the floor and let Allegra doze against his chest for a few minutes until he pulled away to light up another smoke.

'That was for your own good,' he told her.

Starkey held Allegra for another minute. Then, when his leg started to cramp, he stood up and walked her back to the Packard. They exchanged their currencies according to his rate.

'Might be you'll need your sass after all,' Starkey said, as he shut the car door on her. 'It ain't all siestas and garden parties up there.'

*

Aunt Paloma was dressed for a garden party. Tortoiseshell combs adorned her hair and she wore spotless white gloves. She stood on a corner of La Cienega Boulevard under a newly planted palm tree. Their meeting place was just as Paloma had described it on the telephone, right beside a drugstore. Allegra pulled her father's Packard into a parking space and got out of the car.

Her aunt smiled and walked over to her with outstretched arms. Allegra had never felt so relieved. The woman was well appointed. She wore proper hose – Allegra could see the seams through the peep-toes of her shoes. She felt embarrassed by her own bare legs, but at least her skirt was long enough to cover them.

Paloma would have a nice house. It would be smaller than what Allegra was used to, but it would have a comfort-able bed and a clean bathroom where she could wash. Soon, Allegra would find a room of her own to rent. It would be a new life, a simpler one, but it would be better than always owing money, avoiding knocks on the door, skirting the mailbox as if it housed scorpions.

Allegra wanted to find a stable as soon as possible. She hoped to find work exercising horses. Or perhaps she could cook in some rich American woman's kitchen.

'You found me!' said Aunt Paloma. She threw her arms around her niece. 'I'm so grateful you've come, Allegra. After the long silence, we're finally reunited as a family should be. How was the journey?'

'It was fine,' said Allegra.

There had been a few anxious moments at the crossing when the border guard had questioned her, but Allegra was dressed to the nines and she had her best saddle, polished and gleaming, on the back seat. After a brief conversation in English, she had been allowed to pass.

'I can't believe they questioned you like that!' said Paloma. 'Where is your hotel? Should we take lunch there?'

Allegra was baffled for a moment. 'I don't have a hotel, Tia Paloma. I need to stay with you. That's why I'm here.'

The air outside the drugstore turned frosty. A woman had emerged just a moment before and cool air was escaping through the open door. She gave them a disparaging look for no reason at all – they were only standing and talking on the sidewalk; Allegra didn't understand it.

'When you wrote to say you were coming, I thought you were bringing money!' said Paloma. 'Where's your father's money?'

'There's no money, Tia Paloma,' Allegra said. 'He lost it all and then he killed himself.'

Paloma crossed herself. She pulled the glove off her left hand and slapped it repeatedly into her right palm. 'I borrowed these gloves!' she shrieked, and Allegra saw that her aunt was even more desperate than she was. 'I borrowed this dress!'

The pharmacist came out of the drugstore. He carried a broom, as if he intended to sweep them from the sidewalk like so many cockroaches. 'You can't hang around here, you damn wetbacks!' he yelled. He banged at his window with the broom handle, indicating a sign that said: 'NO LOITERING. NO MEXICANS'.

Allegra ushered her aunt into the passenger seat of the Packard. Tia Paloma wept with disappointment that there would be no hotel tea, let alone the financial assistance she needed. She looked at Allegra's saddle on the back seat. It was embellished with silver and baroque tool-work. 'You'll have to sell that first thing,' she said.

'Is it a long drive?' asked Allegra. She would not sell the saddle; she would sell the car first.

'To where?' said Paloma.

'To your house!' shouted Allegra. She was hot and tired.

'It's not a house,' said Paloma. 'It's a stinking little room above a dime store about five miles from here.'

Allegra looked at the car's gauges. She was almost out of gas.

Now as she rode Haywire the last half-mile back to Stationville, Allegra thought of that first day in the United States as one of the most depressing of her life. Haywire quickened his gait when he saw Holt's camp. Allegra's heart quickened, too, as she saw the man without his shirt, washing in a steel pail. The sight reminded her of days spent spying on the jockeys outside their bunkhouse.

Holt was waiting for them, but not anxiously. 'You look like a natural up there,' he commented. He took the reins from Allegra and she dismounted.

'Thank you for this,' she said. 'I loved every minute.'

'You're welcome,' he replied. 'Come by again.'

'I will,' said Allegra. 'And I will join you for picking tomorrow. I could use the extra money.' The truth was that she wanted to see Holt again.

'Your lady-friend is worried about you,' Holt said, and he jerked his head in the direction of the water pump where Mrs Dunn stood watching them with her arms crossed over her chest. Allegra said goodbye to Holt and went to join her neighbour.

'Who is that man?' asked Mrs Dunn.

'He has a horse,' said Allegra. 'He let me take a ride.'

'You watch out for men like that,' said Mrs Dunn. 'Is that man going to feed you, take care of you?' she continued.

'Maybe,' said Allegra.

Mrs Dunn harrumphed in derision, but Allegra could not keep her eyes off Holt, the way he moved with such precision, no energy wasted. He groomed Haywire with long, confident strokes. Allegra watched him, unashamed, as she waited her turn at the pump.

16

At dawn, the farmers' trucks arrived at Stationville to collect their workers for the day. September was a month of harvest. Vegetables lay fat in the furrows, straining their stalks; swollen fruits bowed the tree branches. The farmers would bring along their strongest foremen to protect them from the jostling crowds. Often, the foremen would chalk a mark on the jackets of the men they selected; only marked men were allowed to board the trucks. Others were beaten down with pipes or baseball bats. Sometimes the farmers brought their guard-dogs along, too.

Some days the pickers harvested strawberries. On others it was celery or squash. Every week brought variations to the demands made on a picker's hands. After plucking two thousand strawberries, the skin of a worker's fingers was puckered from the fruits' juice and ready to split open. Peaches, so deceptively soft, rubbed a picker's palms raw with their fuzz. The sweet smell of watermelon rind eventually grew nauseating in the sun. After a few hours, green bell peppers stank worse than the flyblown body of a dead dog.

The heat was as familiar as an irritating relative, but the plagues visited by the insects were intolerable. They were a constant torment. Mosquitoes feasted on the workers' faces. Midges clustered at the edges of their mouths. Horseflies bit them. The sweat wrung from their bodies caused once-comfortable clothes to chafe.

All those painful possibilities lay ahead for Allegra as she left her room and walked between the Rows to where a group of early risers had already congregated. It was six o'clock, a pearly dawn, and Allegra prepared herself mentally for a day of picking. She had worked in the fields during her first few weeks in America but then her uncle Manuel – Tia Paloma's husband – had found her the cleaning job on Lantana Drive. Allegra looked about for Holt. He came over when he saw her and tipped his hat. 'I'll get us on a truck,' he said. 'Stay close.'

The first to pull up was unfamiliar. Agitation rippled through the crowd. A man and a woman got out. They held hands as they approached the workers. The man had a reddish-blond moustache and a long, clean lick of reddish-blond hair across his forehead. The woman had a mousy face, which was held together, it seemed, by freckles and smile lines. She had a wide gap between her two front teeth, which, Mrs Dunn had once told Allegra, was supposed to be lucky.

'My name's Roscoe,' the man announced. 'Roscoe Pepper. My wife and I . . .' he indicated the woman and she half waved shyly '. . . we could use some help with a grove of oranges we got ripened. The pay's no good – seventy-five cents for the day – but there'll be a meal, too. Now, I only need five. I can maybe stretch that to six.'

Immediately the pushing started. Holt forced himself to the front, using his body to thump others aside, his manners discarded. He kept Allegra close beside him. She stopped directly in front of Roscoe Pepper's wife. The woman looked her up and down and said, 'How do you do?' She reached out her hand and Allegra shook it on impulse, surprised by the courtesy.

'Very well, thank you,' she said.

'The job's halfway to Bakersfield, if you want it.'

'Yes, please,' said Allegra. 'Also, my friend Holt. He's very strong – a good picker.'

'I've got two here, Ross,' Mrs Pepper told her husband. She turned back to Allegra. 'I'm Harmony. Harmony Pepper. That's my given name, though I can't hold a tune worth a cent.' She giggled self-consciously at the joke she had told a thousand times. 'You can climb right in back. I've left some sacking there to keep the wind out some.'

Holt helped Allegra aboard and gave her the most protected position – in the middle, behind the cab. Allegra saw Roscoe Pepper shake Mr Dunn's hand and the wiry Irishman and his two oldest boys climbed in. Holt smiled and squeezed Allegra's arm at his good fortune. Today he had work.

They drove north. For a while, the truck joined a high road and they saw the Pacific off in the distance. It made for a good start to the day.

The Peppers' farm lay spread out across two gentle hillocks. The house nestled beside a stream that supported willows, bottlebrush and pipe reeds. It was a scene from a watercolour. Once, eighty years before, some scout had crested one of those hills on horseback and seen this spot for the first time, staked his claim before others saw the natural spring, the groves of bay laurel, the hills where fruit would flourish. That man had been a Pepper for sure, a pioneering Pepper, who had handed the land down from eldest son to eldest son.

Allegra was filled with the kind of covetousness condemned in the Bible. She looked at Roscoe Pepper through the back window of the truck's cab and tried to see something of Starkey in him or Holt, but there was nothing of those men's toughness or strength. What had Roscoe Pepper ever done to deserve security like this?

Allegra soon changed her opinion. The closer they got to the homestead, the more it deteriorated. The subtlety of morning light and the softness of distance disappeared as they juddered along the drive. The house was an unsightly, mismatched construction – a patchwork lean-to made up partly of log cabin, partly of unpainted cypress shack under a tin roof greyed with cabbage-mould. A meagre line of vegetables sprouted from the dry earth of the kitchen garden. The porch sagged beneath a few twigs of furniture.

Roscoe parked his truck in the yard where chickens scratched bad-temperedly; even the cockerel had only two feathers left in his tail. He rattled them together and crowed. Harmony shushed him with a flap of her skirt. Before they were even off the truck, she had retrieved the water bucket and ladle from the kitchen and returned, wearing a hat and a pinafore with holes in it.

The orange trees scrambled up a slope to the left of the house. They were heavy with fruit and bud. Roscoe felt the need to make a speech before they started. He stood up on the rim of the concrete pump tray and took off his hat. Allegra could tell the Peppers were unused to paid help.

'We got near on two hundred trees here. Sanguinellos, they're called. And they come all the way from Italy, Europe. Sanguinellos.' He repeated the name with pride, his only foreign word, an achievement. 'It means blood in American. We call them blood oranges here 'cause the fruit inside of them is red as a nosebleed. I hear they're all the rage in the fancy cafés in town. Mind now for the bees. Those are the hives.'

Allegra looked over at the boxes Roscoe had indicated. 'I shouldn't be around bees,' she whispered to Holt. 'I have to be careful. I take the stings badly.'

Allegra had swallowed a bee at a Sunday-school picnic when she was a girl. It had been hidden from sight in a cup of soda pop. She had been rushed to the nearest mission hospital, her mouth flooded with saliva she could not swallow, her throat closing like a boxer's eye swelling shut.

'We got near on fifty hives in and around this one grove,' Roscoe explained, as he put his hat back on his head and handed out the baskets. 'Pepper Honey is made from pure orange blossom, and it's the sweetest there is. We sell to a few stores and some pretty grand hotels. Harmony drew the label herself. It's got a little queen bee wearing a crown on it – the cutest thing you ever saw.'

Roscoe led them into the orchard and they began a steady rhythm, spreading out silently into the rows.

The bees were a constant presence in the Peppers' orchard. They streamed out of their hives in chaotic black gushes, clotting at the entrance, then separating in space when they took flight, becoming single specks of drifting darkness. Allegra checked each orange before she plucked it. Mr Dunn took a sting early in the day and his hand was the size of a grapefruit by the time they stopped for lunch. Harmony went inside the farmhouse at noon and came back with soup. The weather was too hot for soup, but the pickers were grateful for its saltiness. The goodness of butter beans and barley rushed to their stomachs. They ate their meal in silence. The Peppers did not escape to the paltry shelter of their house: they stuck it out with their workers. They were all in this together.

'My wife's not working this afternoon,' announced Roscoe. 'She's going to rest up some.' At this announcement the tips of his ears turned very pink. Afternoon rest for a farmer's wife meant only one thing: Harmony Pepper was pregnant. Roscoe squeezed his wife's hand before he stood up and dusted off his hat against his denim overalls. She walked slowly back to the house, carefully holding one hand against her belly. Roscoe watched her until she was out of sight.

'My wife's birthed four healthy boys,' said Mr Dunn, proudly. 'When Mrs Pepper's ready . . . Mrs Dunn would be pleased to help her through it.'

'I'm obliged to you,' said Roscoe, but he looked anxious, as if this acknowledgement of his wife's condition was a bad omen. 'It's been hard on Harmony. I've been putting some money aside so as I can take her into a hospital this time.'

They went back into the orchard and, much later, under a high dusk, Roscoe drove them to Stationville. Holt and Allegra hopped off the truck. Before they dispersed, Roscoe Pepper tapped Holt on the shoulder. 'You work good,' said Roscoe. 'I'll come by for you tomorrow, if you like. I just need one hand to help out with a few chores on the farm.'

'Mighty glad to,' Holt said, and tipped his hat. He turned to Allegra and grinned in delight.

In the short time of their acquaintance, she had come to enjoy the sight of his crooked smile. She followed him to Haywire's corral where the horse was waiting for them. Holt petted his nose. 'Would you like to come by for dinner?' Allegra asked him. She flushed at the thought of the two of them alone in her room together. But who would know? Who would care?

'I'd like to shave first,' said Holt. 'I'm not dining with a lady looking like a bum.'

Allegra fed Haywire his oats while Holt sat on an upturned crate, a cobwebbed mirror balanced on his knees and a billycan of water bubbling nearby on the fire.

'Maybe you should grow out your beard,' suggested Allegra, when she saw how the shaving irritated the scars, turning them red; Allegra could tell that Holt had nicked the ridges in places. Minute studs of blood welled up.

'Tried that,' said Holt. 'Only makes them worse. Hair won't grow through the scars, so they stand out like white lines in my beard. Better to stay clean shaved.'

He changed the subject. 'What's all this like for you?' he asked. 'Being poor so sudden. A ways worse than being rich sudden, I bet.'

'I'll be rich again,' said Allegra.

'Oh, yeah?' said Holt.

'I still remember how wonderful expensive things are. I still want them very badly. I miss good soap and pretty clothes. I love paintings on my walls. I love expensive linen.'

'You should have them, then,' said Holt.

'This is the worst it will ever be,' said Allegra. 'I've decided that.'

Her words were a prophecy. Holt dipped the blade of his razor into the billycan and stirred it thoughtfully. 'Believe you when you say that,' he said.

He fished the razor out again and looked back into the crazed glass. Allegra came up behind him and saw her face reflected beside his. She pulled the band from her hair and let it fall free as he watched her. It swung down over her shoulder, bringing a fountain of soft scent with it. Allegra had stolen some of Ivy's expensive shampoo. She had hidden it in a tiny glass jar in her handbag. Holt looked back at her in the mirror. Allegra opened her eyes wide and pressed her lips together hard until they went white. When she released the pressure, blood flowed back, turning them plump and pink. Allegra wasn't watching the effect she had on Holt. She was watching her own eyes. She was steeling herself, daring herself to be something she wasn't. She was transforming into a woman capable of things foreign to her nature. But to be this new kind of woman, she needed an alliance.

Holt reached out and touched her hair. He brought it to his nose and closed his eyes at the smell of it. Allegra didn't pull away. Holt was exactly the kind of man she needed. She leaned over and pressed her mouth to his. He tasted of tobacco and the cheap cologne of the shaving foam.

She flushed with heat as Holt's soft tongue penetrated her mouth. His hands were suddenly all over her body. He wasn't forceful or tender. He was intent. Allegra felt awash with life, resuscitated, like a woman coming out of the vapours to the slap of smelling salts. After a while, she pulled her mouth away from his. Holt would have been handsome without the scars; with them he was unusual but not ugly. When his face was serious, though, he could look menacing. Allegra wondered if he was. The wondering, and the not knowing, made her feel reckless.

Holt wanted to throw her down on his bedroll and have her. It had been a long time since he had been with a woman. They had liked him a great deal before the scars, despite his smaller stature. Now women seemed wary of him, and Holt had never favoured whores. There was something old-fashioned and upright in his makeup. The timing for lovemaking wasn't right for Allegra, though. He felt particularly kindly towards her. Was this the beginning of love? He didn't know. He only knew he wanted Allegra to be around for a long time to come.

'I'll change my shirt and be right over,' he said.

Allegra nodded and started off towards the Rows on her own.

When Holt arrived, fifteen minutes later, he had changed into a clean shirt but wore no jacket. He only owned a canvas one, lined with sheepskin, but he rode in that and it was too dirty for company. Allegra had put on one of her good dresses. She had braided tiny daisies into her hair. They were weeds, which grew beside the stilts of the water tower, but they looked pretty enough. She had placed blankets at angles over the bed and propped pillows sideways to form a rudimentary sofa. She had set the table properly with the few pieces of fine cutlery she owned.

Holt talked to her about Texas, the open space of it. The land sounded like Mexico. Talk of it made her homesick. Holt described thunderstorms that came in low like a steel roof sliding shut over the yellow land. Allegra told him about driving their cattle across the Rio Grande.

She prepared a simple meal for them, using one of the recipes from Lucia's book. She made rabbit stew with celery and tomatoes and wedges of spicy sweet potato.

Holt shook his head in admiration. 'I've never tasted anything this good.'

'You're limited when all you eat comes from a can.' Allegra laughed.

'Your mother taught you to cook?'

Allegra shook her head. 'My mother didn't teach me anything. She passed on when I was a little girl. Our cook taught me – all the best dishes and the peasant ones. That's why I thought I could run a restaurant one day.'

Holt smiled as he sipped the coffee she had made for him. He lit a cigarette. 'Tell me about your restaurant,' he said.

Allegra realized how long the dream had been waiting to escape. The idea had been with her constantly since she had arrived in the United States. She had nourished every aspect of it with delectable details.

'It would be a fine place – not too fancy, but warm. It would be the kind of place you'd bring your girl to, so you could get to know her. There would be red-checked table-cloths, cheap candles and very good sangria. I'd get my seafood right off the boats. We'd make the tortillas before every meal, and I would make the salsa with lots of chilli. In the kitchen, there would be baskets piled with *cilantro* and sacks of lemons. I'd plant a garden out back for toma-toes and runner beans. Also, I would have chickens, because good fresh eggs are very important for cooking. Above the restaurant, there would be a few big rooms for my home.'

Holt took up the story. 'I know the kind of place,' he said. 'Owner says it closes at ten, but they let the last couple stay late – the couple who can't stop holding hands. The help sweeps the floor under their feet and they don't even notice. Years later, that same pair brings their children back to show them where it all began.'

Allegra smiled at his perfect description.

'Might you need a barman in your place?' Holt added. His voice trembled, as if Allegra's answer to this casual question might destroy him.

'I would need a carpenter first,' said Allegra, telling him she had already included him in the plan. 'To make the tables and chairs. I want a wooden bar, too, and lots of shelves in the pantry. In the beginning, I would need a carpenter very much.'

It was decided that easily.

'What would we need to start it off?' asked Holt. He launched himself to his feet and started pacing, a man released from inertia like a pebble from a slingshot. 'How much? That's the question.'

'Enough to rent a good place, some stoves . . .'

Holt picked up her train of thought. 'Plates, dishes, the first provisions. We'd need reliable suppliers. I could strike a hard bargain with them. Can you train a cook?' he asked, and flung his arms around Allegra, nearly throwing her off balance with his boisterousness.

'I could teach somebody.'

'Good. That way you could be at the front door like a candle calling them in. They'd come to see you, Allegra, and stay to eat. You'd be the whole reason for the place!'

'It's a good dream,' said Allegra.

'No!' said Holt. He shook her violently and her head snapped in surprise. 'No, don't you say that to me! Why shouldn't we have it? Why the hell shouldn't we? You think your fancy employees work half as hard as I'm willing to? You think they know what it's like to go without? Or to need something this bad?'

Holt's voice was anguished. Allegra could hear broken glass and broken bones in it. She felt sudden resentment towards her employers, too.

'No,' she said to Holt. 'I bet Miss Charlotte has never known loss.' Allegra thought of her father hanging in his stable. 'She has never known desperation.' She thought of Starkey pumping against her, not even bothering to lay her down. 'She has only ever taken from people, as if she is entitled. She has had an easy life.'

'It's time to take back,' said Holt, and Allegra saw that it was.

'We need a name for our place.'

'Allegra's,' said Holt. 'That's what it'll be called, and people will come there on nights when they've got dreams to dream.'

17

Charlotte bit into one of the apples Allegra had polished and placed in the fruit bowl. She was still floating on a bubble of joy after her weekend in Malibu. She munched the apple and watched Allegra cleaning the icebox. There was a sudden crash from somewhere down the hall, the sound of wood splintering apart against a wall.

'That's another busted door, I expect,' Charlotte commented.

Allegra started moving towards the hallway to investigate, but Charlotte barred her way with an outstretched arm. 'Ivy and Verbena are fighting,' she explained. 'Can you believe it? For once, it's got nothing to do with me. Verbena started throwing things a few minutes before you arrived. I thought I'd rather enjoy it but it's not as much fun as I thought it would be.'

'They are going to kill each other!' said Allegra.

Charlotte shrugged. Allegra took up her cloth again and, haltingly, continued her work.

'It's about Mr Whitewood,' said Charlotte. 'That's Miss Ivy's beau. She's absolutely soft on him and it's getting serious.'

'Miss Verbena does not like him?'

Normally Allegra wouldn't dare to ask such a personal question, but Holt had encouraged her to learn as much as she could about her employers and their habits.

'Miss Verbena doesn't like anybody,' declared Charlotte.

The French windows were open. Charlotte went out on to the deck and plopped down into one of the chairs. She threw her head back, closed her eyelids and smiled up into the sun. Her hair tumbled down. Allegra stopped cleaning and stared at the woman. There was no doubt that she was very beautiful.

Ivy came into the kitchen then, with Verbena close behind her, pleading, 'I don't want you to be a fool, Ivy. It's too soon. It's ridiculously soon. You must see that!'

'I don't want to talk about this any more, Bee. You're my friend, my best friend. You know me. How can you imagine this was my dream?' Ivy indicated the kitchen, the house, and the other women with the gesture. Then she went over to Verbena and touched her arm at that most tender spot in the crook of the elbow. 'I want a husband, Bee, and babies. Don't you? I'm tired of trudging back and forward to auditions and shoots. I'm no great actress.'

'But you're good,' said Verbena. Her face was contorted in anguish. 'You could be very, very good if you tried.'

'That's not the point,' said Ivy. 'I don't want to try. I don't want it like you do!'

Charlotte almost piped up then. She almost confessed that she didn't want it either. It was their fight, though. If she jumped in now, it would only seem as if she was ganging up against Verbena.

'You could have everything, Ivy,' said Verbena. 'Most of all, you could have complete independence.'

'Maybe you want a career –' started Ivy.

'I do want a career!' Verbena shrieked. She was hysterical now that Ivy had misunderstood her so badly. 'But I want you more. I was here for you, don't you see? I stayed in this house because of you, because I love you!'

The room went so quiet that Allegra could hear a cricket singing in the dust below the deck. A hot wind came up from the canyon and fluttered the aspens. Charlotte watched one particular leaf fall from the very top of a tree. As it floated down, it swivelled in the air, catching sunlight, then darkening, then catching sunlight, like a lure on the surface of a pond.

Verbena broke the silence. She tried to pretend her passion had been mere concern. 'Because I'm your friend, Ivy. I'm a true friend who doesn't think you'll be happy with this man.'

'How do you know? You've never loved anybody,' said Ivy. 'You can't know how he makes me feel. And don't tell me I'm naïve. I don't expect to be happy all the time. I only know that being with Nate makes me less sad.'

Verbena had nothing more to say. A tear fell straight down her right cheek, directly in line with the severe curtain of her boyish haircut. It plopped on to the floor. Charlotte stood up and moved into the frame of the French windows. To Allegra, she appeared as the final voter. The side Charlotte took now, the woman she went towards, would be the winner. Charlotte walked over to Ivy and took her hand. 'You should have what you love,' Charlotte said. It had become her motto, a credo to live by.

Verbena stood alone at her end of the kitchen. The table separated her from Charlotte and Allegra, who had frozen beside the sink, and Ivy. Their three pairs of eyes watched her. The kitchen seemed strangely barren, a vast distance across which Verbena could not travel. Verbena's dignity seemed to shrivel before them; she lost stature, and said, in a quiet, deeply sad voice that did not belong to her at all, 'Go and be happy, then. But if you do this, Ivy, your life will never be more. Happy is all you'll ever have.'

'Isn't that what everybody wants?' asked Charlotte, in a tiny mouse's voice.

'Some people want life,' said Verbena. 'The whole experience of it, the good and the bad.'

'I'll just take the happiness,' said Ivy.

'I hoped you'd risk more,' said Verbena. She looked at Charlotte, and offered the woman she despised a compliment: 'I think Charlotte would.' Verbena nodded at the rightness of her pronouncement and left the room. To break the dreadful moment, Allegra picked up her broom and began to sweep the floor.

Ivy turned to Charlotte to keep her position afloat. 'You understand, don't you, Charlotte? Do you think I'm crazy for wanting him?'

'No!' said Charlotte. 'Don't be stupid. Verbena doesn't know what she's talking about. You want a husband and children. That's perfectly natural, Ivy.'

Ivy put her face into both hands and started to sob. Instead of comforting her, Charlotte wanted to run away, to be anywhere but there amid the residue of Verbena's raw need. 'I have to go out,' she said. 'Allie, do you need to go to the market? Get your basket. I'll drive you.'

Allegra fetched her shopping basket from the pantry. Charlotte was already halfway to Verbena's Jordan by the time Allegra caught up with her. She wasn't sure she had understood everything that had been said in the kitchen, or precisely why emotions had run so high, but she was as glad as Charlotte to be away from Lantana Drive, speeding through the dry hills ahead of their own dust.

Charlotte turned south from Mulholland Drive on to Beverly Glen and pulled off the road a mile above Sunset Boulevard. She drove into a narrow parking lot where a wooden cabin housed their local gourmet market. The place was a favourite haunt of the wealthy Angelinos who lived in the hills. It stocked luxuries and homemade delicacies supplied by area farmers and craftspeople. Tables, leafy with fresh produce, framed the entrance. Inside, low-slung lights provided a hushed mood. The store's shelves were stocked with jars of jalapeños preserved in oil and tins of imported Danish biscuits. There were barrels stuffed with string-bag salamis and towers fashioned from the red, waxed wheels of cheese.

'Get anything you like,' Charlotte told Allegra.

Allegra's mouth held a flash flood of saliva. It was months since she had tormented herself with a trip to a decent food store. Now she left Charlotte's side to explore the abundant treats. In the furthermost aisle, she came across a familiar label. On the bottom shelf stood a row of jars with an illustration of a bee wearing a tiara and carrying a fairy's wand. It was the picture Roscoe Pepper had described and there, in whimsical calligraphy, was the brand name: Pepper Honey. Below that, in smaller print, were the words: 'Made from pure orange blossom'.

Allegra took it to where Charlotte was browsing the fresh-produce section. 'Miss Charlotte,' she said excitedly. 'I know this man.'

Charlotte plucked the jar from Allegra's hand. 'Pepper Honey,' she read. 'What does that mean?'

'It is a Mr Pepper who owns the farm. I have picked from his orange trees. They are very special trees from Italy and this is very special honey.'

'Pepper Honey. How funny! We'll have to try it.'

Allegra was unloading her purchases at the cash register when a man's hand reached out and picked up the jar of Pepper Honey from the items she had placed on the counter. Allegra turned to see the enormous figure of a man in a pork-pie hat. It was Mr Pike, whom Allegra had met that one time at the house on Lantana Drive – the sinister man who had claimed he was a friend of Miss Charlotte's.

'I would have thought your boss was sweet enough already,' he said.

Allegra had not expected to see him again. This time, his shirtsleeves were rolled up and Allegra could clearly see the tattoos on his forearms. On the left there was a depiction of a Bible with a sword of fire lying across it. On the right there was a clear illustration of Charlotte Caine's lovely face. Allegra went cold.

'Is the delicious lady herself about?' Pike asked.

Allegra knew the question was fatuous because he had obviously followed them here. The man must have been watching the house. Allegra hadn't noticed him; she hadn't seen a car trailing them as they drove, but here he was. Allegra loosed the fist of her right hand long enough to point to the corner of the store where she had last seen Charlotte, then went back to her transaction without saying a word. She only wanted the man away from her. His breath smelt of sausage meat and garlic.

Charlotte jumped when she saw Pike in the gloom. She

suddenly felt sick. It was a bad day now. It had started out with promise – she would see Liam tonight at a special screening – but Ivy and Verbena's fight, and now Pike's appearance, had turned it sour.

Charlotte spoke first. She went on the offensive. She would not be intimidated. 'You're not performing today, Mr Pike?' she asked.

Pike pushed his body uncomfortably close to hers. 'It's night shows only during the week. I'm free days.' He took a can of dog food from the shelf and examined it. 'They make special food just for dogs?' he commented. 'When there are folks starving? That don't seem right. Twenty-five cents this lot costs! That's a sin, that is.'

He held the tin up in front of Charlotte's nose. 'Remember how we fed the dogs in Florida, Charlotte? We just went out and shot a few racoons and threw their bodies into the cages.'

Charlotte's mind recoiled at the memory. She had watched Pike's pack of mongrel dogs feeding only once. Pike kept his mutts good and hungry. After two days of waiting, they had torn at the still-warm racoons with ardour and come up from their feast with bloodied snouts. The dogs had ripped at each other in their desire to eat, too. The pack's ears and jowls had been ribboned flaps of tattered skin, scarred and healed over, then torn open again at every feed.

'Of course, here in California we make use of the coyotes instead. They're good meat for dogs – coyotes. It smacks a bit of cannibalism . . .' Pike dropped the tin of dog food into Charlotte's basket '. . . but hunger is hunger.'

Pike moved his hips against Charlotte and his hand went down to clasp the round firmness of her left buttock. 'How does that naughty old poem go? "Meat is meat and a man must eat . . ."'

Charlotte forced her way free and moved back into the main section of the store. Pike caught up with her. He spoke in his authentic voice now. Not the put-on Cockney, but all Pike – his rare, real voice. 'Oh, you were so sweet, Charlotte . . .' He closed his eyes in an ecstasy of memory; his eyelids fluttered in a tiny spasm. His mouth opened and the smell of decaying teeth came out. 'It was like fucking open a ripe peach.'

The vulgarity jarred Charlotte loose and brought her back to reality. She was in a store. This was a public place. She didn't have to listen to this. She pushed past Pike and strode towards the entrance. He grabbed her and pushed her hard against a barrel. Charlotte felt his erection against her hip.

'Was it the coarse language that got to you, Miss Fancy-Panties?' Pike asked. He was Cockney again. 'Pretending not to deal in naughtiness any more, are you? Left all that behind, have you? Well, let me tell you a little something. I'm a decent man, so I'll give you options. It's always nice to offer a lady her choice . . .'

Pike's real voice came back at her ear, an unaccented whisper. Charlotte strained to hear it, yet she was repulsed when she made out the words. 'I'll take you, Miss Fancy-Panties, or your money but I'm not going to leave town with neither.'

It flickered through Charlotte's mind that the former might be easier. Before Liam, she might even have acquiesced, but now love was in the way. Her body was Liam's alone. 'I'll get you money.'

'A thousand dollars,' said Pike.

Charlotte swallowed her shock and nodded. Could she find that much? The truth was that she had no idea of her financial situation, and the fact that she had no idea appalled her. She was not a child. She ought to be in charge of her own money. 'A thousand dollars,' Charlotte repeated. 'I think I have that. I can get you that.'

She would lose her chance to buy the house if she had to pay Pike that much.

Pike righted his pork-pie hat. He started to whistle. Charlotte took a few minutes to compose herself. Nobody had witnessed their encounter. Even Allegra, she felt sure, hadn't seen a thing. When she left the store, Charlotte saw that the parking lot was empty, except for the blue Jordan. She got into the car hurriedly and waited for Allegra with both hands on the steering wheel.

She knew she had to devise a plan. She would see Liam that night. Could she tell him about Pike – not everything, but something? Could she admit to knowing Pike, ask Liam for help? If she did, Liam would want to know why she had deceived him about not knowing the man. He would want to know the whole story. She could never tell him that. One day, she might be able to tell him about the men in the park – she loved him that much – but she could never confess the whole ugly truth.

When they reached the house, Charlotte stopped the car at the mailbox at the end of the drive. Allegra got out to collect the few letters. She handed Charlotte a buff-coloured envelope, addressed by hand. Charlotte did not recognize the script, but when she saw the return address, she grew jittery with anticipation.

Once inside, she tore open the envelope and read the note:

> *Dear Miss Caine,*
> *I was so very pleased to receive, in writing, your offer to purchase my home located at #4 Cherrybowl Close, Los Angeles. I find your offer to be acceptable. Perhaps we could meet at a bank or solicitor's office to begin formalizing the arrangements? I await your timely reply.*

There was a rigid signature and below it, in printing, the name Mr Charles McTavish.

Charlotte read the letter three times and held the sheet against her chest. She rushed down the corridor to speak to Ivy but she wasn't home. She went to Verbena's room. She expected a row – she had taken Verbena's car without asking – but Verbena was too desolate to fight.

'That Whitewood man came to fetch Ivy,' Verbena volunteered, when she saw Charlotte at her door. She was lying on her bed, clutching a pillow like a life preserver. 'She called him. She was upset. Naturally, he raced right over to take her away from me, to rescue her.' Verbena's face was long with misery.

'I'm sorry,' said Charlotte. 'But I heard about my house. They've accepted my offer.' She waved the letter towards Verbena, who looked astonished that she could appear so cheerful under the circumstances. 'You'd better get yourself together,' added Charlotte. 'You know it's the screening of my rushes tonight.'

'I'm not going,' said Verbena.

'You have to go,' said Charlotte. 'The studio takes these things very seriously. You'll lose your contract.'

Verbena sat up and wiped her nose with a handkerchief. She could not afford to lose one more thing.

'Besides, Ivy has to be there, too,' Charlotte added gently.

Back in her room, Charlotte thought about Liam. They might be able to steal away from the party for a few delicious minutes alone together. Her body ached for him. Her stomach grew slushy at the thought of his hands, his mouth. Charlotte wanted to show him Mr McTavish's letter. She knew Liam would be thrilled for her. She would speak to Madge about her finances. Surely, with *The Walls of Jericho* due for release in less than two months, a bank would be willing to loan her enough money to buy the house and pay off Pike. That was the answer! She would borrow enough money to do both. Then Pike would be gone for ever. Charlotte was certain she had thought of everything. She was going to have what she loved.

In the kitchen, Allegra unpacked the groceries. There was a can of dog food among the items Charlotte had selected. How bizarre! Allegra thought about Charlotte and Pike. Once again, she wondered how the two of them could possibly be acquainted. Could they once have been friends? It seemed unlikely. Pike behaved more like a stranger who was harassing the actress – he had a tattoo of Charlotte's face on his arm! – yet Allegra hadn't heard her complain about the man to Ivy or Verbena. Charlotte hadn't contacted studio security or the police.

Allegra thought of the way Charlotte's knuckles had gripped the steering wheel as she had driven them home from the market in silence. Charlotte had been afraid and it was Pike who had frightened her. Allegra could not figure out their relationship. There was a secret there. She would speak to Holt about it.

18

When there was a big-budget picture in the making, it was a tradition for Warner Brothers to hold a private screening of some of the footage shot on location. The studio put on a party and showcased several of the more impressive scenes. Select press people were invited to attend. It was all designed to start a positive buzz humming through the town. *Entertainment Daily* would run a piece about the event; the public would begin to talk. Publicity was a big part of the business.

To pad the rooms, and ratchet up the event's glamour quotient, the studio's most beautiful contracted players would be on hand. They were coached to say how excited they were about the picture. It was going to be a huge success! The movie palaces were going to be packed!

Ivy and Verbena had been summoned as part of the crowd to ooh and aah at Selznick's work. Charlotte and Liam were expected to be the luminaries. Charlotte made sure she was right on time. Her car arrived at the studio gates at nine o'clock. Selznick was determined to be European and wouldn't start any function before sunset.

Charlotte sat in her car, waiting for the right time to make her entrance. She saw Ivy and Verbena's car pass by and she waved. The two women ignored her, stone-faced. They each looked out of their own window, ignoring one another. Liam Malone drove himself. His wife sat beside him in his singular Rolls-Royce. Allegra caught a glimpse of Bernadette Malone as she passed. She tried to see what the woman was wearing but the car door hid most of her body from view. A Cadillac passed by next, then several Buick town cars. Charlotte recognized Sam Warner and his wife in one of them.

A boy – Charlotte wondered if it was the one who had worn the harlequin sweater on the day of her Rahab audition – opened her car door. There was a polite little burst of applause from the knots of people about to go into the screening room. Charlotte had dressed well. She was understated in a dress of fuchsia silk that skimmed her knees. A dozen strings of topaz beads swished against each other when she walked. She wore a comb made from porcupine quills in her hair – a touch of the wild to make a statement.

Charlotte felt especially fabulous when she saw Bernadette Malone across the room. The woman was dressed in a frock of brown linen. Brown! To a screening! Charlotte tried not to look at Liam as she was introduced to people whose names she would never remember. The rule, Ivy had told her, was always to acknowledge the money. If a man was introduced to you as a very important investor, you kissed his cheek and lingered for a second. If he kissed your hand, you fluttered prettily.

Selznick kept Charlotte by his side; he seemed very pleased with her. More than once, he called her his 'discovery'. Finally, Selznick asked everyone to settle down. The lights were dimmed. A spot came up at the centre of the screen's curtain. Selznick stepped into it and spoke for five minutes about the project and the challenges of their shoot in the desert. When he was done, Selznick took a seat beside Charlotte in the front row.

Just before the projector began its rhythmic ticking, Charlotte noticed Madge St Claire slipping into the room. Madge held her conspicuous glass cigarette holder like a filament of ice to her lips.

Selznick had produced a good montage. It included action, drama and spectacle. In the darkness, Charlotte felt a hand on her shoulder. Liam was apparently in the seat behind her own. He leaned forward with a casual smile, pretending to impart a commendation into her ear, and said, 'I need to be inside you.' Charlotte wanted to reach back and take his hand, squeeze it in acknowledgement, but she simply clapped with the rest of the audience as the reel blinked and stuttered to an end. The applause was rousing. The audience got to its feet as Selznick announced that there were tables booked at Lulu-Belle's for a late show. A murmur of appreciation emanated from the crowd.

Charlotte stood up and turned around. Bernadette Malone was directly in front of her. The woman clutched a beaded purse in both hands. Her voice was a-quiver with emotion. 'I thought you were just wonderful, Miss Caine, just wonderful. I told Liam I don't know when I've seen a more beautiful woman in all my life. On screen, you have a presence, but in person . . . Well, you're just as lovely as the loveliest thing.'

The back of Charlotte's throat began to sting. The woman was dizzy with appreciation. She had a soft Irish accent, and her voice was soothing, motherly. 'You're very kind, Mrs Malone,' she said.

'Oh, I mean it,' gushed Mrs Malone. 'I think you and

Liam look marvellous together. A taller woman looks so well beside him. I always feel quite hopelessly dwarfed.'

Why didn't Liam take Bernadette away? It was torture to have to converse with her. Charlotte was going to have to destroy this sweet woman's life to have what she wanted. Charlotte met Liam's eyes. They were pained, too. Could she really do this, take him away from his wife? Yes – yes, she could.

'Are you joining the party in town?' Charlotte asked Bernadette.

'Oh, no. I make an appearance for the journalists' sake and because Liam asks me to, but I need to get back to my children. Did you know we have six?' From another woman, it might have seemed like a subtle reminder to a rival of the man's commitments but in Mrs Malone it was no more than maternal pride.

'I did know that,' said Charlotte. 'Liam talks about them when we're working. He talks about all of you.'

Bernadette Malone turned to her husband and gave his chin a quick nip between her thumb and forefinger. It brought a smile to his face and Charlotte saw that this must be an intimate marital gesture Bernadette had employed for years to tell Liam she loved him.

'I'll arrange a car for you, Bernie,' Liam said. 'I need to show my face at this party for a few hours.'

'You go right ahead,' said Bernadette. 'I need my bed.'

'Kiss Aggie,' Liam told her. 'Excuse us,' he said to Charlotte.

'Of course.'

Charlotte watched Liam escort his wife up the stairs of the raked auditorium, away from her. She knew she should go home. She should give Liam up. It was the right thing to do. She might meet somebody else, somebody equally exciting and kind and wonderful. And if she didn't, she would have the comfort of knowing she had done a good thing for a good woman. Even as she thought it, and understood it to be right, Charlotte knew she would not do it.

Selznick delivered a glass of champagne. 'You're a hit,' he whispered. 'I need you to meet somebody very important to getting this picture done.'

The man of whom he spoke was dressed in a blue suit with a Western shirt beneath it and a string tie. He was not wearing a hat but his boots were made of shiny reptile hide and his belt buckle was in the shape of a steer.

'We just call him Mr Texas,' said Selznick. 'Or Tex for short.'

The man bellowed like a branded calf. 'The name's Chip Grogan. I thought you looked fine up there, Miss Caine, just as fine as a nugget in a pan.'

'How kind of you, Chip. Please call me Carlie,' said Charlotte. 'You are coming to the party, aren't you?' She sounded pleading. Selznick watched her work.

'I was planning on hitting the hay. Your kike boss only invited me here to try and squeeze some shekels out of a poor cowpoke.'

'Nonsense,' said Charlotte, as she looped her arm through Chip's. 'It's too early for bed and, besides, I am shy of an escort.'

Chip Grogan tipped the hat that wasn't there and Charlotte walked him out to the parking lot where the studio cars were lined up to drive the partygoers to Lulu-Belle's.

David Selznick threw back his whiskey and looked over

at Sam Warner. 'That girl's a damn gem, is what she is,' said Sam.

'Even if she couldn't act – and she can – I'd keep her on. If our Miss Caine can work the money like that, we're not paying her enough.'

'Sssh,' said Sam Warner, with a finger to his lips. 'We're paying her plenty.'

Lulu-Belle's Revue on Sunset Boulevard was a legendary joint. The place was owned by a consortium of New York businessmen who had hired a wily woman to be the eponymous hostess. Lulu-Belle's boasted a great band and gaudy decor. It was decorated in a combination of Wild West bordello and a vampire's Gothic castle – velvet drapery and gold braiding dominated. While the lure of the place was its sweetened-up sleaze, the tablecloths were crisply starched, the service attentive and the food superb. Ruby-shaded lamps glowed on every table.

There were two bawdy shows a night. A woman called the Yellow Orchid sang achingly beautiful solos and the Six Gun Sisters, a trio of guitar players, plucked out ribald country tunes. Topping off the bill were Lulu-Belle's Love-lies, a bevy of sequined and feathered chorus girls who performed amazing dance displays. It was rumoured that Busby Berkeley drew his famed bathing beauties from Lulu-Belle's stable. The girls were spectacular, leggy, red-lipped and young – taut in all the right places, soft and generous in all the other right places. Their costumes shimmied; their legs and backsides swayed seductively in their risqué costumes. Their delicate bits were ineffectively veiled by strings of beads or strategically placed brooches.

Chip Grogan kept his hand at the base of Charlotte's back as he directed her to their table. She felt his palm slipping around on the satin of her dress, unwilling to be shaken free. She was impatient for Liam's arrival. Lulu-Belle herself showed up, her rampant bosom preceding her. Each breast bobbled like a soft custard on the shelf of her black bodice.

'Are you a guest of the Warners?' she asked Chip, as he kissed her pudgy fingers where numerous rings were deeply embedded in her flesh.

'That I am, ma'am.'

'Well, Mr Warner wants you to know there's a private party just for the gentlemen in the back whenever you feel ready.'

The music grew smoky and dense. A girl came on to the stage and sang a song about waiting and winter. When she was finished, Chip roared his appreciation and threw a few bills at her feet. Charlotte took a five-dollar bill from her purse and tossed it on to the stage, too. The girl singer knelt at the edge of the stage and her eyes, which were spangled with gold dust and ringed with kohl, met Charlotte's and held for a moment before she snatched up her tips and disappeared into the wings.

Charlotte felt heady. She was tired of Chip's braying laughter. Sam Warner came over to ensure they were enjoying themselves. 'Having a good time with my leading gal?'

'She's a firecracker,' said Chip.

Before he could say any more, Charlotte cut in: 'Did Mr Malone arrive yet, Mr Warner?'

'Between you and me, he sometimes uses his wife as an excuse not to attend these events.' To Chip, he added, 'He has so many obligations, and so many children. He's a great father.'

'Good man,' said Chip.

'So, what do you say, Chip . . . Mr Texas? You ready to take a bigger slice of this pie?'

'I would love to, Sam,' said Chip. He snipped the end off a cigar and lit it, puffing to get it started. 'I keep having this good of a time and I might just cut you the biggest darned cheque you ever saw.'

Sam clapped him on the shoulder.

'Normally, I stay clear of the moving pictures. My wife don't like all the bed-hopping and nonsense that goes on here in California. She thinks Los Angeles is a trapdoor straight to hell.'

'That's not how we run things,' said Sam.

'I can appreciate that now,' said Chip. 'You keep your staff in line. You got a decent Christian man in your pictures. I believe I can see myself clear to offer you a bit more of my support.'

'Good man,' said Sam.

'Now, if we could only get some decent Christian men running the business, we'd be all set.'

Sam pursed his lips, then forced them into a smile. Chip Grogan brayed again.

'Let's finish up with the entertainment and I'll find my chequebook.'

Charlotte excused herself from the table. Champagne bubbles fizzed in her brain. A few couples had taken to the dance floor when the music turned sultry. The lights were all the way down. Charlotte saw Ivy's graceful arm extended beneath Nathaniel Whitewood's; their bodies were pressed closely together. Charlotte was surprised that the congress-man was here, but Lulu-Belle's enjoyed a reputation for wholesome naughtiness rather than vice. The whole town tittered about the place and enjoyed its slightly lewd repu-tation. It was all in good fun.

In the corner, Charlotte noticed Madge St Claire in her man's suit and her man's braces, which ran straight down over her flat breasts. Verbena, looking lovely and tragic in black, stood beside her. As she watched, Charlotte saw Verbena lay her head dejectedly on Madge's shoulder. Madge's hand reached up and stroked Verbena's cheek. Her short nails were painted black, so were her lips, and her hand crawled across Verbena's cheek like a pale mantis. Charlotte desperately wanted to speak to Madge about money, but it wasn't the right time.

A young waiter approached Charlotte, bearing a tray of champagne glasses. 'The red one's especially for you, miss,' he said.

Charlotte looked among the glasses and found one reddened with crème de cassis, the sweet blackcurrant-flavoured liqueur that turned plain champagne into a Kir Royale. There was a note scrawled on the cocktail umbrella. 'Chocolate cake out back?' it read.

Charlotte kept the umbrella; she tucked it into her purse. As the music from the band reached its crescendo, Char-lotte looked about for the face she craved. She saw it for a second at the door near the far side of the stage. She followed Liam, the way the course of a river will follow a fissure in the earth.

As soon as Charlotte was through the door, Liam had her in his arms. His lips were on her. His hands dragged the slender straps of her dress from her shoulders and she let them. Charlotte looked around when Liam went on his knees, pulling her stockings down and kissing her between her legs. They were in a narrow alley where the restaurant's trash cans were kept but Charlotte could not smell the reek of tossed-aside things, she could only smell Liam.

'I've been in pain,' he said, 'actual pain, because of you.'

'I know,' said Charlotte, understanding completely.

They were under a light, too close to the door where busboys might smoke or cooks might throw dice when the dinner rush was over. Charlotte was used to finding dark, secret places. She led Liam along the alley to where the backyard of a neighbouring house shared the restaurant's wall. The yard was overgrown with magnolias; the dead blossoms were discarded rosettes kicked aside by their shoes. Liam kissed the silk across Charlotte's stomach as he moved down once more, needing the addictive juice of her, the honey drink of her.

'I can't bear seeing you and not touching you. I think about you every minute. I can't seem to think about anything else. I have to have you, Charlotte. Don't be away from me ever again. Don't ever be away from me.'

Liam was using his mouth to talk and kiss and suck at the same time. Charlotte had to have him that second. The night was steamy on her skin, the fallen magnolias bits of broken moon at her feet. The stars whizzed across the sky above her spinning head in impossible meteor showers. She leaned against the wall and felt Liam's beautiful, eloquent tongue grazing along her slipperiness until she knew she would have to cry out with the magnitude of it, the joy of it. Then Liam was against her again and inside her – hard as glass and fulfilling and necessary.

He said her name over and over again, so that her identity was at the heart of the act: 'Charlotte! Charlotte!' Liam's voice became more ragged; it stretched and frayed until he exploded deep inside her. He cried out then in a release that absolved him of all obligations and all guilt, and set him free.

For Liam, their frantic lovemaking was a return to his youth when he had taken girls, with trembling thighs and cold knees, behind barns-turned-dancehalls. It took him back to the wild, reckless couplings of the days before Bernadette. Liam had forgotten how much he missed sex like that, the raw power of it. He knew now that he could not give Charlotte up. God help anybody who dared ask it of him! She was the craziest sort of addiction, and the loveliest.

'What are we going to do?' asked Charlotte.

'Something,' Liam said. He was still battling for breath in the exquisite aftermath. 'Something.'

He touched Charlotte's face. He felt her lashes against his palm, a fluttering intimacy. He kissed her eyelids. It was not an answer but in the moment it seemed enough for her. Liam fumbled with his trousers and the two of them giggled.

'Promise to see me again soon,' said Charlotte. 'I can't go long without you.'

Liam understood. He shared the feeling. They were two people in a strong current that was pulling them under but, if they could only hold on to one another, neither of them would have to go down into the vortex alone.

Liam walked away from their place beneath the magnolias. Charlotte did her best to straighten herself up. She ran her fingers through her hair and powdered her face, reapplied lipstick. She started to walk down the alley but found it blocked by the figure of a girl. One of Lulu-Belle's Lovelies stood in the shadows, smoking. She had slipped one foot from its scuffed gold heel and stood with it rested on top of the other.

Her face was exquisitely made up but, despite the paint, Charlotte thought she bore an uncanny resemblance to herself. The dancer's eyes were violet, even lovelier than Charlotte's own, but her lips were less generous. They might have been sisters and neither would have been the plain one. Charlotte was about to embark on an explanation as to her presence in the alley, but the girl simply offered her a cigarette. Charlotte took it automatically.

'I'm Daisy Shively,' the girl said. She snapped a lighter and Charlotte sheltered the flame to light her smoke.

'Carlie Caine,' she said.

'I know who you are,' said Daisy. 'You gave me a five-dollar tip. Thanks for that.'

So she had been the girl who had sung the solo, the one who had collected Chip Grogan's bills from the stage floor, and Charlotte's own.

'You're welcome,' said Charlotte.

'I always smoke here in the alley. I heard you,' commented Daisy. 'I thought maybe you needed help at first.'

'Oh . . . no,' said Charlotte.

She felt frantic. Had this girl seen her and Liam together? Had she watched them? Would she tell?

'Then I realized it was only love,' said Daisy, cynically.

'It's not only love,' said Charlotte. Was she going to justify her feelings for Liam to this complete stranger, this tawdry showgirl?

'Who am I to judge?' said Daisy. She had nearly finished her cigarette. 'I came west to be an actress, you know. I got off the bus and met a guy who said he could help me find work. That wasn't quite true, of course. Believe me, the set-up I have now is way better than the place I started out at.'

'You have money coming in, that's good.' Even to her own ears, Charlotte sounded patronizing.

'Yeah, and I work hard for it,' said Daisy. She didn't sound bitter or angry; she wasn't even resentful of Charlotte. 'And look at me now. I'm sharing a smoke with Miss Carlie Caine out by the garbage cans. Makes you realize we're not as different as folks might think.'

Charlotte tried not to take umbrage at that. The girl was right. Daisy slipped her right foot back into her shoe and used it to press the embers of her butt into the dirt. She walked away and turned back only once, to wave to Charlotte with a coy trill of her fingers.

'You're very beautiful,' said Charlotte.

'So are you,' said Daisy. 'So what?'

It was a statement of fact and it made Charlotte afraid. She stayed and finished her cigarette. As she was about to go back into Lulu-Belle's, the proprietor herself came through the back door and out into the alley with a shambling Chip Grogan.

'Oh, sugar,' said Lulu-Belle, when she saw Charlotte. 'You shouldn't be out here. This is the ugly ass-end of my establishment. Seeing backstage tends to ruin the magic of a place.'

Lulu-Belle pointed Chip in the direction of the gate through which Daisy had slunk moments before. 'Just go right through that gate and take a left into the house, honey,' said Lulu-Belle. 'Say Mama Lulu-Belle sent you and that it's on the Warner Brothers account.'

Chip tipped his invisible hat at her. His eyes were glazed; they didn't register recognition at the sight of Charlotte.

'I want the one that looks like that actress bitch,' Chip said to Lulu-Belle.

Lulu-Belle tried to hush him, realizing he was talking about Charlotte in the woman's presence.

'That's Daisy,' said Lulu-Belle. 'Ask for Daisy.'

Once Chip had lurched through the gate, Lulu-Belle looked at Carlie. 'I'm sorry you had to hear that,' she acknowledged.

'What's back there?' Charlotte asked, straining to see beyond the gate where a row of small lit windows ran away into the darkness, like lamps in a mine shaft.

'It's nothing, sugar. I have a clean little dormitory for my dancers back there. I give them affordable rent, a safe place to sleep. My dancers are the best-cared-for girls in the city. They love their Lulu-Belle.'

Ivy and Congressman Whitewood had left the party. Only the diehards and the strays remained, swaying together on the dance floor. Charlotte found Verbena sitting on the floor under the washbasins in the ladies' powder room. Her melted mascara had given her two black eyes.

'I just love her,' said Verbena.

'I guess you do,' said Charlotte, knowing Verbena meant Ivy.

'But that wasn't my mistake,' said Verbena. 'My mistake was telling her I love her. When you tell them, once they know for sure, that's when you're really screwed.'

She looked up at Charlotte, who was still glowing with the aftermath of ecstasy, and in that moment Verbena hated her more than she had ever hated anything in her life.

19

Verbena woke up with a pounding head and a dry mouth. She rolled her face into the pillow. She desperately wanted to go back to sleep but she couldn't. She was due to audition that day – her first job prospect in months – for a picture starring the boy wonder Jackie Gleason. The script was inane, and comedy wasn't really Verbena's thing, but it was work and she was excited by the chance to get out of the house for a few weeks. She steeled herself. She needed to wave her hair and she plugged in her electric curling tongs. She thought about Charlotte and the party at Lulu-Belle's the night before. Charlotte had looked so lovely, so pulled together, while Verbena felt her whole world was unravelling. She wanted to get back at Charlotte somehow. She felt a powerful, primitive desire for revenge. Verbena pulled on her robe and shouted for Allegra to bring her a cup of tea. Instead of the maid delivering it, it was Charlotte who knocked tentatively on her door and came in. Verbena had her curling tongs in her hand, and her arm froze beside her head as she saw Charlotte stretching out the cup towards her, like a peace offering.

'I hope this helps,' said Charlotte.

Did Charlotte think she could be redeemed so easily? Did she think this was some small spat that could be smoothed over with a paltry kindness? Verbena reached around and slapped the cup from Charlotte's hand. It flipped across the carpet, spraying tea. Charlotte's mouth opened in shock and she slapped back. Her arm caught Verbena's, the one holding the red-hot tongs, and they banged into the side of Verbena's face, sizzling there for a second. Verbena screamed at the pain but Charlotte simply turned and flounced out.

'My face!' shrieked Verbena. 'You burned me!'

'You burned yourself, you ugly bitch!' shouted Charlotte, from halfway down the hall.

Charlotte was scared. She hoped she hadn't burned Verbena badly. It had been a terrible accident. The stupid woman had brought it on herself. Charlotte hid in her room until the studio car arrived to collect Verbena. As soon as she left, Charlotte went into Verbena's room and retrieved the keys to the Jordan. She skipped into the kitchen where Allegra was only halfway through a pile of ironing. Charlotte wore a floral wrap-around dress patterned with hibiscus blooms. Allegra could see the straps of her swimsuit beneath it.

'We're going for a spin!' Charlotte declared. 'Take off your uniform and put your dress on.'

Allegra found it odd that Charlotte had started to take her along when she went on random errands. Perhaps it was an indication of the woman's insecurity, her apparent friendlessness, or perhaps Charlotte felt Allegra might buffer her against the unwanted attentions of the dreadful Mr Pike.

Charlotte drove them west towards the Pacific. It took almost an hour to reach the Roosevelt Highway where she turned right. The ocean to their left as they headed north was a bright swathe of blue; the sky was cloudless. The wind whipped their hair and Charlotte smiled to herself the whole way. With the city limits behind them, the beach bungalows and ocean-front mansions of the Palisades receded until the road was a rocky ribbon threaded between the hills.

Away from the cultivated gardens, the native vegetation of California grew low to the ground for survival. The shrubs were all swords and spears, attuned to the desert. Lizards lay petrified on roadside stones, baking their bellies; gulls scratched the sky with their wings as they wheeled overhead. The women did not speak; both seemed more comfortable with silence. After another thirty minutes, they passed a road sign for Malibu.

Charlotte pulled the Jordan off the road into a lay-by. The front tyres were almost nosing over the edge of a cliff when she brought the car to a stop.

'This is the place, I'm sure!'

Charlotte sparkled as she got out of the car. They were in a public lot where a gnarled old tree was scraped with lovers' initials and there were the remains of campfires. Charlotte made her way down a steep flight of metal steps bolted into the cliff-side. Below lay a sliver of beach.

'They're rickety, be careful,' Charlotte warned Allegra. 'Mind the rust.'

Allegra followed Charlotte with the towels and the basket. When they reached the sand, they positioned themselves where an overhanging outcrop of rock provided shade.

Further along the beach, a gaggle of children splashed in the sea, their screams as piercing as the cries of the gulls. They chased each other with swags of seaweed, the horseplay monitored by two nannies. The Mexican women's skin stood out against the pale bodies of the Anglo children and the sugar of the sand. Allegra wanted to talk to the women, speak her native Spanish once more, but she stayed beside Charlotte with her legs bunched up under her skirt. Allegra tried to remain unobtrusive. She wondered why she was there.

Charlotte's attention never left the children. She smiled at their antics every now and then. One of the boys waved and Charlotte waved back, but Allegra didn't think the child recognized her.

'I always wanted a big family,' Charlotte told Allegra.

Allegra did not offer an opinion. Children were a privilege she dared not contemplate in her current situation; she could not afford them. She thought about Holt and what kind of father he would be. The thought made her happy.

One of the children broke free from the group and raced over to them – a little girl, her red curls bouncing on her shoulders, the skirt of her bathing suit flapping against her chubby thighs. She looked no older than six or seven. She came at full tilt to the edge of their towel and stopped dead. In the manner of children, having made the first move she expected them to respond.

'Hello there,' said Charlotte.

'I'm Agnes,' said the girl. She beamed; her two front teeth were missing.

'What a grown-up name!' said Charlotte.

'That's because I'm six,' said Agnes, as if this explained things.

'Are those your brothers and sisters?' asked Charlotte.

'They're all brothers,' said Agnes. 'I'm the only girl. There are six of us . . . And I'm six,' she reiterated. 'Callum is fifteen. He's the oldest.'

'Where's your father?' Charlotte asked.

Agnes shook her head. She looked bored. She glanced back towards the other children. 'Goodbye,' she said.

'Don't go,' said Charlotte. She grabbed the little girl's arm and startled her.

'Let me go,' Agnes demanded.

Charlotte did not. Agnes started to cry and jerked herself free. The two nannies watched Agnes stumbling back towards them with concern.

Allegra stood up. 'I'll go talk to them,' she said.

'I only wanted to meet her,' said Charlotte, 'but I never know what to say to children . . .'

Allegra crossed the sand and introduced herself to the women. They had rural accents but they were friendly enough. The three of them stood and chatted at the water-line while the children scampered between them. Allegra had taken off her shoes and she enjoyed the sea air on her legs as she lifted her skirt up past her knees.

The two maids suddenly waved and called out '*Ola, señor!*' to a man who was descending another shambling staircase, this one from a cliff-top house. He came over to them and Allegra saw that it was Liam Malone, the famous film star, the heartbreaker. Allegra knew Charlotte was working with him on her new picture. He was one of those smiling, affable, dark-haired Irishmen who often turn mean when exposed to whiskey. Allegra had seen plenty of his type in Stationville. None of them looked as healthy and contented as this man, however. The children squealed at the sight of their father; they clustered round him in delight.

'And whose custodian is this?' Liam asked, acknowledging Allegra.

Liam had looked from face to face and identified all the children present as his own.

'I'm with my employer,' said Allegra. 'I'm a maid, not a nanny. I'm here with Miss Caine.'

Liam hooded his eyes with his hands and looked over to where Charlotte sat. He scanned the cliff-top where Verbena's car was parked; its paintwork caught the sunlight and dazzled his eyes. 'Tell your employer I'll come over and say hello to her in a minute.'

Liam loped down the sand, the children shrieking after him, and launched his body into the waves. He needed time to compose himself. He felt jarred that Charlotte had shown up unexpectedly, especially around his children. He was also happy, excited to see her. He needed to cool off.

Allegra walked back to Charlotte whose eyes behind her dark glasses didn't waver from Liam's form in the water. 'It's Mr Malone,' said Allegra, unnecessarily. 'He's coming over to talk to you in a while.'

Charlotte propped herself upright and pressed her lips together to revive the intensity of her lipstick. Allegra had done the very same thing before kissing Holt – she was unexpectedly surprised by the universality of these feminine wiles. Allegra leaned her body against the rock face, hoping she wouldn't be sent back to wait in the hot car. Charlotte didn't banish her, though. Liam came out of the sea, and shook his head like a Labrador. He strolled over to them; his face was chiselled, every muscle defined. 'Hello, Charlotte!' he called out, as he got closer.

His shadow loomed over her but Charlotte didn't strain

her neck to gaze up at him. She kept looking out to sea. 'Hello, Liam,' she said in answer. 'You've met my maid, Allie.'

'Far from home, aren't you?'

'I like the view here,' Charlotte said.

The beginning of a smile crossed Liam's face, but then he became serious once more. 'Those are my children,' he said, quite pointedly. He gestured towards the gang being rounded up by their nannies.

'Yes, we met little Agnes. Where's their mother?'

'Bernadette's up at the house. She's in bed. She's not well.'

'Does that mean pregnant?' asked Charlotte. She pulled her sunglasses from her face.

'That really shouldn't concern you, Charlotte,' Liam said quietly. 'And I think I told you Agnes would be our last.'

'You never know,' said Charlotte.

Liam laughed out loud and Allegra appreciated that he was one of those men who could be described as beautiful. 'Six is more than enough for me!'

'Well, things change unexpectedly . . .'

'I'm very happy with my life just the way it is,' said Liam.

'Especially recently?' Charlotte asked.

Liam couldn't deny that was true, but he couldn't say anything overt with his children there either. This beach was his family's place. Already he had noticed that the Malibu cottage was unutterably changed by memories of what he had done with Charlotte there. Even so, he was getting hard looking down at Charlotte's swimsuit, the fabric stretched thin, and Charlotte's body – so supple and amenable right beneath it.

'God, Charlotte, your voice is so . . .'

'Inviting?' she said teasingly.

'Indiscreet, I was going to say.'

They couldn't help smiling at each other.

'You're all wet,' Charlotte said. She reached up her hand and touched Liam's thigh.

He let her fingers stay there for a second, then gently moved so her hand fell away. He looked back at his children. They weren't watching him; they were almost at the stairs, loaded down with umbrellas and enamel buckets. 'Are you going to the party at the Lava Lounge next Friday?' he asked.

'Yes,' said Charlotte. 'And I'm bringing a man with me.'

Liam shook his head in a kind of dazed wonderment at her gall.

'I'm going to make love to him in secret,' she said. 'I'm going to find a dirty alley and drag him into it.'

A frisson passed between them. Liam turned to go.

'You shouldn't park your car in the direct sun like that. The paint will fade.'

'I don't care,' said Charlotte. 'It's not mine.'

'You should be more careful with things that aren't yours,' Liam said. Charlotte's happy expression changed noticeably. Then he added, chidingly, over his shoulder, 'Spoiled girl.' It was flirtatious. Charlotte turned on her side so Allegra couldn't read her evident joy.

On the return journey, Allegra once again allowed silence to sit between them in the car. Charlotte was sunny; she felt generous. She ought to get to know Allegra better. The woman was in her home every day. It would be a nice gesture on her part to take some interest.

'What's Mexico like?' Charlotte asked suddenly.

Allegra was surprised. Charlotte had never asked her a personal question before. Had their joint adventure at the beach made the actress feel closer to her?

'What's it like where you're from?' Charlotte asked again.

'It's very beautiful there,' Allegra said. She was unwilling to offer more. Her home was a place she kept as a personal belonging. Memories of it were her sole inheritance. Allegra turned her face to the window; her eyes pricked with tears.

'Is your house near the ocean?'

Allegra glanced fiercely at the actress. Was the woman trying to torture her by dredging up what she had lost? Charlotte's face was blithe. 'No, my home was inland,' Allegra volunteered. 'But we used to go to the sea in the summer. We took a house in Cabo San Lucas. It's a small town and there is a white church with big blue doors that open right on to the rocks and the beach. On the beach there, the men fill their donkeys' baskets with ice chips and sell you frozen bananas right on the water's edge. When the tide is right, you can swim out in the sea for half a mile to a sandbank. My father would swim out there with me. Our dogs would swim out, too. We would sit on the sandbank and I would draw pictures in the sand with a shell. When I was on the sandbank, I would look back at the beach and I could see the church rising up like its own island. Sometimes the church looked as if it was the only cargo on a ship, just bobbing on the water, moving God from place to place.'

'How far away is this place?'

'It seems very far away,' said Allegra. She was lost on the

beach in Cabo San Lucas now. Her memories tumbled in on her like an unexpected wave, knocking her off balance. 'It was very unusual then for a Mexican family to take a holiday away from home. The local people found us strange. The little boys from town would watch me with suspicion. One of them liked me. He used to leave shells for me on the mat at the kitchen door – all white. Then he would run away and spy to see if I picked them up.'

Charlotte smiled at the sweet story.

'On those holidays, I would work in the kitchen with Lucia, our cook from home. She would teach me all the dishes she made – the peasant stews and my father's favourites. I became a wonderful cook in Cabo.'

'You'll have to cook something for me,' said Charlotte.

'I would make you ceviche,' said Allegra. 'A very special seafood dish with citrus juice. You would like it.'

'Buy what you need to make it.'

'It's very expensive,' said Allegra. 'I have not made it for a long time.'

'That doesn't matter,' said Charlotte.

Allegra was thinking about cooking in the pristine kitchen on Lantana Drive. She doubted the oven had ever been used. She felt excited by the chance. If there were any leftovers, she would take some home for Holt to try. Ceviche would be their signature dish when they opened their restaurant.

Talking about Cabo San Lucas had made Allegra glad for a few minutes. It had reminded her of her father, his trousers rolled up to his knees, his sandy feet propped up on the wicker sofa beside her own, their baby toes just touching. She remembered late nights by lantern-light when her father had created shadow puppets on the whitewashed walls of their cottage for her amusement. It had been a long time since Allegra had thought of her father without anger. She wiped her fingertips quickly across her eyes; she held the tears in her palm and waited for them to dry there.

'Allie,' said Charlotte, interrupting her thoughts. 'This church . . . Do people ever get married there?'

The Santa Anas had come up during the afternoon. They blew in from the east, dragging the desert with them. The wind howled through the canyon, bowing the high branches of the blue gums.

Verbena was in the living room. 'Where have you been?' she shouted, as soon as Charlotte and Allegra came through the front door. 'You took my car without permission again.'

'You weren't around to ask. I was sure you wouldn't mind,' trilled Charlotte, sweetly.

'Don't use my car again,' said Verbena. 'Get your lover to drive you round in that ostentatious gold thing of his.'

'I don't know what you mean,' said Charlotte. She needed to change the topic quickly. 'You had an audition today. How did it go?'

'How do you think?' said Verbena. She pointed at her face. Charlotte could see a distinct red line, which ran from the brow above Verbena's left eye all the way down her cheek. The bar of the curling tongs had left a serious mark. Verbena had tried to cover it with makeup but it was a bad burn. Charlotte could only hope that it was shallow.

'You've disfigured my face!' shouted Verbena. 'I'll have to visit a doctor. It could take weeks to heal.'

'You can hardly see it,' lied Charlotte.

'It's not come to the surface yet,' said Verbena, woefully. 'Just get out of my sight!'

Charlotte didn't want to go to her room and she wasn't welcome in the living room, so she trailed Allegra into the kitchen. She wanted to sit on the deck, but as soon as she opened the French windows, dust and leaves blew in. She slammed them shut. 'I hate the Santa Anas!' she said. The constant disruption of her hair and the stinging sand made life unpleasant. The wind also made her feel restless, agitated.

'I could stop the wind for you, Miss Charlotte,' said Allegra, 'or make it more tolerable at least.' She, too, had noticed how the peculiar situation of the house enhanced the power of the Santa Anas.

Charlotte frowned at the maid but she was curious. 'How do you suppose you could do that?'

'It's not witchcraft,' smiled Allegra. 'We could plant a grove of trees. They act as a natural wall against the wind. If you choose something that smells pretty, like oranges, the scent will blow up into the garden. It can be very nice. Trees shelter the house. If you plant something with fruit – again, like orange trees – you can have fresh juice for breakfast in the morning.'

Charlotte was charmed by the plan.

Allegra had been thinking all the time of Roscoe and Harmony Pepper and their extraordinary sanguinellos. She was thinking, too, of extended employment for Holt.

'It's a wonderful idea!' said Charlotte. In her mind, it was a parting gift to the house that had borne so much fruit for her – a career, a new home of her own, Liam.

'I know somebody who grows orange trees,' Allegra said.

'He would sell you some, I'm sure – very cheap. I also know people who could plant them for you.'

'Yes!' said Charlotte. 'Let's do it. I can't stand this wind and I'd love the smell of orange blossoms in the house.' She was thinking of the Fleurs de Rocaille perfume. Soon, she would be able to enjoy its scent again. She clapped her hands in excitement.

'What's happening in here?' asked Ivy, arriving in the kitchen.

'We're going to have our own orchard,' announced Charlotte. 'Allie's arranging it for us. Isn't that a blast?'

Ivy rolled her eyes at the ridiculousness of the notion, but Charlotte was delighted. Later, she called Madge and set up an appointment for the following day to discuss her finances. She needed to know exactly how much she had. There might even be enough for the house and to rid herself of Mr Pike without having to take a loan. As optimistic as she felt, Charlotte was almost sure there would be. Still, she didn't want to give away that thousand dollars Pike had demanded. She would prefer to use it to buy furniture for her wonderful new home.

Charlotte considered her situation logically. If the Santa Anas kept blowing, seat sales at the circus would be low and the workers would demand that the circus move on to more lucrative venues. Should Charlotte just wait Pike out? Should she just hope that he would be forced to move on without his money? It was a gamble.

Charlotte would wait until the following Friday. She would watch the tent in the canyon. One day it would be gone, and she would be free. Pike was just an evil chancer. The more Charlotte thought about him, the more she believed he was powerless to harm her. He might go to the police. They wouldn't give a damn about his tall tales. It was private information. No real crime had been committed, had it? Charlotte didn't think so. Besides, Pike had no proof of anything.

If Pike went to Warner Brothers, studio security would rough him up and send him on his way with a warning not to spread malicious lies about their up-and-coming starlet. Either way, Pike didn't really stand a chance. It was only Charlotte's fear of him and his threats that controlled her. Charlotte would call his bluff. She would not pay him off. She would have her house instead. She would fill it with beautiful things. She would fill her mind with beautiful thoughts. She would build a beautiful future with Liam Malone. Pike could go to hell.

20

Allegra smelt Stationville burning from half a mile away.
She had seen the tower of black smoke in the distance as
she walked from the bus stop but had told herself that the
fire must be coming from further to the east or the west.
It could not be her home that was burning. Allegra owned
so little; she refused to believe that littleness could be taken
from her. When she reached the dirt track that formed the
entrance to the settlement, she slowed to a bewildered
stumble. The shanties of Stationville were now no more
than a series of burned lumps protruding from a barren
wasteland. The fire had roared through the makeshift
village, destroying the dwellings and blackening the mud
pathways. Here and there, smouldering bundles emitted
foul plumes. Even the dust of the earth was charred to a
crust.

The shack where Allegra had lived was just a splintered
shape of jutting planks. The iron bedstead she had slept
on lay upturned with its melted enamel legs pointing heav-
enward. The Santa Anas were still blowing, driving the
ashes in drifts against the broken-down fences and piling
them in small hillocks between the railway sleepers. The
weeds had been scorched away.

One of the Dunn boys searched through the debris with
a stick. He unearthed an enamel cup and looked at Allegra
through its burned-out base, using it as a telescope. Mr

Dunn whistled for his son from behind the wheel of the family's truck. The whole Dunn clan was piled into the back of it, seated precariously atop their few remaining belongings – sacks, a coal stove, two surviving chairs.

Allegra walked aimlessly, trying to use landmarks now altered beyond recognition.

'It weren't no accident,' called out Mr Dunn. The creases around his eyes were etched in soot. 'They burned us out. A gang of men from the paint factory was drinkin' in Fletcher's. They took to talkin' about those thugs from Pipe City and their thievin'. They got it in mind to come by and teach us a lesson. The police were called in to stop 'em but they wound up joinin' the fray. They had a paddy-wagon and rounded up anyone who looked Mexican. The police claimed they were obeyin' some law to send all of you back home. They would have taken you, Allegra. It's a blessin' you weren't here to be dumped back over the border.'

'Where will you go, Mr Dunn?'

Allegra noticed that Mrs Dunn was sitting quietly beside her husband, crying. It was the first time Allegra had seen her in tears. The usually stolid woman held a bloodied handkerchief to her face.

'There's strawberries up north,' said Mrs Dunn.

Her voice was a lisp. Allegra saw that Mrs Dunn's two front teeth had been knocked out.

'They came with baseball bats,' said Mr Dunn. 'They had rifles, too, a few of 'em. They shot your friend's horse.'

Allegra's legs gave way. She dissolved like a sandcastle when a wave crashes over it. She felt washed through, diminished, sucked out to sea.

'Hop aboard, if you're comin',' said Mrs Dunn. 'There's nothin' here for you now.'

'I'll stay with Holt,' said Allegra.

Mrs Dunn nodded her acceptance. Mr Dunn put his truck into gear and pulled slowly away. The Dunn boys didn't wave farewell: they were too familiar with goodbyes to bother with them.

Allegra crossed the tracks into the field where Holt and Haywire had made their home. She moved in a daze. Holt sat on the ground with his hat on his knees. There was a stink on the air that made Allegra's gorge rise. The marauders had shot Haywire where he stood and the fire had swept through afterwards. The horse's shiny chestnut pelt was black. His silky mane had melted into sticky globules that ran the length of his neck. Haywire's eyes had rolled back in his head to reveal whites like boiled eggs. The horse's teeth were bared in a grimace of agony, and Allegra wondered if he had been dead when the flames came or merely paralysed by the bullet. Had the horse watched the fire leap towards his face across the tinder grass?

Allegra fell on her knees beside Holt and his arms reached out to encircle her. 'I didn't want to leave him,' said Holt.

His eyes were quite dry. The loss was a fish hook in his gut, a pain too deep for tears.

'We'll bury him together,' said Allegra.

The field was a plain of granite, fired to rock by the heat, as ugly as a strip mine. Allegra wished Haywire could rest in a better place.

'I already tried,' said Holt. 'The ground is stone.'

Allegra felt Holt wipe his face briefly against the shoulder of her blouse. When he tried to pull away, she wouldn't let him go. She held him until his muscles relented and he sagged against her, taking the comfort. 'This is the worst it will ever be,' she whispered.

It was paltry succour but it was all Allegra had to give.

'Said that to myself every day for the past three years. Never once been true.'

'That was before we had our dream,' Allegra reminded him.

'Truck's tank blew,' said Holt. 'Always thought I'd get her running again one day. Never did. Now I got nowhere to go and no-way-how to get there.'

'You do have somewhere to go,' said Allegra. 'I've found you a week's gardening work to start with. You can sleep in the canyon below the house where I work. We'll make you a tent. I've seen camps down there before. I've seen Okie fires from the deck at night.'

'What sort of gardening work?' asked Holt.

'Tree planting for Miss Charlotte,' said Allegra. 'She needs some men to dig in an orange grove.'

Holt nodded resignedly. 'How many trees she putting in?' he asked.

'As many as I say. I can probably tell her she needs at least twenty.'

Holt's scars turned pink and became more obvious and a little frightening when he smiled. 'That's a whole darn orchard!'

'Miss Charlotte's sold on the idea, but the digging will be rough. It's rocky soil in those hills, just like it is here.'

'I'm strong,' said Holt. 'I'm glad of the work, too, Allie. Don't think I'm ungrateful.'

'They have a room for me there,' Allegra said. 'They've been asking me to live in. I only stayed here because of you . . .'

'You won't have to be there long,' said Holt. 'I promise.'

'Can you go to the Peppers' farm tomorrow and see if Mr Roscoe will sell us some trees? I hope he and Mrs Harmony are still there. I know they were planning to look for outside work I think Mr Roscoe might even take on the planting with you, if it means he can make payments on that farm a while longer.'

'Bus to Bakersfield and hoof the rest,' Holt said. He stood up, dusted his seat with his hat, and kicked the shell of his car in despair. Allegra picked up a charred potato sack from the ground and covered Haywire's face with it. 'Your place burned out, too,' admitted Holt.

'I saw it,' said Allegra.

'I got what I could.' Holt had a bundle of Allegra's smoky belongings wrapped in a blanket. He opened it and showed Allegra the contents. The few items of clothing he had rescued were sooty. A photograph of her mother and father on their wedding day was nestled inside her nightgown. He had rescued the coffee tin and Allegra's Sunday shoes. At the bottom of the sad pile, Allegra saw what she had been hoping for. She took its salvation as a sign of her own. Lucia's book of recipes didn't have a mark on it, not even a smudge of ash. It had come through the fire unscathed when nothing else had.

Allegra slept beside Holt that night. They moved his canvas tarpaulin to the very edge of Stationville where the grass was still green. They created a shelter against the fence that had once separated the Border from Pipe City. They were very close to the concrete arcs where the vagrants slept. In the darkness, Allegra felt Holt's muscles stiffen at every noise. She did not think he slept. It made her feel protected and she relished that.

The next morning, after Holt had left for Bakersfield, Allegra went back to the actresses' house on Lantana Drive and asked if she could move into the room beside the scullery, as they had often suggested.

Charlotte, Ivy and Verbena – thrilled by the notion of help on call twenty-four hours a day – chipped in to purchase Allegra a tiny cot with a new mattress. It was delivered that same day and took up most of the space in the room. There was one window high up on the white wall, a table in the corner with a broken leg, and a lamp. There were no pictures; no curtains softened the window. The room was a blank. Allegra listened to the wireless playing in the kitchen as she unpacked her scant belongings. Verbena had instructed her to wash in the pool-house bathroom where there was a WC and a shower. The hot running water would be a luxury. Allegra clutched at the small pleasure.

That first night, Allegra woke at three a.m. with a shudder. Her nightdress was a noose twisted around her neck. She reached for the lamp and allowed its wan light to calm her. Soon, Holt would arrive on Lantana Drive with the Peppers and their trees. Allegra would be able to catch a glimpse of him working in the canyon whenever she wanted to. She got up and took off her damp nightdress. She put her parents' wedding picture under her pillow and cried quietly for a while. Then she paged through Lucia's recipe book to bolster her spirits; she thought about Allegra's by the sea.

*

'I'm glad we don't have neighbours close enough to see this,' said Verbena, from a lookout position at the deck railings. 'It's appalling.'

'I feel sorry for them,' said Ivy.

The two women were watching Holt and the Peppers set up their shanty camp in the canyon below the house. It was the first time Ivy and Verbena had spoken in days and Verbena was grateful for the truce. She had missed Ivy desperately since the party at Lulu-Belle's. She didn't think she could endure one more blow.

Verbena had called her doctor and he'd told her to wrap ice in a clean cloth and keep it pressed against her burn wound for as long as she could stand it. He told her he would visit her the next day. He needed to see the burn to make sure it wouldn't scar.

'I think this is good for us,' said Ivy, self-righteously. 'We need to remember that there's a depression. This is . . .' she snapped her fingers as she searched for the word '. . . authentic,' she said finally.

'It's pathetic, is what it is,' said Verbena. 'Carlie's really showing her roots with this ridiculous scheme of hers. What was she thinking, letting derelicts move in? I'm going to telephone Madge about it. She'll tell the studio. They'll put a stop to it.'

'You can ask Madge in person,' said Ivy. 'She's with Carlie right this moment and they'll be home soon. They went down to the bank to arrange the deposit on Carlie's house. I don't think you'll have to put up with her much longer, Bee. You two never did get along.'

'Because she's an evil little liar,' said Verbena. 'I can only imagine what she's got Liam Malone believing.'

Ivy went over to her. There was something she had been wanting to ask Verbena for the past two months and now seemed as good a time as any. 'Bee,' Ivy started out, in a soft, obsequious tone, 'I know you snipe at Carlie, and we tease her quite a lot, but you wouldn't ever do anything . . . unforgivable, would you?'

'I don't do things I consider unforgivable,' said Verbena.

'You wouldn't expose her in any horrible way, would you? If you knew something private, I mean . . .'

Verbena didn't answer her. She didn't want to discuss it further. She thought about the day she had driven down to the circus to question Teddy Pike. The memory chilled her. She couldn't help feeling she had engendered a rage in the man that might still be burning. She got up and went inside. Ivy stayed to watch Holt and Roscoe set up their temporary home.

The Peppers' truck was parked on a plateau. Holt had slung a canvas awning between two poles he'd hammered into the ground and a high point on the hillside. It formed a basic tent. Before they unloaded the trees, he and Roscoe scrambled up the treacherously steep hillside to the actresses' garden.

By then, Charlotte had arrived home with Madge St Claire after their meeting at the bank. The two women came on to the deck to join Ivy and greet the workers. Allegra stayed in the kitchen: she had dishes to put away. She wanted to rush outside, push everyone from her path, and throw her arms around Holt's neck. For three days, she had wondered if he would return, or simply take off and forget her for ever. But their dream held him in its thrall. Allegra was sure of that now. She restrained herself and listened to the group talk from her place at the sink.

'You must be Allie's friends,' said Charlotte, walking over to the two men. They wouldn't shake her hand – they were filthy – but they took their hats off as a sign of respect.

'Roscoe Pepper,' said Roscoe. 'I'm awful proud to meet you, ma'am.'

'Oh, you're too kind, Mr Pepper. It's very good of you to do the work on such short notice.'

'Holt,' said Holt, stepping forward.

Charlotte stared blatantly at Holt's scarred face. He ignored her inspection. Charlotte wasn't looking at the scars, however. She was thinking she had seen that face somewhere before – and in her memory of it, it was not so damaged. Perhaps she was imagining things.

Charlotte looked over the deck railings at the truck's load. The sanguinellos were well over eight feet tall. The root bulb of each tree was encased in a hessian sack. They were beautiful specimens, leafy and spotted with blossoms. 'They're completely wonderful,' she declared.

'That's the first eight only,' said Roscoe. 'Once these are in, we'll go back to my farm for the rest.'

'They're absolutely perfect,' said Charlotte.

'I can't promise you fruit next year,' said Roscoe. 'A lot depends on how they take.'

'We're not really relying on them to feed us,' said Ivy.

'Well, they'll surely break up the wind some,' said Roscoe. 'They'll be pleased with this stony soil, too. I believe they'll establish just perfect.'

'You don't have children, do you?' asked Ivy, unexpectedly.

Roscoe looked visibly taken aback by the question. 'Me and Mrs Pepper aren't yet blessed,' he said.

'That's good,' said Ivy, thoughtlessly. 'I couldn't bear to think of children living rough like that.'

Allegra was glad Roscoe hadn't mentioned Harmony's pregnancy. Ivy might have made a real fuss about letting them stay if she knew. Charlotte took thirty dollars from her purse and handed it over. Three dollars per tree was the agreed-upon price, but the men needed to buy shovels and picks for their work since neither they nor the house were equipped with enough tools for two men.

'I appreciate it, ma'am,' said Roscoe.

'I'll pay you for the rest of the trees when you bring them, and for your labour – as and when you provide it.'

The project was under way. Holt winked at Allegra as he passed the kitchen window. The two men scrambled back down the hillside, skidding as they went and churning up the loose shale.

'Did you see that man's face?' said Ivy, when they had gone. 'My God, it's like a game of pick-up sticks!'

'Ghastly,' said Madge. 'He must have been in some sort of wreck or a dreadful machinery accident.'

Charlotte was pale. Holt's face had really troubled her. There was a vague memory there . . . She wondered if it was because his scars reminded her of those that criss-crossed her father's hairline. She must find time to visit her father again. The press would be checking up on her, making sure she visited him regularly, waiting to catch her out.

Allegra went on to the deck as often as she could during the afternoon to watch Holt. She saw the men wrestle the trees from the truck. She tossed them a coil of garden hose and they drenched the trees' roots for their overnight stay above ground. In the early evening, Holt and Roscoe drove off in search of supplies.

Allegra caught her first real glimpse of Harmony after they left. The woman wore sturdy boots beneath her loose shift. Her insubstantial figure fussed about her new homestead. Harmony arranged the campsite to her liking. She had balanced a gas stove on a tea crate to serve as a makeshift kitchen. She had been on the road before; Allegra could see that. She had accumulated the necessities of rough living. Allegra could make out a tin bucket, a box containing cans of food, an old quilt that was filthy round the edges, a hand-trowel for burying waste, and a worn Bible.

Harmony appeared different from the last time Allegra had seen her, but she could not identify the nature of the change. She followed her movements between the gaps in the deck railing as the woman gathered a circle of stones together and built a fire in the middle of it. It was nice to have another working woman around the place. Once the flames had caught, Harmony unpacked what looked like a watering can with a narrow spout. She placed dry grass inside it as kindling, then lit it.

For nearly five minutes, she drifted the can back and forward over half a dozen white boxes Roscoe had unloaded from the truck. The Peppers had brought some of their hives with them. At once Allegra closed all the windows facing the canyon. She remembered the bee sting from her childhood.

When he returned from his errands, Holt half scrambled, half dragged himself up the hillside once again, clutching at tufts of weeds until he reached the deck. Madge St Claire and Charlotte were relaxing there. 'Ought to let us fashion you some manner of a staircase down this hill,' he said. 'How else you going to water these trees or enjoy them?'

Charlotte looked dumbly at Madge. She hadn't considered the practicalities. Madge thought the suggestion typical of an Okie. They would invent jobs to keep themselves employed for as long as possible. It was understandable, she supposed, and whoever lived in the house would need the stairs . . . 'I suppose he's right,' said Madge. 'Do you have any woodworking skills, Mr Holt?'

'Been a carpenter my whole life,' said Holt.

'Of course you have,' said Madge, sceptically.

It now seemed that the scars were probably the result of some ghastly wood-cutting accident; a mechanical saw had likely been the culprit.

'Buy what you need, but see to it that you bring Miss Caine invoices for every cent you spend.' Madge turned to Charlotte. 'I'll make sure you aren't being fleeced, darling girl.'

'Mr Holt wouldn't do that,' said Charlotte, and she turned the full wattage of her movie-star smile on him.

From the kitchen, Allegra saw that Charlotte's flirtation had no effect on Holt. She surged with love for the man. Holt doffed his hat and went down the side of the house to wash in the pool-house bathroom. Charlotte and Ivy had agreed that the workers must be allowed to use the outdoor facilities. Verbena thought it dangerous to allow them so close to the house but she had been outvoted – just one more humiliation.

'Thank you for looking out for me, Madge,' said Charlotte, when Holt was out of earshot.

Madge harrumphed.

'You don't seem yourself. Is anything wrong? You don't suppose we're going to have problems with the bank, do you?'

'It's nothing like that. Mr McTavish will have the money for his house by the end of the week.'

'What is it, then?'

'Liam Malone's looking especially happy, these days.'

'That's a good thing.'

'Sam Warner mentioned it to me.'

'Sam Warner should be thrilled that his expensive new picture has a cast that gets along so well.'

'He's thrilled that everybody's happy. He just wants to be certain that everybody understands that this particular happiness shouldn't extend beyond the picture.'

Charlotte flapped that notion away with her hand. 'You're not making any sense, Madge. That's pure nonsense.'

It was Thursday evening when Allegra changed into one
of her two remaining dresses and started down to Holt's
campsite. The hill was very steep and difficult to navigate.
In the gloom, Allegra felt nervous. There were sharp succu-
lents and rocks, not to mention diamondbacks, in the
canyon. Only a week before, she had found one of their
shed skins – with its desiccated rattle still attached – on the
deck.

Holt saw Allegra hesitate on the hillside and jogged up to
her with ease, his strong legs pumping. He reached her word-
lessly and picked her up in his arms to carry her. He slid in
the loose gravel as he descended; Allegra shrieked with fear
and happiness. The Peppers applauded as they arrived at the
fireside, flushed at their bodies' nearness, both breathless.

Allegra had helped herself to some food from the
actresses' kitchen. She was reckless because of Holt. The
dream they shared, the restaurant, was a drug that made
her feel invincible. Over the meal, the Peppers talked about
their farm. They owed the bank on it, of course, but they
would pay every dime back when things evened out. Their
bank manager held the title deeds now, but he had promised
to keep their land from auction for as long as he could.
There would be no foreclosure, Roscoe insisted. Allegra
remembered bankers telling her father the very same thing
about his racecourse.

'Still, we were mightily relieved when Mr Holt came along with an offer to buy some of our trees,' said Harmony. 'I don't know what we would have done this month else.'

'We'd have got by,' said Roscoe.

Harmony pursed her lips and changed the subject by teasing Holt. 'When are you two lovebirds getting hitched?' she asked.

'Soon maybe,' said Holt.

Allegra felt a thrill at this casual remark.

'Well, I can sure recommend it highly,' said Roscoe. He planted a wet kiss on Harmony's forehead. She wiped it away.

Allegra heard a buzzing pass her head and flinched. 'I have to tell you I'm afraid of your bees,' she confessed. 'I once took a bad turn after a sting. I need to be careful.'

'Most of the bees are in for the night by now,' said Roscoe. 'That one's a straggler. Just be sure to stay clear early morning and early night when they come and go.'

'Our bees aren't especially aggressive, Allegra,' said Harmony. 'And their honey's a treat.' She got up and fetched a bottle of milk she had buried, wrapped in newspaper, to keep it cool. She poured it into a saucepan and warmed it over the fire. Then she opened a jar of Pepper Honey and turned it upside down above the pot. A lump of fresh comb plopped out. Harmony stirred it round in the milk with a wooden spoon. 'I wish we had a vanilla pod to add in it,' she said.

Roscoe emptied the last splash from his hip flask into the mixture. 'That'll do just as well,' he said, and they all laughed.

They each received half a tin mug of the warmed milk and clinked them together in a toast.

'To the land of milk and honey,' said Harmony. She tried hard to smile. She leaned back against Roscoe's chest. He took the warmth she offered thankfully. With Harmony's body reclined in that way, Allegra could clearly see her shape beneath the loose dress she wore and identified the change immediately. Harmony Pepper's stomach was as flat and empty as a dry riverbed.

After dinner, the Peppers crawled into their tent and snuggled up together under their quilt. Holt walked Allegra through the orange trees, which stood at unnatural angles in their sacks. Allegra saw the white boxes of the beehives in the trees' shadows and imagined she could hear the furtive industry of insects inside them.

'I'm considering the best route for these stairs I've gotta build,' said Holt. 'Reckon I'll run them from the end of the spur, over there, right down into the heart of the orchard. Have to make them zig and zag some or it'll be too steep.'

'How long do you think it will take you?' asked Allegra.

'How long you want me around for?'

Allegra could see Holt's crazy scars quite clearly in the moonlight. Sometimes they made him look so freakish that it scared her. She closed her eyes and concentrated on the man's beautiful voice, his few words – each one well chosen, none wasted. 'A long time,' she answered.

'Don't want to wait a long time for Allegra's,' said Holt. 'Feel I'm done waiting.'

Allegra considered what she was about to do very carefully before she did it. Then she took in a deep breath and started . . . 'There's a man,' she said. 'He's come to the house before and once he was at the store when we shopped . . .'

'He following you?' Holt asked.

'I think he's following Miss Charlotte.'

'Why? He being a nuisance or something? One of those crazies?'

'No, I think he's known her for a long time,' said Allegra. 'He's very big and very ugly. I'm afraid of him.'

'Miss Charlotte talks to him?'

'That's what's so strange. She pretends not to but she does. She's very afraid of him, too, I can tell.'

'She ever talk to you about him?'

'She talks to nobody about him,' stressed Allegra. 'I don't think she even knows that I've met him because he's never seen us talking but he definitely knows I work for her.'

'If she's afraid of him, why don't she get some hard-nose from the studio to warn him off? They got security men on their payroll. Or she could just go to the police.'

'I'm trying to work it all out, Holt. They don't seem to fit together. His name is Teddy Pike. He works for the Magic Sevens Circus. He's covered in these terrible tattoos. He knows Miss Charlotte for sure. He wants something from her . . .'

Holt stopped strolling and looked right at Allegra. 'She have anything to give?' he asked.

'A lot of money, I suppose.'

'Tell me everything.'

Allegra told Holt what she knew.

He assessed every word. 'We gotta find out what he knows,' he said.

'Why?' asked Allegra.

'So as we can steal it from him and use it for ourselves.'

Allegra remained silent, non-committal.

'We come at it from two sides,' Holt continued. 'You keep your eyes and ears open round the house. Find anything she keeps hidden, any secrets. I'll try and meet your Mr Pike. I'll find him – easy-like, in some bar – and see if he spills anything over a few drinks.'

'You think he's holding something against her?'

'Pretty sure of it.'

'Holt, I don't think I can do this . . .'

Holt took her face gently in his hands. He started to nod rhythmically at her. 'Yes, you can.'

'How do we make Mr Pike share the money with us, if he can even get it from her?'

'We don't,' said Holt. 'Man like that don't share. We got to steal his secret right out from under him. We gotta use it on her first.'

Could she really blackmail somebody? Allegra wondered. She wasn't sure. She only knew, with a deep, resolute certainty, that her dream was tangible. It was right there at the tips of her fingers and it might not come any closer. She had to stretch out and grab it.

Holt helped Allegra back up to the house. It stood in darkness. They sat together by the pool where reflections from the moving water mottled their faces. Holt's scars disappeared in the wash of flickering blue. Allegra leaned forward and kissed him. Their lips touched, then pressed. Holt's hands encircled Allegra's waist; they felt safe and permanent on her hipbones. Allegra let him explore each bead of her spine, then the curvature of her breasts.

Allegra's roving hands encountered a hard lump in Holt's coat pocket and she pulled it free before he could stop her. In the gloom, she could not identify the item. It consisted of two substantial blocks of wood with wire entwined around them. 'What is it?' Allegra asked, as she kissed him.

Holt took it decisively from her and re-deposited it in his pocket. 'Nothing,' he said. 'A kind of tool, is all.'

He pushed her skirt up to her waist. His hands searched between her thighs and parted them. His knuckles nudged, insisted. Allegra gasped and moved against his fingers. Holt's arms were cords of muscle; his chest was a rock. Allegra hid her face against him, but not out of shame. After a while, she found his lips again. She cried out into his mouth as she climaxed.

Holt held Allegra as her body slackened. She wanted to return the favour but didn't know what to do until Holt's hand took her own – firmly, slowly – and showed her.

There was no embarrassment afterwards, only an enduring connection. Allegra couldn't stop smiling; she couldn't stop touching him. Her hands fed on Holt's eyelids, the crease of his elbow, the line of his jaw, his scars. Allegra wanted her body to remember him as well as her eyes did. In the darkness, she was blind and Holt was a new language to be learned by fingertip.

22

Charlotte's father's condition had not changed since her previous visit. She stood beside his bed, looking down at his shrunken form. The sheet was tucked tightly across his chest as it always was. His arms rested in precisely the same position as they always did. His one hand remained dead at his side; the other was pulled into a hooked claw below his chin. The red-pink scars still criss-crossed his forehead and hairline.

Charlotte thought of the scars that marked Allegra's beau's face. That man – Holt was his name – had reminded her of somebody, and the memory, though indistinct, was a threatening one. If only she could place him. He was not somebody she'd known well, she decided, but he was definitely somebody she had encountered before in passing, briefly, somewhere. It was difficult to imagine that face as it must once have been before it was torn up, then stitched back together.

She wasn't sure she was pleased to have the man living in the canyon below her house. Then again, having people camping there might serve as security should Pike decide to walk along the canyon and attempt to get into the house through the garden. Holt and Mr Pepper would be there to confront him before he ever reached her. It might work out well. Charlotte held her father's hand and thought happy thoughts. She need only stay half an hour – that was all the nuns, and possibly the watching press, could expect of her.

That afternoon, she and Madge St Claire would have the chance to visit the cottage on Cherrybowl Close. Charlotte would deliver the banker's draft Madge had arranged for her in person. She would plan how to furnish the place; she would imagine where to place every lovely thing. She thought about opening her precious bottle of perfume – the Fleurs de Rocaille. On her first night in the house, surrounded by boxes, she imagined she would hold a personal consecration ceremony. She would anoint each room with that exquisite scent. It was the scent that took her back. Just the thought of it was enough to evoke memories – though some of those memories were almost unbearable . . .

It was 1925. Jazz was all the rage, so was the Charleston, and Charlotte had been living with her father in Coral Gables, Florida, where they shared a single room in Miss Orteig's boarding house. The postcards from Charlotte's mother were still arriving back then, but they were winding down, the intermissions between them growing longer as the months passed. Patrick Caine and his young wife, Mary, had come to America from Ireland before the war. Now, he worked as a waiter in the University of Miami's student dining hall while Charlotte attended a nearby convent school. Mary had run off.

When her classes let out at three o'clock, Charlotte would take the streetcar from Ponce de Leon Boulevard to the campus and wait for her father's shift to end. She liked the university boys and the pompous faculty who sometimes recognized her and smiled. Charlotte would have liked to learn from them. She received poor grades at the convent. She hated the nuns. They were black crows. Their noses were beaks. Their beady eyes glinted from under their wimples. They pecked and pecked at her, calling her out in front of the others because she struggled with her handwriting.

That summer, the sister superior had written a stern missive to Charlotte's father, requesting he see to it that his daughter was supplied with 'suitable undergarments' for her 'prematurely adult physique'. The note had mortified Charlotte. The sister hadn't put it in an envelope and Charlotte had resisted the temptation to read it until she was on the streetcar on her way home. Once she had sneaked a peek, she couldn't throw the letter away. The sister might expect a reply. Charlotte hated the sister superior for causing her such embarrassment. She hated her mother for not being there to receive the note and deal with the matter.

Charlotte had handed the letter to her father that night. She had stood haughtily before him as he read it. She had decided not to bow her shoulders. That would be an apology for her budding breasts and Charlotte refused to be ashamed. She would make her father as uncomfortable as she was. It was his fault for not noticing, after all. It was his fault for not being man enough to address the necessities of his own daughter's growing up. Instead of Charlotte stooping, it was her father who slumped visibly and said, 'Your mother needs to deal with this.'

'Well, she isn't here,' Charlotte had said. 'It has to be you!'

Her father put the sister superior's letter on his dresser, on top of the pile of his wife's postcards. He left it there.

Early the following Saturday morning, Charlotte took five dollars from her father's wallet while he was still drunk from the night before, and went to Desirée's – the most expensive department store on the Miracle Mile. The lady in the lingerie section helped her, after Charlotte explained that her mother was in hospital with consumption.

'Oh, my,' the woman said. 'Let's get you fitted with something nice, then. There's no need to worry your mammy.' She had a pleasing round face and a big, toothy smile.

'She's dying really.' Charlotte had embellished her story. 'I might never see her again.'

The woman bit her lower lip and gave Charlotte a discount on the two foundation bodices she had chosen.

Charlotte was on the way out of the store when she saw the red glass scent bottle in the shape of a tulip, the red petals like a woman's lips about to whisper a secret. The kindly store assistant spotted her admiring it and took the bottle from its prominent display case. 'Isn't it gorgeous?' she said. 'All the gals who work here are in love with this scent. None of us can afford it, of course,' she whispered. 'Mrs Niemann, who buys absolutely everything, took one look at the price tag and stormed out of the store in a snip, saying it was an outrage.'

The shop assistant came to a decision, looked around nervously, and sprayed a cloud from the atomizer into the air. She showed Charlotte how to walk through the mist.

'That's what the word "perfume" means in French, dear – *parfum* comes from the phrase *par fumée*, meaning "through smoke". You need to accumulate the scent on your skin like a gentle shower of rain.'

It had been the sweetest, most heartbreaking fragrance

Charlotte had ever experienced, smelling as it did of the old South, and morning-after corsages, and loss.

'It's called Fleurs de Rocaille,' the assistant told her.

'Fleurs de Rocaille,' Charlotte repeated deliberately.

'I know a schoolgirl could never afford it,' the assistant added conspiratorially. 'And I'm not supposed to give browsers a sample, but you're such a lovely girl. It seems to suit you.'

Charlotte thought about that perfume for a week. She could get obsessed with something like that – a poem, a picture in a book, a song – but most often it was a desirable item she had come across in a store and which she would visit over and over again. Charlotte drew pictures of the bottle in the back of her schoolbook. Though she could get the shape right, and even the bottle's sparkle, the ethereal smell could never be captured on a flat piece of paper. Charlotte couldn't abandon her desire. The wanting was an actual pain in her stomach that made her sick. The yearning kept her awake at night. She would do anything to be able to see that bottle every day, to keep it on the ugly crate beside her bed. It would be the only truly beautiful thing in her room, in her life. Charlotte wanted to fall asleep near it, swim inside it in her dreams.

She was still thinking about the perfume bottle when July came burning in. She had been wearing her school uniform when it happened, a tartan skirt and burgundy blouse. There were seven of them, all schoolgirls, who jostled on to the streetcar together each afternoon but Charlotte's stop was last. Most of her classmates lived in the emerging suburbs around the Biltmore Hotel with its golf course and tennis courts. Their fathers were bankers and hoteliers and realtors. Their mothers were wives, not flighty dreamers like Mary Caine, who had always coveted maps and one-way train tickets.

Charlotte propped her book bag between her feet and held on to the leather strap that dangled from the streetcar's roof. She swayed with the motion of the vehicle, her over-heated brain jerked alert at intervals by the bell. The streetcars were busy with men leaving work early and women hurrying home with baskets of groceries and niggling babies.

Charlotte had seen the man on previous trips and he had seen her. They had noticed each other noticing. Charlotte felt sure she knew what those half-closed, heavy-lidded eyes of his meant. They were full of admiration and Char-lotte, though still only a girl, was already tired of looking down when eyes like those met hers. As people got on and off the streetcar, the man manoeuvred himself closer to her. Charlotte was being stalked in slow motion. It was oddly stirring. The man moved no more than an inch or two at a time, travelling inexorably nearer until Charlotte felt her breath speeding up. Her heart came alive inside her; she was suddenly aware of it working. She struggled to find moisture for her tongue.

The streetcar stopped again and the man was right beside her, facing her but not looking at her any more. He held the strap beside Charlotte's. His knuckles were white against the distressed leather. His other hand clutched the day-old newspaper. The man wasn't old. He looked like Charlotte's father, only fresher, less worn out around the mouth and eyes.

The streetcar lurched over a pothole and the man's arm

brushed against Charlotte's breast. She did not move away. She did not giggle. She looked out of the windows to where white fences and blue swimming pools rushed by. She watched the pink-painted garden sheds, the lime-green buds about to burst free from the ends of the tree branches. There was a red bicycle, lying abandoned on a garden verge. Its back wheel was still spinning but there was no child in sight.

The streetcar stopped to pick up more passengers and the man advanced another inch. His arm was firmly against Charlotte's breast now. She knew he felt its softness. The man's stiff lips parted. His mouth was dark inside. Charlotte shifted her weight deliberately, ever so slowly pressing back against him. The man swallowed. Charlotte looked up into his eyes, wanting him so desperately to acknowledge something, but he would not stop his false, yet feverish, reading.

Charlotte looked out of the window again. She was acutely aware of random details – a woman washing dishes behind a kitchen window, a bent rake propped against a garage door. The streetcar stopped and the man made his move. He let go of the strap and squeezed Charlotte's nipple between his fingers. It happened so quickly that Charlotte was still drawing in a shocked breath by the time he was reading again. The man's cheeks were red but the blush didn't look like shame to Charlotte. It looked more as if a fire had begun to burn under his skin.

'The next stop is mine,' she said softly.

The man looked at her then, and Charlotte smiled kindly at him. She didn't want him to feel bad. She knew he was probably a nice man with a family. He seemed to take her words as a sign to hurry. They were near the back of the streetcar; nobody was watching. The man used his news-paper as a screen. He forced one of his polished shoes between Charlotte's feet and wedged his knee between her thighs. Charlotte felt something firm yet strangely pliant in his trousers; it rubbed against her belly. The man's breath was ragged now. He slid his hand up under her skirt. He reached the leg elastic of her knickers, up where she was damp and sticky on that summer day. Charlotte felt thor-oughly embarrassed by her own heat but the man's fingers were relentless. His nails scratched her skin where nobody else had ever touched her. The streetcar's brakes wheezed out air and it stopped again.

'This is my stop,' said Charlotte, and she smiled again, holding the attention of the man's eyes with her own.

'Do you travel every day?' he asked.

'Weekdays,' she said. 'After school.'

'Tomorrow,' he said, and he squashed a rumpled dollar, used and grey-green, into her palm.

Charlotte was sure her father would see it on her, the sin – a staining mark she would be unable to conceal. She hid the dollar bill in her sock as she picked up her schoolbag and got off the streetcar. She walked across the campus lawn to the kitchen door of the student dining hall. Her father was sitting there on a trash can, smoking a cigarette. His waiter's jacket was folded over his knees to catch the falling ash. A serving towel wrapped around his neck absorbed the sweat that ran from his temples.

When he saw his daughter, Patrick Caine reached out to muss up her hair. Charlotte felt reassured. She was still his little girl. She would never take the streetcar again. She would be good. She would walk everywhere, no matter how long it took her. Her father reached into his back trouser pocket and handed Charlotte a postcard.

On the front, there was a picture of a red barn. The trees around it were ablaze with colour. The message read: 'Greetings from Vermont'. On the back, Charlotte's mother had written: 'I will learn to ski this winter and can already skate, so Vermont is perfect for me! How's my little girl? Not so little any more, I expect.' It was as if Mary Caine knew what had just happened, even over long distance. The comment was a jibe. Her father didn't seem to have a clue. It made Charlotte angry with him. She felt jealous that her mother had escaped this ignorant, useless man who didn't know what was going on around him, under his very nose. The postcard was signed 'M' but whether this was for 'Mother' or 'Mary', Charlotte could not decide. There were no Xs or Os, not even a quickly scribbled heart. The note was as lean as the woman herself. Charlotte remembered her mother as straight and hard. There had never been a soft place to rest her cheek.

Another man came out of the kitchen, accompanied by a blast of heat. It was Archie, the head waiter and her father's immediate boss.

'Archie,' her father said. 'Guess who's here?'

Her father said the same thing every day. It was stupid. Archie could see Charlotte for himself; he knew she was there. Archie was one of the men who watched her.

'They're offering time-and-a-half for double shifts,' Archie told Patrick. He also lit a cigarette as soon as he could, as if they didn't spend enough time amid the haze of the steamy kitchen.

Patrick looked hopefully at his daughter. 'Can I stay?' he asked.

Charlotte hated the way her father asked her permission for things while still pretending she was a child. 'You can stay,' she answered. 'I'll take the streetcar home on my own.'

Her father handed her the key to their room in the boarding house.

'Miss Orteig is sure to have some dinner for you. Tell her I'll settle up your tab tomorrow morning.'

For once, Patrick didn't suggest that Charlotte take food home from the dining hall's kitchen. Charlotte could smell that it was fish that night. She was always embarrassed when her paper-wrapped package of leftovers stank up the streetcar. People stared at her.

'I need money,' Charlotte said.

She held out her hand and kept it still under her father's nose, not wavering. He gave her a dime. Charlotte pushed the coin down into her sock and felt the dollar bill the man had given her crumple there. She experienced a furtive rush of pride. Charlotte kept her father's dime and walked home, even though it was getting dark. She had been warned about men who hung around parks and street corners after nightfall, but she felt quite safe now — adult, immune.

23

The next morning, Charlotte had slid back the sheet that acted as a curtain between her half of the bed and her father's. His side was empty. His blanket was folded there. The pillow she had plumped for him was undisturbed. He had not come home again. Perhaps he had taken the breakfast shift, too, and slept on the cot in the scullery. Archie turned a blind eye to that. Charlotte sometimes feared that Archie might show up at their room one night when he knew her father was sleeping at the university, but so far he had not.

Charlotte took her towel and her school uniform into the washroom. She chose her best pair of knickers from the box that served as her private drawer.

She lay in the bathtub for a long time. The fractured mirror above the sink was quite steamy when she got out. She could not recognize herself in it. She tied her long hair into two straight braids down her back. She polished her shoes. She gave her father one last chance to be in the room, to say something to her before she left, but he wasn't, he didn't. She took a small jar of talcum powder she had lifted from Ford's Drugs and patted some on her inner thighs. Her legs were tanned brown. She would have to stop being outdoors in the sun: dark skin was so childish and unsophisticated. The white powder left a chalky smudge on her skin, high up where her knickers started – the opposite of a bruise.

The man was on the streetcar after school. Charlotte had known he would be. This time, he came over to stand beside her immediately, not wanting to waste precious minutes. He needed longer to do what he wanted to do. It started as soon as the bus moved forward – the silent, stealthy fumbling. At first, it was his palm, sliding against the powder Charlotte had refreshed in the school washroom after class. Charlotte found the sounds the man made most disconcerting. He grunted out deep, throaty noises. He sucked on thick saliva he couldn't seem to swallow. The man pressed his hardness against her leg again and his fingers explored outside her panties then slipped up into them. It didn't hurt as much as Charlotte had expected. The man rubbed his trouser front against her thighs, pushing so hard Charlotte thought he was going to hurt himself. Suddenly he gasped and shuddered. Charlotte thought he was crying and reached out to take his hand and pat it gently. 'It's okay, mister,' Charlotte told him. 'It's okay.'

The man took his wallet out immediately, wiped his forehead with his shirt cuff, and gave her two dollars.

'It's my birthday today,' Charlotte said.

The man looked at her sharply but Charlotte didn't look away. She wondered if he would be there the next day. She suspected he might be. It had been a lie, of course. Charlotte's birthday had been two weeks before. She had just turned twelve.

The man had met her on the streetcar every day for a week. Then, on a Friday afternoon, the driver had grabbed Charlotte's wrist as she walked past him to get off and said quietly, 'Take another car, girlie.' As he pulled away, he rang the streetcar bell twice.

It was a sound Charlotte would never forget. In later years, when regret came, she would always associate the sound of the streetcar bell with bad decisions, and with a terrible sense of sadness.

Charlotte explained to the man about her ban the next day at the streetcar stop.

'The park's better anyway,' he said. 'Biltmore Park. Be there after five o'clock when it gets dark. There's a bench and a public convenience with a fountain out front.'

Charlotte knew the place he meant. It was near the ancient stone gates that had once led into the original plantation of Coral Gables. She had always thought of it as a private park for the residents of the homes near there – colonial palaces, their ancient oaks bearded with Spanish moss. She had walked through the area once, feeling like a trespasser, and had heard the sound of a piano tinkling through the neighbourhood. It wasn't a park where people ate picnics or children played. The families who lived in this area all had their own walled gardens.

Charlotte's father was scheduled to work double shifts all that week, so Charlotte simply strolled past Miss Orteig and walked from the boarding house to the park. It took her nearly half an hour. The evening was Florida-muggy but Charlotte had brought the tin of talcum powder with her in her purse. At least she wasn't in her school uniform. She wore a yellow sundress that was a bit too small for her now. Her mother had bought it right before she had left for the last time. That had been almost two years before. The straps of the dress cut into Charlotte's shoulders and the skirt was short but it was her favourite thing, the only pretty garment she owned. Charlotte had brought along a flashlight concealed in a brown-paper bag. She had planned everything meticulously. The planning had been exhilarating. She had lain on her mattress the night before and thought about the man's gasping breath. It made her feel squirmy inside. There was a tingle in her belly, like before a fair ride or when she had gone into the circus tent with her father's friend, Archie, to see the freaks.

Archie had taken Charlotte the year before as a treat. One of his friends worked there and he had got them in for free. It travelled through Florida and Georgia in the winter, entertaining the tourists. It went as far north as Chicago in the summer, as far west as California once. Charlotte had loved the danger of the place. Its veneer of magic did not fool her. The women who worked there looked old and tired behind their makeup. Charlotte had only been eleven at the time, but already she knew that the thrill of the circus came from its dirtiness, its transience, its tents of wickedness.

She felt the same way in the park. The place itself was pretty and dusky. The trees shimmered in the last of the sunlight, the first of the moonlight. Leaves hushed and rustled as birds settled. But Charlotte thought she could sense the remnants of furtive goings-on, just as she had glimpsed the darkness behind the glaring circus lights. What lived in the wings was striped and wild. It smelt of wet sawdust and a place where animals were kept.

Charlotte sat on the park bench, crossed her ankles, and opened the book she had packed with the flashlight. She tried to remember the man's face. She knew he was too old for her but sometimes old men did marry very young girls. You saw it in the newspapers all the time, on the society pages.

She saw someone coming across the park towards her. The person tugged a dog on a leash – the kind of fat, fluffy dog refined ladies owned. As the figure drew closer, Charlotte saw that it was a man. He reached her quickly, then didn't appear to know what to say. She put her book down and said, 'I'm Charlotte, by the way.'

'Call me Adam,' he said.

'Adam – like the first man,' Charlotte said.

He laughed. 'I'm the first man, am I? That's going to cost me, I expect.'

Charlotte didn't know what Adam meant by that. He tied his dog to the bench by its leash and it lay down in the sand where people scuffed their feet while they waited. Adam took Charlotte by the top of her arm, not by the hand as she had expected, and led her towards the public convenience. She had imagined they would go around the back of the building where a white bougainvillaea was in bloom, all tangled up in its abandon, but he took her into the men's room instead.

Charlotte was shocked. It stank far worse than any ladies' room. There was a plank of wood hidden behind the door; the man used it to prop the handle closed so nobody else could enter. Had Adam come here earlier today and planned this, as she had planned her part? There was a long porcelain wall with a trough at the bottom. Charlotte didn't know what it was for. She had arrived in a foreign country. The floor had dried yellow crud on it and filth off the bottom of shoes.

Adam pulled her dress up over her head. Charlotte raised her arms so it parted from her body with one swift tug. Adam looked at her exposed skin with what Charlotte knew was love. Then he did something that appalled her, that ruined everything for ever. He took the dress her mother had bought her and tossed it down on the floor so that the splashes of piss soaked into it. The golden yellow fabric turned a dull mustard as the man pushed her down on top of it.

Charlotte kept going back to the men's room for the money. She had done what she had done, and now there was only the perfume, the Fleurs de Rocaille, to make it worthwhile. If she could have that at the end of the ordeal, things would balance out. Charlotte would have traded her body for something valuable.

For a while Adam came to the park alone. In October, when the evenings started to get cold, even in Florida, and the tree bark took on the colour of concrete, he brought a friend along. By December, they came in a gang of three, walking across the park towards her with their three dogs straining against their leashes, moving away from the lighted windows of their homes.

Charlotte endured it; she thought about the miraculous smell of the Fleurs de Rocaille. She thought only of buying the scent. She would own it. It possessed her.

Charlotte returned to Desirée's on 13 December, she remembered the exact date, and purchased the bottle of perfume with a wad of cash. The kindly sales lady she had encountered on her previous visit was not there, but a man had wrapped the bottle in tissue paper and handed it to her in a gold organza bag with ribbons for handles.

'This is a pricey purchase,' the man had remarked, looking at Charlotte distrustfully.

'My mother died,' Charlotte explained, which made the man look away. 'She left me some money in her will and told me to buy something that made me feel special.'

'Then it's a most discerning choice,' the man had said humbly.

There was a small clear sticker on the base of the bottle that read 'Caron' and below that 'Fleurs de Rocaille'.

Once she owned the perfume, Charlotte felt deeply contented for a while. It was like a precious secret someone had entrusted to her. Only she couldn't keep the bottle out in the open. Her father would see it and ask about it. She kept it in its bag, under her feminine rags at the bottom of the private box-drawer her father would never search.

Charlotte kept seeing the men. There were only the three, her regulars, and she wanted the money. There were things she needed very badly. A brooch with a stone the colour of the sea; a pair of golden latticed dancing shoes. Charlotte stopped bringing her flashlight along when she walked to the park. By then she knew the way by heart.

When she got older and thought about what she had done, when she wanted to die because of it, Charlotte told herself that she had been courageous and thoroughly modern. She had wanted certain things and she had found a way to have them. Why those particular items had become so important to her, Charlotte could not work out. They seemed like random choices but they had grabbed hold of her and would not let go.

Years after the summer of the perfume, Charlotte had seen the suit with the fox-fur collar in the window of a boutique. It had a severely cut tweed skirt and a jacket with a voluminous ruff of red-fox fur to soften it. It was very like the one Charlotte's mother had worn on special occasions, only better. Charlotte knew she had to have it. The perfume was wonderful, the brooch was a prize, the dancing shoes were perfect – all of the items she had coveted over the years had been important, but owning the fox-fur suit was an absolute necessity. And she needed the men to help her have it.

Because Verbena had objected to her using the Jordan, Charlotte had called a taxi to bring her to the Order of the Sisters of Charity. The driver had waited for her while she visited her father and now he drove her to Cherrybowl Close.

Madge St Claire was already at the house. Her car was parked in the street. Madge leaned up against the vehicle's hood, smoking. Charlotte paid her fare and got out of the taxi. Madge walked across the street to meet her. Together, they opened the garden gate and made their way up to the front door of Charlotte's dream.

Mr McTavish turned out to be an elderly gentleman with small grey pebbles for eyes and brows like white gorse bushes. The young woman Charlotte had once seen washing dishes through the kitchen window was his daughter. She showed Charlotte through the immaculate house. It was just as she had imagined it. The rooms boasted interesting alcoves and wood panelling. It was a true craftsman's house, meticulously maintained. When they went into the backyard, blue sheets flapped on the line in the gentle breeze.

'I ought to have brought the washing in,' apologized Mr McTavish's daughter. 'It's unseemly.'

'Not at all,' insisted Charlotte. 'I like it. It makes the place feel like a real home.'

When Madge took the envelope from her pocket containing the banker's draft for five thousand dollars, Charlotte didn't feel a qualm. She felt as excited about the house as she had been about the perfume and the fox-fur suit. She had made the right choice. She deserved to have what she loved. Liam Malone had taught her that. Charlotte knew that she had missed Mr Pike's deadline for delivering his bribe. She didn't care. She knew she had spent her money wisely, as an investment in her future happiness.

On the drive home, Madge joshed with Charlotte in a friendly way. She knew she had to talk to the actress about managing her money wisely, but she also knew Charlotte would be an amazing little earner for her over the next few decades. 'You'd better watch your nickels and dimes for the next few months until your picture completion money comes through. Your bank account's not too sound after today's big purchase.'

'I don't care,' said Charlotte. 'I've never been so happy. I don't need money for anything else.'

24

That night Charlotte found it impossible to sit quietly in the living room with Ivy and Verbena. The two women were painting each other's toenails. They had made up and, as long as they avoided the subject of Congressman Whitewood, they were firm friends again. Verbena was all but confined to the house by her appearance. The burn had ravaged her face. The wound was still bubbly and it wept a clear liquid. Verbena's doctor had visited and assured her that it would heal in its own time. He had given her ointment to apply. It was thick and pink and it smelt bad. Verbena had cried about the burn that afternoon but her tears had made it sting even worse. She could not look at herself in the mirror. Ivy had secretly cancelled a dinner date with her beloved Nate to stay in with her friend. She was concerned that the burn might leave a permanent scar. That would be the end of Verbena's acting career. Ivy didn't want to ask her what she would do for a living if she couldn't work for Warner Brothers. She tried to chatter about other things. She needed to keep Verbena distracted. When Verbena talked about the burn, she blamed Charlotte and her temper flared.

Ivy and Verbena had also planned to do each other's hair that evening. They were going to listen to the wireless, and eat a meal they had told Allegra to prepare for them that afternoon. Charlotte had not been included in their plans and she didn't care.

Charlotte knew she wouldn't be able to remain still long enough to enjoy frivolous grooming. Her whole body itched with excitement. She undressed in her room and wrapped herself in the fluffiest towel she owned. It was dark outside; it was always darker here in the hills than in the semi-urban streets of the valley. Charlotte switched on the kitchen light. It illuminated the deck but not beyond it where the pool lay. She went out through the French windows in her slippers. It was muggy; the whistle of the Santa Anas was constant. Below the deck, she could see Harmony Pepper's cooking fire. The mumble of conversation drifted up to her but Charlotte could not make out the words. She could, however, hear Allegra's tone among the voices.

Charlotte left the deck and entered the territory of the night. Here in the garden, plants grew feral and unfamiliar. The high leaves of the blue gums whispered secrets to one another. Wispy grasses planted near the pool's edge tickled her ankles. The water was skinned with dust. It swirled, black syrup in the deep shadows.

As Charlotte's eyes adjusted to the gloom, she stepped into the water, which swallowed her feet and then her legs. Her toes found the grainy bottom. It wasn't too cold, but this was the shallowest corner of the pool and the warmest. Charlotte ducked down until the water covered her shoulders. She gasped. Her skin rose in gooseflesh. She stroked towards the deep end, her feet kicking, then turned on to her back and floated. She could see stars above her head like fragments of windshield glass on the blacktop after an accident. Charlotte let her head relax; sound evaporated as water covered her ears. She could hear the thrum of the night, the hollow thump of her heart. She closed her eyes.

It wasn't warm enough to stay like that for long, but every now and then a tepid wave washed past her. The water tasted oddly salty, Charlotte noted; it had a tarnished copper odour, too. Charlotte's hand touched something. A leaf or a twig? She tried to right her body and stand but she was too deep. She took in a mouthful of water and choked.

Charlotte flailed her arms in an effort to get to the shallow end, but this time her hand struck a more substantial floating object. It was clammy and pliant. It felt horrible. Charlotte tried to swim to the steps but viscous strings wrapped around her neck. They stank. She cried out. She splashed in earnest but her arms were caught in the stinking tangle. She tried to push the mass away and felt sharp teeth. Charlotte retched. Vomit came up and burned her throat. She finally reached the side and pulled herself out of the water. She brushed hysterically at her legs, pulling her knees up under her chin.

Her screams brought Ivy and Verbena running. Verbena carried a flashlight and swung its beam over the water. A bloody clump of entrails, as pink as melted bubblegum and ridged with blue veins, was still wrapped around Charlotte's ankle. Charlotte shrieked when she saw the clotted mess and threw it back into the pool. The splash rolled over the carcass to which the entrails were attached, and brought it to the surface of the water.

The coyote's snarling mouth was frozen open; Charlotte had cut her hand on its death-bared teeth. The animal must have fallen into the pool and drowned. Surely coyotes could swim, Charlotte thought. She was crying; she retched drily.

Ivy turned away and buried her face against Verbena's

exposed collarbone. 'It drowned!' she exclaimed. 'The poor thing drowned. God, how awful!'

Verbena didn't correct her friend. It was clear to her that the coyote's belly had been slit open from throat to hindquarters. The truth of that fact might occur to the others once their shock subsided.

Holt, Allegra and Roscoe Pepper arrived at the pool, having scrambled up the hillside at the sound of Charlotte's screams. Holt picked up the coyote's body by its hind legs and threw it far over the edge of the canyon.

'I'll bury that body for you come sun-up, Miss Charlotte,' he said.

'Damn menace kids, I'll bet,' contributed Roscoe.

Charlotte knew it hadn't been delinquent youngsters. It was Teddy Pike – maniac preacher, circus ringmaster, blackmailer. She had spent his money. She couldn't possibly pay him now. She shivered in shock at the terrible mistake she had made. Only hours ago, her decision to buy the house had seemed so right; now she only wanted that money back to pay off Pike, get rid of him for ever.

Verbena was frightened, too. The minute she had seen that dead coyote, she had known Pike was sending her a message. When she had visited the circus to interrogate him about Charlotte, she had stood beside him as he gutted the very same animal – a mangy coyote – and fed it to his dogs. He had warned her to leave him alone but she had persisted in her questions about his relationship with Charlotte. She had enraged him. This was a warning. Verbena would have to approach him again, humbly, and apologize. She was more afraid of Pike than she had ever been afraid of anybody. He didn't follow the rules of polite society. He was one of those men who worked outside the law and she had little or no experience of men like that.

Verbena glanced nervously round the garden once more before gathering the other two women to her side and escorting them back to the house. 'Go to your room,' Verbena snapped at Allegra, as she passed her. 'And you get back to your camp,' she told Holt and Roscoe. Everybody complied. Everybody was deeply unsettled.

As she lay shivering in her bed, still feeling ghostly entrails encircling her legs beneath the sheets, Charlotte knew that Pike was never going to simply slink away. It had been a foolish hope and now that she had spent all her money on the house, she was terrified of what he might do. Then it came to her: she would be getting more money soon. Madge had explained to her that there was a balloon payment due to her on completion of *The Walls of Jericho*. Charlotte couldn't expect Pike to wait the few months it might take for that payment to come through – and she didn't want him to stay around a day longer than necessary – but surely there was a way to get an advance on the money.

In the morning, as soon as propriety permitted, Charlotte placed a call to Madge St Claire. As soon as her agent answered, Charlotte blurted it out: 'I need money, Madge.'

'What? What's going on, darling girl? Are you all right?'

'I'm fine.' How could she explain this? 'It's my father. He suddenly needs special care and I've spent all my money on the house and . . .' Charlotte's pent-up anxiety surfaced. Tears came. Her knees buckled and she sat down on the floor. 'I don't know what to do!'

It took Madge several minutes to calm her down. 'Sssh, sssh, darling girl. Talk to me. I'm listening.'

'I don't want to lose him,' said Charlotte. She clutched the telephone cord. She twisted it tight. 'I can't lose him. I love him, Madge.' It was Liam she was talking about, Charlotte realized. The shock of losing Liam because of Pike was a fear she had, so far, suppressed.

To Madge, it simply sounded like Charlotte was finally coming to terms with the impending loss of her ailing father. 'We'll get you the money. Calm down now. Tell me everything.'

Charlotte snivelled and her voice hitched as she made up tales about her father's sudden decline, while Madge paged through a ledger of her clients' accounts. Madge controlled hundreds of thousands of dollars on behalf of dozens of performers. It was fraudulent to shift funds from one actor's account to another's, but Madge had done it before in an emergency. This kind of creative accounting was quickly rectified when the studio pay cheques inevitably came in.

Charlotte was due to receive almost five thousand dollars in less than two months' time. Madge flipped the page and came across Verbena Marsh's entry. Verbena's account was very healthy indeed. Verbena had spent little of her own nest egg. She had arrived in Los Angeles with money and a kindly aunt sent regular cheques to augment her monthly earnings.

'I have plenty of money on hand, darling girl. I can advance you as much as you need.'

'Two thousand dollars,' said Charlotte, immediately. She had doubled Pike's demand in case he raised the amount when they met. He was the kind of man who might do such a thing.

'God!' said Madge.

'I need it, Madge,' shrieked Charlotte. 'I have to have it!'

'Fine, that's fine . . .' Madge had to keep this girl happy. 'I'll arrange a banker's draft for you.'

'I need cash,' said Charlotte.

Madge was suspicious but she doubted Charlotte was involved in gambling or dope. She had clients with those problems, and Charlotte didn't display the warning signs. Madge decided she didn't care what the cash was for. There was money coming in. This was a stop-gap measure. 'I'll get it to you in cash, then.'

'Tomorrow, please, Madge. Tomorrow morning.'

'I'll go to the bank this afternoon,' said Madge. She sighed deeply.

When she hung up, Charlotte steeled her resolve. Soon Pike would be gone for good. Madge – smart, savvy Madge – was going to help her. Charlotte felt weak with relief. She had to get the message to Pike before he did anything further to threaten her or raise Ivy and Verbena's suspicions.

As soon as Madge delivered the money, Charlotte would borrow Verbena's car – her permission be damned! – and drive out to the circus grounds to deliver it. She would pay Pike what he demanded, more than he demanded, if necessary. Then she would be done with him for ever. Still, giving away her hard-earned money burned her. As she got control of her fear, Charlotte began to consider alternatives. Was there another way out?

25

Charlotte came into the kitchen that evening and asked Allegra to zip her into her dress. It was five o'clock and Allegra was finishing a hard day's work, anticipating a hot shower, a change of clothes, and a modest dinner with Holt and the Peppers in the canyon. Throughout the day, she had longed for Holt, knowing he was close by, but unable to break away from her chores to see him.

Allegra wiped her hands on a clean towel and attended to Charlotte's velvet sheath, which clung to her body and left her back open to the night. Charlotte was agitated: she hadn't seen Liam Malone for over a week and she would see him that night. They were both scheduled to attend the première of a new gangster picture called *Dark City*, although neither of them had played a part in it. Charlotte wanted to get Liam alone for a few minutes. She wanted to know when they could steal away for another weekend. She wanted to tell him she had purchased the cottage on Cherrybowl Close. She was also still thinking about the Mexican town Allegra had described – the white church on the beach with its blue doors.

Charlotte glanced at her reflection in the glass of the French windows and saw Holt's face outside, staring back at her. His scars did not bother her much any more. The initial shock had worn off. Charlotte still felt that she had met the man before but she had given up trying to remember where.

Holt opened up a cloth he was holding to reveal three enormous oranges.

'I was bringing Allegra these,' he said. 'I didn't mean to disturb you, Miss Charlotte.'

'Nonsense, Mr Holt. Come in,' Charlotte said, as she opened the French windows to him.

'Have you ever tried them?' Holt asked her. 'Sanguinellos?'

Charlotte shook her head.

'I'll open one up for you,' Holt said. He rolled one of the oranges in his hand to free up the juiciness inside, then took a penknife from his pocket and expertly peeled the fruit, holding it out to Charlotte. Both the sight of the knife and the fruit unsettled her. Each juicy segment glistened red. Charlotte put a piece into her mouth where it burst against her tongue in a sweet spray.

Charlotte smiled, a dribble of juice ran down her chin and she wiped it away, self-consciously, with the back of her hand. She laughed at herself. Holt smiled. When he smiled, the man was very handsome indeed. Would it be rude to enquire as to the origin of his scars? Charlotte decided it would be.

'I was thinking about making you that special dinner we spoke about,' interjected Allegra. 'Remember we talked about the ceviche on our way back from Malibu?'

'Your seafood dish?' said Charlotte.

'Yes. I believe I can use the juice of these oranges to poach the fish and the shrimp. It's a very special technique, very delicious.'

'Then I'll invite somebody special to share it with me,' said Charlotte. 'Should we do it next Friday night?'

Saturday night had been one of Allegra's evenings off when she lived in Stationville. As Allegra had anticipated, now that she lived in the room beside the kitchen, she was available all day to cook, clean, iron, and find lost items for their careless owners. The positive aspect of the situation was that Holt now lived less than a quarter of a mile away. Allegra could reach him in the night if she wanted him. But Holt would have no reason to stay after the tree-planting work was finished and he had completed the staircase to the canyon. He and the Peppers would have to move on. What would Allegra do then? She wondered if she would stay in the house and care for Ivy and Verbena, or whether Charlotte might offer her a position in her new home. Either way, Allegra would be a maid. Besides, the likelihood of Ivy staying in Lantana Drive for much longer – her relationship with Congressman Whitewood was going very well – seemed slim. If Ivy moved away, too, Verbena wouldn't stay in the house alone. The studio would insist she take on new housemates. They might even decide to put the house up for sale. It was all very uncertain.

And what about Holt's proposed plan? Allegra wondered. He was supposed to find out where Mr Pike drank and ply him for information. Together, she and Holt were going to blackmail Charlotte Caine, if they could. Allegra pushed her guilt down like clothing in an overstuffed duffel bag. She buckled her conscience closed.

Ivy and Verbena came into the kitchen. Verbena was wearing a pillbox hat with a heavy mesh veil. It was more suited to a funeral than a party but the burn on her face still looked very bad and the veil was the only way to hide it. Both women carried fur coats. It was still too warm for furs but they had elected to carry them to the party.

'I've had a coat stolen from the Lava Lounge before,' said Ivy, diffidently. 'They gave me back a moth-eaten old rag and I was too tight to notice until the next day. They absolutely refused to accept responsibility. I'm not sure it's safe to take furs there.'

'I definitely want to show mine off,' said Verbena. 'What's the point in having one otherwise?'

Charlotte didn't own a floor-length fur. She was tempted to hint to Liam that she would love one as a gift.

'We could take Allie along,' suggested Charlotte. 'She could watch the coats.'

Verbena laughed out loud.

'Take our maid to a première?' said Ivy.

'She can sit in the coat room. She wouldn't be with us.'

'I suppose she could,' said Verbena. 'Put on a fresh uniform, Allie, and be ready to leave in ten minutes.'

Allegra had been hoping for a night off; she was desperate to have Holt to herself for more than two minutes. She wanted to kiss him and make love to him in their secret place in the pool house. She dared to speak up. 'I was hoping to see Holt tonight.'

'You can see Holt any night,' said Verbena. 'Get ready.'

The actresses bundled out of the kitchen, leaving their furs for Allegra to collect and carry along.

'I'm sorry,' she said to Holt.

He saw the disappointment in her face. 'I need to go out tonight anyway,' he said. 'I'm meeting a man for a drink, remember?' He winked at her.

'Holt, be careful!' said Allegra. She touched his face, caressed the fretwork of his scars.

'Do I look like a man who can't handle himself?' he asked light-heartedly.

'I've met Teddy Pike, Holt. He's hard.'

'I've got back-up,' said Holt. He tapped his right trouser pocket where he'd recently replaced the pen-knife and then, inexplicably, he tapped the left one, too.

'Your Miss Charlotte's got pots of cash,' Holt whispered with finality. 'We just need a small piece of it to get away from here and start our restaurant.'

'She's moving soon.'

'Then time's running out,' said Holt. 'I have to find out what I can tonight. I've got to get at whatever she's trying to hide.'

'And what of Mr Pike?'

'Leave him to me,' said Holt. He kissed Allegra hurriedly once more and left.

When they arrived at the Pantages Theatre, the press and the public were waiting in a controlled clump behind velvet ropes.

Charlotte let Ivy and Verbena get out of the car first. She fussed with her dress. If she waited half a minute, she would have the red carpet and the limelight all to herself. Charlotte told Allegra to wait in the car with the driver until the screening was over. She waved as she stepped from the vehicle to the pop and zing of flashbulbs.

During the screening, Charlotte tried to locate Liam Malone in the theatre. She could not find him in the gloom. Perhaps he was seated behind her. She couldn't crane her neck and scour those seats, though. It would be too obvious. She would have to wait. The waiting was agony. When the picture was finished, the Warner Brothers players and their guests moved across the road to the Lava Lounge. Charlotte motioned to Allegra, who was sitting patiently in the back seat of the car. Allegra hurried over to deliver Ivy and Verbena's furs. The women put them on for the stroll along the sidewalk. Charlotte was carried along with the stream of the crowd and the constant press of reporters. She searched for Liam's face. Even Bernadette Malone would have been a welcome sight. Her presence would mean that Liam was there, but Charlotte did not see her, or the man she loved.

The entrance to the Lava Lounge sported a mahogany reception podium and acres of embossed pewter-coloured wallpaper.

Ivy and Verbena took off the furs they had donned less than five minutes before and handed them to the coat-check girl. She hung them up in a special room behind her station and issued each actress with a small gold claim token. Rupert, the maître d', noticed Allegra standing off to one side. 'Can I help you?' he asked sharply.

'She's here to watch our coats,' said Verbena.

'We have a coat girl, Miss Marsh,' said Rupert.

'I know that,' tinkled Verbena. 'But Ivy didn't think her rat-skin would be safe here. She claims her coat was switched on her the last time she visited.'

Rupert tsked-tsked behind his teeth. 'Never!' he declared.

'Oh, be a sweetheart,' said Verbena.

'Very well,' said Rupert, though he sounded distinctly put out. 'In here,' he said to Allegra, as he pushed her through the doorway into the narrow coat room. There were two fashion-house racks on wheels parked in the middle of the floor. They held dozens of coats and a few bare cedar hangers. 'Cashmere on the left and furs on the right,' said Rupert. 'Don't get it wrong. If the fabric ones get covered in fur, we'll have to pay for professional cleaning.'

When the door shut, Allegra could hear the distant music of a band through the walls. They were playing Irving Berlin's 'Puttin' On The Ritz'. There was a wooden stepstool resting against one wall and Allegra sat down on it. She was exhausted. She listened to the music and wished Holt was with her.

Charlotte opened the door and threw her coat at Allegra. 'Sneak out in a minute and watch us dance,' she said.

Allegra waited half an hour, then left the coat room and explored into the lobby. Rupert was nowhere to be seen. She hung back in the archway to the club's main lounge and took in the scene. An enormous fountain was the room's centrepiece. It spurted blue-coloured water. A hidden bubble machine in the basement pumped huge rainbow orbs through discreet grates in the floor. The bubbles soared and drifted by the hundred overhead where they caught the light of the blue chandeliers before they sank and popped on the ladies' naked shoulders. The band was dressed in white tails; their brass gleamed.

Near the centre of the room, Allegra saw Charlotte, besieged by admirers. With a champagne glass in one hand and a cigarette in the other, she dipped down to kiss podgy studio executives and heavy-jowled financiers.

As Allegra watched, Liam Malone walked up to Charlotte and kissed her cheek. He had his daughter, Agnes, with him. He held the little girl by the hand. Agnes was dressed up as a fairy in a gossamer costume with tulle wings on her back and a crown on her head. She held a wand of glittering rhinestones. Charlotte looked nonplussed at the child's presence. Allegra remembered how awkward her employer had been when they had met the little girl at the beach.

Allegra suddenly became aware of somebody standing beside her. Another woman was also using the huge potted ficus tree as a hiding place. Allegra recognized her as one of the photographers she had seen outside. There was a camera bag at the woman's feet and a Graflex slung around her neck. She offered Allegra a cigarette.

'I don't smoke, thank you.'

'You speak English,' said the woman. She stated it as a fact. It was not intended to be condescending.

'Yes, ma'am,' said Allegra.

'Good for you,' said the woman. 'It'll help you here in America. You'll do well with good English.' She held out her hand. 'I'm Dorothea. Dorothea Lange.' They shook like gentlemen and equals.

'Allegra del Rio.'

'Pretty,' said the woman.

Dorothea suddenly snapped Allegra's picture, then clamped her cigarette between her lips as she dug in her pocket for a pencil. She asked Allegra to spell her name as she wrote it down in a small notepad.

'You're a professional photographer, Miss Lange?' Allegra asked quietly.

'I'm trying to be,' said Dorothea. She spoke in a clipped,

matter-of-fact way. There was no nonsense about her. 'I'm not working officially tonight. I'm just a friend of an invited guest but I can't stop snapping. It's an addiction. At the moment, I have a government contract to document, in photographs, the appalling working conditions in this state. I'm working especially hard with our migrant labourers.'

Allegra wanted to tell Dorothea about her experiences in the fields, how Stationville had been burned, how Haywire had been shot, but the story seemed too long and too poignant to convey.

'I spend my days surrounded by the most desperate need, then get invited to something like this.' Dorothea dropped the ash from her cigarette on to the floor, condemning the whole place with the gesture. 'It's unbelievable. This morning I saw a child buried. He had starved to death. Starved in California where you can pick fruit from trees at the roadside! He had a teenage mother, an unfortunate. Her milk had dried up and she didn't realize it. She knew nothing. She was no more than a babe herself. I don't blame her.'

A waiter passed them, carrying a silver tray heaped with chilled lobster tails.

'Have you ever had your photograph taken before?' asked Dorothea.

'Of course,' said Allegra, then felt rude at her abruptness. This woman had spoken with her as an equal, an intelligent equal. 'I come from a good family, Miss Lange. Now I have to work as a maid but it was not always that way for me. I'm here to watch the coats for my employers. They are actresses.'

'Contract girls?' asked Dorothea.

'Yes. Actually, one of them is Charlotte Caine . . . Miss Carlie Caine.'

'I know the name. I hear she's going places.'

Something tugged at Allegra's skirt. It was Agnes. 'It's me!' said the little girl. 'And it's you!'

'Miss Agnes Malone,' said Allegra, as she knelt down to look the little girl in the eye.

'I'm Titania really,' Agnes confided.

'Queen of the fairies,' said Allegra. 'You're having a special night out with your papa?'

Agnes nodded excitedly. Dorothea Lange watched the interaction with interest.

'We're going to have a tree house in our elm,' announced Agnes. 'The boys are building it but my father's helping them.'

'That will be fun,' said Allegra.

Agnes nodded again. 'I baked a cake with my father this weekend,' she said. 'It was a chocolate one. What did you do?'

'I did some washing. I helped my friend plant an orange tree.'

Liam, who had apparently been looking for his daughter, strode up to them.

'It's Allegra from the beach!' Agnes told him.

'Ah, Miss Caine's maid,' Liam said. 'Of course, I remember.'

'Can I stay with her?' asked Agnes. 'Please!'

'Would you watch her for me, Allegra? I mean, only if you're here working in some capacity.'

'I'm watching the coats and waiting to go home,' said Allegra.

Liam pressed ten dollars into her hand. 'If she falls asleep, just lay her down somewhere and keep an eye on her.'

'I'm not tired,' said Agnes.

'Do as you please, then,' said Liam. 'But mind Allegra. She's in charge.' He turned to Allegra. 'Don't take any nonsense from this little miss.'

'No, sir,' said Allegra.

Agnes stuck out her tongue at the back of her father's retreating head. 'I'm not sleepy at all,' she announced.

Ten minutes later, Agnes fell asleep on Allegra's lap in the coat room – a flushed, dishevelled fairy with a scraped knee and a gap in her smile. Allegra didn't want to put the child down on the cold floor. She held the limp body in her arms, amazed at the acute angle at which Agnes could bend her neck without apparent pain. Allegra tried to get comfortable on the wooden step-stool and failed. She pressed her knees together with her ankles buckled out to the sides in an attempt to provide the sleeping child with a lap. Her arms were stiff and numb. She stared at the fur coats and longed for the guests to collect them so she could go home. Dorothea Lange came in and snapped a photograph before Allegra had time to sit up straight.

Dorothea smoked another cigarette and they listened to the sounds of the party together – glasses smashed, women squealed, men fell over, bellowing drunk, and ripped their tuxedos. Allegra and Dorothea remained quietly companionable for a further five minutes. There didn't seem to be any need to talk. The sounds told the story of the party as well as the photographs would.

'Did you get the pictures you needed?' whispered Allegra.

Dorothea nodded. 'Oh, I've captured the true spirit of the event,' she said.

Another hour passed and Dorothea said goodnight. Allegra tried to stay awake after that but failed.

Verbena stood dejectedly beside Madge St Claire and watched Ivy on the dance floor with Congressman Whitewood.

'Plenty of fish in the sea,' said Madge.

'I don't know what you mean,' said Verbena.

'Oh, Verbena darling. You don't have to lie to me. I lost somebody, too, you know. She married. Why do you think I always wear black? I'm in mourning for a beautiful girl.'

Verbena was too sad to deny it any more. Instead, she said, 'I thought you were just incurably unhappy.'

Madge laughed. 'Hold on to that deadly sense of humour, Verbena darling. You're going to need it.'

Verbena sipped gin from a tall glass. There was lots of lime zest in the tonic and it tasted delicious. She didn't even care that it stung the burned corner of her lip. She had polished off three of the drinks already, even though she knew gin made her melancholy.

Madge saw the burn up close when Verbena lifted her veil to drink. She had been told about the incident in great detail, of course, but she hadn't believed it was as bad as Verbena had made it out to be. Now she saw that the burn really was quite serious.

'God, that burn does not look good,' Madge said. 'Is it healing at all?'

'I don't want to talk about it,' said Verbena. 'Unless you're going to tell me I can sue Charlotte over it.'

'I'm not going to tell you that,' said Madge.

Verbena glared at her. 'I need to leave actually,' she said. 'I'm meeting somebody.'

'Really?' said Madge, knowingly.

'And the somebody is a man,' said Verbena. 'I need to see a man about something.'

'Well, I'll be up at the house tomorrow,' said Madge. 'I need to drop some cash off for Charlotte. Actually, it's for her father . . .'

Verbena didn't want to know anything more about Charlotte, or her pathetic father, or her relationship with the dreadful Mr Pike. Verbena had sent a messenger to the Magic Sevens Circus that morning. He had returned to tell her that Mr Pike would see her at midnight that night at the Soggy Dollar Bar. It wasn't the kind of place Verbena would ever willingly frequent but at least nobody there would know her. She simply wanted Mr Pike out of her life. Would he demand money from her? Verbena didn't know what to expect. She only knew she couldn't risk his displeasure – or whatever it was she had engendered in him – escalating beyond the mutilation of coyotes.

Allegra woke to see the anxious face of Liam Malone looking down at her. He was shaking her angrily. Before Allegra had the chance to realize that she was cold, that a weight was missing from her lap, Liam demanded, 'Where's my girl? Where's Agnes?'

Allegra looked dumbly around the room. It was late. Most of the coats were gone. There was no way Agnes was hiding among them unseen.

'She was asleep,' said Allegra. 'I fell asleep, too. I thought I would feel her if she moved . . .'

Liam didn't wait around for further explanations. He didn't waste time on reprimands or rage. He turned decisively and threw open the coat-room door, shouting his daughter's name as he went. Allegra stumbled to her feet. She followed in Liam's wake as he threw open the washroom door and scoured the interior. He checked under the maître d's stand and behind the foliage of the enormous ficus trees. Rupert was questioning Liam, trying to calm him down, uncertain as to the nature of the trouble. Liam ignored him. By the time Liam reached the open front doors of the Lava Lounge, Allegra was only a step behind him.

The street was still busy with cars taking weary partygoers home. Street lamps washed the night in acid yellow. Pink neon signs announced their messages in the window of a soda shop. Liam looked east then west, like a man contemplating the careful crossing of a street. Over the way from the Pantages Theatre there was a small urban park, half the size of a city block. Its trees were tall black spirits taking flight up to heaven in the dark. In the middle of the park there was a marble fountain. It gurgled cheerfully and there, sitting on its far rim with her feet in the water, was Agnes Malone. A large, squat man sat beside her. He held the little girl's patent-leather shoes in one of his beefy hands. Liam saw his daughter's red curls first. He shouted her name again, burst into the street, narrowly missing a taxicab that honked its affront. He bounced off its hood and kept running. He reached Agnes and whipped her up into his arms so violently that she shrieked in fright and started to cry. Agnes pressed her face against her father's chest as he soothed her with soft words.

When Liam pushed Agnes's hair back from her face, he saw no damage, only the fear he himself had caused by jerking her out of her quiet contemplation of the fountain. Liam Malone turned to the man, who seemed calm, unmoved. Liam experienced a rage he was not familiar with, something primeval and raw. He turned and passed Agnes to Allegra, who was the only person nearby. The maid redeemed herself by doing the smart thing and carrying the little girl back across the road and into the Lava Lounge. Now Liam was free to express himself without fear of terrifying his daughter further.

He wrenched the man up by his thick throat and threw him against the rim of the fountain. He might have snapped his spine and killed him instantly. 'Did you put your fucking hands on my daughter?'

The man raised both hands in the air as Liam forced him back until the bald bulge at the back of his head dipped into the water. Liam wanted to push him under and hold him there. It would be so easy.

'I never touched her. I never touched her.'

The man spoke with a Cockney accent and Liam suddenly thought he had seen him before. He had not liked the look of him then either.

'Who are you? I saw you at Miss Caine's house. You're with that maid of hers. You and that Allegra planned to take my child!'

'Allegra?' He sounded confused. 'No, I don't really know Allegra. A little girl walked out here and I sat with her, that's all.'

'Agnes wouldn't do that. She would never cross a street alone. We've taught her . . .'

'I was worried for her, all alone, a little mite like that. I thought I'd sit with her until her mummy or daddy came by for her. Now you have, and no harm's been done to nobody.'

Liam was confused. He had been drinking all night. He had been intoxicated by Charlotte's closeness on the dance floor. He wasn't equipped with the full faculties he needed to interrogate this man. Liam clutched at his pounding head, and the man took the opportunity to sit up and squirm off to the side. He kept his hands up in a position of surrender. Liam saw his white palms and the blue of his tattoos in the gloom.

Agnes was alive. She was unharmed. Liam should be joyful. Her dead body had passed so clearly through his mind during his few frantic minutes of searching. He had seen her laid out on a slab, all colour extinguished from her red hair, as if the light of her spirit had resided in her curls.

'I'm not one of them, Mr Malone. I'm not one of them that meddles with little girls. I'm very good with little girls, actually.'

Liam nearly flew at him then. He ought to crush this man now, before he did harm to some other man's family but what he said next stopped Liam completely.

'You ask my friend Miss Charlotte Caine about me. She'll tell you I'm a good friend to little lost girls.'

The realization that this odious man was claiming to know Charlotte threw Liam completely off-guard. He stepped back long enough for the man to take off down the road, running at a sprint Liam wouldn't have imagined possible. His coat-tails whipped out behind him for a few seconds, disturbing the night, then he was gone.

Liam tried to think. If what the man had said was true, Charlotte had lied to him. She had told him that the man was Allegra's friend. Whatever the truth of it, Liam wanted his daughter in her bed under his roof, and he wanted answers from Charlotte Caine. He walked back to the Lava Lounge.

'She's fine, Mr Malone,' said Allegra. 'I only closed my eyes for a moment. She's not even crying . . .'

Liam wasn't interested in this Mexican maid's excuses. Agnes did look fine and she said, 'He came in and got me from Allegra. We didn't want to wake her. He said there was a turtle in the fountain. I wanted to see the turtle. He took me to see it but I didn't see it. You came and got me before I saw the turtle!'

'You're fine, Aggie,' said Liam, as he clutched her. 'It's not your fault.'

Charlotte showed up in the foyer then, unaware of the drama that had unfolded in the preceding five minutes. 'I've been looking for you,' she told Liam.

She was disconcerted by the sight of Allegra, Agnes and Liam all standing together, solemn-faced. 'What's happened?' she asked Liam. 'Is everyone all right?'

'I could be asking you that, Charlotte,' he said. 'Who exactly is that man . . . that man you pretended not to know? And don't you try and lie to me again.' He was holding out his hand as he spoke, as if he wanted to slap her face with it.

'Pike was here?' Charlotte asked, in a whisper.

'He tried to take my daughter,' said Liam, with unmasked

rage. Whatever Charlotte was involved in, Liam knew it must never be allowed to touch his family again. He could never risk his daughter, he realized, with a flash of clarity. What was he doing anyway?

'I can explain it all,' said Charlotte. 'I didn't want to worry you . . .'

'He said he was a friend of yours.'

'He's not,' said Charlotte. 'Of course he's not.'

'Then call the police and have him dealt with.'

'I can't do that! Please trust me.'

'I can't trust you if you won't tell me what's wrong,' said Liam, sadly. 'And I won't have my family exposed to people like that.'

He bounced Agnes higher on his hip for comfort and turned to leave. 'I'm taking my baby home,' he said. 'But if I see that man again, ever, I will kill him. Right now I wish I'd done it five minutes ago when I had the chance.'

Charlotte tried to clasp Liam's jacket but he pulled away. 'Don't go, Liam! Please don't leave me,' she begged hysterically.

'Just tell me the truth! We can go somewhere quiet. Aggie will sleep in the car. We can talk. People make mistakes in life. Mistakes can be forgiven. You can tell me all of it now, Charlotte.' Liam leaned in to her and said, despite the proximity of his daughter, 'Don't you know I love you?'

It was Charlotte's chance. She could purge, tell Liam everything. He might decide to love her anyway, love her still. He might not. 'It's really nothing,' she said.

Liam looked up to the sky in exasperation. 'Beautiful Charlotte,' he said, and his voice was weighed down with pain, grief even. 'I can stand any ugly truth but I can't deal with these pretty lies you keep trying to sell me.'

Charlotte stumbled back at his rebuttal and dropped down drunkenly on the floor, showing her stocking tops. Allegra tried to get her to her feet – Charlotte's lipstick had smeared up one cheek to form a false smile at odds with the abject misery on her face. Liam might claim to love her, but Charlotte knew he could never sustain that love if she told him the truth. 'One day, I will explain everything . . .' she tried.

But Liam had already gone.

26

A couple necking on the banks of the Los Angeles River in Frogtown saw the body bobbing lazily in the shallows. It floated face down, its limbs tangled in tendrils of algae. The man mistook the shape for a discarded mannequin at first. Despite his girlfriend's protestations, he leaned out from the bank and poked the figure with a stick. It turned over in a slow, sludgy roll to reveal a face that was blue with bloat but which had once clearly belonged to a human man.

The couple scrambled backwards up the bank and ran to a nearby store to call the police. A uniformed officer with a name badge that read 'Pennington' arrived and explored the crime scene. The victim was fat with putrefaction. The water had distorted his body, turning it into a bloated bag of skin wrapped in a heavy coat. One personal attribute was immediately obvious, however. The man had been completely bald.

Two representatives of the detective division arrived twenty minutes later. The senior man's name was Isaac Bobdanovich, an unpopular whiner who was always sensing the onset of some unlikely illness. His junior was Aloysius Shaughnessy, a dim, muscle-bound, ginger-haired Irishman with no ambition.

When Officer Pennington saw the two detectives approach, he knew the case would never be solved. He doubted Bobdanovich and Shaughnessy would even put a name to the victim. They were the duo the Detective Division assigned to a case when nobody cared about it. They had been given this case because the dead man was obviously a shadow-walker, someone who loitered on the outskirts of society. Pennington dreaded the day the body of a businessman – or, God forbid, a rich white society girl – landed up in Bobdanovich and Shaughnessy's patch. Fortunately for them, Frogtown's victims were usually on the fringe. It was an unsavoury neighbourhood.

'You think he got washed out from the valley?' asked Pennington, trying to get the investigation started.

Bobdanovich nodded.

'He's been in the river a good few days,' volunteered Pennington. 'And it rained last night, so the water levels are high.'

Pennington knew he would make a better investigator than either of these two men. He ought to apply for a promotion, take the exam, but he couldn't keep the dream of being an actor – the next Liam Malone – out of his head.

'So, he must have fallen in upstream a few days ago. The current would have carried him all the way to Long Beach if the weeds hadn't hooked him.'

'You think this was an accident?' asked Bobdanovich. 'He just fell in?'

Bobdanovich parted the corpse's jacket. Beneath the coat, the victim's white shirt was soaked to his skin. The fabric provided an opaque window on the innumerable tattoos that ornamented his body. 'I reckon he's been done in,' said Bobdanovich.

'Maybe,' said Shaughnessy, reluctant to embark on a

homicide investigation when the paperwork required for a death by misadventure was far less onerous. 'It could still be an accident. A fall and subsequent drowning, something like that.'

Pennington drew their attention to a distinct bulge at the man's hip.

'What's that?' he asked.

Bobdanovich pulled out a thick tube of tightly rolled-up paper. It was a magazine.

'Just his reading material,' said Shaughnessy.

Bobdanovich tossed the magazine on to the weeds and fished out the corpse's wallet. He opened it. Because it had been folded tight, the few greenbacks it contained were barely wet. 'It wasn't a robbery,' said Bobdanovich. 'He's still got cash on him. No identification, though.'

The action of retrieving the wallet had given Pennington an idea. He carefully unfurled the magazine. As he suspected, its inner pages were dry, too. Pennington knew the issue. It was a copy of *American Woman's Weekly*. His wife had purchased it and told him it featured a great article on Carlie Caine caring for her father. The actress looked delicious in the pictures. Pennington felt a physical stirring. He carefully turned the pages, peeling the sheets apart, and noticed something. The autograph was clearly legible. Carlie Caine had written her name right across her own image.

'Look at this,' said Pennington. 'The guy met Carlie Caine. She signed the magazine.'

'Carlie Caine the actress?' asked Shaughnessy.

'Yeah,' said Pennington.

'She's some dame,' commented Bobdanovich.

'Looky here,' said Shaughnessy. He held up the corpse's

right arm to reveal the tattoo of Charlotte Caine. 'The guy was a real fan.'

'Think we got reason to pay her a visit?' asked Pennington.

'I sure do,' said Bobdanovich. He didn't really. It was just an excuse to visit a glamorous actress in her home. He didn't want to go but he could see that Pennington did. It was never a bad idea to have a blue owe you a favour.

'Well, I ain't going,' Shaughnessy declared. He thought all actresses were stuck-up bitches.

'I'll go, sir,' said Pennington.

'Don't get too excited, kid,' Bobdanovich said. 'It's a bar fight. I'm telling you that now.'

'We ought to get him identified, though, right?' Pennington said. 'Tell his family at least?'

Bobdanovich shrugged.

'He look like a circus man to you?' Shaughnessy suddenly asked. 'He's got a lot of tattoos. The work's definitely home-done. It's good, though.'

'Why don't you find out if the circus is in town?' Bobdanovich told Shaughnessy. 'Inform his family, if you can find them, but don't make any promises about bringing the culprit to justice. I'm telling you right now, we're never gonna solve this one.'

He stood up and turned to Pennington. 'So, Wonderboy, you gonna go question that gorgeous movie star for us or not?'

'Yes, sir,' said Pennington.

'Remember, you owe me one,' said Bobdanovich.

A reporter from the *Los Angeles Times* arrived in time to snap a few pictures of the body, the most gruesome of which appeared on page four of the publication the next day under the headline 'Nameless Corpse Surfaces in City Wash'.

Allegra saw the newspaper first. She glimpsed the grainy image of familiar tattoos over Ivy's shoulder as the actress sat at the kitchen table, nibbling a slice of toast and reading the society pages. At first, Allegra couldn't believe the evidence of her own eyes. The photograph clearly showed the corpse of Mr Pike. There was no mistaking that body of art. Allegra's heart went into double beats. What did this mean? How had Mr Pike died? What did it mean for Miss Charlotte, for Holt? What did it mean for their plans now that Mr Pike was dead?

Allegra's thoughts were jumbled and incoherent. She had to talk to Holt. When Ivy finished with the newspaper and left the kitchen, Allegra snatched the page up and went out to the edge of the deck. The stairs were not in place yet, so she scrambled down the hillside to the Peppers' camp. She was relieved to find Holt alone. Roscoe had taken Harmony back to their farm in the truck. The couple would return the next day with the last of the sanguinellos.

'Holt!' said Allegra, urgently.

He saw the distress in her face and leaned on his shovel. Allegra grabbed his hand and pulled him behind the canvas shelter where they couldn't be seen from the house.

'Look!' she said, flapping the newspaper under Holt's nose.

Holt tried to read the jiggling type but couldn't. He had never seen Allegra this frantic.

'He's dead!'

'Slow down, Allegra,' said Holt. He took the newspaper from her and looked at the article. His face changed subtly.

It hardened. A pulse flickered at the point of greatest tension on his jaw. 'Shit!' he said. He dropped the hand holding the newspaper to his side and began to pace. 'Oh, shit!' he said again, as he slammed the paper against his thigh.

'What does it mean? What happened, Holt?' Allegra asked.

'It means I'm done for. That's what it means.'

'Why?' asked Allegra. 'What did you do?'

'Nothing, I swear. I just met up with him. He drank at a bar out by where they got their circus set up. A bar near the river called the Soggy Dollar. We spoke. I bought the drinks. I got him talking about Miss Caine. I told him I knew the maid who worked for her. He knew your name. I told him you were at a première with her that night.'

So that was how Pike had located them at the Lava Lounge. Holt had given him their whereabouts. 'Did he tell you anything?'

'No. He was sharp, suspicious of me right off the bat. He didn't tell me anything. He never gave me a hint as to how he knew her. But, Allegra, that bar is right on the river. They've got a kind of deck that hangs out over the water.'

'So?'

'So, I was seen there drinking with him at this place and now his body is found in the river. I promise you this: he left. Then I left. I didn't see him again.'

'So?' asked Allegra again. 'Why are you so worried?'

'Police pin things on men like me.'

'You don't have a motive to hurt him. You didn't even know him.'

Holt scanned the paper again. 'Bar fight!' he said. 'Says right here the police suspect a bar fight.'

'But why would they suspect you? Mr Pike could have got into it with anyone.' The thundering in Allegra's chest slowed. She looked at the sky where two hawks duelled among the updraughts.

Suddenly Allegra remembered. 'He did get into it with someone! He came to the Lava Lounge and Mr Malone almost killed him for talking to his daughter. Mr Pike was alive and well at the Lava Lounge after he left you at this bar. You couldn't have been the one who hurt him.'

Allegra did not disclose the details of falling asleep and thereby allowing Agnes to fall into Mr Pike's hands. She was ashamed of herself for that.

'Mr Malone had more of a reason to kill him,' said Allegra. 'Mr Pike took his daughter.'

'Okay, okay,' said Holt. 'But who's more likely to get fingered? Me or some Hollywood dreamboat?'

'If you didn't do it . . .'

'I've done other things.' Holt stopped walking.

'Like what?' asked Allegra.

'Allegra, do you believe I want to be with you, to have our place together?'

'I do believe that,' said Allegra. 'But I have to know. What have you done?' She felt tears pricking the corners of her eyes. He was going to tell her something terrible and ruin everything.

'We'll talk tonight. I need time to think.'

'Could all this work out to be good for us?' asked Allegra, in a tiny voice. 'Miss Charlotte wouldn't want anybody to know she knew a man like that, would she? We could still go ahead with our plan, couldn't we?'

She was talking directly about blackmail now, not around

the subject but about it. Holt looked at his boots. He scuffed the dust.

'Isn't this what we wanted?' Holt didn't answer her. Allegra felt cold to her core but she reached out and squeezed his hand. 'Desperate times,' she said to Holt.

'Desperate measures,' he finished. 'Right now, get that paper back to the house and see what Miss Caine does when she reads it.'

'I don't think she reads the news.'

'Leave it out where she can't miss it, then. Watch her face when she first sees it. Because I think Miss Caine had more reason than anybody to want Pike dead.'

For an actress who ought to be able to disguise her emotions, Charlotte's reaction to the newspaper article was very revealing. She couldn't hide her shock. She picked up the paper and held it very close to her face then put it down. She took it into the living room, then came back into the kitchen with it and threw it in the garbage pail. When she finished her coffee, Charlotte threw the grounds from the bottom of her cup directly over the article. She looked up to see Allegra watching her. 'What's wrong with you?' Charlotte demanded.

Allegra went silently back to her work.

'You're always watching me,' she said angrily. 'Stop it!'

Charlotte sat down at the kitchen table. Pike was dead. He was dead! She tried to breathe evenly to calm herself. She swallowed and couldn't get her own saliva down. She went out on to the deck. Below her, Holt was already working. What was she going to do? Was there any way Liam could have been responsible for this? And why did

Allegra look so damned intent? Had the girl ever seen her with Pike? No, Charlotte was sure she hadn't. The first time Pike had visited, Allegra had been outside, cleaning the pool. They hadn't encountered one another. The second time, Pike had accosted her in the grocery store, then left. Allegra had been at the checkout and wouldn't have seen him that time either. The Lava Lounge! Pike had taken Agnes but Charlotte had been inside the whole time. No, Allegra had never seen the two of them together. Besides, Allegra was a simple girl from Mexico. She had a little breeding, perhaps, but she wasn't ever going to say a word to the authorities. These foreign girls were afraid of the police. Charlotte began to calm down. There was nothing to link her to the dead man. A happy thought suddenly presented itself. Pike was gone! She didn't have to give him any money! The two thousand dollars Madge was due to bring round that day could go towards her trip to Mexico with Liam. What had seemed like disaster was really good fortune. Pike was out of her life. She had her house! She had Liam – almost. Her father in his bed at the convent was sure to die soon. She was going to have it all.

Allegra came out on to the deck just then. Charlotte glared at her coldly. 'What?' she demanded.

'Mr Malone is on the telephone for you.'

Charlotte took the call in the entrance hall. It was the only line in the house – exposed to eavesdroppers, but there was no alternative. 'Liam,' she said delightedly.

'Have you seen today's *Times*?' he demanded. His voice was frantic.

'Yes,' said Charlotte.

'That man of yours is dead,' he hissed, in a whisper. He, too, was on an insecure line, it seemed.

'He's no man of mine,' said Charlotte, crossly.

'God, Charlotte! Do you know what this means? He's a filthy chicken-hawk I almost came to blows with on Saturday night and now he's dead!'

'Who saw you with him?' asked Charlotte.

'What do you mean? It happened. I wanted to kill him.'

'But you didn't,' said Charlotte. 'Did you?'

'Don't be stupid,' said Liam. 'The last time I saw him, he was running away like a whipped dog. But I'm attached to this mess because of you, because of some twisted secret relationship you have with this man but won't tell me about . . .'

'I will tell you,' said Charlotte. 'And it's nothing. You're making it bigger in your mind than it actually is.' Charlotte knew she would be able to come up with a lie for Liam, something bad enough to be believable but nowhere near as bad as the truth. She had plenty of time to get her story straight before she saw him again. 'Did anybody see you talking with him?' Charlotte asked.

'Agnes saw –'

'Agnes is a child,' interrupted Charlotte. 'She'll do as she's told.'

'And that bloody maid of yours . . .'

'Allie would never breathe a word.'

The line was quiet for a few seconds. When Liam spoke again his voice had calmed significantly. 'You're right,' he said. 'Charlotte, this is all too dangerous. First, there was you and me, and now this. If it got out, any of it, I'd be ruined.'

'I'll explain it all to you. Please meet me, Liam. Meet me tonight. I need to see you. I'll tell you everything . . .'

There was a pause on the line. When Liam spoke again, Charlotte heard the need in his voice, too.

'Where?'

'A nice quiet hotel. You check in and I'll meet you there.'

'Nine o'clock tonight. The Palm Gardens Inn off Beverly Glen.'

'Yes,' said Charlotte. 'I'll be there. And what about the weekend? Can you steal away for a few nights?'

'This weekend?' Liam sounded unsure. 'I could try. Bernadette thinks I'm shooting but it's been cancelled at the last minute. I haven't had the chance to tell her that yet.'

'Don't tell her, then. Come to dinner next Friday night at my house. Allie's going to cook us a special Mexican dish and then we're going on a surprise escape. Liam . . . that man – he was a bad man and some other bad man finally did him in. That's all. He's gone. We're safe.'

'I hope you're right.' Liam let out a strained breath. Part of him wanted to run away from Charlotte and feel safe again. He would count his blessings and thank his God that he had not been caught out as a philanderer. Another part of him desperately wanted to be with Charlotte. He wanted to see her, kiss her, taste her one last time. Would there ever be a last time? Would he ever not want to make love to her?

There was a knock at the front door. Allegra passed Charlotte in the hall on her way to greet the visitor.

'This thing with the tattooed man better be over, though,' threatened Liam. 'I mean it, Charlotte.'

'It is over,' promised Charlotte. 'Liam, it's going to be

fine. It's going to be beautiful. I have to go now. We have a guest.'

Allegra opened the door and stepped aside to reveal a policeman.

Charlotte hung up the phone. Her head wanted to explode. She was simultaneously filled with joy at the idea of seeing Liam that night and the terror of seeing a uniformed officer on her doorstep.

'I'm Officer Pennington from the Los Angeles Police Department,' the man said. 'I need to ask Miss Caine a few questions.'

They went into the living room and sat down. Charlotte requested tea; the officer wanted coffee. Allegra was loath to leave the room but there was no legitimate reason for her to stay. She was afraid she might miss a crucial titbit. Her mind tripped and stumbled. What should she say if the police officer questioned her? She needed Holt's help with this. She didn't want to volunteer the wrong information and blow their chances, their dream.

Charlotte assumed the role of a society lady. 'How can I help the police, Officer Pennington?'

'I'm making general enquiries about a suspicious death.'

Charlotte's face froze in surprise. Her pretty mouth made an O. 'A death!' she exclaimed theatrically. 'Whose death? I don't know any dead people.'

Pennington handed her that day's newspaper. It was his only photograph of the victim. The pictures taken by the coroner at the mortuary had not yet been developed. 'Do you know this man?' Pennington asked.

Charlotte took the newspaper from his hand and studied it for a long time. She had decided to deny everything, but two questions had to be answered: who had killed Teddy Pike and how had the police connected his death to her?

'I don't know any people who look like this,' Charlotte answered. 'Why have you come to me?'

'It's silly, really,' said Pennington. He felt hot and he stuttered when he spoke. The lady certainly was easy on the eye. He would try to get her autograph before he left . . .'The dead man had a magazine on him with your autograph in it.'

Charlotte wanted to laugh out loud. That was all! They had found the magazine she had signed for Pike on the day he had first confronted her at the house. Her gaze was guileless and assured. 'I sign thousands of autographs, Officer Pennington.'

'I guess so,' said the officer. 'You don't remember this man, though? He's pretty hard to forget with all that ink.'

Charlotte shook her head. 'It's possible I signed the magazine for somebody else and they gave it to him. I don't recall this man in particular. I'm sorry.'

'He had your face tattooed on his arm,' said Pennington.

'Oh,' said Charlotte. 'That's rather an unappealing thought.'

Allegra came in with a tray.

'Lovely!' said Pennington, as he took his cup of coffee from it.

Charlotte hoped the coffee was cool. She wanted the man to drink it and go. Instead, Pennington turned unexpectedly to Allegra. 'I don't suppose you know this man?' he asked.

Charlotte had dreaded this moment. Would Allegra mention that Pike had taken Agnes from her at the Lava

Lounge? Allegra looked her directly in the eyes and Charlotte saw something cold and hate-filled there. Something she had never seen in Allegra before.

'No,' said Allegra. 'I don't know this man.'

Charlotte felt something twist up inside her when she ought to feel relief. Why had Allie lied for her? Was it simply to keep her job?

'Well, it was a tenuous lead at best,' said Pennington.

'I'm sorry I couldn't be of more help,' said Charlotte. She stood up.

Pennington had only enjoyed one sip of his coffee but he was clearly being excused. He put the cup down regretfully and stood up. Miss Caine was a busy lady, he supposed. He didn't need to take up any more of her time.

Before he could leave, however, somebody else arrived. Allegra responded to the knock and opened the front door to Madge St Claire, who was holding a cloth bag with the logo of the Western Federal Bank on it. 'Oh, God, Carlie. Why are the police here?'

'Some poor deceased unfortunate had my autograph on him. It's just routine . . .' She was trying to push Pennington graciously out of the door.

'What dead unfortunate?' asked Madge.

'It's really nothing, Madge. He was a derelict, I suppose. He was probably going to sell my autograph. I don't remember him – I don't even remember signing it.'

'So my work here is done,' said Pennington.

'Well, you shouldn't be questioning my client, officer,' said Madge, in a punitive tone.

'Leave it, Madge,' said Charlotte. 'The officer was just going.'

'I mean, there are undesirables running rampant all over the county,' said Madge. 'By God, Carlie's got a bunch of them living on her doorstep. Take a look for yourself.'

Madge ushered Pennington into the kitchen and out on to the deck. Allegra went along with them. Holt stopped working at their sudden appearance behind the railing. He shielded his eyes with his hand to stare back up at them.

'One look at that fellow's face tells you he knows his way around a knife.'

Allegra was outraged. She wanted to slap Madge. How could she throw Holt to them as a suspect like that?

'Mr Holt is in Miss Caine's employ,' said Allegra. 'He's not a vagrant.'

She wasn't going to stand quietly by and see Holt labelled a criminal.

Pennington seemed really interested in her for the first time. 'I didn't get your name . . .'

'That's our maid, Allie,' interjected Charlotte. 'Mr Holt is her beau. She's naturally protective of him.'

Madge threw her hands up. 'Now you're allowing the help to carry on together!' said Madge. 'Honestly, there's no hope for you.'

'Oh, Madge,' said Charlotte. 'They have the right to be in love.'

'But it is true that the man is working for you?' Pennington asked her.

Allegra sensed in the officer a degree of sympathy for the labouring man.

'He's my gardener,' said Charlotte. 'He's planting some trees and building a flight of stairs down the hillside for me.'

Holt, who couldn't hear their conversation, had gone back to digging.

'Well, he's working like a coal-miner,' said Pennington.

'He's fine,' said Charlotte. 'I've never had a moment's trouble from him. Allie,' she announced with finality, 'show Officer Pennington out.'

Allegra walked Pennington to his car.

'Is it true what Miss Caine said?' Pennington asked her. 'You're sweet on that Mr Holt fellow?'

'We're in love,' said Allegra, simply.

Pennington stuck out his lower lip and nodded his understanding. 'Those are interesting scars he's got.'

'A horse threw him through a fence wire.'

'Oh,' said Pennington, with apparent relief. 'That explains it. I was concerned for a moment because I've only seen marks like that once before. They're pretty distinctive. You see . . .' Pennington plucked a long slender stem of grass from the flower bed and checked its flexibility. 'Imagine this is a wire,' he said. 'A long, fine, strong bit of wire.' He moved behind Allegra. 'May I demonstrate?' he asked. He placed his hands on either side of her head and tightened the grass stalk around her neck. 'This is what we call a garrotte.' He spoke conversationally as he tightened the stalk to breaking point. 'It can be a bit of strong twine or a piano cord, almost anything slim and flexible enough, but a good bit of wire is best. You attach some wood to each end. That way you can get a good grip on it. If the victim is quick on his feet and street-smart, he'll get his fingers in behind the wire before it closes too tight. He'll struggle to free himself . . .'

Pennington loosened the stalk and pulled it further up

Allegra's face till it fell between her lips like a bit in a horse's mouth. 'Sometimes the victim will get the garrotte up this far in his struggle, but then it gets caught right between the teeth and, as it's tightened, it cuts through the flesh of the cheeks and tears the skin right back to the jawbone.'

Allegra appreciated that this was exactly how such wounds might be caused. She thought of how she had found the pieces of wood and the wire in Holt's pockets when they had made love in the pool house.

'It's a nasty little weapon,' said Pennington. 'But deadly effective.'

He threw the stem back into the flower bed and got into his car.

'Most victims don't survive that sort of sneak-up attack. But your friend got his scars in a . . .What did you say? A horse-riding mishap, was it?'

Pennington left Allegra standing in the drive, processing what he had told her. He had completed his part of this pointless investigation. The case of the tattooed man was going into the unsolved files as soon as he got back to the station. If Bobdanovich and Shaughnessy wanted to bother discovering the ugly bastard's name, they could go ahead and do it without his help. Pennington was done with it. On top of everything, he had forgotten to ask for Carlie Caine's autograph.

Inside the house, Madge had slumped into the sofa.

'Why wouldn't you let him leave, Madge? My God, you kept on and on at him . . .'

'Well, excuse me,' said Madge. 'I came all the way up here to bring you your money.'

'Oh,' said Charlotte. She didn't want to cause suspicion by not taking the cash after begging for it. She reached out and accepted the bag. 'Thank you, Madge.'

Verbena came into the room. She was moving in a trance. Her eyes were shadowed with dark rings. She still wore her nightgown. 'What's been going on?' she asked.

'Nothing,' said Charlotte.

Verbena turned to go. She was dragging her feet. Charlotte thought she had seemed almost sprightly during the preceding few days. She had believed Verbena was finally bouncing back after her low period. She also thought the burn looked a little better this morning.

'She is awfully blue, isn't she?' commented Madge.

'She's so changeable,' said Charlotte. 'I just avoid her, these days.'

'Now, Charlotte,' said Madge, moving to the edge of the sofa to underline her seriousness. 'That money is a loan. You'll have to repay every dime when your completion payment comes through. I've had to move cash from other clients' accounts to accommodate you. I hope you won't make a habit of this. I just thought that since it was for your father, I'd do my best to help.'

'I understand perfectly,' said Charlotte.

She couldn't tell Madge, or indeed anybody, that the man in the bed at the Convent of the Sisters of Mercy was not her father.

27

The invalid living at the Convent of the Sisters of Mercy, the man Charlotte Caine visited regularly, was not Patrick Caine. The real Patrick Caine had been killed in a fire in the University of Miami kitchens one Thanksgiving Day.

Witnesses said he was drunk. He had caught his sleeve on the open flame of a gas stove. It could have happened to anybody, the ensuing report said, but Patrick Caine had been carrying a bottle of cheap rum in his breast pocket. It had burst and the liquor had fuelled the flames. Patrick had run shrieking from the kitchen, a howling human torch. He was a fast runner and nobody could catch him. He eventually collapsed near the administration buildings where his charred body left a black mark on the lawn. By the time two undergraduates had smothered the flames with their sweaters, Patrick Caine's face was unrecognizable. They had covered his body for the sake of dignity but students claimed they could smell the stench of cooked flesh for days afterwards.

The dining-hall kitchen had been blue with policemen by the time Charlotte arrived to travel home with her father that night. She had nine dollars in her pocket from her detour to the park, and she thought the police cars were there to carry her off to jail.

'Is this his daughter?' one of the officers asked.

A scullery boy nodded and stepped back so he didn't have to look at Charlotte when they told her the news.

'Is your father Paddy . . . Patrick Caine?'

'Yes,' said Charlotte. 'He works here. I've just come from school.'

'Awfully late to be getting in from school, isn't it?' asked the officer.

'She does her homework in the library till his shift is over.' It was Archie. He had stepped forward to save her.

'Uncle Archie,' Charlotte said. She had added the 'uncle' for effect. 'What's happened?'

'Your dad's had an accident, Charlotte.' Archie moved closer and put his arm around her waist. 'It's a terrible, terrible thing. He's dead, baby girl.'

'Are you an uncle by blood?' asked the officer.

'Her mother's brother,' said Archie.

It was a lie, of course, but Charlotte didn't interject. She had no idea how to find her mother. She didn't want to go to jail with the policeman or to a reform school, or an orphanage, or wherever the authorities might take lost girls.

The policeman had been relieved. It was Thanksgiving, after all, and he didn't want to spend his evening driving round looking for a facility with a safe bed for this girl. The uncle would get her home to her family. 'Have your mother stop by and pick up the death certificate from the coroner,' said the policeman.

'I'll break the news to my sister, officer,' said Archie. 'I'll do all the necessaries. Take the burden off her.'

'Good man,' said the officer, as he officially handed Charlotte into Archie's care.

They had walked out of the cafeteria together. Archie's hand never left its harbour above Charlotte's hipbone. The policeman put his hat back on his head and glanced across the grounds to where three medics were lifting the body bag on to a stretcher. It was a long way to run on fire, he thought. An ambulance rolled across the lawn to collect the stretcher, leaving deep tyre marks in the virgin grass. Even from that far away, Charlotte had seen the black patch left by her father's immolation. He must have burned and burned.

Charlotte laid her head against Archie's chest in appreciation. She had never been so afraid before.

'Don't you worry, baby girl,' Archie had said. 'I'll do right by you.'

And she'd replied, 'Okay.' Not believing him for a second.

Charlotte and Archie had never spoken about the mutual lie that had initiated their relationship. Their decision to move forward together had never been verbalized. It had just happened. Sometimes, when she was very angry with him, Charlotte wondered if Archie had only been waiting for his chance to be alone with her so that he could take advantage. Once or twice, she had even thought he must have seen her father's death as fortuitous, a vicious twist of fate in his favour.

Together, Archie and Charlotte had collected her few belongings from Miss Orteig's boarding house. They didn't mention her father's death to the old spinster. Archie had stayed at the University of Miami just long enough to collect one last pay cheque. Then they had taken a train across the width of Florida to the Gulf coast. By the time they saw the water again, they were different people.

Charlotte and Archie slept in separate beds for the first week of their acquaintance, and then, one night, unprompted, Charlotte had slipped in beside him. From then on, they had slept together. The warmth they shared was not entirely venal. Though he managed it sometimes, drink had long ago made the act of love a challenge for Archie. He intended to use Charlotte in a more novel way.

Once, Charlotte had calculated their age difference as twenty-one years, though she couldn't be sure Archie had given her his real date of birth. He had assumed Patrick Caine's name and sometimes used that man's birth certificate – which Charlotte had found among her father's papers – as identification when he registered for jobs or signed on for relief.

Archie sold Charlotte's father's good watch and anything else of value that had once belonged to the real Patrick Caine. He moved Charlotte into a squalid room but he took her shopping in the best boutiques. Archie had formulated a strategy. He spent what money he had on finery for Charlotte. She had always known what was beautiful, like the perfume and the fox-fur suit. She had exceptional taste in clothing. Archie made do with one very good suit and one that could pass at night.

When he felt Charlotte was ready, Archie took two rooms in the finest hotel Fort Myers had to offer. They reserved a table in the middle of the dining room and waited. Archie said a man, the right kind of mark, would eventually notice her. Charlotte understood her part but she was sceptical about the likelihood of success.

Archie was right, though. It happened on the second night. Charlotte felt the eyes of one particular man on her. At first, she was coy. Archie was her father in the scenario they had planned. Charlotte laughed at Archie's jokes, ate prettily, and grew giggly on a single glass of sherry. The following night, she let her eyes meet the man's as he dined alone at his nearby table. During the evening, Charlotte's looks grew more brazen. The following afternoon, the man sat two chairs away from her in the parlour as she listened to a string quartet. In the buffet line at dinner, the man asked her to meet him behind the swimming-pool pump house later that evening.

On that first occasion, Archie's calculations had been perfect. He had arrived just as the man was unbuttoning Charlotte's blouse. Archie began a tirade of abuse. He accused the man of attempting to deflower his daisy-fresh daughter. The man was a chicken-hawk and a degenerate! Archie intended to inform hotel management – and the police – of the man's debauched behaviour. The man paid up, of course. He had to avoid the scandal at any cost.

The game worked every time, in every hotel. Now and again, Archie showed up on the scene too late and Charlotte was forced to follow through with the deed. Once, Archie had stayed in the bar and the man had hurt her badly for more than an hour before leaving her sobbing at the base of a tattered palm tree. Charlotte had fled to their room in her torn dress to find Archie passed out on the bed in his second-best suit.

Once, Charlotte thought she might be expecting a baby but the next man had been very rough. He had brought her bleeding on and it was over. She never shared these details with Archie. Sometimes, for comfort, she would reach out and hold his hand across the dinner table when they were between marks. Charlotte liked it most when the linen was snowy and the crystal gleamed, and Archie would whisper lyrics to her as the orchestra played:

What'll I do
When you are far away
And I am blue?
What'll I do?

When I'm alone
With only dreams of you
That won't come true.
What'll I do?

Charlotte and Archie had spotted Howard Warner on their last night in the Biltmore Hotel. They were back in Coral Gables again, only a short walk from where her father had died. They had moved restlessly across Florida for years, working the big hotels then the smaller ones, running out of marks and money. They were broke and had planned to check out the next morning, when Archie noticed Howard entertaining two women with brash anecdotes at the pool bar. Charlotte had been wrapped in a gauzy beach robe and Archie had pulled it gently from her shoulders. He had told her to go buy herself a drink.

Howard Warner had watched Charlotte cross the deck towards him, her long perfect body snaking between the statues of various Greek gods that edged the pool. She removed her sunglasses when she reached the shade of the bar, and ordered a Cosmopolitan. Charlotte hated the taste of the drink but the glass looked good in her hand, the red liquid against her lips a promise of sinful things to come.

She made eye contact with Howard who reached out his hand immediately. The other two women slunk away: they knew when they were topped.

'Howard Warner,' he said.

Charlotte pouted the way Archie had taught her. 'Charlotte,' she said.

'You ought to be in pictures, Miss Charlotte.'

They both laughed at the hackneyed phrase.

'So they keep telling me,' Charlotte said.

'But they can't make it happen,' he said. 'And I can.'

'I suppose you're a movie palace mogul, Mr Warner? Or a talent scout?'

'I'm a Warner, like I said.' He paused. 'I'm one of *the* Warners.'

'You're one of the Warner brothers?' Charlotte said, wide-eyed, but cynical.

It was so tricky a lie to authenticate that Charlotte thought the man must be telling the truth. Either that or he was very new to the game of deception. Had she run into another, less astute Archie? Was this man also conning the bored, wealthy folks at the Biltmore that summer?

'I'm their cousin, actually, but I work with them all the time. I sometimes draw their attention to exceptional opportunities.'

'Do I look like an exceptional opportunity to you?' Charlotte fluttered her eyelids.

'Exceptionally exceptional,' Howard said.

Charlotte smiled and sipped her drink. The alcohol rushed to her temples and into her eyes, making her vision wobbly. 'My father agrees with you,' she said, tossing her head in the direction of her sun chair, where Archie was pretending to read a newspaper. Howard looked over at him. 'Are you on vacation, Miss Charlotte?'

'No, my father's a very important engineer.' Just so this man knew she was protected. She was not simply another hussy working the pool bar alone. 'He's consulting on a bridge they're building in the Keys. That's his thing – bridges.'

'How fascinating!' said Howard. He felt the need to impress this sensational girl. 'Did you know that Johnny Weissmuller broke a record in this very pool in the late twenties? He worked as a lifeguard here, doing swimming demonstrations for the guests after he won his Olympic medals.'

'Did he?' said Charlotte.

'Nice man, Weissmuller.'

'I suppose you know him well,' said Charlotte.

'I sure do,' said Howard. 'Of course, MGM make the Tarzan pictures, but we mix in the same circles. Weissmuller was on the verge of bankruptcy when they offered him that part. Olympic swimming isn't a very lucrative career but motion pictures made him rich again. That's their power – they can take an ordinary person and turn them into a hero.'

'Just imagine what they could do with an exceptional person,' said Charlotte.

She knew she had played the conversation perfectly. She picked up her half-empty glass by its stem and walked slowly away. She felt Howard Warner's eyes watch her go. Perhaps one last lure? 'Do you eat dinner, Mr Warner?' Charlotte discarded the question over her shoulder.

'I do,' he said.

'So do I,' said Charlotte, casually, and she continued back to her chair.

'Who is he?' asked Archie, without looking at her. He kept pretending to read, as if he hadn't noticed their conversation.

'Some film baron, or pretending to be,' explained Charlotte. 'He'll be looking for me in the restaurant later.'

'Good girl,' said Archie.

He took the glass away from Charlotte and drained it.

Apparently, bedding Charlotte Caine was not Howard Warner's primary objective. It was better than that. He wanted to discover her. It was becoming fashionable for young actresses to be 'discovered' by talent scouts and whisked away to stardom. It made a great story for the papers. Archie realized quickly that Howard Warner was genuinely interested in getting Charlotte to California. Howard had come up to their table and shaken hands with Archie. He had produced a business card, and immediately opened negotiations for Charlotte's screen test. Charlotte sat quietly by until Archie smiled at her.

'Is this something you might like to do, baby girl?'

'I might like to try, Daddy,' Charlotte said. 'I think I'd make a great actress!'

The secret message in the words passed between Archie and Charlotte in the intimate way she loved. They were both natural-born players.

'Nothing's too good for my baby girl,' said Archie. 'Though I couldn't possibly expect you to chaperone her all the way to Los Angeles, Mr Warner.'

I don't trust you with my daughter. That was what Archie was actually saying. *You're mad if you think I'm letting her out of my sight. Not yet, anyway. Let me get to know you better, and I might let you at her.* Both men understood the deal.

'If only her dear mother was still alive . . .'

'Is there any way you could make a quick trip out west, Mr Caine?'

'I'm a busy man, sir,' said Archie. 'I have no time for wild goose chases.'

'What if I could guarantee her a part?'

'I might steal away for a few days for that. I could get Charlotte settled into a suitable place. What do you say, baby girl? Would you enjoy a couple of months in sunny California?' Archie turned again to Howard Warner. 'My Charlotte's looking to her future, Mr Warner. She's too headstrong for marriage . . .'

'I haven't met the right man yet, Daddy.' Charlotte sounded wounded. 'You know that.'

'There are lots of eligible men with fine credentials and solid bank accounts out west,' said Howard.

'Let me make a few calls,' said Archie.

That night he booked a call to the west coast and took it in their room. Charlotte knelt on the bed at his feet, willing herself not to be too disappointed if their investigation exposed the man who called himself Howard Warner as a fraudster. Archie reached Jack Warner, who acknowledged his cousin's legitimacy with some reservation. Jack backed Howard, though, and agreed to 'take a look' at Charlotte. There were no guarantees, Archie could hear that, but they were broke and it seemed like an opportunity. Archie hung up the telephone and rolled Charlotte over in the bed, his weight pressing down on her.

'I think you're going to be a star, baby girl,' he said.

There had been no money for train tickets. They had packed Charlotte's best clothes into her biggest trunk and skipped out on their bill at the Biltmore Hotel as soon as Howard Warner had checked out. They had enough money for a taxi to the nearest shunting yard, then Archie had shuttled Charlotte's trunk of clothes from boxcar to boxcar on his back. It was a wretched, exhausting journey that took the better part of a week. Charlotte was frantic with worry that Howard Warner would go off the boil, forget her, grow tired of waiting, have too much time to reconsider his decision.

'You've got him hooked, baby girl,' Archie assured her. 'You've got that big fish on the line. He ain't going nowhere.'

Charlotte wanted to arrive in California looking her best. That proved difficult. She washed in station washrooms, never able to bathe properly. She needed hot tongs to curl her hair. Instead, she slept with it in rags, nestled in the crook of Archie's shoulder against a pile of baggage or mail sacks and, once, a lumpy pile of potatoes from some Midwestern farm town.

Archie always tried for an empty boxcar, or one with a mother huddled inside surrounded by a clutch of barefoot children. In the boxcars, people behaved as they did in elevators – they ignored one another. They didn't speak. They viewed with distrust each new traveller who jumped aboard. Archie guarded Charlotte like a treasure. His eyes flashed from side to side with suspicion all the way to Utah.

Outside Carson City, two new men jumped aboard. They wore silver-studded belts and silver boot buckles, like most of the drifters who hailed from silver country. Twenty minutes later, near Lake Tahoe, a third man hopped into their car. He was small and mean-looking, a compaction of sinew and violence. He had a deck of cards with him.

The moment Charlotte saw that deck, her heart sank slowly into her stomach, like a rock settling to a riverbed through deep water. She experienced a premonition of a catastrophe that could not be avoided.

At first, Archie ignored the men, who started up a game of poker by lantern-light. They passed around a dented hip flask. Charlotte felt Archie tremble beside her; his body ached for the cards and for the whiskey. He twisted. He couldn't get comfortable, but Charlotte wouldn't release his arm from around her no matter how hard he wriggled. Eventually, he wrenched free by force and Charlotte knew she had lost the struggle. Thank God there was no money to wager. Archie might lose Charlotte's mother-of-pearl hairbrushes, but what use would these men have for those vanities? There were some pieces of paste jewellery in Charlotte's trunk. They might want her perfume or her suit with the fox-fur collar for one of their cheap girlfriends. Charlotte would fight to the death for those. What else could Archie barter? Charlotte felt she knew.

Archie whispered quietly to the three men, who looked surreptitiously at her. Archie did not. He could not meet her eyes. Charlotte began to take the rags from her hair and twiddle each curl into shape. She did it with a kind of exhausted resignation. The dealer dealt the cards.

Archie won for a while. For several hours, he held his own. When the hip flask was empty, one of the men produced a full bottle of rye from his bundle. Charlotte slept. Perhaps, for once, Archie would quit while he was ahead. If he made enough for a hotel room, Charlotte might be able to bathe and wash her hair before she met Howard Warner again.

She woke to one of the men shaking her. He was skinny but very strong, one of the two with the silver-embellished belts. Charlotte saw that his buckle was in the shape of a curled snake.

'Wakey, wakey, Sleeping Beauty,' the man said.

Charlotte rolled on to her back and sat up.

'I'm the winner!' he declared. 'Bet it's been a while since you've been with a winner.'

Charlotte looked at Archie. He was hunched down in the corner, rocking on his boot heels. She brushed some straw from her skirt and stood up. Perhaps the man would let her lead him behind the packing crates. Else the other men would be able to watch, and Charlotte was damned if she'd give them that satisfaction. Quite without warning, the man slapped her face hard. The slap, when she had been completely acquiescent, stunned her. Charlotte realized in a flash that this was part of what the man needed from her. The eager, hateful look in his eyes told her that. She didn't expect much help from Archie but she was afraid of her face being marked for her meeting with Howard Warner. Charlotte backed away from the man and raised an admonishing finger at him. 'Not like that,' she said.

The man slapped her again. Archie got to his feet and stumbled across the boards of the boxcar like a doped steer. His hands were outstretched to strangle. Archie never reached the man who had assaulted Charlotte. One of the other two smashed the empty rye bottle against his skull and he went down. The man leaned over Archie, who was holding the back of his head with both hands, and stuck the jagged end of the bottle into his face, moving it back and forward like a carpenter turning a screw.

Archie bellowed and flipped over. The three men kicked at him in turn. They were working as a team. Even though they had boarded the train separately, Charlotte now understood that all three of them knew each other; they preyed in a pack. When Archie stopped responding to the beating, the men lost interest in him. The small one, the one who had jumped aboard last and alone, ran his fingers over Archie's body, like a man taking advantage of a sleeping woman. He nimbly turned out Archie's pockets and felt along his seams for hidden swag. He discovered a few coins and took Archie's watch off his wrist.

Charlotte knew her body was next for those nimble fingers. The small man looked up at her. He was all in shadows but his hands came forward into the light. They held something – a slim coil of wire stretched between two wooden dowels. He pulled the wire apart to show it to her. It gleamed, as honed as a silver razor's edge in the gloom.

One of the silver-buckled men looked out through a gap in the boxcar door.

'Shit!' he said. 'Bulls!'

Charlotte hadn't noticed the train slowing. The three men jumped clear of the boxcar in a scramble of limbs. Station bulls – transport policemen issued with truncheons – leaped aboard. They were assigned to clear out any freeloading undesirables before the train reached its station. Down on the tracks, Charlotte saw one of the bulls grab her fleeing assailant. The small man landed a punch in the uniformed guard's throat, pulled free from his grasp, and climbed a fence into the yard of a house that bordered the line.

Charlotte had rushed to Archie's side. His wounds were terrible. She tried to help him. The train had entered the station by then and had all but come to a stop. Charlotte had slipped down on to the platform, directly into the arms of a nun wearing the traditional habit. The nun had helped her with soothing words and a nurse's calm, practical response to an emergency. Charlotte's saviour had introduced herself as Sister Olivia and she had seen to it that Archie was transported to the Convent of the Sisters of Mercy. She had assured Charlotte that he would be cared for there. She had allowed Charlotte the use of the telephone in her office. Charlotte had found Howard Warner's card in her luggage and placed a call to him, explaining that her father had been attacked. Since Howard knew Archie Welch as her father, Charlotte was forced to continue the charade. Howard Warner was shocked for her. He honoured his promise of a screen test and she was signed up as a contract player. She earned herself a minor part in Warner Brothers' next picture.

In fact, Charlotte's father's unfortunate beating might have won her more sympathy from Howard and Jack Warner than she would ordinarily have received. His condition might have helped her career. Nobody was insensitive enough to question how the attack had occurred. Nobody had discovered they had travelled as stowaways in a freight car. Howard assumed they had been the victims of desperadoes who had jumped aboard the train to rob the first-class passengers in true Wild West tradition. Mr Caine had undoubtedly put up a struggle and paid the price. Eventually, when Mr Caine passed away, any questions surrounding him and his accident would be buried for ever.

Sister Olivia believed Charlotte's story. Everyone at the Warner Brothers studio believed Charlotte's story. It had become the back story of Charlotte's life, and it would have stayed that way, everything would have worked out perfectly, if not for two unconnected but equally devastating attributes of the two people Charlotte hated most: Teddy Pike's long memory and Verbena Marsh's unrelenting spite.

28

Charlotte considered Pike and Verbena as she lay in Liam's arms on the hotel-room comforter. Pike and Verbena's worlds would never have connected if not for her. Their incongruent lifelines would never have crossed. Fate was so unknowable and so cruel. But Fate could be benevolent, too, Charlotte thought. At that moment she was in Liam Malone's arms. They were stretched out side by side, fully clothed, holding each other. They hadn't bothered to pull back the bed sheets. For the first time since they had initiated their affair in Malibu, they were alone together without making love. Liam had come through the hotel-room door angry, prepared to interrogate, and seen her waiting for him. Charlotte had been ready to face his anger. Her eyes had been filled with tears when he arrived. She had never seemed more like an innocent girl than she did at that moment, and Liam had softened to his core, infused with love for her. He had kissed Charlotte until her lips were sore, holding her face in both his hands, devouring her. He could taste his own tears mingled with hers as they kissed and he had thought, without embarrassment, that he was crying with the happiness of loving someone so completely. The kissing had slowed. They were both exhausted by the intensity of it. Eventually, without words, they had lain down together, tangled up in each other's limbs.

Liam stroked Charlotte's back through her thin blouse.

She rocked him gently. Liam had fallen asleep like that. Charlotte was still awake. Neither had spoken a word. Liam had forgiven Charlotte without her having to share any deception or any truth, and now she knew she would never tell him the story of her life. With Pike dead, there was no need. Charlotte still suspected that Liam might have killed the man – just for her. And if he had, he was guiltless. Pike had deserved to die. Liam was not only Charlotte's lover but her rescuer, too.

In her room in the house on Lantana Drive, Verbena also lay on her bed, rocking, but she was alone. She felt icy all over. Her hands were curled into fists at her chest. She could not get the previous night out of her mind. It ran over and over like a looped section of film. Verbena had been very afraid and that had made her angry, and because she had been so angry, she had killed Teddy Pike.

Verbena had met the man at the Soggy Dollar at midnight as planned. He was very late and she had waited nervously in her car in the bar's parking lot, her anxiety building. When Pike had finally arrived in a taxicab, he was dripping with sweat and his face was a storm cloud. He leaned into her window and said, 'Come inside. I need a drink.'

'I am not drinking in a place like that, Mr Pike.' Verbena had been determined to retain some dignity during what was sure to be a mortifying exchange.

Pike walked round the front of the Jordan and opened the passenger door. His sudden weight in the seat beside her had rocked the vehicle.

'I've had a God-awful night, Miss Verbena.' At least, his

Cockney accent was gone. 'So, tell me, what the fuck do you want?' Any pretence at civility was absent.

'I want to apologize if I offended you with my visit to your establishment . . .'

'What?' said Pike. He was lost. 'What are you talking about?'

'I think you sent me a message the other night . . . in my pool . . . and I wanted you to know that I'm deeply sorry if I caused offence. I mustn't be so nosy. It's a dreadful fault of mine.'

Pike had started to laugh then. 'You're all right, my lovely,' he had said. He was Cockney again. 'That wasn't for you . . .'

Verbena's curiosity was piqued by that admission. She couldn't leave it alone. She had to know. 'It was for Charlotte?' she asked.

'You just said you shouldn't be so nosy,' Pike had said pointedly. 'Stay out of this, Miss Verbena. If you know what's good for you, you'll stay out of it.'

Verbena realized she was close to knowing the truth about Charlotte. Charlotte – that thieving bitch, that destroyer of dreams, that usurper of real talent – was hiding some ghastly destructive truth about herself, and this rancid bastard wasn't going to give her the satisfaction of knowing what it was. By that time, she had been shaking with frustration and loathing. 'Just promise me you'll destroy her with it, whatever it is.'

Verbena didn't care how Charlotte's story became public, as long as it did. Somebody, even though it wouldn't be her, was going to pull that scheming whore down off her pedestal and Verbena was going to witness her fall. That would be enough . . .

'A secret's got no power once it's out,' said Pike. 'It needs to stay a secret to be valuable to the person whose secret it is, see?'

Verbena could not believe what she was hearing. Was she to have no compensation after everything that had been taken from her? She lifted her veil. She needed to smoke a cigarette and calm her nerves. Pike took out his lighter. In the flare of its flame, he saw Verbena's face clearly.

'What in hell have you done to yourself?'

How dare he ask? Verbena had tried to cover the oozing sores on her face with powder, but it had clotted to form an unsightly, crusty pancake.

Pike laughed. 'I could give you a part in the freak show with that face, if you like.'

Verbena's rage bubbled over. She made a sound of fury – a throaty, strangled, pent-up scream – and she slammed her fist sideways into Pike's face, hoping to hurt him, to give him a painful nosebleed. The car door popped open on his side and Pike half scrambled, half fell out, cursing her. Verbena leaned over and pulled the door shut behind him. She turned the key and revved the engine. Then Pike did a stupid thing. Instead of walking behind the Jordan and into the bar, he walked in front of it. His ugly bulk was illuminated clearly in the headlights and Verbena pressed her foot on to the accelerator. She hit him hard, hard enough to snap both his legs at the thigh. He dropped to the ground. Verbena didn't see him again. She felt his bulk beneath the Jordan's wheels as she drove over him. Pike's coat must have been caught up on the undercarriage. She dragged him quite a way.

Verbena sat, shivering uncontrollably, for a few minutes.

Nobody came out of the bar. No new cars pulled into the parking lot. When she got out of her car, and saw Pike's torn, bloody corpse, it lay only three feet from the railing that separated the parking lot from the river.

Verbena only had to roll his body over once before the gravity of the hillside took him. There was a dull little splash when he reached the bottom.

Verbena drove home shaking. What she had done hadn't quite sunk in. As far as she could tell in the dark, there was some damage to the Jordan's front bumper but no visible blood. Charlotte was always borrowing her car. Verbena would blame the dents on her. Only after she had showered, and washed her hair, and climbed into bed, did the shivering finally stop.

She had woken up believing it had all been a dream. She had cried and lain on the carpet of her bedroom and prayed, though she didn't really believe in God. After she had worn herself out with regret, she sat at her dresser and suddenly noticed that her burn hurt significantly less. A dark scab had formed in the night. Soon, that scab would fall off, revealing fresh new skin that would be too pink at first, but eventually smooth and lovely. In less than a week, there would be no sign that anything had ever damaged Verbena's exquisite face. It was a sign. She knew that she had been forgiven. God had forgiven her. Her perfectly restored face would be the proof of her own innocence. Pike had been a rotten man and she had merely been the instrument that had dispatched him. Verbena felt reborn. Perhaps she was a believer after all. Nobody was going to make her feel small and useless. She was Verbena Marsh! Nobody would ever know she was a killer. She would leave her room and face the people in the house. Soon she would face the world outside again. She was Verbena Marsh and, Hollywood and all its crap aside, she was the world's greatest actress.

29

Allegra was in turmoil after Pennington's garrotte demonstration. She kept reminding herself that – if what the officer had told her was true – Holt had been the victim of an attack, not the perpetrator, but why had he lied to her about his scars? Pondering that kept Allegra awake all night.

In the early morning, she went on to the deck to watch Holt working, but she did not call out to him. She still didn't know if she wanted to confront him with what Officer Pennington had told her. Did she even want to hear the truth? Did she love him enough to hear it, whatever it was, and accept it?

Allegra didn't visit Holt in the canyon for lunch as had become her habit. He had worked alone all that day, digging platforms into the hillside to accommodate the steps he was going to install. It was hard, heavy work. Once or twice, Allegra had caught him looking up at the kitchen window, hoping for a glimpse of her, but she had shrunk back into the room, half afraid of catching his eye. By evening, however, she was desperate for him. Her longing outweighed her uncertainty.

Allegra went to the kitchen window again at five o'clock and saw the Peppers' truck parked beside the campsite. They had returned from their farm where they'd gone to collect the last few sanguinellos. The young trees, tied to the old truck's bed, looked lovely, deep green against the straw-coloured canyon grass. The Santa Anas had stopped blowing as mysteriously as they had begun but the trees would be there as a buffer when next the winds came through, trailed by dust.

During his trip, Roscoe had also apparently found time to purchase lumber for the proposed stairs. Holt helped him drag the boards from the truck and stack them on the lower slopes of the hillside. Roscoe had returned with a post-hole digger, too. Allegra recognized the tool from her days on the racecourse: the labourers had used one when they built new corrals. Holt went to work with it, driving the cups into the rocky soil as deeply as he could to give the posts a strong foundation. He would be at this task until it grew too dark to work. Roscoe and he would probably toil through Friday, too, securing the upright posts and setting the risers and handrails in place. The staircase would be ready for the party on Friday night. Allegra would tell Miss Charlotte that she could take her guests down into the canyon to visit her new orchard. The staircase would not be a pretty construction, though, even with a coat of whitewash.

Just then, Allegra noticed a black police car following the rut the Peppers' truck had created, moving slowly but determinedly towards the campsite.

Officer Pennington drove cautiously over the uneven terrain. He had taken back roads up from Ventura Boulevard until he discovered the empty plot used to reach the undeveloped canyon land.

Allegra knew she would not be able to hear the officer's questions, even from a position on the deck. It would be agony to watch Holt being interrogated and not be able to discern if he was answering to the officer's satisfaction. Allegra tried to lose herself in a whirlwind of work. She made a shopping list for the groceries required to make her ceviche. She could not avoid the kitchen window, however. Her eyes were drawn to it. Allegra watched Pennington. She watched Holt.

'Morning,' Pennington said to Holt and Roscoe. He showed them his badge. 'Can I have a moment of your time?'

Holt dropped the post-hole digger reluctantly. The three men moved into a clump of shade offered by one of the orange trees. Harmony was left to tidy the campsite.

'I noticed you from up on that deck yesterday,' said Pennington, indicating the actresses' house above them.

'Noticed you right back,' said Holt.

'What's the trouble here?' asked Roscoe.

Pennington produced the newspaper story of the body found in the Frogtown wash and tapped the photograph of the man's tattooed body. 'Have you ever seen this man?' he asked.

Holt mimicked Roscoe's genuine perplexity and shook his head.

'He hasn't been hanging about?' asked Pennington. 'You've never seen him with Miss Caine, for example?'

'Nope,' said Roscoe. 'We don't see much of the comings and goings of the house from down here. My wife and Holt here and me, we stay down in the canyon. We work late, try to make an honest dollar.'

'His name was Theodore Pike,' said Pennington. 'And I expect he was also just trying to make an honest dollar.'

Holt was surprised to hear the detective use the man's name. So, they had identified the body. 'His kin tell you that?' he asked. 'They say he was an honest, working man?'

'He doesn't have any family,' said Pennington. 'We located his place of work. That's how we know his name. He's been with the Magic Sevens Circus for many years. We tracked them to a site off the one-oh-one, not twenty miles from here.'

Roscoe slapped Holt in the chest with the back of his hand. 'I seen their posters up,' he said to Holt. 'They got a deck of cards on them.'

'That's the place,' said Pennington. 'Circus types aren't generally talkative but they sure are vengeful. I expect if I told them who we thought the guilty man was, they would take the whole business out of police hands.'

'You talking rough justice there, officer?' said Holt.

'We like to get our man, one way or another,' said Pennington.

Roscoe looked bewildered by the nuances he sensed flying above his head.

'Some folks just don't like to talk much,' said Holt. 'Don't mean they're guilty of nothing.'

'No.' Pennington pretended to agree with him. 'It just means they're secretive, afraid to be caught out in a lie. How'd you come by those unfortunate scars, Mr Holt?'

'Fell from my horse,' said Holt.

'That's what your girl told me. You still got that horse, Mr Holt? Because he'd be a bit cut up, too, after an accident like that, I imagine.'

'He's dead,' said Holt.

'That's convenient,' said Pennington.

'Haywire – that's my horse's name – got killed by police. They torched the camp I was living in. Took a shotgun to him.'

'It's likely he was diseased then, or so misused he couldn't be saved,' said Pennington.

'He weren't diseased,' said Holt. His eyes glinted. 'And he weren't misused.'

'We'll surely keep a lookout for anything strange from now on,' volunteered Roscoe, trying to be the peacekeeper.

'You do that,' said Pennington. He tried one final line of questioning. 'You ever taken a drink at the Soggy Dollar bar in Frogtown, Mr Holt?'

'Don't know the place,' said Holt.

'It was a favourite watering hole of our poor dead Mr Pike.'

'Said I don't know it,' said Holt.

'Well, I'll reassure the folks at the Magic Sevens of that,' said Pennington. 'Just in case they take it into their heads to do something foolhardy. I'll surely give them your name and let them know you've been helpful.'

Pennington raised his hat to Harmony as he returned to his car. She was washing towels in a bucket. She stopped her work and watched the officer leave. She gave Roscoe a nervous glance.

'He says he'll tell that man's friends you're not involved,' said Roscoe. 'That's decent of him.'

Holt laughed coarsely. He didn't bother to explain.

Roscoe was surprised by his apparent bitterness, though. 'What's going on, Holt?' he asked. 'You're acting strange. Are you privy to something we ought to tell the police about?'

'Already told that officer everything,' said Holt. 'Don't know nothing about that Mr Pike. Don't know how he got himself killed.'

'Well, okay, then,' said Roscoe.

As soon as she saw the police car moving away, Allegra hurried out into the garden. The preceding fifteen minutes in the kitchen had decided her. The sight of Holt in possible danger had reassured her that she loved him. She didn't care if he was dangerous; he wasn't dangerous to her. Allegra wanted to be with him. She would do anything to make that happen.

Allegra crouched on her haunches and skidded down the bank in an uncontrolled scramble. Holt grabbed her as she nearly tumbled into the canvas siding of the tent. He clutched her tiny lithe form to him, taking advantage of the opportunity to embrace her, holding her longer than was necessary.

Harmony looked over at them. She smiled at Allegra and the girl smiled back at her. Harmony still wore the loose pregnancy shifts that flapped pathetically against her empty, concave stomach. Allegra felt a pang of sadness for her. Harmony must have sewn half a dozen of them as soon as she learned she was having a baby. Allegra had also noticed that sometimes Harmony would touch her belly unconsciously, then her hand would slide away, having found no swell there to reassure it.

'Allie and me need some time,' Holt told Roscoe. 'Got plans to make.'

'This job should be done in a few days,' said Roscoe. 'We'll all have to move on then.'

'Exactly why we gotta plan,' said Holt.

He led Allegra between the orange trees to the far end of the grove. The canyon was lilac with dusky shadows. The air was still bright, but the small chills of Fall had taken residence in the dips and valleys, turning them crisp. The stalks of the blue rye had grown brittle. Allegra could hear the distant sawing sound of the Peppers' bees. She hoped they were back in their hives at this hour.

'What did that policeman want with you?' she demanded.

'Fishing around about Mr Pike.'

'Why's he asking you? You never knew the man.'

'Trying to pin it on someone. I look the part, I guess. He mentioned the Soggy Dollar bar. People saw me there. Bartender saw me. The police ask, they'll remember me. People remember my face, Allie. And if they can't pin it on me proper, they'll leak the word to his circus friends that it was me.'

'We have to do something!' said Allegra.

'Gotta move fast. It's days now, not weeks. We've gotta get some money. We gotta go, you understand?'

Holt had taken Allegra by the shoulders and was shaking her like a rag doll. Roscoe glanced over at him in concern, and Holt pulled her against his chest in a fierce hug to show his intensity was only frustration, not anger.

'How did you cut your face?' Allegra asked, into his shirt.

She did not look at Holt. She kept her eyes focused on his top button, the triangle of tanned skin between his collarbones. Her voice was a vulnerable tremble. Holt's shoulders slumped. He could not avoid the subject any longer. He slid down with his back against the newly planted tree. Allegra sat beside him. She did not want to let go of his hand. She was afraid that if she lost the connection she might not find it again.

'I am a carpenter, that part is true. Had a good job in Texas, working lumber in a yard till the depression closed it down. I moved from place to place. When I had nothing left, I took to playing cards and throwing dice for a few dollars. I jumped a train in Nevada, trying to get here to California, and met up with a couple of guys who were working the route. They were loners, drifters like me, living on cans of beans and their own wits. I watched them take a few men with a marked deck. I figured out what they were up to. We sort of fell in together. We jumped that line for three months, getting on and hopping off the same route between Carson City and Los Angeles. When things got tough, or a loser didn't want to pay up, one of them took to using a bottle. The other had a mean short blade. I fashioned a wire with some wood . . .'

'A garrotte,' said Allegra.

Holt didn't ask her how she knew the weapon. He was too involved in his own tale to pause. 'I didn't like it when the other two started taking advantage of women. It made me sick to my stomach, Allie. You gotta believe me. I never took nothing from a lady nor ever hurt one, I swear, though I stood by when I saw it going on – I have to be straight about that. It's hard for me to tell a thing like that to you. It's an ugly thing, but I said this would be the truth and it is. This is the all of it . . .'

Holt took a chance on Allegra's eyes then. For a moment, he managed to raise his glance to hers, then looked at the ground once more.

'Partners like that don't last. After a time, one of you is

going to turn on the other. That's what happened to me. Woke up with a blade at my throat. Went for my wire; it was gone. One of them had taken it off me while I slept. They'd also stolen my share of our takings from that run. My own wire was round my neck. I'm smaller than most other men but I fought for my life. I got the wire loosened some, pulled it up from my neck but it caught me in the mouth and tore through. They would have killed me but I managed to roll to the door, fell out into the dirt, walked four miles back to Carson City with my face torn in two. A mission took me in and healed me up. That part about the sisters helping me out was true. I stole Haywire from a horse farm near Santa Clarita, but I loved him. That part was true, too.'

Holt stopped talking. There was a jarring pause before he started up again. 'Didn't know where I was heading until I met you, Allie. Now I do. I want our own place, our restaurant by the sea with a home above it and happiness in it. Been looking for a new dream to dream for so long that I didn't believe I'd ever find one. But I have one now, and I believe I can make it come true – if you're in it.'

Allegra remained silent. She squeezed Holt's hand a little but she didn't look at him.

'You ever do something you're near dead ashamed of?' Holt asked her.

Allegra nodded. 'I gave my body to a man I didn't love. His name was Starkey. It was my first time and he gave me some dollars for it.'

Holt twitched beside her. His hand squirmed in hers but he did not pull it free. 'You don't never have to do that again,' said Holt. 'I'll make sure you don't.'

Allegra smiled a weak smile. She had told him. He had told her. It was the truth and they had come through it.

A solitary bee suddenly landed on Allegra's forearm. She froze; she held her breath in terror. Holt noticed her muscles seize up. 'Stay calm,' he said. 'Take a look at him. Take a proper long look. Bet you never have before. He won't sting you for nothing.'

Allegra moved her arm, bringing the bee closer to her face. The movement was tentative but she wanted to show Holt that she trusted him. Allegra examined the bee closely as it moved in tight circles on her forearm. After a few moments, it took off with wing beats so rapid they blurred the air around them.

'They're quite wonderful, really,' Allegra said. She felt oddly at peace with the creature now.

'When you ain't afraid to look.'

'We've lost our chance at Miss Charlotte's secret, haven't we? I mean, with Mr Pike dead there's no way to get any money, is there?'

'I'm gonna borrow Roscoe's truck and go see those circus folks. One of them might know something,' said Holt. 'It's our only chance.'

'It's almost dark, Holt,' said Allegra. 'Can't you go tomorrow?'

'I've gotta get my own answers before that officer visits them again. He might finger me to them. If he does that, I'll never get a word out of them. They might even wanna kill me.'

'Go now, then,' said Allegra.

'Have you searched her things?' Holt asked.

'I'll do it tonight,' said Allegra. 'It's so strange in the

house . . . Miss Verbena won't leave her room and Miss Ivy's hardly ever home any more. She's always out with her Mr Whitewood. Miss Charlotte is so happy today that she can't stop smiling. I don't know what any of them's thinking.'

'Find something we can use,' said Holt. 'In a few days, it's too late. We gotta go!'

They kissed and Allegra clambered back up the hill. She heard Roscoe's truck start up behind her. By the time she reached the deck, Holt was gone. The canyon was silent except for the rhythmic banging of Roscoe's hammer. He had started to nail the steps of the staircase in place.

Allegra heard the wireless come on in the living room. Charlotte was listening to *American Bandstand*. Allegra was fuelled with purpose. She would search every nook and cranny, every purse, every cupboard, every diary page, every secreted-away envelope until she found something. She went to work, looking through Charlotte's drawers. It was too late for Allegra still to be working. If she was discovered, her presence in the actress's room would be suspicious, but she had no choice. Sometimes she started at an unexpected sound and stood jack-rabbit still, listening.

There were very few markers of Charlotte's life before she had moved to California. Allegra came across the bottle of perfume she had seen before, the exquisite twist of red glass with its seal still intact. This item, above anything else she knew of the actress, unsettled her. She could not explain it to herself. The woman had plenty of money to replace any perfume she might finish. Why had this bottle never been opened?

Allegra's heart was thumping in rhythm to Roscoe Pepper's hammer. Her face was red with heat and blood. Suddenly she recalled that once, months before, she had come across Verbena in Charlotte's room. Verbena had been going through some papers from Charlotte's suitcase. Allegra eyed the suitcase. It was pushed far back on top of the armoire. She would not be able to get it down without making a noise. Searching it would take time, too, and she would not be able to replace it quickly if she heard Charlotte's shoes in the hallway. She would have to find time to open it the next day.

The telephone rang. It was Allegra's job to answer it, and she hurried quietly down the hallway to where the instrument vibrated on a table.

The woman on the other end asked for Verbena Marsh, and Allegra called her from her room. Verbena's end of the conversation was composed of a few spare words. She said 'Yes' and 'I understand' and 'Yes' again. She hung up and turned to Allegra. Instead of scolding her for hovering within earshot, she said dazedly, 'My aunt died.'

They were both still standing there in a frozen tableau when Ivy bounced through the door, squealing delightedly, her left arm extended to display a two-carat diamond engagement ring.

30

As he drove north, Holt thought about escape. He could just keep going, following Route 101 all the way to Oregon. He would steal the Peppers' truck, abandon Allegra, leave the whole mess surrounding Mr Pike's death behind him and head into Canada. He could cut lumber, fight fires. There was work in the opposite direction, too. There was palm-planting in Las Vegas and freeway-building in Phoenix. There was always rough-necking in Dallas. He would find a place for himself.

But he could not abandon the idea of owning the restaurant with Allegra. That dream had him in its clutches.

A gauge on the dashboard of the Peppers' old Ford truck showed that the tank was almost empty. At seven o'clock Holt stopped at a gas station. He bought some homemade lemonade, which the clerk decanted into an old Coca-Cola bottle for him. Holt pulled off the road near a farmer's dam outside San Bernardino and sipped his drink in the shade of an arroyo willow. Clouds were roiling in from the mountains. Holt felt his destination drawing closer in the near dark.

Five miles further on, in a field beside an abandoned cannery, Holt saw several tents pitched higgledy-piggledy among a dozen caravans. The sky behind the scene was black with thunderheads. The evening's gloom dulled the circus's already worn colours, turning the place all purple and shadowed. Holt pulled the Ford off the road at a corrugated-iron gate.

There was no big top. There was obviously no show that night. The circus was on its way to a larger town. This site was just an overnight stop en route. The surrounding farms didn't provide enough patrons to make putting on a show worthwhile.

The campsite was at rest, except for a crew of Chinese acrobats who spoke in angry, incomprehensible exclamations as they practised their contortions. Two girls with dancers' bodies stood chatting beside one of the tents. As Holt drew closer, he saw that they weren't girls. They were middle-aged women. The illusion of youth held up only from a distance. A striped monkey paced across one woman's shoulders, its tail curled around her neck like a noose.

'I'm here about Mr Theodore Pike,' said Holt.

'He ain't around no more,' said the monkey-woman. 'There's no jobs going neither,' she added.

'Don't need a job,' said Holt.

'I took you for a wire walker,' said the monkey-woman. She raised her hand to her face and indicated the places that corresponded to Holt's scars. 'I've seen that before after a bad high-wire fall.'

Holt nodded. 'Who do I talk to?'

'About what?' asked the monkey-woman.

'About Mr Pike,' repeated Holt.

'You can talk to Juno. He's taken over.'

The monkey-woman pointed to a caravan with a barred window. Normally it would be parked near the entry gates and used as a ticket office. Inside the small, barred room, a man sat on a stool with his legs propped up on the slender counter, an ice pack on each knee. When Juno saw Holt approach, he volunteered, 'It comes from the stilts. They put a wicked strain on the knees and ankles.'

He spoke with the phoney British accent affected by ringmasters the world over. He had adopted Pike's role completely.

'May I help you, good sir? Tickets for the young ones for tomorrow night's show, perhaps? You'll have to drive over to Pasadena to see us, though. We're moving on in the morning.'

'I want to talk about Mr Pike.'

Juno's face grew wary. 'We lost our Mr Pike. It was a sad business.'

'I know that,' said Holt. He took a chance. He knew his scars made him look mean, but this place was used to freak shows. It ran one of its own. 'I'm the one the blues plan to pin it on.'

Juno leaned forward and held on to the window bars like a jailed ape. 'Why do they think you done it?' he asked.

'Look at me.'

Juno examined Holt, then shrugged. 'Because you look the part, I expect,' he said, understanding.

'I only met Mr Pike once,' said Holt. 'We shared a drink in a bar.'

'Lucky for you,' said Juno. 'Had you known him better, you might've wanted to kill him.' He roared with laughter. 'Didn't make friends easily, our Teddy.'

'I need to speak to someone who knew him,' said Holt.

Juno considered Holt for a long time. 'Talk to Dainty. Dainty Delightful. She's in the pink caravan round the side.'

Holt nodded his thanks and went off in the direction Juno had indicated.

'You work the high wire?' Juno called after him.

Holt ignored the man; he pretended not to hear him over another grumble of thunder.

He found the pink caravan and knocked on its siding. 'Miss Delightful?' he called. He felt silly using the name.

A woman the size of a small child opened the door.

'Miss Delightful?' Holt asked again.

'It's Dainty,' she said cheerfully.

She was the littlest person Holt had ever seen, though her proportions were more or less those of an adult woman. Her hands were a bit too big, and so was her head, but her body was sweetly curvaceous. 'I need to talk to someone about Mr Pike. Mr Juno sent me over to you.'

'Ah, lover,' said Dainty, with genuine sympathy, 'Mr Pike's gone. He's dead, my dove.'

'I know that,' said Holt.

Dainty spoke in a maternal manner. She had seen that Holt was in his mid-thirties, but she had still assumed the mothering role.

He wondered how old she was. Could she be nearing fifty? It was impossible to tell.

'Are you one of his boys?' Dainty asked.

'No,' said Holt, unsure of what she meant. 'I don't think so.'

'He had a good few. In every town we visited regular, a boy or girl would show up. Mostly it was a boy. They were braver, I guess. Their mamas had all told them that our Theodore was their daddy. It must have happened four or five times. Our Theodore was what you call prolific. He used to tell them that if they were his, they'd have come out with tattoos all over them. Most of the boys didn't find that funny, but Teddy did. I'm sure he must have been a disappointment to them. He wasn't the fatherly type.'

'Not looking for a father,' said Holt. 'My name's Holt.'

Without any introductory smattering of rain, the heavens opened and dumped water down like a torrent from a pail. Dainty grabbed Holt's shirt at the stomach to pull him inside. She was standing on the top step of her caravan but she still reached no higher than his waist. 'Come in out of the rain, Mr Holt,' she said.

Inside the caravan, Dainty moved about in the darkness, lighting lamps. Holt felt as if he had crept into a doll's house. The size of the furniture was disconcerting – it was made for Dainty – but the everyday objects, the kettle, the clock, the cups and saucers, were standard size.

'We have a carpenter here. Over the years he's made me a few bits and pieces.' Dainty indicated the wardrobe and the kitchen cabinet.

'Real nice,' said Holt.

'It's where I feel right,' said Dainty. 'We all feel right here . . . in the circus, that is. It's why we joined up, I guess. Some are born into it. Some find their way here. Are you looking to feel right, Mr Holt?'

'Happy where I am,' said Holt. 'Got a girl I love.' He was quite surprised that the statement came out so easily.

'Theodore once had a girl he loved,' said Dainty. 'In his way.'

'Was it you?' Holt asked.

The conversation had turned personal awfully quickly, though Dainty didn't seem offended.

'No, not me!' said Dainty. 'Teddy's girl was a beauty. It was a sad thing, really. She wasn't his, you see. She belonged to another fellow. Teddy pretended not to care but he mooched over her for a long time after she left. Me, I had my own man. Ernie was his name and he was our human cannonball. He got shot out of that cannon like a bullet twice a day for twelve years, then died of a sneaky wasting disease. It doesn't seem fair . . .' Her high, girlish voice had grown wistful. 'I did share a bed with Teddy for a time, out of mutual loneliness when Ernie died, but mostly we just had our art in common.'

Holt searched her body for tattoos. He didn't see any but his inspection made Dainty smile. 'My tapestry's too small to showcase much,' she said. 'But Theodore was an enormous canvas and we had some fun with him. He was picky, mind you. Tea?' she asked suddenly.

'Take coffee, if you're offering.'

'I surely am,' said Dainty, and she hopped from her chair and busied herself at the Primus. She seemed happy to keep talking as the rain pounded on the caravan's roof.

'Our Teddy liked his tattoos to mean something,' Dainty said. 'They had to tell a story. He was most particular about that. He used tattoos to mark special days in his life.'

'You did his tattoos?'

'I did,' she said proudly. 'I'm quite the artist.'

Holt looked at her tiny hands. He imagined their agility with a needle and ink. Dainty put the kettle over the blue gas flame and pulled a book out from a shelf. She placed it on Holt's knees. 'That book was Teddy's,' she said. 'I took it from his caravan as a keepsake when we heard he had died. See? He kept all my sketches, my doodles, the practice drawings I'd do before I'd commit to skin. He saved every one of them.'

Holt opened the book to reveal a world of fantastical imagery. There were mermaids and sailors, centaurs and seductresses. Each image was in Dainty's unique style, each was a work of great detail and originality.

'Of course, Teddy didn't go in for fancies, being a practical sort of a man. He preferred meaningful things. He liked fire and brimstone. Mostly, he liked depicting events in his life or images that were powerful to him.'

Holt paged through the book. He came across a picture of a strongman balancing weights on a bar above his head. Dainty glanced over at it. 'Teddy had that one on his chest,' she continued. 'He asked me to do it for him when he got his first job as our strongman out of Tuscaloosa. He would lift me over his head and then he'd lift Jenny, one of our regular-sized girls. It got some laughs. Theodore had a talent for showmanship and for cards. He was a great sleight-of-hand man. Only fools accepted a game of cards with Teddy.'

Holt was taking in every word Dainty said, trying to glean the meaning from the information. He needed to get from Theodore Pike to Carlie Caine. He had to connect the two of them. 'Was Mr Pike ever married?' he asked.

'Teddy never took a wife. I always thought that was odd for such a religious man but, then again, his faith was flexible. He wasn't often cold in his bed, if you know what I mean, judging by the kiddies who keep popping up.'

'He was religious?' asked Holt.

'Oh, Theodore had zeal. He claimed he was called or ordained, or whatever,' said Dainty. She suddenly seemed to realize that she knew nothing about this man she had invited into her home. She grew wary. 'If you knew him, Mr Holt, you'd know that about him for sure,' said Dainty. 'Why exactly are you here?'

'There's no harm for you in my questions, Miss Dainty, or for this place. I promise you that.'

Dainty took Holt at his word. She handed him a mug of coffee and sat on the edge of her bed with her teacup resting on her knee. 'Well, Teddy was somewhat famous for his religious shenanigans. He did funerals and gave last rites. He was quite a novelty, what with all those tattoos. He made a bit of money handling snakes at Christian crusades, and he would heal the sick at those revivalist tent meetings in Mississippi and Alabama. It was all show. The snakes had no teeth and half the time the people he cured were only buddies who owed him a favour. He had one special mate named Archie Welch, who could play blind like a genius. Old Archie got trotted out at every state fair, till some folks started recognizing him and his amazing recurring blindness. That's when Teddy came to live with us. A circus needs a man like that. We do a lot of our own ceremonies in private. It was all legal and state-sanctioned, too. Teddy posted the proper documents off to Tallahassee, or wherever, every time. It's an easy move from religion to circus work. It's the same business really – entertaining folks.'

Holt glanced down at the book again. He was looking at a picture of a burning Bible. A sword pierced it. 'The police think he may have died in a fight . . .'

'That seems likely. Teddy was always fighting with somebody. He thought the whole world owed him money. If he could bleed an extra nickel out of a deal, he would. He ruined many a fair piece of business by pushing it too far. I expect, that last time, he just pushed the wrong person.'

'I wonder if Mr Pike ever mentioned a woman named Carlie Caine?'

'I don't recall that name,' said Dainty. 'Teddy didn't mention names often. He spoke fondly of Archie Welch, of course. He lost touch with him, too, eventually. You can't keep a friendship going on the road, and Archie didn't want nothing more to do with Theodore after what happened with that girl of his . . .'

'What girl?'

'I don't recall her name but she was a breathtaker. She was the beauty I mentioned before. The one I believe Teddy fell hard for. She was with Archie when he joined up with us for a time in Florida. This was a good few years ago, but I saw Theodore watching that girl with those needful eyes of his. One night, he and Archie took to playing cards in the ring, sitting in the middle of the sawdust, throwing long shadows out from under the spotlight. They had their rear ends resting on buckets. They had a hay bale for their poker table. The stakes got higher and higher. Word spread through the camp until half of us were looking on, watching from the front row, holding our breath.

'I knew how it would turn out. Archie Welch – bless him – was one of life's born losers. He was a drinker and a gambler, but he showed up with this girl who looked like an angel. Where he found her, I'll never know. The word "angel" doesn't rightly describe her face – she had blonde curls and quite dark brows with chestnut-coloured eyes.

'I'd long before resigned myself to the body God gave me, Mr Holt, but the sight of that girl made me yearn to be a regular woman. I yearned for the long bones she had, and for the way men watched her. I wanted to be that girl. While she was with us, I lay in bed at night beside my Ernie with an actual stomach ache, crying with my longing to be her. She was valuable, just because of the way she looked, the way nature had put her together. In fact, she was worth three hundred and twelve dollars . . .'

'What?'

'That was the bet. Archie couldn't cover it. Where would Archie Welch get three hundred dollars? He washed dishes for a living at some university canteen. I guess Teddy knew that. He wanted the girl, you see. He let Archie run up his bet, knowing he would put the girl up eventually. Oh, they were supposed to be friends but I watched Teddy play Archie while they played that game, giving Archie enough rope to hang himself with until he offered up the girl. Teddy even made it seem like it was Archie's idea. I saw her on the other side of the tent while it was happening. She was watching Archie lose her with a dull kind of acceptance. I could have stepped in and asked Ernie to put a stop to it on moral grounds. Teddy respected Ernie. He might have listened. And she did look awfully young, that girl. But I didn't ask. She was too beautiful to be allowed to have everything. I wanted Teddy to have her, to ruin her. I was that jealous.'

Dainty stopped talking. Her lower lip quivered with shame. Holt didn't speak. Together they listened to the rain on the roof for a few minutes.

'What happened next?' coaxed Holt.

'Teddy won the hand and he wanted the bet honoured. Archie begged him to leave the girl be, but Teddy wouldn't hear of it. Archie didn't have the guts to prevent it. Teddy picked up a horse blanket and took the girl into the woods beside the camp. There was a canopy of kudzu growing out of control in the trees and it made a kind of tent. He took the girl in under the kudzu and did what he wanted to do to her.'

Dainty Delightful had started to cry. Her tears rolled down her cheeks, fully formed, the same size as any adult's tears.

'Late in the night, hours afterwards, I could still hear that girl sobbing. I saw Archie go in under the kudzu and carry her out. He took her to the tent he was sharing with the Chinese. Archie had been staying with Teddy before then but, after what Teddy did that night, he couldn't. Moving out, then moving on was Archie's small act of contrition, I guess.'

Holt turned the page of the book on his lap and saw an ink drawing of two intertwined wedding bands. Lying across the picture, trapped between the pages, was an envelope bearing the seal of the state of Florida.

'That girl's name wasn't Carlie Caine?'

'I can't remember, Mr Holt. Carlie Caine? It's not familiar but it's pretty-sounding.'

'She's an actress now,' said Holt.

'That explains it. Actresses always have such lovely names, don't they?'

It occurred to Holt that Miss Caine might have used a different moniker before coming to Hollywood. He despaired. He would never be able to find out her real name unless Allegra unearthed some of her personal papers.

'She was some girl with that blonde hair and those brown

eyes.' Dainty was reminiscing. 'I'm not sure I ever did learn her name.'

'So you don't know of any connection between Pike and a Carlie Caine?'

'I'm sorry.' Dainty was distressed that she couldn't help the man. 'I don't know any woman called Carlie. Never have.' She thought for a second more and her tiny brow furrowed. 'I guess Archie's girl might have been called Carlie. Archie married her the next day, you know. It was pretty unpleasant if you ask me – Teddy practically forcing himself on her the night before, then Archie marrying her the next day. I suppose Archie felt he was making something up to the girl, though she was too young for marriage, of course – so many of them are. Teddy did their wedding service as a favour to his friend, Archie, and as a penance, I suppose. I remember him posting off the wedding licence. Archie never got it because he used our address and he had left us long before the certificate came back from the authorities. The circus picked up its mail in Tallahassee every few months . . .'

'Could this be it?' asked Holt.

He held up the envelope he had discovered in Mr Pike's book of tattoos.

'Oh, there's another one,' said Dainty. 'I thought I got them all. He had a box full of them in his caravan and I posted them back to state, to see if they can locate the rightful owners. That one was in the book?'

Holt opened the envelope and Dainty did not complain. She was looking down at the page.

'I tattooed those wedding bands on Teddy's back the night Archie and his new bride took off. The girl couldn't stand to stay – she couldn't stand the sight of Teddy, I expect. How she could stand the sight of her own husband after he'd allowed Teddy to have her, I don't know. But she sure made an impression on our Teddy. He marked their marriage on his body. He marked her face on his right forearm. I'd call it an obsession.'

Holt had been reading the sheet of paper the envelope contained as Dainty spoke. In it, the state of Florida acknowledged the marriage of Mr Archie Welch to Miss Charlotte Caine. Dainty was half reading the sheet over his shoulder. She snapped her finger. The noise, so close to his ear, startled Holt.

'Charlotte!' said Dainty. 'Not Carlie . . . Charlotte. Now I remember. I did know her name after all. Her name was Charlotte Caine.' She tapped the paper Holt held. 'Though I suppose this makes her Mrs Charlotte Welch, assuming old Archie is still alive.'

By the time Holt arrived back at the canyon below Lantana Drive, the house beyond the deck was in full darkness. The rain had not reached here. As desperate as Holt was to see Allegra and tell her about the evidence he had found in Dainty Delightful's pink caravan, he knew that his presence in the house at night would be unwelcome.

He parked the truck a fair way from the campsite so its engine wouldn't disturb Roscoe and Harmony. He needn't have bothered. As he passed the Peppers' tent, he heard Roscoe's tractor-snore coming from inside. Harmony, however, was sitting, wrapped in a blanket, beside the campfire.

Holt sat down beside her and nudged her playfully with his shoulder. 'Didn't think I was coming back with that old truck of yours, did you?'

Harmony squished her lips to one side the way she did when she was trying to hold back a smile. Then she let it free. 'Guess I had my doubts,' she said.

'Brought it back safe and sound. Put some gas in her, too.'

'Ross never gave it a second thought. He loans the last decent thing we own to a near-stranger then he sleeps like a . . . baby.'

Even the word was difficult for Harmony. They sat together quietly for a few minutes. Holt used a stick to poke the embers. In the still air, the sparks rose like fireflies.

'Mr Holt,' asked Harmony, and Holt knew something serious was coming. 'You fixing to bring trouble down on us?'

'No, ma'am,' said Holt.

''Cause Ross and me ain't got the strength for that.'

'Ain't gonna bring trouble on you, Harmony. You and Roscoe been friends to me. My first friends in some time.'

'Sometimes friends bring trouble even when they don't mean to.'

'I'm moving on soon, maybe even tomorrow.'

Harmony nodded at that. She was relieved. 'Are you taking little Allegra with you?'

'Aim to,' said Holt.

Harmony looked closely at him. Her own eyes glittered with bits of the fire. 'You're going to be a good man to that girl?'

'Aim to be,' said Holt.

'Are you a good man, Mr Holt?'

Holt considered that. 'Done bad things but Allie knows them. I told her the whole of it.'

Harmony nodded gravely again. 'A man who's done bad things ain't the same as a bad man. It all gets weighed in His scales at the end.'

'Reckon I'm about balanced.'

'Sometimes balanced is the best a man can hope for.' Harmony got to her feet, using Holt's knee as a hand-rest to lift herself up. It was how she said she liked him. He rested his hand on top of hers for just a moment. It was how he said thank you.

'I think you're a good man, Mr Holt. I think the scales are hanging somewhat in that direction.'

'You go see if that husband of yours is ready to give you another baby,' Holt said.

'The cheek of you!' said Harmony, and she swatted Holt's shoulder.

Holt stayed quietly beside the last of the embers, steadying himself, knowing that the day ahead would not be a quiet one.

Holt and Roscoe began working at seven o'clock the next morning. They wanted to get the staircase finished. Holt wanted Roscoe to get his pay before he and Allegra confronted Charlotte Caine, then fled. Roscoe broke for coffee at ten o'clock and Holt took the opportunity to choose a few ripe sanguinellos from the trees. He carried three perfect specimens up the hill to the deck.

When he peered through the glass of the French windows, he didn't see Allegra in the kitchen: he saw Charlotte Caine. She was sitting at the kitchen table, poring through a small leather-bound diary. She appeared to be counting days off on the calendar, turning the pages back and forward, counting again. Holt rapped, and Charlotte closed the book hurriedly before opening the French window to him. She was flushed, lovely with excitement, and Holt saw that it would be hard to fleece her, but he could do it. He would do it.

'Allie's not here, Mr Holt. I've sent her marketing,' Charlotte saw disappointment on his face. 'I'm having a small soirée tonight and Allie's cooking up something special for us.'

'I know,' said Holt. 'I brought these for her. She needs them for what she's making.' He presented the oranges.

'I'll take them for her,' said Charlotte. She took the fruits and placed them in a bowl on the counter. 'Was that all?' she asked.

'For now,' said Holt.

'Have you ever been to Mexico, Mr Holt?' Charlotte asked suddenly.

'Never,' admitted Holt.

'Neither have I, but I'm going down there this weekend,' Charlotte bubbled. 'We're going to a place Allie knows, a beach town with a white church on the sand, a white church with blue doors where they do weddings.'

'Sounds pretty,' said Holt. He must ask Allegra about the place.

'Do you have children of your own, Mr Holt?' Charlotte asked.

'No, ma'am,' said Holt. 'Ain't never been married.'

'That doesn't necessarily mean anything,' teased Charlotte, with a giggle.

'No children,' said Holt, more firmly.

'I think children are important,' said Charlotte. 'Don't you? I think children hold a couple together.'

'Mr and Mrs Pepper don't have no children and they do just fine,' said Holt. 'Guess it depends on how much two people love each other.'

Charlotte considered that. 'I believe you're right. Children or not, love is love. It ought to be enough.'

Holt tipped his hat again and started back towards the campsite.

'Is my orchard ready?' Charlotte called out.

Holt turned back to her. 'Yes, ma'am. Stairs should be finished by tonight. Could bring your guests down for a drink, if you like.'

Charlotte clapped her hands. 'We'll do that!' she said. 'And I'll see to it you're paid, too. In fact, let me take care of that now.' Charlotte went into the hallway and returned a few minutes later with several ten-dollar bills. 'There's a bit extra there for a job well done.'

'Obliged,' said Holt. 'I know Mr Pepper could sure use his wages.' He went back down the hill.

He tried to get back up to the house to see Allegra several times that day. Each time, the kitchen was busy with people and he could not get a private moment to speak with her. He worked with Roscoe on the stairs. The Santa Anas had started up again. The wind was a constant irritation, blowing sand into their eyes as they worked and stinging their skin. Holt took comfort in the fact that the police had not come to see him that day. He was nearly done with his commitment to finish the job for Roscoe's sake.

From the kitchen, Allegra listened to the discordant cacophony of Holt and Roscoe's hammers. She had spent the whole day tidying the house and had just started preparing the food for dinner. The three actresses, each of whom had invited a guest to attend the evening's party, suddenly wanted the place spotless. Allegra had scrubbed, washed, dusted, cleaned, put fresh flowers in the living room and made up the beds with crisp linen. In the mid-morning, Verbena drove her to the grocery market and Allegra collected the ingredients she needed. When they returned to the car, Verbena pointed at the hood and exclaimed, 'Somebody's smashed up my car!'

Allegra saw the damage to the front bumper. 'Oh, Miss Marsh! Did they leave a note?'

'No, there's nothing.' Verbena looked about in exasperation. The lot was practically empty.

'Should we ask inside if anybody heard anything?' suggested Allegra.

'We didn't hear anything,' said Verbena, angrily. 'Why would they? There's nothing to be done. I'll have to pay to get it repaired. People have no manners.'

'Perhaps it happened yesterday, or even before . . .'

'Nonsense!' said Verbena. 'It just happened now. My car was in perfect shape this morning when we set out. Didn't you notice? There wasn't a mark on it.'

Allegra hadn't inspected the front grille before climbing into the passenger seat, but Verbena was so furious that she had to agree. 'Yes, I think it was fine this morning.'

'Right,' said Verbena. 'You're quite right, Allie. Now let's get home.'

When they returned, Liam Malone's beautiful gold Rolls-Royce was in the drive and Verbena manoeuvred her blue Jordan neatly in beside it. Allegra went directly into the kitchen to start preparing the ceviche. The best of the day was gone. Allegra saw that Charlotte and Liam were sitting together in the pool house. It was where Allegra and Holt had made love: she thought of it as their place.

Charlotte and Liam were talking intently and sipping champagne. Their conversation seemed too intense for such a frivolous drink. A few times, Liam's hand went up to his forehead and pushed his hair back with exaggerated pressure. It was a gesture Allegra had only ever seen made by men under extreme stress. Charlotte was smiling, though. She clasped at Liam's hands in desperation. At one point, she slid off her sun chair and actually went down on her knees before him, imploring with upturned eyes. Allegra wondered what news could make a woman so happy and the man she loved so anxious? The answer hit her with a jolt. Suddenly, beyond the window, she saw Liam reach forward and pull Charlotte violently against him, holding her as if he could never bear to let her go, and Allegra assumed that everything was going to be all right between them. She wondered if her suspicions were correct; she tried to remember when last she had washed Charlotte Caine's soiled cloths.

The Santa Anas blew dust and dry leaves against the French windows with ticks and rustles. It blew Charlotte and Liam back inside. They passed Allegra in the kitchen. They seemed unsteady on their feet. Were they both already drunk, or had some decision with mind-reeling consequences made them stumble? They went into the living room to await the other guests.

Allegra knew Holt wanted to speak with her but she couldn't find the time to break away. She didn't want to see him until she had fulfilled her half of their bargain. She had to complete her search of Charlotte's room – she had to see inside that suitcase – before she could honestly tell Holt that she had looked everywhere for clues as to Charlotte's secret. Allegra would wait until the party was well under way and the guests were drunk; then she could resume her snooping with little likelihood of being caught.

There was a thrumming expectancy in the house because of the party, but Allegra's anticipation came from the fact that this was probably her last evening on Lantana Drive. It was, perhaps, her last night in California, possibly even in the United States. If Holt had found proof of Charlotte's secret and had decided, based on its severity, how much they should demand from the actress, they might leave that night or early the next morning. Allegra was saying goodbye to cleaning work. She was sealing her future to Holt and their restaurant. She was terrified and giddy at the same time.

The telephone rang. Allegra answered it with wet hands and an urgent sense of time ticking away. The voice on the other end was plummy.

'Could I speak with Miss Verbena Marsh?' said the man. 'It's Mr Owens of Owens and Green in Boston. It's regarding her aunt's estate.'

Verbena came to the telephone in her bathrobe; her hair was sticky with a special conditioner she made from eggs and stale beer.

Allegra went back into the kitchen to work on the ceviche. She rubbed crushed garlic and coarse salt into the lobster meat, and allowed it to steep. She diced the thick white fillets of fish into bite-sized pieces. She finely chopped an amarillo pepper and two tomatoes. The red onion she sliced into transparent slivers. She boiled water on the stove.

Verbena came in after about ten minutes and sat down, looking bewildered. 'She left me everything,' she said, in a daze. 'I'm an obscenely rich woman.'

'Oh, Miss Marsh,' said Allegra.

Verbena looked at Allegra like a woman looking for answers. 'I wonder what I want to do now?' She sounded completely lost. 'I'd better get going. I've invited Madge to this silly party of Charlotte's and I ought to be ready when she arrives.'

Allegra dropped a dozen peeled shrimps into the boiling water and blanched them for thirty seconds. As side dishes, Allegra arranged a platter with corn on the cob and wedges of sweet potato drizzled with butter. She placed a large bowl of black beans in its centre. She mixed tequila and beer with fresh lime juice to form a fizzy cocktail and stocked a tray with martini glasses.

Around six o'clock, she heard the doorbell ring several times. Before she could get to it, however, she heard one of the women answer it. She heard greetings and the smack of exuberant kisses. She assumed Ivy was welcoming Congressman Whitewood. From the living room, she heard the chink of glasses. Laughter drowned out any discernible speech. A needle scratched along a record groove, then music began to play.

Allegra was hot and sticky from working all afternoon. She ran warm water into the Belfast sink and closed the scullery door to wash in private. She stripped down to her slip and ran a soapy washcloth over her body, hurrying, worried that somebody might barge in on her. She wet her hair and ran a comb through its tangles. She dried herself on a fresh towel in her room off the kitchen and changed into a dress Ivy had given to her rather than throwing it away. It was blue and far nicer than anything she usually wore around the house. Allegra was tying her hair up when Charlotte came into her room without knocking. Her face was pink with joy. Some of the champagne sloshed from the glass she was carrying.

'Oops,' Charlotte said, and her laughter tinkled up through her nose along with the sweet bubbles. 'I asked him, Allie. He said he would!' She clung drunkenly to the wall. 'We're going away together to the beach in Mexico for the weekend. We'll have three whole days together. Don't breathe a word . . .' Charlotte tried to raise a finger to her lips. It landed on the side of her cheek instead. 'Would you bring us some more drinks? I want to keep things celebratory.'

Allegra didn't ask what Charlotte was celebrating. She felt she knew. She had to ensure that Holt got the chance to threaten Charlotte before she left for Mexico. She felt sick to her stomach just thinking about it. She also wondered how they would get away after the transaction was completed – there was only the Peppers' truck . . .

Liam Malone appeared at the door and held Charlotte round the waist. His face was quite white.

'Don't squeeze,' Charlotte said. She pulled his hands away and rubbed her stomach tenderly, as if he had injured her.

'You have guests waiting,' Liam told her.

Charlotte kissed him deeply, then flitted from his grasp, saying, 'Bring in some ice, too, Allie.'

As soon as she was gone, Liam lit a cigarette. It took him two tries before the tip glowed to life.

'How is Agnes, Mr Malone?' Allegra asked quietly. She still felt guilty about losing the child at the Lava Lounge.

'Oh, she's just fine,' said Liam, dismissively. 'I'm sorry if I overreacted that night, Allie. I was out of my mind when I thought I'd lost her.'

'I'm glad she's well.'

'I need to ask you something. It's very hard for me, believe that. I find myself in a very unfortunate situation, a terrible situation . . .'

'Because of your wife . . .'

'No – well, yes, but not only because of her. I have another difficulty.'

Allegra wondered what Liam could want from her, even if her assumptions about Charlotte's delicate condition were correct.

'Thank God, Charlotte's been a gem about it. She recommended Mexico the minute she informed me. I didn't even have to ask . . . but I need some assistance.'

'If I can help, Mr Malone . . .'

'How does one find a discreet doctor in Mexico?' he asked. To his credit, Liam looked deeply ashamed. He hung his head.

'A doctor?' Allegra was confused. 'In Mexico, the big cities have hospitals but I think in Los Angeles you would get better care.'

'I don't want a hospital. Jesus!' Liam began pacing the small space. 'I want a woman who knows what she's doing. I'll pay anything. I want Charlotte to be cared for. I understand it's not that complicated, if you know the right – the best – people.'

Allegra suddenly knew what he was talking about. In her shock, she tried to be thoroughly modern in her response. 'When are you going?' she asked.

'She wants to go right away. I understand that. She told me to bring some clothes when she invited me over. I have a suitcase packed in my car so we can leave as soon as I can drag her away from this party.'

'Tijuana is just over the border. You could ask there.'

'I can't just stop on a street corner. Shit!'

'You need a *curandera*, a medicine woman. One of them might be willing to help.'

Liam threw his cigarette down on the floor of her room and crunched his shoe on it. 'I love her, Allie. You should know that. I don't know why it's important for me that you know that, but it is. When I'm with her, I know what happiness means. Aside from money, aside from things and fame, there is still simple happiness and I feel it most when I'm with her. I can't think of it as a baby, a real little baby, else I won't be able to help her through this . . . She's being so wonderful about it. She keeps talking about not hurting my wife unnecessarily, of making sure the children aren't hurt by our actions . . .'

Liam broke down then. He turned and left the room, wiping his eyes. Allegra knew she had to speak to Charlotte. Her employer and her employer's lover were approaching their dilemma from two completely different angles. It was a despicable misunderstanding. In Liam's mind, there was no notion of a glorious weekend away. He had no intention of ever enduring a hasty divorce and remarriage. Charlotte was already quite drunk, though. How would Allegra convey such a sensitive message to a tequila-muddled brain?

Slowly she went to the kitchen counter and mixed all the ingredients for the ceviche together. She watched the luminous flesh of the fresh fish turn cloudy from the acid in the sanguinello juice. The shrimp and lobster poached in the citrus, too. Allegra spooned the ceviche into wine glasses and carried them through to the living room on a tray.

The guests ooohed and aaahed at the sight of the bright spectacle. They tasted and sighed.

'This is wonderful,' declared Congressman Whitewood. He was speaking too loudly. 'The best I've ever had.'

Allegra bobbed a curtsy of thanks.

'You should have your own restaurant,' said Ivy.

'Yes, Miss Ivy,' said Allegra. 'I hope to.'

The partygoers were already in an advanced state of dishevelment. Shoes had been discarded. Eyelids drooped.

Allegra went back into the kitchen and washed up. An hour later, she placed an ice block from the cold box in a silver bowl and slid an ice pick and tongs down beside it. In the living room, bodies were now tangled on the sofas. Lamps were lit and a stick of incense and several candles burned. The air was fragrant with eastern spices and whiskey. Verbena and Madge St Claire were kissing. Allegra didn't believe it for a second but they were fused together like a man and a woman, their bodies straining for contact, their hands roaming the expensive fabric of their dresses. Charlotte laughed. Allegra felt drunk. The smells were overpowering; the lighting was strange.

'Have you seen a ghost, Allie?' asked Charlotte. 'You're as white as snow.'

The room went quiet. Everybody stared at Allegra. She could hear the gramophone needle scratching against the paper label at the centre of the record; it had finished playing minutes before. The atmosphere was expectant, still. Madge's hand moved against the silk of Verbena's dress, kneading her nipple to an erect point. It was the only movement in the room.

'I just remembered!' shouted Charlotte. She was talking far too loudly. 'We should go down and see the trees I've had planted. They're so beautiful. You'll have to mind the bees, though.'

'Bees?' slurred Liam.

'The Okies have brought some beehives with them. They're down in the canyon near their campsite,' explained Verbena.

'Are those people still here, Charlotte?' said Madge. 'If you're not firm, you'll have to get the police in to run them off.'

'They're still working,' said Verbena. 'They've been building a staircase down to Charlotte's orchard.'

Ivy squealed and leaped to her feet. Congressman Whitewood followed her. 'We should go and look at that!' she squawked. 'Maybe we'll see the bees. Buzz! Buzz! Buzz!'

'It's the middle of the night,' said Verbena, but Ivy dragged her to her feet.

She wasn't sure if it was because she was so drunk, or because Madge's lips were so sweet and soft, but Verbena felt she didn't mind Ivy marrying Congressman Whitewood any more. It was good just to be her friend again. Verbena was rich. She didn't have to compete with anybody any more. She could just buy what she wanted. The realization was illuminating. Verbena was so happy with the way the evening had ended up that she complied with the others' plans.

The two couples went towards the French windows, towing Charlotte and Liam behind them. Allegra followed in their wake but she stopped when they went out on to the deck. When she was sure they were leaving the house, she turned away from them and walked down the hallway to Charlotte's room.

32

The last electric filament of sunlight singed the tops of the faraway mountains. The women's high-pitched chatter was jarring in the quiet. An owl screeched at them from a gum tree and they shrieked back in surprise as they made their way along the spur towards the top of the new garden stairs. Below them in the canyon, the kerosene lamps of the Peppers' campsite glowed. Charlotte could make out three figures – Roscoe, Harmony and Holt – standing quietly in the darkness, watching their approach.

'I'm not climbing all the way down there,' said Verbena. 'I'm in silk.'

She was somewhat disappointed. She had been quite excited about kissing Madge amid the scent of orange blossoms.

'Don't you want to see the bees?' asked Ivy.

'Not enough to tackle that many stairs. I'm very drunk, you know.'

'Me, too, actually,' added Ivy.

'Charlotte, this is ridiculous,' said Madge. 'It's a bloody Hooverville down there.'

'It's their home,' replied Charlotte. 'For now, at least. It's all they have.'

'Beautiful Charlotte,' said Liam, softly. 'I love your heart.'

At that the whole group went silent. They had all assumed

an affair and nobody had really cared. Now that it was love, it was serious. It would have consequences.

'We should take a drive instead,' said Madge, always politic, always smart. 'Why don't we go to the Dairy Queen for some ice cream?'

'Yes,' said Congressman Whitewood. 'Let's take off.'

He began to usher Ivy, Verbena and Madge back along the path.

'Thanks for a lovely evening, Charlotte,' said Madge.

'Yeah, it was swell,' said Whitewood.

They blew her kisses with booze-soaked breath.

'Call us from Mexico,' said Ivy. 'Or we'll see you when you get back. Whatever!'

Charlotte watched them lurch around the house to the drive.

'There's going to be a scandal,' she heard Verbena's voice sing in the distance. 'Shit!' she heard Madge declare.

An engine started, then another. The cars drove off and there was silence again.

Inside the house, Allegra had dragged Charlotte's suitcase from the top of the armoire on to the bed. She opened it, expecting to search along the seams for the concealed hiding place as she had witnessed Verbena doing. Instead, Allegra saw something astonishing. The suitcase contained, in plain sight, a large green bank bag stuffed with cash.

Liam could hear the cicadas in the canyon. He stood alone beside the woman he loved, surrounded by desert. For a moment, it was hauntingly poignant.

'If you don't like them here, I'll have them leave,' said

Charlotte, who thought Liam was assessing the squatters. 'If you don't like Allie, I'll let her go, too.'

'You can't fire her now,' said Liam. 'You might need looking after next week, even a bit of nursing probably. I'll try to stop by most days, of course.'

'What do you mean?' asked Charlotte.

'After . . . Mexico, you'll need some discreet care. I don't think the procedure is especially pleasant.' He crossed his chest with his fingertip. 'God forgive me.'

Allegra arrived, bemused by her discovery of the money, beside them. She looked down at the campsite and saw a vignette of her future if she didn't find a way to take that money away from Charlotte Caine. If she and Holt were careful, it might be enough to finance their restaurant. But Holt was right – they couldn't just take the money and run. Charlotte would surely set the police on them. If they blackmailed her, however, Charlotte would never contact the authorities and their departure would be a welcome relief.

Allegra pulled her eyes away from the canyon and listened to Charlotte and Liam, who were face to face in the middle of a harrowing conversation.

'We can't have a baby together, Charlotte,' said Liam. 'I wish we could.'

'But you love children,' said Charlotte.

'Yes, and I have six of them already with my wife.'

'I don't want our baby to be a bastard. There's plenty of time to sort things out. We could be married by the New Year.' She smiled as if Liam wasn't grasping her point. This was just some silly, laughable misunderstanding that would be cleared up in a few minutes.

Allegra could see that Holt had started up the hillside towards them. Was he going to confront Charlotte now?

'Once we're married,' continued Charlotte, 'nobody will count the days. We can say the baby came early.'

'A divorce?' said Liam, incredulously. He actually laughed. 'Oh, Charlotte, what have you got into your silly head?'

'Mexico,' she said. 'That little church . . .'

'No,' said Liam. 'A little back room where they'll erase our mistake in half an hour. You'll be as right as rain by Monday. I've said I'll come with you. You won't be alone.'

'I will be alone,' said Charlotte.

It was said as an epiphany. Her eyes went wide with the realization. Her face was imbued with the expressionless calm of deep understanding.

Holt came over to them, breathing heavily from the climb. 'We're nearly finished,' he interjected. He was under the impression that they were discussing the staircase. 'We just have this last step to see to and we'll be . . .'

Liam ignored him.

Charlotte made a final desperate bid. 'I'll make you happy, Liam. You'll have a real marriage at last.'

Liam looked torn. Was there still time to be married to a woman he truly loved? Would his children forgive him? He didn't think so.

'You can't get married,' Holt said.

'What?' said Charlotte, stunned by this absurd interruption.

'Because of this,' said Holt. He held out an envelope with the seal of the state of Florida in its corner. 'Because you're already married.'

It was a chancy gambit. Charlotte might say she had

divorced Archie Welch years ago, but even if that were the case, Holt could tell from the look on Liam's face that the man knew nothing of his lover's past.

Charlotte turned on Holt. 'You treacherous dog,' she whispered. 'What do you think you know?' She spun towards Allegra. 'And you! How dare you tiptoe around behind my back?'

All the rage Charlotte had been suppressing for the past few minutes flared into her skin. 'How dare you blackmail me after all I've done for you, you unspeakable bitch!' She lashed out at Allegra and scratched her face. Holt grabbed Charlotte to stop the attack and Liam grabbed Holt. There was a messy struggle, pushing and shoving, before the two men finally pulled the women free of each other. Liam slammed Allegra against the topmost post of the staircase handrail and held her pressed there. Holt was restraining Charlotte's arms but the actress was still screaming. Her fury was now directed at Liam.

'It's our baby!' she screamed. 'It's our baby. The baby we made together in Malibu. Do you remember Malibu, Liam?'

Liam's eyes were wet. 'I remember every minute with you, every breath of you, Charlotte. I fell in love with you in Malibu and it tore my life apart.'

Charlotte was crying, too. 'Then be with me,' she said. The fight went out of her and Holt loosed her arms so that she could hold out her hands to Liam. 'It's so simple. We should have what we love. You told me that.'

'I have a wife!'

'You don't love her,' said Charlotte. 'Not the way you love me.'

'And there's Agnes and the boys . . .'

'You'll still have them! You'll have them and you'll have me.' Charlotte's legs buckled and she almost went down on her knees. 'Aren't I worth it? Aren't I worth anything?'

'It's not that.'

Charlotte stopped suddenly. Her eyes cleared of tears and it seemed her understanding clarified, too. A stillness overtook her whole body. 'It's the baby,' she said, with absolute certainty. 'I'll get rid of it, then. That's what you want, isn't it? It's appalling timing. I understand that, my love.' She touched Liam's face. 'I'll get rid of it for you.'

'Shut up,' Liam said quietly. He couldn't stand it being put that way. That he alone would be responsible for this abortion when it happened. That God would read his name on the sin. 'Shut up!' he roared. He slapped Charlotte hard across her face.

'Enough!' said Holt. 'The lady's in distress, can't you see that?' He turned to Charlotte. 'Calm down, Miss Charlotte. There's a baby? All this shouting can't be good for it.'

Perhaps because he had acknowledged the baby, expressed concern for it, Charlotte turned round in Holt's arms and clung to him, weeping.

'Is everything okay up there?' It was Roscoe Pepper. His voice sounded from halfway up the hillside. He was coming to see what the fuss was about. They could make out the aura of his lantern moving through the grass.

'I'll wait to have a baby. I can wait until the time is right,' said Charlotte. 'I'll get rid of it this weekend in Mexico.'

Liam's face went into his two hands, like that of a boy in deep shame. 'What have I done?' he asked nobody in particular. 'What have I done to you?'

'You made me happy,' Charlotte said. 'Anything bad that was done to me was done long before I met you.'

Liam took a deep breath and tried another tack. He had long since given up any sense of propriety. This achingly private argument had been conducted in front of the help. He didn't care. He only wanted it to be over. 'Charlotte, try to understand. I married my wife because she was the kind of woman she is. She's solid and good and loyal. I was with you because you're the kind of woman you are.'

Charlotte moved from Holt's arms into Liam's. Liam caressed her cheeks and pushed her hair behind her ears. Roscoe arrived to witness the moment.

'You're beautiful and exciting and men want you . . .' Liam continued. 'Not for babies, though, Charlotte.' He kissed the top of her head. 'Can you understand that?' He held her face in his hands and lifted it so he could look directly into her eyes.

'Okay, okay,' said Charlotte. She was throwing dreams away. 'I don't need babies,' she said. 'I can give that up.' The ultimate thought came to her. 'I can even give up the house. I don't need my own house, Liam. I only need you.' Charlotte laughed. Relinquishing her house would have been inconceivable to her fifteen minutes before, but now there was only Liam, and keeping him, and having him make love to her and wanting it. 'I love you so much,' she said.

He had to be harsh, Liam could see that now. He had to end this, with pain if necessary. He couldn't give her what she needed. He was drunk. It was all too much. 'And I love fucking you, Charlotte.'

It took several seconds for the comment to sink in.

Charlotte seemed to inflate slowly. She grew in stature

as she pulled away from Liam. She drew in breath. She used all the power of her pent-up steam, raised her arms and slammed her palms into the middle of Liam's chest with such force that he stumbled backwards.

For a second, Charlotte thought of how Liam had taken the rabbit from its cage in the desert when they were shooting in Palm Springs, and how it had kicked and kicked at him when he was only trying to set it free. In the half-second it took that image to race through her head, Liam scrambled for balance on the topmost step. Then the board tilted. It was the last board, the one that had not yet been nailed home. It came loose with a snap and a clatter. Liam's arms flailed in the air. Allegra saw the disbelief in his eyes as he disappeared over the edge of the slope. His legs thrashed wildly but he didn't make a sound as he crashed through the handrail and bounced off the stairs.

By the time they all reached the edge and looked down, Liam was motionless. His clothes were torn in places. He was bloody. He lay face down, his arms and legs splayed, but his neck had turned all the way round so that his face looked back up at them. His startling dark Irish eyes reflected the moonlight and a few cold, gold chips of stars and an otherworldly emptiness.

33

Harmony reached the body first. She swung the beam of her kerosene lantern across Liam's face and screamed. Roscoe and Holt hurried down to her, skidding in the dust. Roscoe took his wife in his arms, turning her eyes away from the scene.

'He's dead!' shouted Holt.

Above the crest of the hill, he could make out the white circles of Charlotte and Allegra's astonished faces. The two women came to life and slid down the hill together. The back of Charlotte's dress was torn and dirty by the time she reached the place where Liam lay.

'No,' she said softly. 'I just pushed him . . .'

She fell down beside Liam's twisted torso and grabbed it as if she could shake the life back into the man. She recoiled from the hideous sensation of embracing the dislocated body and fell back on her elbows in the dirt.

'Someone should call the police,' said Allegra. 'I'll do it. I'll go.'

'No!' said Holt.

Everybody looked to him for advice. Even Roscoe seemed willing to follow Holt's lead.

'How?' asked Charlotte. 'How? How?' She kept repeating the enquiry.

'You killed him, that's how. We all saw you shove him.'

'It was an accident,' said Charlotte.

'Don't matter,' said Holt. 'You'll go to jail for it.'

Allegra turned and pounded Holt's chest feebly with her fists. She wanted, needed, for him to stop. In that moment she hated him. His cruelty seemed unbearably harsh.

'I didn't mean to,' said Charlotte. 'I love him.' And then, hopelessly, to Liam's body, 'I love you.' She pulled herself up and stood with tears streaming down her face.

'We have to call an ambulance,' suggested Harmony.

'Ambulance?' said Holt. 'The man is dead. His head's half torn off, for God's sake.' He paced for a few seconds, massaging his temples, trying to get the thoughts flowing inside his head again. 'Already got that damn blue sniffing around me through no fault of my own. I'm in the crosshairs because of you, Miss Caine. Because of you and that Mr Pike.'

He flapped the envelope containing the marriage certificate manically in the air. Despite all the chaos, he hadn't let it go.

'Miss Caine here is a married woman.'

'I don't understand,' said Harmony, her voice quavering. 'Why does it matter if she's married? Isn't Mr Malone married, too?'

'It matters because her studio doesn't know about it,' said Holt. 'They're pushing her as their fresh new starlet. She's lied on her contract, I'll bet. Worse still, she's philandering with a married man who has six children . . .'

At the mention of Liam's children, they all glanced at the body again but it was too terrible to contemplate.

'Who's your husband, Miss Caine?' asked Harmony. Despite everything, she was polite, in awe of the actress.

'He's in care,' said Charlotte. 'He should have died. I wish he'd died . . .' Her voice trailed off.

'Ain't going to prison for the likes of you,' said Holt.

He held an accusatory finger in Charlotte's face. She looked terrified but also blank. She was drunk and all of this was an inexplicable nightmare. Holt addressed the small assembly.

'Here's how it's gonna be. Miss Caine and Mr Malone left for Mexico tonight. The guests at the party knew they were going –'

Allegra interrupted, speaking quietly to Charlotte, 'Ivy and Verbena will both say you left together. Mr Malone brought a suitcase. He said it was in his car.'

'So you've gone to Mexico,' said Holt. 'You've taken off together and might never be seen again. The rest of us were leaving tomorrow anyway.'

'What do you plan on doing with the body?' asked Roscoe.

It was as if they were discussing a remote problem. Everything was hypothetical. Nobody imagined they would do the things they were contemplating. Holt turned to look at the final hole, the one they had already dug for the last sanguinello tree, which they had not yet planted.

'Grave's already half dug,' Holt said. 'We put him in it. We cover him over so the coyotes don't get at him.'

As if it had heard Holt's words, a coyote howled in the darkness. It sounded jarringly close.

'No,' said Charlotte. She was frantic. 'I'll call the police. I'll say you pushed him, Mr Holt.'

'Allegra saw you do it,' said Holt. He had expected this of Charlotte. He wasn't angry.

'A famous actress's word against that of a Mexican maid and a vagrant who are admitted lovers?' shouted Charlotte. 'Who do you think they'd believe?'

'They'd believe it if four of us said it,' piped up Roscoe.

'You didn't see anything!' screamed Charlotte. 'Mr Holt pushed Liam. He murdered him. I'm going to call Madge. She'll fix it.'

Holt reached out and slapped Charlotte smartly across the face. She recovered from the blow and faced him without cowering. She didn't even raise a palm to her cheek to cool the burn. Allegra saw that Charlotte was a woman who had taken her fair share of beatings. The realization shocked her more than anything else she had witnessed that night.

'Nobody's gonna fix this for you, Miss Caine. Believe you know that,' said Holt.

Charlotte took his glare head-on. Yet again, powerfully, she felt sure she had seen the man somewhere before . . .

'I can't put him in the ground.' Charlotte went down on her knees and took Liam's hand. 'He's still warm.'

'Roscoe and I will do it,' said Holt.

'I want no part of this,' said Roscoe. 'Harmony and me will pack up our truck and leave this very minute.'

He started to move away, helping his shocked wife, but Holt grabbed his shoulder. 'You're in it, Roscoe. You ain't walking away. You're gonna help me out of it or, God forgive me . . .'

The threat remained unfinished but Roscoe saw Holt's resolve. 'I'll just put Harmony in the tent,' he said.

While Roscoe settled his wife and gave her his hip flask of brandy to sip, Holt issued orders. 'We got two shovels. We dig in shifts. Gonna be heavy work.' He pointed at Charlotte. 'You're going to help us, Miss Caine. Bring some candles from the house, if you got them. Bring lanterns, too. Get sensible shoes on your feet.'

Allegra hugged herself as she listened to Holt, awaiting her instructions. She was so cold. Her senses were numb.

'Allegra,' said Holt. 'We'll be leaving soon, too.'

He was still saying 'we', Allegra noticed. She found she was grateful for the word.

'Pack whatever you wanna take, then get back down here to help,' Holt continued. 'We're all in this together.'

'I can't dig,' said Charlotte, plaintively. 'I'm expecting a baby.'

'I'll do her share,' said Allegra. Harmony had also been affected by Charlotte's statement. She came to the entrance of the tent.

'Where am I going?' said Charlotte.

'You can come with us,' said Harmony. 'We'll go back to the farm. You can stay as long as you like. You'll need help until the baby comes, at least. I'll look after you.'

Roscoe did not object. He was as bewildered as any of them. Having failed to deliver so much of what he had promised Harmony when he married her, he could not deny her this.

'I can't live on a farm,' said Charlotte.

'Well, you're gonna,' said Holt, with finality. 'Unless you got somewhere else to go where nobody'll recognize you.' He gave Charlotte a shove that started her up the hill.

'She won't leave her home . . .' said Allegra.

'She's leaving it tonight,' said Holt. 'And she ain't coming back. Take whatever you want from the house, whatever we can fit into Mr Malone's car.'

'What about her agent? What about Warner Brothers?' asked Allegra. 'Won't they all be looking for her?'

It seemed pathetic to be worrying about details at a time like this but Allegra felt she had to.

'They'll think she took off with Mr Malone. Everyone will think it.'

'There's money in the house,' said Allegra. 'A lot of cash. I found it in Miss Charlotte's room.'

'Take it all,' said Holt. 'We've gotta get away from here. The police'll put you in jail or send you back to Mexico, if they think you're involved in any of this. This is the dream, Allegra. It's dirty and ugly and it don't come any closer on its own. Now we gotta run towards it.'

Allegra managed to nod. 'I'll watch Miss Charlotte in the house,' she said.

She ran up the hill until she caught up with Charlotte's struggling form, twisted in the satin ropes of her torn dress.

Holt said to Roscoe, 'Dig.'

It took them three hours to complete the hole. The men dug until their falling sweat dampened the dust around them. When they broke for ten minutes every hour to catch their breath, Allegra took over while Charlotte held a lantern for her. They listened for the return of Verbena's car in the silent darkness of the canyon. They didn't hear it. Allegra looked at Charlotte's face. It was grimed with dirt and tears. Her hair was dishevelled and sticking to her cheeks. She was still beautiful, the most beautiful woman Allegra had ever seen, and what had all that beauty brought her?

Holt went over to take the shovel from Allegra. In the darkness, he misstepped and kicked hard against a solid object. His foot went through it with a splintering crunch. It was one of the Peppers' beehives. Holt pulled the toe of his boot free and bees spewed out, befuddled and furious.

They rose in a cloud that couldn't be seen in the dark orchard but which could clearly be heard. Their combined buzz was a chainsaw in the night. Allegra tried to brush them away.

'Bees!' Allegra shouted. 'Holt, bees!'

Realization dawned on Holt. Allegra could not take stings. More than one or two might kill her. He grabbed the canvas awning from the side of the Ford and wrapped her in it, throwing her face down on the ground. Harmony hurriedly zipped herself into her tent to keep the insects out. Charlotte whimpered and slapped at her body as the bees surrounded her. Holt took her ferociously by the top of the arm and threw her under the covering with Allegra. The thick canvas protected the two women. Roscoe shouted instructions to Holt, who tried to follow them. The two men stood still. There was nothing they could do. They took the stings.

When the worst of the swarm's fury and confusion had passed, Roscoe and Holt picked up Liam's body and tossed it unceremoniously into the bottom of the pit they had prepared. They shovelled dirt in on top of it.

Liam Malone – movie star, father, all-round nice guy – was gone.

Wrapped in the tight bag of their canvas shroud, Allegra and Charlotte could do nothing but look at each other. Their faces were close enough to kiss. Both trembled in the aftermath of a terrible personal quake. So different in appearance, each recognized herself in the filthy face of the other. Charlotte cried again. Each of her half-dozen stings burned. Holt's quick thinking had kept Allegra from danger.

Eventually the noise of the bees subsided. It was replaced with the relentless scratching of the shovels against hard ground. It was a sound Charlotte would always associate with tragic endings.

The airlessness beneath the canvas didn't cause Allegra to panic. It made her light-headed, almost joyful. The hopelessness of her situation brought her a profound peace. She thought about Allegra's by the sea, the taste of Lucia's special sangria swirling in a wine glass like the juice of blood oranges.

'I've been stung,' Charlotte called out, in despair.

'We've all been stung,' said Holt, gruffly. 'Shut up!'

Charlotte and Allegra eventually fell asleep. When Allegra woke, Holt had removed the canvas from around her. There was no visible grave in the place where they had been digging, only the flat, unforgiving desert sand raked over and camouflaged with pebbles and a few dead branches from the chaparral brush. In a few days, the Santa Anas would blow the face of the orchard clean and the site would be invisible.

'The bees are starting to head out,' said Roscoe. 'You girls better go wait for us in the house. Holt and I will bring the truck up to fetch you.'

Harmony sat quietly under the last morning stars. She was wrapped in her quilt; she rocked herself. Holt threw the tarpaulin into the Peppers' truck. Dead bees rained from it like fragments of charcoal. He collected his paltry possessions from among the detritus of the campsite and loaded them, too, for the drive up to the house.

Harmony roused herself and went over to where Charlotte still slept. 'Have you decided if you're coming with us?' Harmony asked. 'If you don't, you're on your own. If you do, you'll be cared for. You can stay with us for ever, if you like.'

'The movie . . .' said Charlotte, drowsily.

'All that's over now, Miss Charlotte,' said Harmony. She held Charlotte's head against her breast and stroked her hair.

Allegra saw Charlotte rest her whole weight against Harmony's body in complete surrender.

'You'll be a mama soon. I'll help you with the baby,' Harmony said. Her face lit up at the thought. 'I'd be glad to do it.'

Charlotte allowed Harmony to escort her up the hill for the last time. Roscoe and Holt drove the truck out of the canyon. After a few minutes, the place was as empty as it should have been, except for the sanguinello trees and the burrows of the lean coyotes.

It was six o'clock in the morning by the time Allegra and Charlotte moved quietly through the house, gathering precious belongings. Allegra found there were only a few things she wanted to hold on to. One was her mother and father's wedding picture in its silver frame. The other was Lucia's book of handwritten recipes.

Holt and the Peppers waited on the drive.

'She can help us out with the bank,' Roscoe said to Harmony. 'Make that payment on the farm that's due.'

'We can't ask her to do that!' said Harmony.

'Sure we can,' said Roscoe. 'She'll be getting a room and board from us. We'll be doing her a favour by keeping our mouths shut.'

Allegra and Charlotte met at the front door in silence.

Holt saw a large bag in Allegra's hands. If that was the cash, there was a lot of it, enough.

'I own a house,' said Charlotte to nobody.

Holt had taken Liam's keys from his pocket before they buried his body and now he used them to open the dead man's car. He didn't look back at Charlotte as he threw Allegra's bags into the trunk of the Rolls-Royce. 'Forget all that,' said Holt. 'Get used to forgetting it.'

The Peppers didn't want to stay any longer. Roscoe revved the Ford's engine as Harmony helped a somnambulant Charlotte into the back. Holt walked over to Roscoe and handed him a brick of Charlotte's money. 'You've earned it,' he said.

Roscoe did not thank him. He did not wave goodbye. He was a Christian man and he felt physically sick at himself. Roscoe knew the way home, however. He drove his old Ford on to Lantana Drive.

Allegra watched them go. She felt weak and hot. She turned and retched into the flower bed but only water came up. Holt caught her before she fell. 'Holt,' she said. 'I think I took a few stings after all.'

Harmony sat in the back of the truck to keep Charlotte company on the trip. She peeped inside Charlotte's suitcase and found a silk bathrobe. She held it up and smiled condescendingly.

'It's a farm, Miss Charlotte. You won't get any use from the likes of this. You don't want folks recognizing you as a glamorous actress, do you? You'll be a farm hand for a while, just until you decide where you're going next. I can look after the baby till you get situated.'

There was no traffic on the road at that hour. Roscoe drove until the hills receded. The land grew flatter. Buildings grew sparser and more modest. They left the verdant lawns of the suburbs behind them. The earth here was scorched by sun and fire. They drove for thirty miles until, for a few brief minutes, Charlotte saw the shimmering blue of the Atlantic.

It was her turn to rummage through her suitcase now. She found the gold organza bag she was looking for. She opened it. From inside, Harmony saw her retrieve a red glass bottle in the shape of a tulip – a beautiful thing. Charlotte reached her hands over the side of the truck and pulled the stopper from the delicate bottle. The seal was fragile with age and the wax cracked into tiny bits. Charlotte tipped the bottle upside down. The wind whipped the scent away before either of them could catch the ghost of its fragrance – just as Charlotte had intended. The Fleurs de Rocaille splashed a trail behind the truck on the blacktop. When it was empty, Charlotte dropped the bottle. It smashed to crimson splinters, each one sharp enough to cut the skin.

For a second, Charlotte thought she smelt Liam, or was it the sweet, warm scent of chocolate cake just from the oven? Roscoe turned the truck inland then, on to a road that pulled them further and further away from the sea. From there on, California was dry, a place of dust and rocks – and the flowers that survived there were small and dull and spiky.

34

Ivy and Verbena only started to worry about Charlotte's whereabouts on Tuesday evening, and it was Ivy who called for help on Wednesday morning. She didn't call the police; she called the Warner Brothers security office. A man who looked like a banker in a pinstriped suit arrived at the house on Lantana Drive. Apparently Mrs Malone had already called them the previous day, asking when her husband was expected back from his location shoot.

Under duress, Ivy confessed that she had waved Charlotte and Liam off on Friday night as they left together for a weekend in Mexico. Verbena confirmed the story. It was true that neither of them had actually witnessed the couple's departure but both women were reluctant to admit where they had really been late that Friday night. Congressman Nathaniel Whitewood had driven straight to the Beverly Hills Hotel, checked in under his chauffeur's name and spent the entire night making love to his fiancée. Verbena had joined Madge St Claire at her home in Westwood and spent the night there. Neither woman was willing to confess to her illicit affair, least of all to representatives of the studio.

Madge St Claire arrived, in her role as agent, to support Verbena during the questioning. 'Where's that maid of yours?' she asked, when she noticed her ashtray hadn't been emptied.

Ivy looked around the messy living room and shrugged. 'Maybe Charlotte gave her the weekend off,' she said. 'I see those Okies have finally gone, too.'

'The weekend off? It's Wednesday!'

Ivy glanced into Allegra's room and saw most of the maid's belongings were gone. 'I think she's run away with her beau, too,' she volunteered.

Madge and the security officer went out on to the deck and looked down at the abandoned campsite. The grass was flattened and there was a ring of stones surrounding a charred pit where their fire had been.

'I think Charlotte's just off having some fun,' said Ivy. 'Leave her alone. She'll be home tomorrow or on Friday at the latest. Don't you agree, Bee?'

'I don't really care what Charlotte does any more,' said Verbena.

For the first time in months, she felt free. She had received a second telephone call on Sunday evening from her aunt Honor's attorney in Boston. He apologized for disturbing her on a weekend but he thought she would want to know that the contents of her late aunt's will had included a letter. The executor read it to her over the line.

I have always felt an affinity for the untenable situation in which you have found yourself, Verbena, as a romantic of a different and socially unacceptable sort. I have silently commiserated with your pain and difficulties for many years but, due to my own marital situation, have never found it appropriate to offer salve. I hope you shall now enjoy the happiness and fulfilment that only financial freedom allows. I trust you will follow your heart, as I never found the courage to do.

As a result of this news – and the disclosure of the actual bequest amount as being well in excess of half a million dollars – Verbena was feeling charitable, dizzy with liberation.

'Wait until Friday,' said Ivy.

Both actresses knew that Liam Malone had scenes to shoot on Friday – he had mentioned it at the party – so the couple was bound to be home by then. They wouldn't miss any actual work, but Liam was starting to risk a serious indiscretion. If he stayed away any longer, his wife would have to be told that he was with another woman. His children would find out about the affair. Everybody knew that Liam Malone would not risk his relationship with his children . . .

When the telephone rang on Friday afternoon, Verbena snatched up the receiver prepared to bawl at Charlotte. The female voice at the other end of the line was unfamiliar and coolly apologetic. The woman introduced herself as Sister Olivia from the Convent of the Sisters of Mercy. She explained that she needed to reach Miss Charlotte Caine urgently. When Verbena explained that Charlotte was unavailable, Sister Olivia told her that Mr Patrick Caine, Charlotte's father, had passed away peacefully in the night. Decisions regarding his interment needed to be made. Verbena promised that Charlotte would be told as soon as she could be contacted.

On Monday, when the couple had been missing for two weekends, the press started to put two and two together. Charlotte Caine hadn't gone away for a quick break: she had done a moonlight flit, and one of Hollywood's leading men had done it with her.

By the following Wednesday, the situation had grown more intense. Charlotte still hadn't returned and nobody had heard from her. Ivy and Verbena were, by then, astonished. Madge St Claire was deeply concerned. She had to make decisions regarding the burial of Patrick Caine on Charlotte's behalf and it was more responsibility than she felt she was being remunerated for. The little voice inside Madge's head insisted that something bad had happened to Charlotte. She was also experiencing enormous anxiety about the large sum of cash she had advanced to her from Verbena's account. She might have to get seriously creative with her accounting to cover the error. And if Charlotte's completion money didn't come through, Madge knew she risked accusations of fraud.

At the studio, management was in uproar. Liam Malone had disappeared, too. It was increasingly clear that the two stars really had gone off together. By the end of the second week, lawyers, accountants and agents were in day-long emergency meetings about the situation with *The Walls of Jericho*. The police and the United States border patrol were notified. Private investigators were hired. Mrs Malone was hysterical. Fortunately she had access to her husband's accounts and did not find herself in financial need. Bernadette Malone maintained that Liam adored her and his children. He would never leave her. The police, who had seen Charlotte Caine's picture in the press, were sure he had done just that. Rumours were rampant that Liam Malone had been stashing money away for months in preparation for his separation from his wife. It was true that Bernadette found the accounts far lighter than she had anticipated but Liam had enjoyed spending money: he loved horseracing, he treated friends to fine dinners – it all added up.

Liam Malone's ardent followers speculated that he was on a distant island somewhere in the middle of a blue sea, using an assumed name. How could he abandon his fame? his fans asked. The Hollywood insiders felt they knew. The life of a star wasn't all it was cracked up to be. The news of Liam and Charlotte's bold move made headlines for weeks, then months. Without its stars, *The Walls of Jericho* was shelved. If the errant couple ever did return – the Warner Brothers attorneys threatened in every press statement they made – both Liam Malone and Charlotte Caine would face prosecution for breach of contract. Mrs Malone sued the studio. The studio sued the production company. The production company sued a well-known insurance agency, which held the 'assurance of completion' policy on the picture. The insurance agency was bankrupted by the settlement of the claim. Tens of thousands of policy owners, who had paid their premiums despite the economic ravages of the depression, found themselves with no cover.

Bernadette Malone ultimately sought to declare her husband's departure abandonment, but she never applied for a divorce. She'd be damned if Charlotte Caine would ever be allowed to call herself the legitimate Mrs Liam Malone. Let the two of them live in sin and God curse them. Mrs Malone set about poisoning all six of her children against their father. The boys cleaved to their mother and mollycoddled her all their lives. Only Agnes never lost her affection for her father. She missed him sorely. She tried very hard to understand why he had never contacted her.

She mourned the loss of him. When her first son was born, she named him Liam.

With no leads as to the missing couple's whereabouts and nobody left to sue, the debacle eventually quietened down.

Ivy Stone married Congressman Nathaniel Whitewood at the Bel Air Country Club. Verbena, looking pale and too thin, was her only bridesmaid. The couple had decided on a honeymoon in Mexico. This news had been reported in the society pages months before the event. The day before her wedding, Ivy had received a letter from Charlotte Caine. She managed to keep it a secret, except from her closest friend. That evening, Verbena sat on Ivy's bed and, sworn to secrecy, read the single page. It was unquestionably in Charlotte Caine's handwriting.

> *My darling Ivy,*
> *Who else can I trust? I need you to do something of great importance for me. Liam and I are in Mexico. I can't tell you exactly where. Please, please, please can you say you've seen us while on your honeymoon and that we are looking well and relaxed? Just make it all up as you like. If you describe us as blissfully happy, you will be right. We have bought a house and love it here – all the sun and sea is good for us. We are sorry for Mrs Malone and her children but you don't have to say anything about that. Say you won't disclose our location to anyone. We deserve to be left in peace. Thank you, dearest Ivy. I know you will help me now that I need it most.*
> *Best wishes,*
> *Charlotte*

'Will you do it?' Verbena asked.

'I don't see why not.'

'The bloody insurance company could subpoena you to tell where they are, for one. I'm sure the studio would like to get their hands on them, too.'

'That insurance-company man blew his brains out right after the judge's ruling,' said Ivy. She was trying on her veil and the sight of her made Verbena's chest hurt. 'I don't care a jot for the studio. Tomorrow I'll be a married woman.'

She began to think about how she would describe seeing Liam and Charlotte in Mexico. Nathaniel would back her up. He adored her. He was a bona fide politician now. He lied about everything.

'I don't care about the studio either,' said Verbena, wistfully. She had applied to attend the University of California at Berkeley.

Ivy drifted into the ennui of wedded life and Verbena moved on, too. Verbena and Madge St Claire grew closer but never declared themselves a couple. Even in Hollywood, it wasn't done. Verbena found her calling as a scholar and eventually won a position as a lecturer in the emerging field of women's studies in the 1960s. Berkeley was building its reputation on an ethos of progressiveness and Verbena had fallen in love with the place, its eager young students, its eccentric values. She was sometimes questioned by reporters as to her knowledge of the events of the fall of 1935, but the period in her life when she had been a glamorous actress caused her acute embarrassment. Verbena declined any interviews that she feared might delve into her pre-Berkeley past.

In 1972, when she was in her mid-sixties, Verbena Marsh won the Pulitzer Prize for a groundbreaking non-fiction book she had written about the role of lesbians in American society. As a result, she was lauded and ostracized in equal measure. Verbena had always lived her life at the two extremes of the scale of experience. She relished controversy. At times, she had even been tempted to reveal her role as one-time murderess, but she never did.

When Verbena died at the age of eighty-seven, Ivy Stone-Whitewood was conspicuous at her funeral. The beloved congressman's widow wanted her support and admiration for Verbena to be known. Ivy contributed an obituary to the *Los Angeles Times*. Her love for Verbena took up a whole page.

Charlotte Caine had arrived on the Peppers' farm in a state of shock. Harmony had gone into Bakersfield that first day and purchased some hair dye from the drugstore. It was expensive, a real indulgence, but she needed it for Charlotte. Together, out by the water pump, they washed Charlotte's blonde crown away.

'When the wave comes out, you'll look completely different,' said Harmony. 'Nobody would ever know who you are.'

Charlotte rocked herself for comfort. She didn't answer. She had always been vain about her hair.

The Peppers were stoic and strict. Harmony wouldn't allow Charlotte to go into town for months. She claimed it would be dangerous for Charlotte to be seen. She might be recognized. Charlotte grew fat and lazy on the farm. She helped with the chores. Even she was surprised by how quickly age and ugliness descended on her face. The sun splattered her nose and cheeks with freckles. Drudgery brought on wrinkles. Charlotte grieved for Liam. She never recovered from the loss of him. At night, before she fell asleep, she would think of Liam coming out of the sea and how cool his thigh had felt against her palm when she had reached out to touch him and found that he was real.

In some of her dreams, before Liam fell, she caught his shirt and steadied him. The scare of the near-accident sobered both of them and smoothed over their anger. In these dreams, Charlotte gave up the baby; she gave up her career, even her house. She chose to be satisfied with what she had, and with the time she could steal to be alone with Liam. She chose to be happy with the size of her life.

Charlotte read about Ivy's impending nuptials in the newspaper and wrote to her, asking for a favour. She followed Mrs Malone's tirades and the ensuing litigation in the press. She thought about running away from the Peppers, of moving on, but she had nowhere to go. There was no Archie Welch to tell her what to do. There wasn't even a Theodore Pike, who might have taken her in if he was still alive.

Charlotte's pregnancy progressed. As a treat, when she went into labour, Harmony presented Charlotte with an issue of *Movie Mirror*, which she had purchased in town especially for the occasion. It had a glossy shot of Hollywood's latest starlet on its shiny cover. The sight of the lovely unknown girl made Charlotte laugh insanely. Harmony presumed it was the pain.

A boy was born to Charlotte Caine at a quarter past three in the morning. She never saw him. She had lost a lot of blood during the delivery and, with no midwife in attendance – though she had pleaded for one for hours – she never regained consciousness.

As Charlotte slipped away, her last thoughts were of herself as a child. She was five or six years old and her mother was bathing her in an enamel tub. The water was warm and they were laughing together. Charlotte had always believed she had no fond memories of her mother but now, at the end, here one was – dredged up from somewhere deep inside her, long forgotten. Charlotte knew that her mother must have been going out with her father that evening because she was wearing the jacket with the fox-fur collar, which she only chose for the most special occasions. In the memory, her mother was so joyful, so light. She was feeling playful and she produced a bottle of perfume with a crystal stopper. How could Charlotte ever have forgotten this? Her mother opened the bottle and, mysteriously, as if she was performing a ritual, she poured one golden drop into Charlotte's bathwater.

'There,' her mother said. 'That will make you beautiful all over.'

Then Charlotte's mother leaned over to kiss her on the forehead, but before the kiss alighted, they were both gone.

The Peppers called the boy Moses after the biblical foundling. With no official papers for Charlotte, and unsure what they had planned to do with her once the baby came, they buried her in their family graveyard.

Moses was a delight to his parents, though the neighbours often commented that they couldn't imagine where he had come from. They didn't mean to be cruel but both

Roscoe and Harmony were plain-looking folk and this boy was so handsome you couldn't help but look at him. It seemed odd how tall and dark he was. He was almost pretty enough to be called beautiful.

Allegra sometimes thought about writing to Charlotte. She had no address for the woman but she thought that if she wrote to the Pepper Family Farm, and included the district in the address, the letter might reach the right woman.

'No point,' Holt had said. 'Peppers and her need to tie up their loose strings. Got our own future to worry about.'

The morning after Liam's death, Holt and Allegra had crossed the border into Mexico in Liam's gold Rolls-Royce. For a day and a half, Holt felt sure he was going to lose her. Allegra's face was warped by the swellings around the bee-stings. Her throat was bloated, her breathing staccato and soft. Eventually he stopped at the house of a *curandera* near Los Cabos who nursed her for a few days.

As soon as Allegra could focus her eyes again and smile a little, Holt helped her back into the car and they left.

They passed back and forward through the borders between Mexico and the United States several times in the following weeks. Holt counted their money and felt ebullient. Allegra felt nauseous. She could not forget the sight of Liam at the foot of the staircase, his neck at that grotesque angle, the bruising of his snapped bones turning his throat as purple as the encroaching dawn. She could not forget how Charlotte's face had looked, less than six inches away from her own, as they had lain together under the tarpaulin.

Holt and Allegra ended up on the southern tip of Florida, tired of fleeing. It was two months since Liam's death and nobody was chasing them. They had left the Rolls-Royce in Mexico and bought a new Chevrolet truck, which Holt polished and showed off with pride. On a long, lonely stretch of road one night, Holt had reached out to Allegra and taken her hand without turning his attention from the road. 'Desperate times . . .' he had said.

The phrase was an umbrella that encompassed every-thing they had done, every treachery they had committed together.

'Desperate measures,' Allegra had whispered back.

One Sunday morning in early 1936, Holt and Allegra were walking up Worth Avenue in Palm Beach when they came across a building for sale on the beachfront road. Allegra was drawn to it because it was a two-storey block in the Spanish style with wrought-iron balconies and terracotta roof tiles. They crossed the street to get a better look.

There was a large plot of land in the back, and Worth Avenue was exclusive but busy with people, even on a weekend morning. Allegra imagined the entrance glowing with lanterns, a great wooden door that would always be open, a courtyard with ivy-covered trellises and a fountain.

'It's sure close enough to the sea,' said Holt.

'It's Allegra's,' said Allegra.

'We'll put in an offer and we'll open our restaurant here.'

'No,' said Allegra. 'First we'll make ourselves a home.'

Just then, a streetcar rolled by and rang its merry bell. They both turned to watch it pass. Streetcars were fading out of fashion, and not many cities still ran them. The increasing rarity of the vehicles made them quaint and charming.

'I like streetcars,' said Holt. 'Something about them. They're old-fashioned and . . .' he sought the right word '. . . kinda innocent, I suppose.'

'I can't think of anything nicer than a streetcar running past my door every day,' said Allegra. 'Just the sound of its bell makes me happy.'

Afterword

For her grandparents' sixtieth wedding anniversary, Jacinta Holt wanted to treat them to something very special. She was leaving for college that Fall, and she thought a unique gift would show them how much she cared for them, how much she thought of them.

As soon as she saw the book of photographs, Jacinta knew what the perfect gift would be. She had seen it in a local store, displayed in a tower of several dozen copies. It was large, designed to grace a coffee table, with enormous photographs on almost every page. Jacinta loved photography – she was hoping to take a class about it at college.

This particular book was a collection of images by the celebrated Dorothea Lange, who had earned a following as one of America's great photographers. Miss Lange's reputation was built on the extraordinary work she had done documenting the Great Depression. She ranked alongside Ansel Adams in critical acclaim. As Jacinta had paged through the book, she had come across a photograph that reached out and grasped her. Good art should evoke a visceral response, but Jacinta's reaction was due to something else entirely – she believed the woman in the photograph was her grandmother.

From her mother, Jacinta had learned that her grandmother had been a maid in Los Angeles during the depression, and here was a picture to prove it. The simple caption read: 'Mexican maid – Allegra del Rio – with privileged child'.

It was a dramatic image. In it, the lighting was low, mottled with shadows. The woman's long hair was a black sweep across half her face. Any sparkle in the image came from the form of the sleeping child – a little angel with her mouth open in total relaxation and her eyelids closed like rice-paper blinds. The girl's wings were all cheap sequins and glued-on glitter. Her silky dress shone in a sliver of light. Her two little feet pointed, pigeon-toed, towards each other and she was at peace. The woman who held her could not rest, however. Her face showed exhaustion.

Jacinta wrote, hopeless of a reply, to Dorothea Lange's estate. The letter explained that Jacinta believed her grandmother was the subject of one of Ms Lange's portraits, and that she would love to have a copy of the print for that grandmother's sixtieth wedding anniversary. She enclosed a cheque.

Unexpectedly, two weeks before the celebration, a large envelope arrived at the post office and Jacinta went to collect it. It was stiff with protective board and, when she opened it, she saw that Miss Lange's estate had kindly printed her a copy of the picture, as big as a fair-sized window. It was beautiful.

Jacinta was delighted. She took the print to a framer and paid extra for a rushed job. On the night of the party, they closed the doors of Allegra's for a private gathering, which included only friends and family. Jacinta's two brothers were there, and her two uncles and their wives and children – her innumerable cousins.

After dessert, Jacinta presented the gift wrapped in silver paper. Grandma Allegra tore the paper from it with a smile of delight on her face. Then she went quite blank. Grandpop Holt came up to his wife and steadied her; he had always been doting, always protective. Suddenly, as her grandmother looked at the picture and blinked in stupefaction, Jacinta feared that she had done a stupid, awful thing. She had reminded her of a terrible time in her life. Her grandmother had often refused to tell Jacinta and her brothers tales from her past, especially about her depression days when times had been very hard. How had Jacinta miscalculated so badly? She wanted to cry. 'Grandma, I'm sorry. I didn't think. I thought you would like it.'

Grandma Allegra's face softened. Wrinkles had done little to detract from the loveliness of her kind eyes. 'I do like it, Chica,' she said. 'I had almost forgotten, that's all. I remember that night so clearly. That little girl . . .'

Jacinta saw Grandpop Holt squeeze his wife's hand. 'Who was the child?' she asked.

'I don't remember her name, Chica,' said Allegra. She had turned enigmatic, yet Jacinta felt sure her grandmother was lying.

'We'll hang it in the restaurant,' said Grandpop Holt. 'Right here above the fireplace. Good to have reminders.'

'"Be sure your sins will find you out,"' quoted Grandma Allegra, as she looked at her younger self holding the sleeping child.

'No, no,' said Grandpop Holt. '"Remember whence your blessings come."'

Acknowledgements

A world of thanks to Mari Evans and all the wonderful, learned and passionate women at Penguin – thank you for keeping the faith!

Psst
want the latest gossip on all your favourite writers?

Then come and join us in . . .

THE
BOOK BOUTIQUE

. . . the **exclusive club** for anyone who loves to curl up with the latest reads in women's fiction.

- All the latest news on the best authors.
- Early copies of the latest reads months before they're out.
- Chat with like-minded readers as well as bestselling writers.
- Excellent recommendations for new books to read.
- Exclusive competitions to get your hands on stylish prizes.

SIGN UP for our regular newsletter by emailing
thebookboutique@uk.penguingroup.com
or if you really can't wait, get over to
www.facebook.com/TheBookBoutique

KAREN MAITLAND

COMPANY OF LIARS

The year is 1348 and the first plague victim has reached English shores. Panic erupts around the country and a small band of travellers comes together to outrun the deadly disease, unaware that something far more deadly is – in fact – travelling with them.

The ill-assorted company – a scarred trader in holy relics, a conjurer, two musicians, a healer and a deformed storyteller – are all concealing secrets and lies. And at their heart is the strange, cold child – Narigorm – who reads the runes.

But as law and order breaks down across the country and the battle for survival becomes ever more fierce, Narigorm mercilessly compels each of her fellow travellers to reveal the truth … and each in turn is driven to a cruel and unnatural death.

'A richly evocative page-turner which brings to life a lost and terrible period of British history, with a disturbing final twist worthy of a master of the spine-tingler, such as Henry James' *Daily Express*

'An engrossing fireside read . . . a compelling mystery' *Daily Mail*

'Combines the storytelling traditions of The Canterbury Tales with the supernatural suspense of Mosse's Sepulchre in this atmospheric tale of treachery and magic' *Marie Claire*

KAREN MAITLAND

THE OWL KILLERS

England, 1321
Welcome to the Dark Ages

In the heart of the countryside lies an isolated village, where pagan Owl Masters rule through fear, superstition and murder.

When a group of religious women ill-advisedly settles outside the village, they awaken dangerous jealousies. Why do their crops succeed? How do their cattle survive the plague? Are they concealing a holy relic which protects them from harm?

The Owl Masters cry 'Witchcraft' and sharpen their talons. As torment and hellfire rain down, the women must look to their faith to save them from the darkness spreading across the land.

Fear is a question of what you believe.
And death alone the answer.

'Powerful, very enjoyable, very intelligent, very gripping' Simon Mayo Book Club, Radio 5

'A fast-moving, grisly story' *Daily Mail*

'Scarily good. Imagine The Wicker Man crossed with The Birds' *Marie Claire*

'A chilling Gothic thriller' *Tatler*

Lucinda Riley

HOTHOUSE FLOWER

As a child, concert pianist Julia Forrester would linger in the hothouse of Wharton Park estate, where exotic flowers tended by her grandfather blossomed and faded with the seasons. Now, recovering from a family tragedy, she once more seeks comfort at Wharton Park, newly inherited by Kit Crawford, a charismatic man with a sad story of his own. But when a years-old diary is found during renovation work, the pair turn to Julia's grandmother to hear the truth about the love affair that turned Wharton Park's fortunes sour . . .

And so Julia is plunged back in time, to the world of Olivia and Harry Crawford, a young couple torn apart by the Second World War - and whose fragile marriage is destined to affect the happiness of generations to come, including Julia's own.

Lucinda Riley's heart-rending storytelling embraces war-torn Europe and the exoticism of Thailand as she examines the messy tangles of love.